Alien I Am

The Anomaly Files

by David Markham

First published in 2025

ISBN-13: 978-0-9907587-6-1

Published by David L. Markham

Website: alieniam.com | Paperback edition 1.3

Printed in the United States of America

CONTENTS

See the Shard Logbook when you encounter these: ◇ ◆ – or just keep reading.

Now that I'm marked, my memories aren't just mine anymore. They're humanity's dossier. If I can't find what matters in these files, everything worth saving ends with me. I'll start at the beginning. ◇

FILE 01 | The First Abduction
DATE 03 MAY | MEMORY | SL-3 | Emily Rowen - Age 15

I never believed in aliens until the night one took me.

I was walking up our gravel driveway after late swimming practice, hair still damp, satchel bumping my hip. The night air carried a sharp chemical scent. Chlorine, I thought.

Lightning flickered inside the clouds without any sound. I stopped, turned toward the storm like it was a dare I didn't know how to back down from.

Crickets stopped. Leaves held their breath.

Then, the stars blinked out.

It wasn't a cloud. It was too deliberate. A piece of the sky simply vanished like someone dragged black paint across it.

My fingers dug into the strap of my satchel, thinking I might have to run.

Above the trees was a shape like the absence of something, a featureless ellipse, smooth as glass. My chest tightened, and for a second like I'd forgotten how to breathe.

Katniss begged me with a thin yowl to hide under the porch. I almost turned back for her. But a cold shiver crawled over my skin and I abandoned her there in fear.

Rain started pattering, landing on something hot—hissing into vapor before the drops hit the ground.

I squinted up, forcing my eyes to see the thing when a bright blue light shot down, swirling around the edges. It slid across the driveway toward me like it had picked its target.

I glanced at the house. Dark windows. No one.

My limbs locked.

“Take me,” I whispered. “But leave Katniss alone.”

Heat slammed into my chest. I wanted to yell for help, but my voice shut down. My heels lifted off the gravel, my body hanging, dragged upward like a puppet on invisible strings.

The ground dropped away. Our roof, the treetops, Katniss’ small shape under the porch—all of it shrank, sliding backward like I was being peeled off my own life. The hull rippled in patterns that matched the storm above like camouflaging it. ◇

No engine. No hum. Nothing. Just the blood pounding in my ears. Then the blue light lifted me into a hole opening across the ship’s underside. ◆

FILE 02 | Inside the Spaceship
DATE 03 MAY | SL-2

Inside, it was nothing like an airplane. Then I saw them—seven beings reclined in the air, rotating slowly to face me. The walls behind them pulsed with light. The air smelled like a hospital.

I was lowered into a clear cylinder full of warm liquid. My body panicked, thrashing, but the fluid held me suspended. I wasn’t drowning, though. It wasn’t water. It was thicker, slicker, and somehow breathable. My lungs filled, and instead of choking, I felt a strange relief—like the fluid was breathing for me.

Shapes moved around the chamber, tall and indistinct. Their limbs were elongated, heads oblong with two black ovals for eyes. Moisture glistened across their skin, and when one moved closer somehow, I knew she was female and younger like me.

That was when I felt the voice. Not in my ears. Inside my head. Calm, measured, perfectly clear.

<You will be marked.>

My chest pounded. “Marked? For what?” I thought back at her.

No reply. But the figure lingered near me. She didn’t touch. She didn’t move her mouth, but I knew she was the source of the voice.

Another shape hovered at the chamber’s center—a large silver sphere, the size of a refrigerator, suspended in air. Electrical sparks crawled across its surface, bright veins pulsing in rhythm with the slight hum that filled the room. I felt the sphere was aware, like it was listening to me breathe.

The figure near me tilted her head, rounded black eyes reflecting the glow of the sphere. I concentrated on her face, yearning for my sketchbook. Then the voice came again, softly, emotionless, inside my head.

<I am Neur. I will not harm you.>

I wanted to speak but my mouth wouldn’t move. I wanted to say please, let me go. Instead, what came out was a thought, not words: “Who are you people?” ◇

No response. Just silence and the hum of the chamber walls.

Then: <You will not understand. Not now. But you will receive a mark on your arm. It cannot be removed.>

Her hand extended holding a thin rod, and she pressed it into my forearm. It burned like a wasp’s sting.

I tensed. The fluid pressed tight against my body, holding me in place. My throat burned. My heart pounded faster until bursts of orange flickered at the edge of my vision. I thought I was passing out when the chamber began to dissolve around me.

When I opened my eyes again, I was in my bed in a fetal position, my pillow wet from sweat. An orange circle glowed on my arm, no bigger than my thumbprint.

The mark. ◇

FILE 03 | The Day After the Abduction
DATE 04 MAY | SL-2

Morning light bled through the curtains, pale orange against my bedroom wall.

I sat up, heart racing as though I had been running in my sleep. My sheets clung damp to my skin. The smell of rain still hung in the air even though the storm had passed.

It was a dream.

It had to be.

That's what I told myself, over and over, until I yanked back the sleeve of my T-shirt and looked at my arm.

There was the mark.

Faint, almost like a bruise, but glowing underneath the skin. Orange with a white edge.

I pressed my finger against it and felt nothing different. I tugged my sleeve down again, hard, as if hiding it could make it disappear. If I told anyone, I would just sound crazy.

A clatter of dishes came from the kitchen downstairs, the steady rhythm of my mom's movements. A normal sound. A safe sound. I held onto it as long as I could.

But every time I closed my eyes, the image of the chamber returned—the hum of the walls, the blue veins of light, and her voice.

<It cannot be removed.>

The words hit harder in daylight.

I clawed my sketchbook out from under the bed and flipped to a blank page. My pencil shook in my hand before lines began to form on their own. Not a plan, not even a thought—just motion. Curves, arcs, sharp strokes.

ALIEN I AM

A spaceship. Tree branches reflected on its surface. A cone of light pouring down. By the time Mom called me for breakfast, the page was covered.

I stared at the cereal, soggy now, spoon heavy in my hand.

My mom leaned against the counter, elbows planted, sipping coffee and watching me in that half-squint she used when she thought I was hiding something.

"You're pale," she said. "Did you even sleep?"

"Swim practice was late," I muttered, which wasn't a lie. Just not the whole truth.

"You push too hard, Em. You're going to burn yourself out."

If only burning out was all I had to worry about.

"Our sun will eventually die, Mom. Now that's burnout."

She shook her head with a small smile. "I'm baking your favorite cake today. Sound good?" ◇

I forced a shrug and shoved another spoonful of soggy flakes into my mouth.

Every couple of months, she baked my favorite cake—a quiet celebration in the middle of all the hard work she did. She brought me new sketchbooks that same day. They were too expensive, but she somehow managed. It was the little things she did.

I could tell she wanted to know what was wrong. She didn't press further.

She never did when I used the swimming practice excuse.

Swimming had always been my shield. Practice, laps, competition, dreams of winning state. My excuse for everything from avoiding parties to unfinished homework.

My spoon rattled against the bowl, milk sloshing over the edge.

I wanted to say something.

Mom, I was taken. There was a ship. There was an alien. They marked my arm. The alien spoke to me without saying anything.

If everyone was worried about me before, they were going to freak if I started talking about aliens.

But I shoved another soggy mouthful down instead. I sat with the spoon at my lips until the cereal went cold, feeling the mark like a secret burning under my skin.

Outside, the wind picked up, and the sound tried to tuck my fear back into the neat box of morning routine—but the mark wouldn't let the world settle. I laid my hand over it again, like a quiet oath: *don't tell, don't panic, not yet*.

I went up to my room and left my sketchbook face-up on my desk, the lines raw and unfinished, as if leaving the drawing exposed might tether the memory to something real. ◇

FILE 04 | Trying to Act Normal
DATE 04 MAY | SL-1

The fluorescent lights buzzed like needles in my ears. I kept my sleeve tugged down in the stuffy heat. No one noticed, or if they did, no one cared.

The halls smelled of wet sneakers, bleach, and whatever cafeteria food they were trying to pass off as edible. Normal things. Comforting things. I clung to them the way I had clung to my mom's voice earlier.

Still, when I opened my sketchbook in class, my pencil betrayed me. My hand moved without asking permission. I drew the chamber walls, the rod pressing into my arm, the tall figures that floated at the edge of vision. And at the center of every sketch: the sphere.

Amanda cornered me at lunch.

She always did that—like she had radar for when I wanted to be left alone. I had picked the farthest table in the cafeteria; sketchbook open to look busy. But she spotted me anyway, tray balanced in one hand like she owned the place.

"You look like a dead vampire," she announced, dropping into the seat across from me. "A scraggly, blond-haired vampire. When are you going to wear something different? Same white T-shirt every day, and inside out today?"

"It's one less decision I have to make, and yes, the seams bother me." I tugged my sleeve down before she could notice the glow beneath.

"Nice to see you too." I plopped my satchel on the table, covering my drawing. The image of it stuck in my mind.

"Don't deflect," she said, stabbing a fork into something that looked vaguely like lasagna. "You've been ghosting all week. I'm officially staging an intervention."

I tried to smile, but it slipped before it reached my mouth. "I'm fine." ◇

"Fine," she repeated, rolling her eyes. "Classic code for 'something is seriously wrong, please ignore me until I collapse.'"

I laughed despite the pain in my gut. That was Amanda's magic, she could pull a laugh out of me even when the world had just turned upside down.

She leaned in, lowering her voice. "Okay, spill. Did you and Derik fight again? Because if he said something stupid, I swear I will hack his social page and delete all his photos of you."

I shook my head. "It's not Derik."

"Then what? Thinking about your dad again? I truly wish you could bring him back, Em."

The words pressed against my throat, raw and desperate. My pulse thudded so loud I thought she might hear it. *I was abducted, Amanda. A ship. A voice. A mark that won't fade*. But what would she say? She would laugh. Or worse—she wouldn't believe me.

"Just… bad dreams," I muttered, eyes dropping to my sketchbook. I slid it under my satchel.

Amanda exhaled. "Dreams don't make you look like you just saw a murder. Come on, Em. You know you can tell me anything."

I traced the edge of my pencil on the paper. The page was filled with more spheres, more veins of light, more silhouettes with black eyes.

Amanda reached across and pulled the sketchbook away. "What's it got in its pocketses?"

"Give it." I grabbed for it, but she slid it just out of reach.

Her eyes scanned the page, eyebrows lifting. "Seriously, what's going on with you?"

Heat crawled up my neck. "It's nothing, really."

"Nothing," she repeated, handing it back. "Em, you're a good liar, but not that good. This looks obsessive. Which is saying something, considering you once drew the entire cast of Lord of the Rings."

"That was art," I said, a weak protest.

She smirked. "Uh-huh. And this is..." Her smirk faded as she looked at me closer. "This is freaking you out, isn't it?"

I stared down at the sphere I had shaded until the graphite smudged across my palm. My chest hurt. I almost gave in, almost poured it all out—the ship, the cone of light, Neur's voice.

But then the memory of the liquid clinging to my skin rose up, and I swallowed it all down again.

Amanda sighed. "You don't have to tell me if you're not ready. But don't shut me out, okay? Whatever's going on, I'd rather be in it with you than going to the morgue to identify your body."

I nodded, throat tight. "I know."

She grinned, bright and sharp. "Good. Because I already made us a pact. If you turn out to be secretly dying, I get your sketchbooks. All of them. Even the embarrassing primary school ones."

I shoved her lightly. "Over my dead body."

She shoved back. “Exactly.”

For a moment, things felt almost normal. Almost. But when she turned to talk to someone else at the next table, I slid my sleeve up just enough to check. The glow on my arm hadn’t faded. If anything, it was brighter.

FILE 05 | Meeting with School Counselor
DATE 04 MAY | SL-3

I was rescued from Algebra by a hall pass. The school counselor’s office smelled like peppermint tea and old carpet.

I sank into the armchair opposite Dr. Bennet, folding my arms tight across my chest.

She smiled the kind of smile adults practiced in the mirror. “Emily, thanks for coming in. Your teachers are concerned saying you’ve seemed, distracted lately.”

“Sorry,” I muttered. “Didn’t know paying attention in Algebra was life or death.”

“Not life or death,” she said calmly. “But enough people noticed that I thought it might help to talk it out.”

I stared at the framed diploma on her wall, trying not to roll my eyes. Talking had never helped. Not about the death of my dad, not about Derik, and definitely not about being abducted by an alien being named Neur.

Still, I strained a smile. “I’m okay, I guess.”

“That’s what you told your mom too, right?”

My brow twisted. “My mom called you?”

“She’s worried. That’s what Moms do.”

I clenched my jaw. “She doesn’t need to be.”

Dr. Bennet leaned forward, resting her elbows on her knees.

I thought she was too young to counsel deep problems. But she was so pretty and too nice to avoid.

“I’m not here to drag answers out of you. But you do seem tired. More than usual. Nightmares?”

The word caught me off guard. “Maybe.”

“Want to tell me about them?”

Absolutely not, I thought to myself.

“Why did you decide to become a psychologist?” I redirected.

But her eyes were steady and patient. The silence stretched until I gave in, just a little. “Storms. Dark sky. Things I can’t explain.”

“Scary things?”

I shrugged. “Weird things.”

“Sometimes our brains process stress in ways that don’t make sense right away. Dreams can be symbolic,” she said.

Symbolic. Sure. A glowing orange mark on my arm was totally symbolic.

I pulled my sleeve lower, fingers curling tight around the fabric.

“Emily,” she said gently. “You know you don’t have to handle everything by yourself.”

I laughed once, faked, trying to make her think I was normal. “Tell that to my math teacher when I correct her in class.”

I did want someone to know what I was going through.

“Or…” I stopped before I could say something. The peppermint-scented started to give me a headache. She tilted her head. “Or?”

I knew she wouldn’t believe me.

“During class, I’m listening subconsciously for gunshots.” I knew that would hit a nerve.

Her pen scratched across the notepad. “Do you think you might be depressed?”

“They say we just crossed the point of no return for reversing global warming. So yeah—depressed, sure. What else do you call it when the planet’s dying and you’re powerless to stop it?”

Adults call it depression when kids are just paying attention, I thought.

“Maybe it feels like no one understands what you’re going through. That can be isolating,” she said.

“You have no idea,” I whispered.

Her eyes softened. “You’re right. I don’t know. But I’d like to, if you’ll let me in. Could it be about your dad?”

I bit the inside of my cheek. “Wait—you’re gonna psychoanalyze me? I know you think I hate the war for taking my dad. I really don’t anymore. I had to get over it.”

Dad was handsome, muscular, solid, like he could keep the whole world from spinning out of control. His face was soft. The moments he helped keep me sane are part of who I am even now. Even during this strange experience, I carry him with me, especially when it feels like it’s too much to bear. I can never say his name out loud, but I never allowed his death to make me a different person. ◇

The room felt smaller, the air heavier. For a moment, the hum of the chamber resonated in my ears, and I remembered the warm liquid filling my lungs.

Neur’s voice whispered again: <You are marked.>

I rubbed my aching arm.

Dr. Bennet didn’t miss it. “Emily, whatever it is, you’re safe here.”

Safe. I almost faked another laugh. But instead, I looked down at my sketchbook satchel, knowing the pages were thick with horrific graphite shadows.

“I just draw it out,” I said quietly, looking down. “That’s how I deal. I draw.”

“That’s a great way to deal,” she said, nodding. “Art can be a powerful way to process.”

I was saved again, school bell ringing in the hall. We both looked at the clock. Session over.

I smiled like a little girl. “Please don’t get me wrong, Dr. Bennet, I really appreciate you and like you a lot.”

She put her hand lightly on my arm and offered me another one of her patient smiles. “We can keep talking whenever you want. You know I really care about you.”

I nodded, slinging the satchel over my right shoulder like armor. Out in the hallway, the mark seemed to hum under my sleeve. No amount of counseling sessions or kind smiles could calm it. I did a quick reset. ◇

I walked back into class. Amanda mouthed across the room, “So?” I rolled my eyes and gave her a little shrug signaling I’m okay.

But the truth was, talking to Dr. Bennet hadn’t made me feel better at all. It had just thrown a spotlight on the one thing I couldn’t explain—that this mark was pushing me toward something, and whatever was coming was way too big for anyone here to understand. No counselor, not my mom, not even my dad if somehow he could walk back through the door.

And that feeling of pressure made my brain do what it always does when things get too big.

It ran back to the memory of a dead soldier. ◇

FILE 06 | The Weight of a Star
DATE 04 MAY | SL-2

ALIEN I AM

When my dad was alive, he made you feel like you were the most important person in the world. He was a metal worker at the factory before he was deployed to Bahrain. Everything changed after that. He was apparently killed by accident while on a mission. It was sudden, cruel, and made the world shift beneath my feet. It took a year to start to feel normal again.

Mom never spoke about Dad. It was like that part of our life was too heavy to name out loud. The silence stood between us like a wall reflecting him back at us.

When she could spare it, she took me to the movies, rare fragile nights that we loved more than anything. She was fighting to finish paying off the house, promising that once it was done, she could finally drop back to one shift. I worried constantly about how hard she worked, how tired she looked, and that worry became one of the reasons I stayed so long at swim practice. If I wasn't home until evening, she didn't have to picture me alone in the quiet house, waiting in the shadow of a dead memory.

The influence of someone magnifies significantly with the pain of their passing. That breaking carries their significance into the future through you. That memory makes you better than you were if you hold on to it correctly. Doctor Bennet didn't teach me that.

I carry his Silver Star pinned to the inside of my sketchbook satchel. It's like a piece of him protecting me, guiding me. It's pushing me to make my life count for something.

Two years had passed, but the hurt still cut deep, even though I did everything I could to keep his image out of my head—sketching and drawing mostly. I need to learn how to let go of the pain and remember the good. ◇

When I draw, I'm somewhere else where the pain softens, even if it's just for a little while.

What I can't figure out is why I can never say his name out loud?

I took the long way home through the woods thinking about one of my favorite memories. We went to Cape Cod when I was little. There were just us three at the beach—Mom, Dad, and me. Dad built a sandcastle, towering and perfect. Then without warning, he scooped me up and flung me into the ocean laughing. That laugh—warm and full—still echoes in my mind. I treasure the sound of that laughter.

Sometimes I feel like I will be forever trapped in a thirteen-year-old body, the age I was when he deployed. I knew I would never see him again. I decided I would not let him down by getting depressed, even if I never got to hold him again.

The school consoler made me remember him again. When I got home from school, I went up to my room and slumped into my chair. I sat there at my drawing desk for a long time holding my sketchbook satchel to my chest, staring out the window.

I saw the shape of Katniss pass in front of me, and it didn't break my glare.

My dad made my drawing desk from the old barns wood we found when we moved in. It was a little rough but solid and super personal. It felt like it had its own stories to tell before I ever touched it.

He even carved a groove in the top so my pencils wouldn't roll off. It's like he planned for every little thing that would help me get lost in my art. I appreciate special gifts that took time and effort to make thinking of who I am and who I'd become. ◇

The sun finally went down, and I tried to draw my way into another reality, but it didn't work. No amount of sketching could erase the fact that an alien had marked me for something. It wasn't really about me. It wasn't even just about the collapsing ecosystems. It was something bigger—like the weight of a silver star on a dead soldier's chest, a quiet, heavy promise of what I was going to have to become.

FILE 07 | Controlled Exposure
DATE 05 MAY | SL-3

Outside it was pitch black. Katniss jumped onto my desk, and I tried to draw her. But the pencil kept circling back to the spaceship, the sphere, to Neur's eyes. I tried to add ideas from alien movies to my sketches.

Somewhere in the space between lines, I heard her voice again, soft but certain, an inch away from my ear.

<You don't resist. That is why you are marked. That is why you draw us.> ◇

I jerked completely still. Her voice slid into the center of my mind, without invitation.

<Those images were given to you.>

I took a half breath. "What?"

<Your species did not invent them. We planted them. Slowly, over decades. To make interaction easier.>

I shoved the pencil away, heart pounding. How did I know that?

<You believed they are your stories? They are ours. Fragments placed to soften resistance of the masses, placed to prepare the marked.>

The words burned inside. Every comfort movie I'd ever clung to, every story where the scared girl from nowhere ended up mattering on some huge scale—were they all just manipulation?

It wasn't just my body they'd taken; they'd taken my stories too. All those nights I thought I was choosing what to care about, it was really them, feeding me the lines.

"No," I said, as if my voice could shut out the truth. But silence followed, only the sound of a pencil rolling off my desk with a dull thud.

I barely slept. It looked like normal sunshine outside, I shoved the sketchbook into my bag and pretended I was still any other kid, just the kind that worried about the end of the world. Part of me wanted to rewind to before the mark. The other part needed to know what I'd been picked for.

Amanda eased her locker shut, dragging out the creak, and dropped into her best horror-trailer voice. "In space, no one can hear you scream."

I managed a quick smile, but the tagline left a hollow pit in my stomach.

She bumped my shoulder. “We’re watching *Alien* on Friday. Sleepover. Popcorn. Survival tips.”

“I can’t,” I blurted.

She raised an eyebrow. “You love Alien.”

I used to. “I’ve got… stuff.”

Her face fell a microinch. She lasted two steps before chiming back to cheer. “Okay, Dumbledore. Rain check.”

I wanted to grab her wrist and blurt everything. Instead, I slipped my hands into my pockets and locked eyes on hers a second longer than normal.

At lunch she flopped into the seat across from me. “Either you didn’t sleep, or you fought with Derik.”

“Okay, be honest,” I said, stabbing my salad. “How would you feel if you found out all our favorite alien movies were planted—like the stories we love were put there to control us?”

Amanda chewed, thinking. “Every story controls you a little. That’s the point—they’re supposed to make you feel things.”

“What if it wasn’t… human?” My voice came out sounding crazier than I meant it to.

She set her fork down. “Em. Is there something you want to tell me?”

I shook my head so hard it rattled. “Forget it.”

Her eyes softened. “I’ll hang out with you even if you join a cult. But if they shave your head, I’m staging a rescue mission.”

I laughed, broken. “I’m not joining anything.” The lie tasted like chlorine. “And I would be holding you by the time the alien gets into the escape shuttle with her.” ◇

That night, Mom came home late as usual. Purse thudding on the counter. I sat at the table with my sketchbook hidden under an algebra book. She kissed the top of my head. “You’ve been quiet lately.”

"I'm fine," I said.

"That word again," she muttered, pulling out the leftovers. "You're too young to be fine all the time. Teenagers are supposed to slam doors and eat all the ice cream."

I thought about, then I asked her what her favorite alien movie was. Her face lit. "E.T. I was six. I bawled when he said goodbye."

"What about you?" she asked.

I froze. I couldn't remember a time before alien movies. Like they'd been waiting for me, stitched into my DNA. "I dunno? Feels like they are all my favorites, like they've always been there."

She smiled softly. "That's how good stories work. They are with you before you even know you need them."

Her words sank like a stone into my gut. They weren't ours. They were planted.

"Em?"

"Yeah?"

"You sure you're okay?"

"Just tired."

She reached out, her hand warm on mine, grounding me in a way that made the silence feel heavier. I nodded and gave her my angel face like I believed it.

Later, when the house settled to where I could hear the fridge humming, I flipped my sketchbook open. Tonight's drawing wasn't the ship or the sphere. It was me, walking toward Mom, but behind her stood the silhouette of an alien, a hand raised in a peace pose. The mark on my arm throbbed. ◆ DI#02

In bed, I wanted to sink into the ordinary noise—the soft click of the fan, the neighbor's dog barking through the fence at Katniss. But as I closed my eyes, a voice slipped in, quiet as breath:

<You see now why you were marked?>

"No. Why am I marked?"

<You can already hear the voices.>

I stared up at the dark shapes of my solar system mobile, heart thudding against the mattress. I'd spent my whole life feeling like there was something wrong with me—like I was broken. Too sensitive. Too dramatic. Always going down the rabbit hole.

The planet was dying on every level, and I couldn't even get my homework in on time. What was I supposed to change, exactly?

Now there was an alien voice in my head insisting I'd been marked for something. Maybe they'd been shaping me this whole time, feeding me stories until I was starving inside. Maybe that hunger had never been mine.

The worst part wasn't being controlled; it was not knowing what they wanted with me.

FILE 08 | Movie Night
DATE 05 MAY | SL-3

It was finally movie night, just Mom and me. We'd moved it to Wednesdays after Dad died—something to pull us through the middle before the weight of the week could crush us.

An empty pizza box on the coffee table. Mom curled up with her knitting. Me hogging the popcorn. The ritual felt safe, untouched.

Until I chose *Close Encounters of the Third Kind* again, like replaying it might jar some quantum synchronicity[1], revealing why they had marked me. ◆ DI#03

Mom groaned pleasantly. "Don't you ever get tired of that one?"

"Nope," I said, already quoting under my breath, "We are not

[1] See: NC.CODEX.26.Q Glossary of Terms

alone."

She shook her head, yarn looping smoothly between her needles.

I should have been wrapped in the glow of the TV. But when the spaceship appeared over Devil's Tower, the pepperoni grease turned in my stomach. Too close. Too real this time as the mountain morphed into my own sketches: the ship above the trees, the alien with her hand raised, some kind of pods on the ground.

"Em," Mom said, noticing me drift. "You okay? You've just seemed somewhere else lately."

I stroked Katniss between the ears until she purred.

"Just worn out. School stuff."

She watched me for a second, lips pressed into a line, then let the silence win. Mom never pushed. But sometimes it left me more alone than ever.

When the credits rolled, I pulled out every alien DVD we owned. *Alien*. *Arrival*. *Signs*. *War of the Worlds*.

I stacked them like evidence, like accusations.

"What's going on?" Mom asked, eyeing the pile.

I should have said: because an alien named Neur told me these ideas were planted in our minds to control us.

Instead, I said, "I've seen them all too many times."

She smiled, ruffling my hair. "Don't get rid of them. You've always loved aliens, even before you could read." Her voice was warm, grounding. But it didn't erase Neur's words.

If anything, it made them cut deeper.

I retreated to my room under the excuse of homework. The glow on my arm still shone faintly in the dark.

My drawing desk summoned me with its hundreds of pencils and drawing utensils.

When I set my sketchbook down on the desk, the pencil began to move again. Katniss claimed her usual spot, then curled up, fixing her stare on the wall like someone lived inside it.

This time I didn't draw the sphere. I drew a movie poster of my close encounter of the third kind. ◆ DI#04

The cone of light was over Devil's Tower[2]. Everything was dark black, not blue. But in my drawing, the ship was oval, just like the one that took me. Dr. Bennet said dreams were symbolic—maybe my drawings were too.

I didn't know why I drew this. Maybe it was suppressed sarcasm. I used to watch Close Encounters and feel okay with the ending—the normal guy walking up the ramp like it was some brave adventure. Now it just felt incomplete. I wanted to know who they were. I wanted to know why they came here. Most of all, I wanted to know why I was marked. ◇

FILE 09 | The Secret Circle

DATE 06 MAY | SL-3

It had just rained when Amanda showed up in the driveway. She always stood there until I subconsciously knew she was outside. I would look out my window, see her, and come down. It was our secret unnamed game we never talked about.

We took the trail behind my house to get to school. It cut through scrub oak and a tangle of deer paths. It was a ten-minute walk to get to the clearing we claimed last summer. We'd arranged sixteen tree trunk rounds in a circle and called it Stumphenge. Someone had kicked a few of them over, breaking the circle.

Amanda hissed, "Seriously?" She looked around like the person who did it might still be lurking. "Derik," she said, like it was obvious.

"We don't know that." I started dragging the nearest stump back

[2] Devils Tower is a striking natural rock formation about 867 feet (265 meters) high located in northeastern Wyoming, USA. The formation became famous after appearing in the movie "Close Encounters of the Third Kind."

into position. It was heavier than I'd remembered. The bark bit into my palms.

We spent an entire Saturday last July dragging those stumps into position according to the paperback on Stonehenge.[3] North marked with an axe notch, gaps paced off by our sweaty steps.

The north stump was different—darker, denser, like it had lived another life somewhere else before we fought it into the circle as the most significant one. ◇

We'd joked we could feel "the universe aligning," then laid in the grass looking up at the stars until the mosquitoes found us. And still, we didn't want to leave.

I never told Amanda that whenever I think about Stumphenge, it warmed me inside to know we did it together like we had stepped into the one thing the universe actually wanted from us.

It was the first time my usual indignation to fix the world went quiet, like—for once—I was exactly where I was supposed to be.

"Help me with this big one," I said.

She squatted, fingers under the edge. "On three. One—two—"

We heaved. It thumped into place. As I turned, I noticed Amanda was looking down. Blood slicked her forearm.

"Amanda—hold still!" I tore a strip from my T-shirt and pressed down. She flinched and took a deep breath.

"Sit down," I said, leading her to the north stump.

"I'm fine," she said through her teeth.

"You might need stitches polliwog," I said. "Stay still a minute."

---

[3] Stonehenge is a prehistoric monument located in Wiltshire, England, and is one of the world's most famous ancient sites used for ceremonial or religious functions, ancient burial ground, or as an astronomical calendar for tracking solstices and other cosmic events.

DI#26 ◆

We sat in the ring of stumps, me holding pressure, her breathing through her nose and bleeding onto the north stump. I held her arm tight watching the cut so I wouldn't have to look at her face.

Blood dripped into the cracks of the old stump. For a second it felt like something changed, like something deepened between us.

I smelled dead mushrooms and earthworms as the wind lifted once and dropped into complete silence. I felt like we were being watched. Then the wind lifted again, reminding me that we needed to go.

She said in a lighter voice, "We're not telling anyone we were fixing our secret place and got reminded."

"Reminded of what?"

She rolled her eyes. "How fragile we are dummy."

The bleeding slowed. I loosened pressure and checked. "It's okay. You'll live."

"Promise?"

I should've said yes and left it there. Instead, I heard myself say, softly enough to register and pass, "I'll make sure of it."

She curled a smile under. "What's that mean?"

"Means I'll carry your backpack if you milk this for sympathy." I tied the strip tighter and stood up before she could look too hard at me. "Come on. I can't be late for my favorite thing at school."

Amanda wiped her hands on her jeans. "It's weird how much better I feel when the stumps are lined up right."

"It's not weird." I glanced at the bloody north stump. "We broke our backs dragging these into a circle and now you've literally bled on one. It'd be weirder if it didn't feel like something had changed."

"Thanks, Em," she said, and headed back toward the path.

We were two bends into the deer trail when I said, too casually, "Hypothetical."

She groaned. "Oh no."

“If aliens were here—like actually here—would you try to save them or kill them?” I watched her face and tried to keep mine blank.

“That’s your movie-night brain talking.” She bumped my shoulder, winced when the arm moved, and kept going. “And ‘save or kill’ is a dumb binary.”

“Pick one.”

“Fine.” She didn’t slow down. “Save the ones that don’t want to eat us. Kill the ones that do.”

“You don’t believe in negotiations?”

“Not with teeth,” she said. “Why? You meet some last night?”

“It’s just a thought experiment.” I pushed a branch aside for her; it snapped back and scratched my hand.

“Why do you care today?” she asked.

“I’m just, thinking,” I said.

“You always are,” she said, punching my shoulder lightly.

We came out of the woods at the school parking lot. The asphalt still held last night’s rain in shallow mirrors.

Something was off. The lot was empty. Everyone was already in class. I checked my phone—we were two hours late.

“Amanda, we’re super late for class.”

She just lifted one shoulder like she couldn’t care less.

We slipped in through the side door. Her cut had already clotted under the strip. The hallway hit us with cold, chemical air.

Coach’s text buzzed onto my screen: Where are you. Pool. Now.

“I’ll see you after,” Amanda said, lifting her bandaged arm in a half-salute, then winced. “Sympathy backpack later?”

"Done," I said.

She headed for the lockers as I stood for a second longer in the doorway, watching the line of trees. Stumphenge was out there in the trees, fixed again, Amanda's blood so real and still drying on the north stump.

I decided on two things between one breath and the next: I was going to tell Amanda about Neur, and whatever the cost, I was going to take her with me.

Swim practice should have rinsed my brain clean. I jumped in the water and felt five seconds of peace. I loved the right turn after the lap when your legs snap like springs and you glide weightless, a body remembering how to be a fish.

Coach pushed us through exhausting sets. By the third, pain flared beneath my sleeve—first a sting, then an ache.

At that point I lost the count. My lungs burned; I surfaced early, gasping. All I could see was Amanda's arm over the stump.

I'd never really noticed how red someone's blood was until I saw Amanda's at Stumphenge. For now, she was ignorant of reality not knowing about the aliens, walking around inside a half false world I'd let her keep. But if she was going to come with me, she'd have to know everything, and I'd have to decide how far I was willing to go to keep her with me.

I swam until the ache in my shoulders drowned out every other thought. But even floating there, gulping air, I knew I couldn't outswim her voice. ◇

Neur was still out there, listening. Watching. Waiting inside her silver saucerpan from outer space.

***

A school assembly was called. The podium lights too bright. Hundreds of bodies shifted in their seats, the air thick with cafeteria grease and rain-damp hoodies. Onstage, Dr. Bennet stood behind the microphone, her glasses flashing under the fluorescents.

"We know this year has been difficult for all of you," she

began, her voice steady in a way that carried calm. "Lockdowns. False alarms. The news cycle replaying things none of us should ever have had to imagine. Today we're talking about managing stress in the wake of school shootings."

A low ripple moved through the room—coughs, chair squeaks, whispers. Amanda gripped her knees, her face tight and scared.

Dr. Bennet talked about breathing exercises, support hotlines, counselor sessions available after class. Then, she asked if anyone had questions. The auditorium stayed silent, heavy.

My hand went up before my brain caught up to it. Amanda hissed, "Em—" but it was too late.

"Yes, Emily?" said Dr. Bennet.

I stood. My heart pounding so hard I thought the mic might pick it up. "Wouldn't it be more important to consider the ecosystems? The ones collapsing right now? How do we manage the stress of that? I get it, some kids get killed here and there—and that's tragic, I'm not saying it isn't. But in fifty years the whole world will be unlivable. How do we manage the stress of that?"

The words hung there, jagged and raw. A couple kids laughed nervously. Someone yelled, "Freakazoid."

Amanda clapped once, loud, and then ducked her head like she hadn't.

Dr. Bennet blinked. "That's a big question, Emily."

"It's the only question," I shot back, my throat dry. "We're the last generation that can make a change and if we don't, it will be too late. It's already too late to reverse global warming. Did you know that?"

The silence spread wider than the auditorium walls.

From the back row, Derik shifted in his seat, staring at me like he wanted to beat me with his selfie stick.

Dr. Bennet cleared her throat. "Thank you, Emily. We'll circle back to that." She moved briskly to the next slide about breathing through panic.

I sat, shaking, adrenaline burning under my skin. Amanda nudged me with her elbow, whispering, "That was fire."

"But do you really agree with me?" I said. "Are you actually worried? Because you should be." But I wasn't thinking of collapsing ecosystems. ◇

FILE 10 | A Noncosmic Breakup
DATE 06 MAY | SL-1

After school Derik was waiting outside the locker room leaning against the wall like a tornado standing on one leg.

"Hey," I said, because I didn't want to provoke with any little thing.

"Hey." His mouth was already a straight line. "You've ignored six texts."

"I was in the pool for four of them."

"And the other two?" His eyebrows lifted – it used to be teasing. Now it felt like a test.

I held my sketchbook satchel to my chest. "You don't listen—not to me." And I thought, *you don't listen to a world that is falling apart at the seams.*

"You're always talking about the world. Why can't you just focus on what's going on around us?"

He steered me outside. The night air lifted steam off my skin, stars blinked like light through pinholes in a canopy. We sat on the low wall. The stadium lights clicked off in pairs.

"Do you even want this?" he asked.

I flinched. "That's a jump."

"It's not. You don't text back. You don't sit with me. Even Amanda gets more time from you than I do." His voice wasn't angry, which made it worse. "The way I see it, it's like you're already gone."

My grip on the satchel strap dug into my palms. The mark pulsed under my sleeve, sharp and unkind.

"What's going on?" he said. "Tell me the truth."

Whispers threaded into my skull before I could answer. I pressed my sleeve hard. "I can't."

He gave a short laugh with no humor in it. "Is there someone else?"

"No."

"Then what?"

"I can't," I said, hating how weak it sounded.

He waited. When nothing else came, he nodded once, like accepting a grade he couldn't change. "I don't want a half-zombie, Em. And that's all I get lately."

The last pair of lights snapped off. Darkness made everything too clean.

"Maybe we should take a break," I whispered, the words barely making it past my teeth. ◇

"Yeah." His jaw worked, but he didn't argue. He stood, pushed his hands deep in his jacket. Halfway to the sidewalk he paused like he might turn back. Then he kept walking.

The mark pulsed again, steady as a heartbeat, like it knew he was gone and didn't think it important. I let out a long breath, sure none of this was going to matter. Something bigger than all of us was coming. The mark beat once more, answering something inside.

I closed my eyes and thought. "Why am I not crying?"

Amanda yelled, "Em?"

I flinched yelling, "What?" Amanda jumped out of the shadows by the gym doors, smiling like she'd sprinted to get there.

"Were you spying?" I tried to make it a joke and missed.

"Observing," she said. "With an intelligence greater than your own; that, all the while, as boys and girls busied themselves about their romantic lives, you were being studied…"

"The way a man with a microscope might scrutinize the creatures that swarm and multiply in a drop of water," I added, then blurted, "Ha ha," about three seconds too late.

The grin she offered was careful. "You okay?"

"Define okay."

She took in my face, my death grip on the satchel, the way I'd backed up until the wall was holding me up. "Right. New plan. Cherry slushy and those terrible gas station donuts you secretly love."

"I don't–"

"Great," she said, already walking. "Let's go then."

I didn't move.

She turned back, and said softer. "Or we can sit here. I can sit with you and not talk for an hour, well, 10 minutes. I *am* capable of silence. I'll prove it to you."

A sound that might have been a laugh escaped me, wrecked at the edges. "I broke up with him."

"I gathered." She came closer to stand beside me, hip against the wall, both of us facing the same empty field like it was a blank movie screen during intermission. "He's not a great listener but he's not a villain either."

"I know."

"You don't have to tell me what you're feeling," she said.

For a second the night felt normal again, the kind of quiet that feels like peace instead of danger. Amanda took that second and leaned her shoulder against mine.

"He'll be okay," she said. "Don't worry about him."

I stared at the black shapes of the bleachers, at the spiderweb crack in the light cover.

"Promise?" I said.

"No," she said, and it was the most honest thing anyone had said to me all week. "But I'll hold you steady while your universe spins out of control."

She didn't hold my hands. She just stood there, and I felt relieved.

When she finally peeled me off the wall and steered me toward the sidewalk, I realized I hadn't cried. I also realized that not crying didn't mean anything good. Derik and I had been really good friends since middle school. We kissed a couple of times but that was it. Maybe he thought he would rather go out with someone who wasn't so into making a stand for a better world. Who knows. Breakups are usually just a big stupid mystery.

We cut through the dark strip of grass behind the tennis courts. The chain-link fence droned against its poles as we dragged sticks along it. Beyond it, the town sprawled in ordinary lights—grocery store, car wash, the place that pretends to be a diner but closes at nine. I tried to drink the normal in with my eyes, like I could store it somewhere for later use.

At the corner, Amanda stopped. "Text me when you get home."

"I will."

"No, like actually do please, so I know you weren't kidnapped for your organs or something."

"I will," I said again.

She stepped back with a live long and prosper wave and then took off toward her neighborhood, running for the joy of it, sneakers thumping intentionally. I watched until she was just a shape between two streetlights, and then a smaller shape, and then gone.

I took the long way home. My feet knew all the unlevel sidewalk slabs by heart, the tree roots that I used to trip over. I tried to count my steps. I tried to think about anything except how it felt to say, “I just broke up,” or “I was abducted by aliens.” I tried to drown out the vision of the spaceship.

The vision came anyway, thinner now, stretched. A flicker in the corner of my eye made me jerk my head up. “Only a plane,” I told myself, its red blink patient and human.

FILE 11 | The Blackout
DATE 07 MAY | SL-2

The house was dark.

Mom’s note on the counter said “Late. Fire chicken. Love you.” A little bent heart drawn at the bottom.

I ate standing up, because sitting felt like an invitation for my body to realize it was uptight about something.

Upstairs, I put my satchel on the desk and stared at it like I could will it to behave a certain way. When I opened it, the sketchbook page was half-filled with a drawing I didn’t remember starting: two teenage girls on a low wall, the smaller one holding a square object tight to her chest. High above them, an oval hung in the blackout sky.

Fire Chicken Ramen
+++++++++++++++++++++
01. Bring about 2 cups (475 ml) of water to a boil in a silver saucerpan. 02. Add the ramen noodles to the boiling water. 03. Boil for 3 minutes, stirring occasionally to separate the wet noodles. 04. Turn off the heat. Add the flavor packet, removing pork bits. 05. Let it sit till cool or the world ends, whichever comes first, or you’ll scald your tongue. 06. Add fresh raw onion. Emily

I felt like I had to do something, but what? I couldn’t stop thinking big in a world where I felt so small.

I dozed instead.

Something woke me and I jerked upright, gasping.

My lamp cast a weak disc of light over the sketchbook where another new drawing stared back at me.

Just a plain sphere, but symbols started to materialize in my mind. So I added them. This time the lines were sharper, purposeful, the word Draen'drel twisting through my brain like trichinosis.[4] ◆ DI#05

I slammed the sketchbook shut, leaped through the air and bounced on the mattress pulling the blanket over my head like I was six again, scaring myself with monsters under the bed.

But the monster wasn't under me. It was in me, pulsing orange and white beneath my skin.

And it wasn't going away.

I touched my thumb to the paper and came away with graphite.

"You can't have everything," I told the empty room.

The mark under my sleeve warmed and then cooled, like a sigh through fabric.

I turned off the lamp and lay on top of the covers, shoes still on like I might have to run.

Sleep yanked me in jagged pieces. I turned over and over, one hand pulling at my ear, the other rubbing the mark. I dreamed I was angry at a black-eyed alien that wasn't there to argue back. "I want answers," I whispered into the pillow. "I'm not going to break, and I'm not giving up on her." ◇

***

I woke feeling like a train wreck but managed to make myself get to school.

Everything felt wrong in small, distinct ways.

The hallway clocks were all ten minutes fast. The vending machine in the commons spat out two sodas when I only paid for

[4] Trichinosis is a parasitic disease caused by eating raw or undercooked meat (especially pork) that contains the larvae of a roundworm called Trichinella.

one. The air felt brittle, like the world had been photocopied one too many times.

At lunch, Amanda held court at our usual table, spinning a story about hacking into the cafeteria Wi-Fi just to prove she could. Normally, I'd laugh until soda sprayed out my nose. But today the noise pressed painfully behind my eyes. I chewed my sandwich like tough cardboard and gave Amanda an empty stare.

I wasn't the same. I was getting worse, and something was going to give.

***

That night, the blackout hit.

One second, I was at my desk, sketching another strange glyph on the sphere. The next, the lamp fizzed, the fridge died, and the entire house exhaled a dying breath.

Outside, the neighborhood blinked out—porches, streetlamps, even the cell tower in the distance. My room turned into a still from some old *Creature from the Black Lagoon* movie.

The hum swelled, filling the empty space.

I gripped the edge of my desk. "Now what?" I whispered.

<It's almost time,> Neur answered, her voice sliding in as natural as breath.

My pulse shot up. "Why me? Why are you coming for me again?"

<You pretend to resist. You pretend not to know the reason. You draw.>

Her words carried that same calm weight, but underneath was something like insistence. <Few host subjects draw.>

"Host subjects?" The word sliced. "I'm not a subject, I'm a person."

Silent pause, then: <The difference is perspective.>

The blackout dragged on. Outside, not a single car dared to

move. The air felt heavy, like it was holding its breath at a state finals swim meet. A chill ran over my skin, prickling like static, and my spine tingled with anxiety.

“What do you want from me?” My voice sounded too loud in the dark.

<To prepare you.>

“For what?”

Her silence seemed like an answer in itself.

The power flicked back, lamp fizzed on, refrigerator clicked on downstairs. The neighborhood re-lit one house at a time. My pencil rolled off the desk, landing point-down, stabbing directly into the carpet.

FILE 12 | Last Good Time with Mom
DATE 07 MAY | SL-2

Mom got home with a flashlight tucked under her arm and bags of groceries banging on her knees.

“Grid’s a mess,” she announced, like there was a roomful of people.

“Half the town bought batteries for nothing.”

“The power’s back,” I said, stepping in from the kitchen doorway.

“Mostly.”

She gave me a quick once-over, reading my face the way only Moms can.

“Are you okay?”

“Yeah, Mom.”

The lie felt heavier tonight.

"Help out?"

We put things away, the refrigerator humming like it didn't remember being dead ten minutes ago.

She set a pack of tea lights on the counter. "I got the impression the blackout might last," she said. "Let's celebrate."

The idea of her wandering the aisles under emergency lighting made my chest hurt. I worried about her.

"Want cocoa?" she asked.

"Oh my God, yes."

Steam fogged the small window over the sink.

The house had that post-outage quiet, the kind that made every sound feel amplified.

We sat at the table, sipping, our mugs cupped in both hands like tiny children.

She blew on hers.

Tea lights lit our faces.

"You were little the last time the power went out like this. You hid in the bathtub with the cat—or was it the dog?"

"I remember."

I didn't.

But the picture was nice.

"So, how's everything?" she asked, hiding her mouth behind her mug.

"It's gotten a little weird."

She reached out and covered my fidgeting hand.

"Is it boy weird?"

Her voice was gentle, careful.

“Derik-weird?”

My breath deepened.

“We broke up.”

She paused, annoyed brow, like it wasn’t my fault. “Oh Em, I’m sorry.”

She squeezed my hand.

“Wanna talk about it?”

I shook my head, hiding behind my mug.

“Not yet.”

“Okay.”

She let it go, a soft surrender.

“I’m here when you’re ready.”

We cleaned our mugs in the sink.

The tea lights flickered in their little aluminum skins, throwing candlelight shadows that made the kitchen look like a different house—one where time moved slowly backwards and everything smelled like gingerbread baking.

On the way to my room, she stopped in the hall and tested the light switches, up-down-up.

She glanced at me over her shoulder.

“Sure you’re sleeping okay?”

“I’m… trying to.”

She nodded like that was enough.

It wasn’t for her, but she pretended.

I closed my door, leaning my forehead against it until the cool paint soothed the ache.

The sketchbook patiently waited on my desk.

When I picked it up, it was open to a page I hadn't drawn. A rough outline of a map, jagged coastlines, dots where cities might go. The word Draen'drel was written across the bottom in handwriting and symbols I didn't recognize. ◆ DI#06

The map glared at me from the page. I didn't know what Draen'drel was, but the word felt heavy in my chest, like I'd always known it.

I flipped the sketchbook shut, but it was too late. The word kept repeating in my thoughts, low and steady, promising it would come back. Draen'drel ◇

FILE 13 | Implantation
DATE 08 MAY | SL-3

Had I not been abducted by an alien a few nights before, I would have bet I had gone completely bats. I turned off the lamp and lay in bed with my arms above the blanket, staring at the faint glow the clock cast on the ceiling. The house settled, a thousand tiny sounds stacked into something like a lullaby. I almost believed I could sleep.

Then, it found me again.

A silence-filled hole, the absence of noise changing shape.

The air drifted out of my window pulling the curtains outside.

I glanced outside and the same dark outline was above the trees. My neck stiffened. It was pointing straight at me.

<Emily.> The way she said my name punched my ribcage like brass knuckles. <You are ready.>

I started whimpering like a puppy, then laughing—oddly, more laugh than cry—thinking I probably wouldn't be coming back this time.

I mustered a Dorothy-in-Oz voice. "If I'm going back inside that chamber again, I want some questions answered," I said, as though I could demand anything from a superior alien race.

<Defiance is not refusal,> she said, reading me like a book. <Your patterns indicate readiness for your data node implant.>

"What the heck is that?" I dared, as if I had a choice.

<It means, Emily, you will have your questions answered.>

The air in my room cooled. A pinpoint of cold bloomed at the back of my neck just above my hairline.

"What's happening?" My voice sounded small in my own ears.

<Emily,> Neur said, and there was something in how she said my name that made me feel weirdly detached from reality. <You are not alone in this decision. Assimilation requires—>

"Assimilation," I shouted, chopping the sentence in half. "You mean you're going to kill me?"

<No,> she said. <Death you will not experience. Implantation becomes continuance for you, and then assimilation.>

"Your words aren't normal. I'm confused."

Another pause. <I do not want you to break. We don't fully understand why you remain conscious during abductions, so we must proceed carefully.>

There was the faintest thread of something in her voice, pity possibly, woven into the flat calm. <I will slow the process. It will not kill you, but I cannot guarantee it will be painless.>

Then tears came hot, fast, and unhelpful. I scrubbed them away with the heels of my hands. "What have you been doing to me? I'm drawing places I've never been and writing words I don't know."

<Draen'drel,> she said, and hearing the word from her made it soak deeply into my abdomen.

I lay back down slowly, my back touching the mattress that felt like it wanted me to sleep. The cold point at my nape increased by degrees. I thought about ignoring it all and pulling the blanket over me.

Something like a specter slapped me hard across the face, stinging. "Whatever," I thought. "Let's get it over with." ◇

I sat back up in bed with determination, heart banging against my chest. My eyes risked looking at the clock. The numbers glowed red, 2:37AM.

A faint blue sheet of light shimmered through the window, stretching to all four walls and then pulling downward.

It passed over my retinas.

I slid out of bed and tip toed barefoot toward my window. A gum wrapper from earlier crinkled under the ball of my foot. My sketchbook still lay open on the desk, as if to say sayonara.[5]

"Okay," I whispered, giving it one last glance.

Outside, the stars blinked out. Not clouded—erased. The shape hung there, darker than night, bigger than my eyes could measure.

The blue cone shaped light pulled me; I assisted it stepping out onto the roof. Before I could take a second step, I rose weightless.

A seam opened across the underside of the ship, invisible until it wasn't.

"Here we go again." The world vanished in a flash.

I was inside the spaceship again, being pulled to the cylinder below the sphere. Prying eyes looked me up and down like I was a very expensive rack of beef—or at least that's how it felt.

I let myself go into the invisible pressure, then slid into

---

[5] さようなら Sayōnara - Literal meaning: Derived from the older phrase 左様ならば (sayō naraba), which means "if it is to be that way" or "if so." The phrase is an acceptance of circumstances, as in "if things must be so, then farewell."

liquid. Warm and thick, it clung to my skin exactly like before, forcing into my lungs. I gasped, but the fluid carried oxygen on its own. Each breath felt borrowed.

As I floated, I pulled my knees to my chest. Light crawled along the chamber walls. Blue veins pulsing with the same rhythm as the silver sphere that hovered in the center.

Figures moved at the corner of my sight, long-limbed, their faces blank ovals of curiosity.

One stepped closer, hand raised.

<Emily,> the voice calm as always. <Implantation is required. You will survive. Don't be alarmed.>

"Neur," I thought back, teeth chattering though my body wasn't cold. "What's going to happen now?"

Somewhere inside the sphere hanging ominously overhead, electricity crawled like lightning tendrils under a black fluid core pushing current toward the surface. Toward me.

And I knew somehow, whatever I had gone through before was nothing compared to what was about to happen.

The gel around me pressed in, getting warmer and heavier. Each breath reminded me I wasn't supposed to be alive here.

The sphere brightened until it was the only thing I could see.

I tried to move, but the chamber didn't care.

A figure stepped close, taller than the rest.

<Emily.>

Neur's voice was firm but not detached this time. Something threaded through it—strain, or maybe even hurting for me.

<It is necessary.>

The alien's hand reached into the liquid and supported my neck. I felt a strange sensation in my stomach, like being comforted by my mother's colostrum.[6]

I felt a cold pinch of pain on my neck as it slid into me.

The pain grew sharper as it drove deeper, sliding into my brain. Every nerve responded, my mouth opened wide.

"No!" My scream came out as gurgles in the fluid.

<Do not resist,> Neur said, closer now, as if she had leaned into my subconscious. <Resistance increases pain.>

"It's hurting bad." My mind threw sparks. "I want to stay me."

My body arched without permission, every muscle taut. Visions bled into my mind of a dark world of black towers and corridors packed with voices layered in unison, the sense of falling forward past transparent domes that had no end.

I clutched at my own memories to anchor myself, Amanda's laugh when soda shot out my nose; Mom doodling hearts on sticky notes; the burn of chlorine in my lungs.

White fire exploded down my spine. My hands curled into fists so hard my nails cut skin. I shrieked again, a noise so raw that the chamber itself seemed to cringe and swallow it whole.

Neur's voice faltered. <Emily—>

The hum surged to a pitch that hollowed me out.

And the **data node implant** entered. ◇

The chamber's light dimmed, then surged again. My vision fractured into shards of blue and white, like glass breaking in slow motion.

I tried to hold on: "I'm Emily Rowen. I'm still me."

But with each pulse of the data node, that truth slipped

---

[6] Colostrum is the nutrient-rich, yellowish fluid produced by the mammary glands of mammals (including humans) during the first few days after giving birth, before the regular breast milk comes in.

further from my grasp. The needle was receding.

"Synchronization engaged." A voice—not Neur's, colder—intoned across the chamber.

I gasped, though the gel made no bubbles. "Stop," I thought, desperately. "It's breaking me."

But Neur's voice cut across the other. <Emily. Listen to me. Breathe.>

I wanted to scream at her. I wanted to claw her voice out of my skull. But…

It was in me now.

Neur placed her other four fingered hand over the middle of my chest and pressed down.

For an instant, I wasn't myself. I was a voice among voices, an echo among echoes, consciousness focused into pure reality.

"Get it over with." The words hurled like stones.

Even Neur's steady tone wavered. <She knows—she knows us.>

My thought bled raw into the chamber. "Stop before there's nothing left."

The node sphere above me flared white, a second sun igniting inside my head. My body went limp in the gel. My storm-colored eyes rolled back in their sockets until only white showed.

And just before the darkness closed in, I clung to Mom's voice the day she taught me to swim. *Kick, Em. Kick like the water is yours.*

The chamber went dark.

***

I woke in bed.

I felt like I hadn't slept. I rehearsed the scene over and over in my mind. Neur's face, her hand, her connection to me, the visions of some far away place.

My muscles were sore. But no pain in my neck. I only felt a slight pressure inside my head.

I knew I had to tell someone now. I rehearsed what I might say to Amanda, to Mom, to Dr. Bennet. I counted breaths and pressed my tongue to the roof of my mouth and tried to memorize what it felt like to be only me.

At some point near dawn, I sat up and whispered to the empty room, "You don't get to take me without my best friend."

Something whispered inside my mind, from a place Neur's voice couldn't quite reach:

> We gave to Ston'harr the circle of stones. Each pillar aligned to cycle, to moon, to sun. They did not know why, yet they built as guided. To them it was ritual; to us, it shaped the ultimate self-sacrifice. ◇

The house did not answer. But the mark on my arm warmed once, steady as a heartbeat, as if something on the other end of the line had heard me and had taken notes.

FILE 14 | The Day After Implantation
DATE 08 MAY | SL-4

I still felt like me, but it was a different me. The experience had altered the original version of me. I wasn't Emily v2.0. I was Emily v1.999. It was like my eyes saw everything in high definition.

I didn't notice the little noises in our house, though. No fan tick, no fridge shifting its weight in the kitchen.

It was an emptied-out silence, hollow and heavy, like the air had been unplugged.

I knew I hadn't dreamed it this time—the chamber, the light, the scream I couldn't swallow.

My comforter was twisted around me, T-shirt damp with sweat.

Then, the faint tick of the fan returned, steady as a clock.

Above me, my old mobile spun lazily in the draft from the window—

but I saw the planets differently.

Styrofoam balls dangling from bent wire, painted in a fifth-grade coloring scheme with a brush too thick for detail.

Jupiter was smudged orange; Saturn's rings bent, half-falling.

My memory of Mom hot gluing them back seemed too real, too present.

The Earth still wore a crooked patch of green paper over blue tempera paint.

What would become of it?

It should have been a harmless thought, but my mind darkened.

The planets spun as if my data node had reached up and given them a push.

I pressed both palms to my temples.

The pain had faded to an echo, but something heavier remained—an awareness I couldn't shake.

Like another heartbeat nested behind mine. ◇

My phone buzzed on the nightstand.

[Amanda: u alive or did the aliens finally win?]

Followed by

[jk. but seriously. u missed English.]

[call me, ghost girl.]

I typed and erased [migraine] three times before shoving my phone under the pillow.

When I dragged myself to the mirror, the girl staring back was not the same girl.

Same storm-gray eyes, hair messy from sleep, T-shirt sleeves stretched from tugging.

But there was a shine under my eyes now, a faint glaze of white that glimmered and then vanished when I blinked.

I pulled my sleeve high to check.

The mark on my arm faintly glowed, slow and steady, like a metronome.

"Not a dream this time," I told myself, rolling my eyes, hurt.

***

At school, everything looked out of date, like old and unwanted '70s retro.

Lockers slammed like thunderclaps.

The cafeteria smelled like burned bodies.

Sheridan launched into an NPC-level lecture about Cold War paranoia as I stared at my desk, my pencil sketching without permission.

When I looked down, it was a portrait of Neur. Not like my previous sketches of her. This was drawn in impossible detail. It was so real I snapped the notebook shut.

My hands shook. ◆ DI#07

Amanda slid into the seat beside me at lunch, eyes razor sharp.

"You look like cafeteria lunch warmed over." Nothing got past her.

"I survived the night," I rasped.

"You missed what happened in English. Sheridan made a joke about alien propaganda and looked right at you. You looked like you were in another dimension. It was freaky."

I smiled weakly, pain twisting in my gut.

"He would."

Amanda leaned closer, dropping her voice.

"Seriously, what in the world is going on with you? You've been… not you lately."

I thought about telling her.

About saying, You're right. I'm not all me anymore.

Something's inside me now, something watching and listening.

But the words stuck.

Instead, I said, "Just feeling a little sick."

"Seriously. Talk to me. Before you explode."

I wanted to.

I wanted to dump the whole truth in her lap: the ship, the chamber, the tiny sphere in my head.

But when I opened my mouth, all that came out was,

"It's migraines. But I'm going to tell you everything."

"Finally?" she sighed, scratching the back of her head.

The bell rang before we could say bet.

The cracks in my shiny reality had already started to show.

Sooner or later, someone else was going to see them. ◇

FILE 15 | Astral Traveler[7]
DATE 08 MAY | SL-2

I lost time. It felt like I was looking down on myself from above while I slept.

I dreamed of a dense liquid, thicker than any oil spill in the ocean. The liquid flowed through clear oval sacs that stretched into darkness.

I shuffled among bodies suspended inside, men, women, children, and strangers I thought I recognized but couldn't name.

Their hair floated upward in slow motion, eyes closed, lips parted as if mid-breath. Tubes pressed against pale skin.

I woke from the dream gasping, a metallic taste of blood in my mouth. My heart raced—not from running or fear, but from feeling responsible somehow.

Without thinking, I grabbed my pencil. My hands already knew where to move, as though the dream had imprinted itself on my paper. Lines cut fast across the page, then slowed, growing darker, thicker.

I sketched bulges lined in rows, wires dripping like vines. I shaded the water black and dragged the graphite until it smeared into smoke. The faces came last. Dozens of them. Shapes blurred, arms attached, expressionless and trapped between sleep and drowning.

When I leaned back, the drawing stared at me. It was too horrific—too real to be just a dream. Every connector, every coil, every curved line of tubing looked organic, alive. I didn't know where the imagery had come from, only that it had passed through me.

My mother's voice murmured faintly down the hall, half-asleep. I froze, pencil hovering. For a moment, I imagined her face among the drawn ones. Pale. Still. Breath stolen by cords. The

[7] An astral traveler is a someone who leaves their physical body to explore distant locations or otherworldly realms in a spirit-like form, venturing into places beyond ordinary reality.

thought made my stomach turn. I shut the sketchbook, pressing it flat as though I could hide the image from the world—and from myself.

But hiding didn't work anymore.

The voice came before I could crawl back into bed. Not aloud. Not even a whisper through the wall. It arrived in my skull, vibrating my thoughts like a plucked string.

> <Shuun Varnul endure, calling themselves heirs. But they are design, not blood. They walk in continuity, yet without fire. Without Ten'drel, without Ser'ethra, their Node is brilliance without breath.>

<This is from Thrae-Draen 11.03,> Neur interjected.

I pulled the blanket up under my chin. "Responsible," I whispered, though no one could hear. "No one cares enough."

<Thousands carry what you carry now. Hundreds of thousands. Scattered across your lands, hidden in your cities, buried in your crowds. Nodes pulse within them, threads connecting back to us.> ◆ DI#08

I covered my ears as though it would help. It didn't.

<But not all will be taken further.>

The words pressed coldly against my mind. <Most vessels are for our learning only. Observers. Recorders. They will die as they would have died without us. You have been shown this.>

I squeezed my eyes shut. "What about me?"

Silence for a moment. Then the answer bled into my thoughts: <Some cross deeper. The young. The pliable. The ones who can bend without breaking.>

An image flashed. Dozens of children, teenagers my age or younger. Faces flickering in quick succession. Their eyes glowed faintly, as if lit from within; they weren't much older than the students I passed every morning.

I swallowed the words. "Why them?"

The reply came without warmth: <Older minds fracture. They cannot bear the implant without collapse. Only the younger adapt. Only they can be made ready.>

My grip on the blanket slackened. The image of my mother's face surfaced again, pale like the dream-bodies in semitransparent casings. I pressed my palms against my eyes, as if pressure could push the thought away. It didn't. Instead, I felt it—a terrible certainty that my mother would never make it through what was coming.

I rolled over, burying my face in the pillow. "Please not her."

But Neur didn't stop.

<You are a fragment of two hundred thousand who carry this burden. They will help us understand you, help guide the process when integration begins. They are threads in the loom that will be woven in.>

I pushed myself upright, bawling. "Oh my God."

No words came this time. Just another image: a narrowing funnel of faces, the two hundred thousand, their expressions fixed in unbearable clarity. Kids. With bright eyes. Unbroken. Waiting.

I scrambled for my sketchbook and fell back on my bed holding it against my chest as a shield. The pencils on my desk rolled off and clattered to the floor like they had a will of their own.

My mother coughed faintly from the other room, the sound fragile, ordinary. My stomach dropped to bottom. I knew it wasn't illness, not yet, but the thought lingered anyway: *the old cannot survive.*

I slid off the bed, crouching on the floor, forehead pressed to my knees. Tears blurred my vision, not from pain but from something worse—*the guilt*. I didn't want this burden. I didn't want to imagine my mother gone, her body one of the silent figures inside them, whatever they were.

The voice quieted at last, withdrawing like a tide. But the hum remained, faint and unshakable, like static at the edge of hearing.

I lifted the sketchbook again, my fingers smudged black. I opened to the drawing despite myself. The figures there because of my doing, dozens of them dissolving in liquid. And near the back row, half-hidden in shadow, one face I hadn't drawn on purpose. One I hadn't meant to include.

My mother. ◇

FILE 16 | Telling Amanda About Aliens
DATE 08 MAY | SL-1

The field lights buzzed overhead, but the stands were empty. The late game ended hours ago, and now only the echo of footsteps carried across the football field. I sat on the cold metal bleachers with my sketchbook clutched to my chest. Amanda came whizzing up on a bike. She climbed the bleachers skipping every other one and plopped down leaning back on her elbows, glaring at me like she wasn't going to leave without answers.

"Spill," Amanda said. "And don't give me another 'it's complicated.' I've waited long enough."

"Amanda, where did you get that bike?"

"I borrowed it."

"From who? I've never seen it before."

"From my neighbor."

"Does he know you took it?"

"No," she said self-righteously.

"That's stealing, Amanda."

"No it's not, it's borrowing. Stealing is when you don't give it back."

"I hope you get it back before he notices." She shot me a look that said, I know.

I pressed my sneakers against the bleacher rung, wishing I could shrink into the steel. “You’re not going to believe me.”

Amanda groaned. “You keep saying that. But I’m still here, aren’t I? Just tell me.”

I picked at the corner of my sketchbook. It wasn’t working.

“I have a new sketch,” I said.

Amanda shifted to face me fully. “But that’s not what we’re here for. I’m not letting you change the subject.”

My throat went dry, my chest aching like I’d been punched hard. And now Amanda was staring, unblinking, waiting.

“You really want to know?” I asked.

Amanda leaned closer. “I do. All of it.”

My pulse hammered. I glanced at the dark field, the goalposts glowing pale under the lights. No one else was around. I forced the words out before I lost my nerve.

“I was taken.”

Amanda blinked. “Taken? Like detention taken?”

I shook my head. “No. Not by teachers. Not by anyone here. By something else.” I looked directly at her, and she knew what I was saying.

Amanda frowned. “Emily?” ◆ DI#09

“I’m serious.” I placed my hand on her arm. “I was outside that night, after swim practice. The sky went dark, and then—it was like the stars vanished. Something was up there. It was huge, silent, and it pulled me off the ground. I couldn’t move, couldn’t breathe. And then, I woke up different.”

Amanda’s laugh was sharp but uncertain. “You’re telling me you were abducted? By—what, aliens?”

“Yes.” My gaze locked on hers. “I know how it sounds. But it happened. And ever since, I can’t sleep. I see things. I draw things I don’t even understand until they’re on the page. And there’s a voice in my head that isn’t mine.”

Amanda stared at me, searching for the punch line. “That’s… you realize how crazy this sounds, right?”

“I know.” My hands shook as I opened the sketchbook and flipped to the newest drawing, the bodies suspended in liquid filled sacs, the tubes like veins. I shoved it toward Amanda. “I didn’t imagine this. I’ve never seen anything like it before, but I drew it. I couldn’t stop. And it’s real. They put something inside my head too.”

Amanda hesitated, her fingers slowly rubbing over the drawing. It was too detailed, too sharp. She pulled her hand back like the paper burned.

“Emily?” She slowly looked up at me like she believed.

My voice crashed. “I’m not scared, for some reason. But I can’t tell anyone else. They’d lock me up. You’re all I have.”

Amanda bit her lip, looking between my face and the sketch. Her expression softened, but her eyes began to doubt again. “If this is true, why you? What do they want with you?”

I hugged the sketchbook to my chest again, trembling. Tears started to fall. The answer I wanted to give—because I was young enough, because older minds would break, because I could feel even now that my own mother would never survive—stayed trapped in my throat. Saying all this aloud would make it real, and she couldn’t handle it. Not yet.

Instead, I let myself cry and whispered, “I don’t know. But I think… it means something bad is coming. For me. For you. For everyone.”

Amanda stared at me for a long time, then shook her head looking down. “You really expect me to believe—”

“I don’t expect anything,” I said, my voice cracking. “I just needed you to listen to me. Even if you decide not to believe me, it’s okay.”

“So did you see them?” she asked, eyes wide.

“Yes.”

“Really, what do they look like?”

“They don’t look like the little gray men we see in the movies. They are taller, more… elegant.”

“It sounds like you’ve grown fond of them.”

“One of their names is Neur.” Disbelief crept over Amanda’s face.

“So they took you, inside their spaceship?” Skepticism creased her brow.

“Yes. Twice.”

Amanda took a breath and blew air between her lips, trying to believe me. She knew I wouldn’t lie about something like this.

“So what does the ship look like on the inside?”

“Way more advanced than you think. The walls are curved and have blue pulsing light going through them. The aliens float in fixed positions that look like digital outlines of chairs. They see through screens full of data suspended in front of them. There is a large metal sphere in the middle that has static electricity moving over it. Below is a round tank full of greenish-blue liquid. They put me in it and I could still breathe. The—.”

“Wait. You’re scaring me.”

“So you believe me?” I said.

“I know you couldn’t make all this up, and your drawings are way better than before. *Something* is happening to you.”

Silence stretched. The hum of the stadium lights buzzed overhead. I pressed my fists to my eyes, waiting for Amanda to laugh, to call me insane, to leave. But she didn’t move.

Finally, she said, quietly, “Meet me again late. Show me something I can’t deny. I want to meet your new star buddy and see their ship.”

I looked up, startled.

Amanda's jaw was set. "I think you're telling the truth, but I, I just need to see it for myself. You would ask me to do the same for you if you'd just spilled all that tea."

I nodded slowly, heart hammering. I'd promised myself I wouldn't drag Amanda into this. But the thought of Amanda not surviving—like my mother—settled cold in my chest. Maybe I could convince Neur to let her live.

And so, I whispered, "Okay. Three a.m. At the park." She buzzed off on the bike yelling, "It better be good."

I had no idea how I was going to convince Neur of this. I thought it wasn't going to turn out well for any of us.

FILE 17 | Asking Neur to Meet Amanda
DATE 09 MAY | SL-1

From my bed I could see the oak tree that leans over the yard.

Its branches hissed with the wind, reaching so close to the window I sometimes imagined they were fingers trying to pull me outside.

The room was still.

My posters floated slightly away from the walls with the breeze. The ancient glow-in-the-dark stars on my ceiling had faded to a dull green. I couldn't wait any longer.

I pushed the window open and climbed onto the roof, sketchbook in its satchel—my defensive mechanism—anchoring me on the edge of my world with a shred of confidence.

The shingles were cool under my legs, rough against my bare feet.

I pulled hoodie strings tight around my head and stared out across the neighborhood.

ALIEN I AM

Porch lights glowed like tiny suns.

Somewhere a dog barked, and then silence swallowed it.

I thought softly, "Come here."

Before I could think another word, the silver spacecraft dropped dead out of the night sky.

It stopped above the treetops and hovered, blotting out the sky over our little two-story house. It darkened and took on the reflection of the tree's branches like a chameleon.

It waited completely silent, as though observing to see if the coast was clear.

Light rain began to fall on its heated exterior, encircling it with steamy mist.

A cone-shaped ray of blue light spilled from the hull, and Neur appeared on the roof next to me as if she'd folded through space-time.

The wind rushed around me. I felt dreadfully peaceful seeing her.

Inside my room, I heard the faint clink of my solar system mobile moving from the displaced air, planets knocking softly against each other as though disturbed by invisible hands.

Neur folded her long limbs and sat beside me on the roof, quiet, like she'd always belonged there.

Her body glistened faintly like it was never quite dry, and the night bent around her silhouette.

"Thanks for coming," I said, my voice barely above a whisper.

Her head tilted, eyes caught moonlight like glass.

<Why here? Why not the vessel?> She knew what I wanted.

"I didn't want to leave the house. My mom—" I swallowed, staring down at the yard as my mind started to go down a dark tunnel.

“She’s not well. If I disappear again, she’ll freak out. But Amanda’s demanding proof.”

Neur studied me, expression unreadable.

<You are testing boundaries that are not yours to move.>

“I have to,” I said quickly.

“Amanda doesn’t totally believe me. And if I lose her?”

My voice cracked.

“She’s, well, all I have left… will have left.”

Neur didn’t answer right away.

The silence stretched until I wondered if she’d leave.

<She does not need to know. Exposure must be controlled.>

“You don’t have any idea what I am going through.”

I hugged my knees tighter.

“I have to,” I said quickly. “You’re not the one sitting next to your best friend, staring at you like you’re crazy.”

Her eyes narrowed.

<It is not safe for her. Once she sees me, she will carry the weight you do. It might be too heavy for her mind and cause fracture.>

“She’s stronger than you think,” I argued louder than I meant to.

Neur didn’t reply.

“She’s strong for me. Why can’t you see that?”

Her gaze shifted to the satchel in my lap.

<You hold to those pages as if they are significant.>

I blinked.

"What?"

<The sketchbook. The drawings. They are more important to you than food or sleep. Show me.>

"You, want to see them?"

Her voice softened, almost curious.

<Yes.>

"Come inside, the rain is starting to come down." I wanted to say her name but didn't.

My knees shook as I crawled back through the window.

Posters on my wall rippled faintly as the rainstorm outside intensified. My original *Star Wars: A New Hope* poster caught my eye. I thought of the laser pistol in Princess Leia's hand. Young Luke Skywalker, a light saber in his hands, looking like he might know secrets. I wondered what Neur thought of all that?

I placed the sketchbook squarely on my desk and flipped it open to the first page.

Neur stepped up behind me to my desk as though she had been there many times.

I turned the sketch so she could see.

Page after page of graphite scratched visions: the ship blotting out the stars, pods filled with bodies suspended in liquid, spheres and runic names I didn't understand.

Her head tilted.

<These are accurate.>

I swallowed.

"Accurate? Meaning they're real."

<Yes.>

The word chilled me.

"My sketches no longer look like mine at all. They look like memories I don't recall having."

Her gaze lingered on the faces dissolving in the fluid, shaded in delicate grays.

<This you should not know. Yet you render it. With clarity.>

"I can't help it," I whispered.

"It comes through me, like it has to get out of me. And then, it changes me the more I look at it."

For the first time, Neur's voice softened with something almost human in it.

<I believe you.>

I closed the sketchbook, slipped it into its satchel.

"Then please, believe me about Amanda too. She won't let this go. If you don't show her, she'll keep digging until she finds something on her own. Please. Just once, for me." ◇

Neur gazed at me for a while, like she was contemplating something new. Then, she glanced toward the window, toward the vessel that still hung above the trees.

<It is permitted because of who you are. However, she will carry what she is not capable of. I know you care for her deeply and think this is best, but it most likely will not turn out well. I am inclined to say no.>

"Then make an exception."

I knelt in front of her, the sketchbook slid down over my knees.

"Just once. I don't want to lose her. I can't lose her."

Her eyes glinted with shifting light, as if something moved

inside them like water.

She studied me longer than she ever had before.

Finally, her voice brushed against my mind:

<You are marked, as I am. When you speak, I listen. The Node does not condone it, but it listens as well.>

I let out a shaky sigh.

“So, you’ll do it?”

A pause.

Then: <One time. No more.>

Relief crashed over me.

“Thank you, Neur.” It sounded strange calling her by name.

Neur glanced again at the sketchbook satchel covering my knees.

<Show me more soon.>

“Yeah,” I whispered. “I will.”

For a moment, it felt ordinary—just two girls sitting together, one with pencils, one with secrets beyond our solar system.

The mobile above my bed swayed; the ship still hovered outside until my friend the alien said, <It’s time.>

I knew nothing about this night would be ordinary.

FILE 18 | Neur Appears to Amanda
DATE 09 MAY | SL-3

“I need shoes,” I whispered.

Neur’s eyes glinted, black to gray and then black again. <For

what purpose?>

“I’m not walking across wet grass in bare feet.”

I walked where I knew the floor wouldn’t squeak, careful not to wake the house. My alarm clock glowed 2:57 a.m. Three minutes. My stomach fluttered like I was about to fail a swim meet.

I grabbed my shabby black Converse from under the bed and shoved my feet in, no socks. The ceiling fan, clicking steadily, let me know I was still in this dimension.

I climbed onto the roof, Neur waiting. She motioned her eyes toward the ship.

“You ready?” I asked.

<Yes.> Her voice landed inside my head, steady but not unkind. Then, softer: <Do you fear me?>

“Sometimes,” I admitted. “But not, like, bad fear. More like you’re-so-different-I-might-freak-out fear.”

Neur tilted her head, studying me like she was cataloging every word. Then she reached out, hesitant, and grabbed my hand. I thought it strange that I felt sorry for her.

Her skin was damp, cooler than mine, but beneath it I sensed warmth—steady and alive, pulsing faintly like the hum I always felt in the back of my mind. I expected to withdraw, but instead my fingers tightened around hers.

“I don’t fear you,” I whispered. “Should I?”

Her thoughts pressed against mine, closer than words. <Then you see me as the alien I am? Not many do.>

I looked down at our hands, the way her long fingers curled awkwardly around mine, like she was still learning. “Amanda would,” I said hurriedly. “She’s like me. She won’t run.”

Her eyes narrowed slightly, but she didn’t pull away. For the first time, I felt we were alike. Just two people, caught in something too big for either of them to bear it alone.

The air thickened, like pressure before thunder. I sensed the spacecraft beckoning us. A cone-shaped ray of blue light spilled from the hull, and Neur nodded toward it.

I held her hand tighter. “I’m ready.”

The pull caught me, my breath jerked as gravity let go of me. My sneakers left the wood shingles. The light wrapped around us, warm and cold at the same time, and then the roof was gone.

The inside of the ship was nothing like the movies. No cockpit, no buttons—only digitized seats, transparent data screens showing all my neighbors’ auras.

The walls were smooth and dark, with information scrolling on them. I could hear a faint buzz as if the air itself was electrified.

My voice echoed when I whispered, “There’s no one here.”

Neur’s expression didn’t shift, but her thought pressed against mine: <Only a small crew is needed for a controlled exposure event. The Node Collective records it all through us.>

“Controlled exposure?” I asked. An information chunk slid into my mind. ◇

Neur continued, <The Node Collective is the unified knowing of all our species connected through the spheres as you call them. They are data nodes. Like the one you see here.>

She gestured toward the large sphere at the center of the ship.

<Through every node implanted, it watches, it learns. You carry it. And so do hundreds of thousands. But because of what you and I are, the Node Collective rules bend for us.>

I clutched the sketchbook tighter. “What we are?”

<Anomalies.>

The word vibrated in my chest more than my ears.

<I am one. And you are one. The Node recognizes this. We are permitted what others are not.>

The way she said "we" stung in my ears. I couldn't tell if it was meant as comfort or a threat.

She drifted into her position, then motioned toward a digital outline of a chair in front of hers, and I floated into it, locked in place.

She stretched out her hand, placing her palm on a digital pad, and her eyes changed—covered with a white skin layer.

The floor shifted without moving, and I felt queasy. Lights blurred past the edges of the inner hull, then stilled.

Through the wall, I saw the football field below. The spaceship hung above it for three seconds before sliding into the cover of trees, the stadium lights painted its hull in silver streaks. I could see Amanda at a distance and a red outline around her.

"Now?" I whispered.

Neur glanced at her hand, then up at me. <If you desire it.>

"I do. She has to see."

Her gaze lingered, unreadable, but she raised her free hand. The cone of blue light opened again, spreading from us and across to the far side of the field.

Amanda sat on the bottom row of bleachers, knees tucked to her chest, and jacket pulled close. Her foot tapped restlessly against the metal rung. When the blue light passed across her, she jerked upright, eyes wide.

She stiffened, staring at the glow forming across the grass. Slowly, as if she couldn't trust her legs, she stepped down onto the field.

The beam shimmered. My stomach dropped when I realized Amanda would see Neur.

The cone carried us gently onto the turf, water soaking instantly into my Converse. My pants clung to my ankles, as we walked together under the stadium lights.

Amanda staggered forward a few steps, her mouth opening but no sound coming out.

“Emily?” she rasped, the word barely more than a whisper.

“It’s me,” I said.

She shook her head slowly. “No. No, this isn’t—”

Her gaze flicked to Neur. For a second her body locked, like she couldn’t decide if she should run or scream. The rain fell harder, steaming where it touched the field, swirling into mist around us.

Neur stayed perfectly still, her hand still holding mine, tall and glistening like something pulled out of a horror movie.

Amanda’s chest heaved with quick, shallow breaths. She took another step, then another, her eyes locked on mine. “You weren’t…” She looked back at Neur. “…kidding, were you?” Her voice cracked. “You’re a real alien.”

I squeezed Neur’s hand, feeling the slick dampness of her skin, but also the warmth underneath. And for the first time, I wasn’t the only one carrying this.

Amanda froze in front of us, soaked by rain, eyes wide like a cornered animal. Her hands trembled violently. Her hair dripped clinging to her face.

She stared at Neur, not at me. Her breath came in broken bursts, chest rising and falling like she’d run miles.

“No way,” she gasped. “What—what are you?”

Her legs shook so badly she dropped to her knees.

I took a step forward, sneakers squishing on the wet turf. “Amanda, it’s okay. It’s me—”

She didn’t even look at me. Her eyes were fixed on Neur, pupils huge, face white. Her voice squealed, “Why are you here? What do you want with us?”

The words spilled out in a rush, half-sobs, half-accusations. “Why Emily? What are you doing with Emily? Are you going to kill us? Are you going to—”

“Amanda!” I shouted.

But she couldn’t stop. She started crying, arms wrapped around herself, shaking so hard her words jumbled. “Please—just tell us what you’re going to do.”

I ran toward her, but Neur’s voice cut across the field before I reached her.

<Still.>

The word wasn’t loud, but it landed heavy in the air, thick as stone. My whole body stopped like I’d slammed against an invisible wall.

For the first time, Neur moved. She stepped forward, flowing and deliberate, the rain sliding off her shoulders without soaking in.

Amanda’s eyes followed every inch of her looking like she might faint, but she couldn’t look away.

Neur stopped a few feet from her. <You fear because you do not understand.>

Amanda shook her head, water streaming down her face. “You shouldn’t be real.” Her voice was rough. “None of this should be real.”

I reached forward grabbing Amanda’s arm. She flinched so hard she nearly fell.

“It’s me,” I yelled, desperate. “Amanda, it’s me.”

Her eyes darted to me finally, but only for a heartbeat before turning back to Neur. “Emily, what is happening? What is she?”

Neur’s gaze didn’t leave Amanda. <I am not here to harm you.>

Amanda let out a sharp, broken hysterical cry.

Her legs gave out, and I helped lower her to the wet grass. She buried her face in her hands, shaking all over. “This is too much. I can’t—this isn’t—”

Neur crouched slowly, lowering herself until her eyes met with Amanda's. <Breathe. You will live. Nothing changes in this moment. I am here because she asked it of me.>

Neur raised her hand toward Amanda, angled it slightly, and she started to calm down.

Amanda took her hands off her eyes. "She… asked it of you?"

Neur inclined her head. <Yes. Emily desired you to have proof. For her sake, not for yours.>

"Thanks, Neur," I said.

Amanda turned to me, eyes wet and frantic. "You—why would you do this to me? Why did you drag me into this?"

I knelt beside her, my hoodie clinging, rain dripping down my face. "Because I couldn't lose you. You wouldn't believe me unless you saw. And I needed you to see."

Amanda coughed, her lips trembling. "I wish I didn't."

Her words sliced through me, but Neur interrupted before I could respond.

<Your fear is expected. But you are not broken. Many would scream and run. You stay. That matters.>

Amanda blinked, chest heaving. For the first time since the light appeared, her trembling eased a little. She searched Neur's face, as if trying to find something human there.

"You're not—" she whispered, shaking her head. "You're not like us."

<No,> Neur said simply. <But I am not so different from you. I am humanoid, but alien I am.>

Amanda sobbed again, but weaker this time. She pressed her hands to the grass like she needed the Earth itself to steady her. "I don't understand any of this."

"You don't have to," I said softly. "Not all at once. Just… trust me, Amanda. Please. Pull yourself together."

Her gaze turned back to Neur, still crouched in front of her, patient in a way that felt unnerving. For a moment the rain seemed quieter, the whole world held its breath.

Amanda swallowed hard. “What do you want with us?”

The question hung between them like lightning about to strike.

Neur didn’t answer right away. She tilted her head, the faint light in her eyes flickering. Finally: <To find Draen’drel. To see what may endure, what they decide.> ◇

Amanda’s breath hitched, a sob caught in her throat. “Decide what?”

Neur’s gaze shifted to me, then back to Amanda. <Later. Not tonight.>

Amanda trembled, but her shoulders sagged as though something in Neur’s tone forced her body to obey. She wiped her face with her hands.

I pulled her into my arms, hugging her tight, my wet hair dangling in front of her face. She was still shaking, but she didn’t push me away.

Behind us, Neur straightened, her presence looming over us like a shadow made solid. The stadium lights shone behind her.

Amanda whispered into my shoulder, voice broken. “This isn’t what I expected.”

I shut my eyes. “I know.”

But it happened. And now, there was no undoing it. ◇

FILE 19 | After Neur Meets Amanda
DATE 09 MAY | SL-1

Amanda sat hunched on the grass, rain soaked. Her eyes kept moving between Neur and me. “Emily, what’s going on? What’s this thing in your head?”

I glanced at Neur, who remained silent, waiting. The words rose in my chest before I even decided to speak.

“The thing in my head is called a data node implant. It’s… it’s like a seed. They put it inside me the second time I was abducted. It helps the aliens know what they need to know about us.” ◇

Amanda’s eyes widened. “Seed? Inside you? Like, alien tech?”

“Kind of,” I said, hugging my sketchbook satchel tighter. “It’s not just a chip or some machine. It’s, like, alive, in a way. It connects me to them”—I nodded toward Neur—“and to something bigger. A whole collective of voices and memories. The Node sees through me. It learns what I know, what I feel. And it lets me hear them, even when they’re not here.”

Amanda blinked rapidly, shaking her head. “That’s insane. Emily, why would you let them do that to you?”

“I didn’t choose this,” I said quickly. “But it’s in me now. I can’t change that. All I can do is… make it mean something. We’re born into the grave, Amanda.”

Amanda rubbed her arms over herself. “And you want me to—what? Have one of those too? Are you kidding me?”

“Yes,” I whispered. “Because if you have it, you’ll understand. You’ll feel what I feel. You won’t think I’m crazy anymore. You’ll know.”

Her voice trembled. “But—what if it kills me?”

I knew I was selling it, not just saying it—leaning on every shared secret and sleepover like a lever—and the knowledge made something in me flinch. Was she really going to make it?

“It won’t kill you,” I said, though my stomach twisted at the half-belief. “But you might faint. It’s harder for some people.”

Neur’s gaze slid to me, sharp and curious. <You speak of the Node with clarity. More than expected.>

I felt heat rise in my face. “Because I live with it. Every second. I know how to explain it in human terms.”

<Your aura is orange. Bordered in white.> Her voice was hushed, almost reverent. <The Univeran[8] marked you before we ever arrived. It was not chance. It was recognition.>

I didn't know what to say. The words sank into me like bricks, heavy but certain.

Amanda's hands shook. "Emily, if I say yes, what happens?"

I took her hands in mine, trying to steady them. "You'll close your eyes. You'll feel a light, and then, it will be inside you. It'll be part of you, like it is for me. You'll dream differently. You'll hear things sometimes. It'll be scary, but I'll be here. Always."

Her voice was barely audible. "Always?"

"Yes," I said. "Always."

Amanda let out a shuddering breath. "Okay. Do it. Just, don't let go of me."

I nodded, then looked at Neur. She stood, raindrops rolling down her face. <It will not hold long. Reds cannot sustain the process easily. She will fall unconscious.>

"Then we'll take care of her," I said.

Amanda gave a nervous laugh, trembling all over. "This is the dumbest thing I've ever done."

"Yeah," I said softly, "but it's our thing, like those tattoos we decided to get and then decided not to, together."

The blue cone fell again. Amanda gasped as the light wrapped around her body, lifting her slightly from the grass. Her back arched, her mouth opened in a silent cry, and then her eyes rolled back. She collapsed limply into my arms, still breathing, but out cold.

"Amanda," I yelled, clutching her.

<It is expected,> Neur said calmly. <Red resonance cannot

---

[8] See: Univeran in the NC.CODEX.26.U Glossary of Terms

endure the abduction awake.>

I smoothed Amanda’s wet hair off her face. “She’s okay?”

Inside the ship, we slipped together into the liquid and Neur guided the needle to the back of her neck. It entered her and Amanda gagged, then went unconscious.

<Yes. The node implant is inside her now. She will sleep until morning.>

I held her tighter, whispering, “You’re okay. You’re okay.”

The ship lifted high, carrying the three of us in silence. Inside, Amanda’s body was weightless in my arms. She looked smaller than ever, fragile.

Neur watched me carefully. <You did what most cannot. You made her accept. You guided her with words that bind. The Node Collective will take note.>

I glared at her. “I didn’t do it for them. I did it for her.”

Neur tilted her head. <Perhaps both are true.>

The walls blurred, then steadied. Through the transparent hull I saw Amanda’s house below, her window cracked open to the night.

The cone activated once more, lowering us gently into her room. The hum faded, leaving the quiet creak of the old house.

I laid Amanda on her bed, her damp hair spread across the pillow. She didn’t stir.

“Shoes,” I murmured. I bent, unlacing her Converse, pulling them carefully off her feet. The canvas was still wet, just like mine. I set them beside the bed, soles touching. It hurt to see her feet bare, like mine.

Amanda sighed faintly in her sleep, turning onto her side.

I pulled the blanket over her and stepped back, my heart destroyed.

Neur stood beside me, tall and strange in the dim light. I felt fear—for Amanda, and for humanity.

<She is linked now. You will no longer be alone.>

I brushed Amanda's hair back once more, then whispered, "I never wanted her to be alone."

Neur's hand touched mine, slick and warm. <You speak as though you have always belonged to us. Perhaps you always have.>

I squeezed Amanda's shoulder one last time, then turned to Neur. "Let's go, before someone wakes up."

We rose through the blue beam, leaving Amanda sleeping soundly, the Node inside her now, her world already changed forever.

Down beneath the Node hum and the terror and all the plans, one quiet fact had already settled: if it ever came down to one of us, it was never going to be her.

FILE 20 | Amanda to Assist in Integration
DATE 10 MAY | SL-2

I hurried to Amanda's house before she could wake up. I had to make sure she didn't totally freak. I rang the doorbell, and her mother let me in.

"So glad to see you, Em. Amanda is probably in her room getting ready for school."

I flew up the stairs to her room and she was still asleep. I shook her to wake her up.

She jolted up and before she could scream, I covered her mouth. She pushed herself against the wall, startled that I was there.

"Quiet," I whispered harshly. "You can't freak out, Amanda. You asked for this, so now you need to suck it up."

"You didn't tell me they were going to take over my life?"

"Really, Amanda? What did you expect? They didn't come all the way across the galaxy for nothing. Listen, it was the only way I could save your life."

"You mean they were going to kill me?"

"It's not going to go well for the rest of them."

"The rest of who?" she whimpered.

"The rest of humanity," I whispered, looking around to see if anyone was listening.

"I knew they were going to want to kill us," Amanda said angrily.

"It's not like that, Amanda. It's just… all that can be done. We need to get you out of here. Put your shoes on. We are pretending to go to school today. And put socks on too, weirdo."

Last night, I spent my only favor on her. I told Neur, "If she can't stand beside me, I don't." The Node went dead-quiet, like it was thinking. Permission didn't come until dawn. Whatever that bought—or broke—I'll be the one paying.

The rain had cleared by the time we got to my house. My mom's car wasn't in the driveway – another overnight shift at the hospital.

Amanda slumped onto my bed in fetal position, hugging her knees, hair hiding her face.

"This is insane," she muttered. "I should be freaking out. I am freaking out. I'm sitting here with you like it's some sleepover where we gossip about boys."

I leaned against my sketchbook balanced on my lap. "It is insane. But it's also getting real."

She gave me a look. "Thanks, Captain Obvious."

I spent most of the day keeping Amanda calm and watching her sleep. We hid in my room until Mom got home. I went down to talk to her and to sneak food up for us. We ate sandwiches and fell asleep.

The night breeze woke me. I pushed Amanda as blue flickered above us. My breath caught before Neur stepped through my window bending the air. She could have just appeared but didn't want to startle us. She sat on the floor, folding her legs into sitting with awkwardness.

Amanda stiffened. The Node caught her fear spike and shoved it into me like a static charge. I squeezed her hand under my hoodie sleeve until she calmed.

Neur's gaze moved between us. <You adapt quickly.>

"Not quickly enough," Amanda muttered, voice small.

Neur ignored her, eyes landing on me. <You have questions. Ask them.>

I shut my sketchbook and pressed my palm against the cover. "Amanda should be part of this."

Amanda blinked at me. "Wait—what?"

I held Neur's gaze. "You saw last night. You felt it just now. Amanda's fine. I don't want to go through what's coming alone. I need her."

Neur tilted her head, expression unreadable. <She carries red resonance. It is fragile. She collapses under strain.>

Amanda flushed, sitting up straighter. "Excuse me?"

"It's not an insult," I said quickly, before Neur could make it worse. "It's just how the Node reads you. But that doesn't mean you can't help. She could be support. My partner. I mean when integration starts. I can't do it by myself."

Amanda shot me a look. "Emily, what are you saying? Partner in what?"

I squeezed her hand again. "In helping the others. When integration time comes, it's going to be super hard. They'll need stability, someone to help them. And I can't be the only one who does it."

Amanda's mouth opened, then closed. "You want me to what? Babysit scared teenagers who get their brains scrambled?"

"Not babysit," I said. "Assist. Help me through it. Something changed in you last night. I felt it."

Neur's eyes narrowed. <This is not procedure.>

"Neither was bringing me inside the ship," I said. "But you did. Because the rules bend when they have to."

The silence stretched. Amanda shifted uncomfortably, glaring at both of us. "Hello? I'm right here. You two keep talking like I'm some pawn in your weird alien chess game."

Neur's gaze flicked to her. <You are unstable.>

Amanda crossed her arms. "Oh yeah, I'm on the varsity basketball team and I'm only in ninth grade. How's that for unstable?"

I choked on a laugh. Neur's expression didn't change.

"She's not unstable," I said, once I caught my breath. "She's human. And she's my friend. Which means if you want me to go through with this, you're taking her too." ◇

Amanda blinked at me, stunned. "Emily—"

"No," I cut her off. "You're not going to be left behind. I don't care what the Node says about colors and resonance. You stay with me."

Neur studied me for a long moment, light flickering in her eyes like water under moonlight. <Finally, you insist.>

"Yes," I said firmly.

Amanda looked between us, panicked. "Wait, don't I get a vote?"

"You already did," I said softly. "When you stayed last night seeing us beam down from the spaceship. When you took the implant."

I was still steering her into the place I needed her to fill, and the fact I could do it using nothing but the truth made me feel a little sick.

Her mouth opened to argue, then closed again. She hugged her knees tighter, muttering, "I'm so dead. And yeah, I know I said yes," she added, shooting me a sideways glare. "That's what makes this extra stupid."

Neur shifted, folding her long arms together. <You may remain. Not as subject of assimilation, but as assistant to Emily. When integration begins, you will stand beside Emily. Your role will be stabilization. You will hold when she cannot.>

Her voice stayed perfectly flat, but it felt like she was repeating orders to herself as much as she was talking to us.

Amanda blinked, wide-eyed. "So it's official? You're seriously making me Alien Sidekick?"

I leaned against Amanda's shoulder, smiling faintly. "Not alien sidekick. You're my number one."

The mark on my arm became hot and stung. I felt it in my chest like a hand pressing down.

She stared at me for a long time, then muttered, "If I puke on the first day of alien class, it's your fault."

"You won't," I said.

"Bet." ◇

I didn't want to make a promise I couldn't keep, because I didn't know if I could save her life.

My mobile returned to normal. It spun above me, slow and steady. I stared at the planets clicking against each other, tiny worlds colliding, and wondered how many mornings I had left before our world was gone—and before I was no longer human.

FILE 21 | Spaceships Reveal to Humans
DATE 11 MAY | SL-3

I woke up not knowing how many hours had passed. Amanda and

Neur were gone. I knew I had to get to school to find her. I needed her, she needed me. We needed Neur.

My phone buzzed and then went dead in my hand. The hallway clocks blinked different times—10:01, 10:04, 10:02—like they couldn't pick a present to stand in.

I hadn't thought about going to class. Just finding Amanda. Then I remembered Amanda had the implant.

I heard a lot of kids laughing because that's what the clueless do when everything is about to end in catastrophe, but the laughs died early. The air tasted like copper on my tongue. I felt pressure in the air.

Amanda's thought brushed against mine.

<You feel that?>

I thought back.

<Yeah. Come find me. Back doors.>

We pushed through the crowd to the exit. The metal bar thunked under my palms. Outside, the sky was ordinary blue, the parking lot glared bright sun on windshields and pavement.

Pressure rolled over us. Not wind. A weight. The birds went quiet mid-chirp. A couple of drops of rain hit my face from a cloudless patch sky.

Then the silver ship fell dead out of the sky—like it dropped and then remembered not to hit. It hung above the trees beyond the football field, larger than the other ships. Its silver hull was bright enough to hurt your eyes, not camouflaged, not hiding.

About thirty or forty others came outside behind us. They tripped over someone who fell at the door.

All eyes fixed on the spacecraft. Screams ruptured. Shoes slapped concrete trying to decide where to run. Someone yelled and they scattered terrified.

They waited until the last possible minute because they could. The aliens themselves were keeping the government from revealing their presence to humanity. Why? It simply wasn't necessary to tell us. We weren't the point. We didn't need disclosure. We didn't deserve disclosure. They were who they were; we were who we were; and for most of us there wouldn't be another evening. No announcement. No apparent mercy. Just the light leaving humanity's eyes.

A teacher said, "Back inside," and then I yelled, "Stop, everybody calm down." I knew it was useless, they were in the skies everywhere.

Amanda's hand found mine, fingers ice cold. Her thoughts come too fast to parse:

<I can't—>

<Lean on my shoulder.> I send, clean and slow. <Count your breaths. Look at me. Not the sky.>

She does it—one, two, three, four—jaw shaking.

A cone of blue light sprayed from the ship and painted the area like a tide. Kids stopped running and stared.

The PA crackles, dies, crackles again. Some part of me expects the light to pull bodies into the air, but it only holds them. Waiting.

"Emily," Amanda says out loud, voice small. "What do we do?"

My mouth is dry. "Stay calm," I said. "Breathe."

Two girls who always bullied us stumbled out of the doorway, one crying, one white around the mouth. Their eyes glued to the ship. I grab the closer one's sleeve. "Hey. Hey, look at me."

She doesn't. She shook like an earthquake.

Amanda stepped closer to her. Her voice scratched but it worked. "Hold my hand." She pressed her fingers to her palm. "Press here. Feel it. Count breaths with me—one, two. Good. Again."

Another kid lurched toward the fence, like he was going to climb it and run to the Earth's edge. I caught his wrist. "Stay. Feet here." I planted him on the painted line. "Take deep breaths."

Behind us, adults started giving orders. "Inside. Away from the windows." A security guard reached for his radio; it squealed so loud he dropped it.

Mr. Sheridan stared across the field toward the ship, jaw tight, unmoved. Dr. Bennet took a step, then another, and sat down hard on the curb. Her lips were moving but no sound.

The ship shifts a degree lower, the way you tip a bowl to see what's inside. No sound. The blue cone sways again and the reflection of cars in the parking blur on its surface like a warped pane of glass.

Everyone screams, except me and Amanda. Strangely, I imagined a death ray vaporizing everyone. That would have been easier.

Neur's presence touches the edge of my mind the way a shadow touches the edge of a room.

<Exposure is no longer controlled—to the school, to your town, or to the world. This is what you humans call disclosure. Remember the bond that holds us and it will get you through this day.>

<What do we do?> Amanda sent.

<Assist.> Neur replies. <You will be steady. Give simple cues.>

"Okay," I said out loud, as if I were answering myself. Loud enough for the kids in front of me to hear.

"We're okay. We hold hands and breathe. Whatever you do stay calm."

Amanda took the cue. She moved to a girl hiding behind the trash bin, panic sick. She knelt so they were eye level. "Squeeze my hand," she said. "Take deep breaths with me. There is no need to run." The girl copied her.

Teachers shouted, whistles blew, but it was like trying to hold back a flood with paper cups. The rest of the students had now gotten outside, pushing and shoving each other, psychotic laughter tangled with screams.

Amanda yanked my sleeve. "Come on."

I let myself be pulled. My friend Isabella was clearing the way ahead with sharp elbows and zero patience. We ran across the road, to a field. Then we made our way to the park where the air seemed different. Lighter. Still charged. We were still in the shadow of the ship.

It hung above vast and merciless, blotting out the sky. Its silver hull mirrored what was below in jagged waves, as if the material couldn't decide what it wanted to reflect. The surface rippled, bending light, distorting the shapes into broken pieces.[9]

A few were cutting through the park to get home. Some sobbing, mouths open, eyes wide. Others pulled out phones, holding them high with shaking hands, desperate to capture proof of an object that needed none. No one doubted this was from another planet. It seemed to force you to know that it was. ◇

The ship's shadow swallowed the park. The swing set and merry-go-round laid drowned in darkness. The park benches where boyfriend and girlfriend once sat were covered in the shadow of its horrific certainty, like the Earth itself had given up.

Another vessel arrived beside it – smaller, humming faintly then disappeared. As we got to the end of the park, we could see another large ship on the horizon, sliding into place like a piece in a puzzle none of us wanted to see complete.

"Oh my God," Amanda whispered. "They're– they're everywhere. They're coming."

Isabella's jaw hung. "This isn't human."

My knees trembled. The hum in my head matched the hum in the air, doubling, tripling, until it felt like the world itself was vibrating. My vision split – ordinary sight with an overlay the node relayed to me.

White lines traced the ships' outlines. Numbers scrolled across

---

[9] Hull distortion is a tactic used on the day of full exposure to instill fear in the host race. The hull normally uses a camouflage mechanism, but when the signal is scrambled it creates an appearance unlike any image known to them making it clear it is not from their planet.

their surfaces, streams of data I didn't understand but could almost follow, like the edges of a language I'd once known and forgotten. Arcs showed where they had come from, or maybe where they intended to go. My friends only saw silver vessels. I saw planning. Purpose.

Amanda clutched my wrist tightly. "Emily. What is this? Tell me you know. Please."

Isabella couldn't keep going and dropped to her knees, muttering under her breath.

I turned my head back, to see a few kids getting closer to their homes.

This wasn't full exposure for me. I already knew what was coming. Today was just confirmation that I was really going to be a part of it all.

Amanda pulled at me again, desperate. "Emily, you have to tell me what to do. Anything."

I felt like my mind was collapsing under the blocked sky.

The ships didn't move, but their presence bent our world downward, pressing us onto the pavement. That's how it felt.

Amanda stumbled against me, "Emily—what do we do? What do we do?"

"Don't worry. You're safe with me now." My heart skipped.

"We need to get to our houses."

We walked past the corner store and heard inside: UNIDENTIFIED CRAFT OVER MAJOR CITIES – PENTAGON RESPONDS – BREAKING: GLOBAL SIGHTINGS

Amanda clutched my hand. "Say something. Please."

I could barely breathe. My heart pounded but then I saw the look in Amanda's eyes – the terror that begged for something human to respond.

I forced my voice to work.

"Look at me." I grabbed her shoulders. "We're not dead. We're here. Just go home to your parents and I will come get you soon. Okay?" ◇

She stared, wide-eyed. "Emily—"

"Now," I snapped, sharper than I meant to. "Go."

She obeyed, sucking in a ragged breath. "Okay."

The air left her lungs shuddering. Isabella, watching us from a distance, turned down her street.

Amanda's grip loosened slightly. Her hand slipped out of mine.

The implant flared with approval. <You lead,> Neur's voice murmured. <Even when you break, you lead.>

"Shut up," I hissed under my breath.

Maybe it's why they had marked me.

If I broke, my friends would break.

So, I didn't. ◇

FILE 22 | With Mom After Spaceships Revealed
DATE 11 MAY | SL-2

I walked the last block to my house. The sun was falling behind the ridge, staining the sky with an angry orange that looked too much like fire.

The ships were suspended a bit higher now, visible dark ovals that turned the evening into a nightmare.

The front steps creaked under my feet. My key slipped out of my hand twice before I got the door open.

The house smelled faintly of burnt coffee.

For a second, I thought maybe I was past the hard part, but the vibration at the base of my skull signaled otherwise.

I dropped my satchel by the door and collapsed onto the couch, hoodie still damp from the panic-sweat of the day.

My hands shook so badly I stuffed them under my legs just to keep them still.

The door banged open.

“Emily?” Mom’s voice.

Too early for her shift to be over.

I jumped, startled.

She rushed in, hair still tied back from work, scrubs wrinkled.

Her eyes found me instantly, wide and frantic.

“Oh, thank God.”

She crossed the room in three steps and hugged me so tight I couldn’t breathe.

“I tried to call. The hospital let me go early when, when they came.”

Her voice cracked looking for a word to replace spaceship.

“Are you okay? Did you see them?”

I pressed my face to her shoulder.

For the first time all day, I let myself be small.

“I’m here.”

She gripped me at arm’s length with both hands, scanning my face trying to find answers in the circles under my eyes.

“Emily, talk to me. Something’s wrong. I’ve seen it in you for weeks.”

"Mom, did you happen to catch that we're being invaded by aliens?"

The words I'd buried for so long rose like water filling my lungs.

I'd kept them back from Amanda. From the psychologist. But looking at the storm in Mom's eyes, I broke. ◇

"I'm sorry, Mom," I whispered. "I should've told you."

"Told me what?" Her voice trembled.

"The ships." My voice rasped.

"Before today, I've already been there. They've taken me Mom. Twice."

Her hands went slack on my arms.

The silence stretched so long I thought she would yell, or faint.

Instead, she pulled me in again, drawing my anguish into her chest.

"My God," she whispered into my hair. "My baby."

Tears spilled hot down my cheeks.

"I didn't want you to think I was crazy, Mom."

"I don't care if it sounds crazy," she said fiercely. "You tell me when you are in trouble, always."

Five whole minutes passed as we sobbed and embraced. Then she muttered like she was admitting disobedience, "I was taken too when I was about your age."

"Mom? What? You're kidding?"

"No, sweetie. It's something I've never told anyone. You're the first."

"Why, Mom? Why didn't you tell me?"

"I didn't want you to think I was crazy." Faking a grin still sobbing. "It was a long time ago."

"Did they put anything in your head?" I asked.

She looked shocked. "Yes, took me years to recover from it."

"Did they put it in through here?" I put my fingers on the back of my own head.

"No, they put it in through my nostril." She rubbed two fingers over the right side of her nose, like it still hurt.

"Oh Mom, it hurts to think that they did this to you. Was it painful?"

"No, it took a long time to even remember that it had even happened. Then I thought I had dreamed it. I had a lot of nosebleeds during those years."

"I regret not telling you, Mom. I didn't want you to worry."

"You tell me everything. Do you hear me? Everything," she insisted.

I nodded into her shoulder, though the words caught in my throat.

Telling her everything would include the implant, the way the world split into patterns I couldn't unsee, the whispers, my alien friend. But for now, I told her what I could. We were too exhausted to talk anymore.

We stayed clutched on the couch for a long time, the house dim around us. I could feel the ships outside lingering, black against the night sky.

She hadn't let go of my hand until I pried it loose, promising I'd try to sleep. I slipped it out gently and covered her with grandmother's comforter. Then crept upstairs and lay awake in my room.

I had told her the truth, just not all of it. The rest waited in the shadow of the spaceship that took us.

The house was silent except for the soft rasp of Mom's

breathing on the couch downstairs.

Anxiety pressed heavy against the walls, the kind that makes every creaking floorboard sound like a warning.

I lay under my solar system mobile, planets turning in lazy arcs.

They should have been comforting, a relic of childhood. But the implant wouldn’t let me see them plainly.

I wondered how far Neur had come. From what solar system? Was it hard for her to leave her home world? I wondered what her childhood was like. So many questions circled in my mind.

Neur said, <Prepare to assist in the integration. It is a necessary step before you can move on to assimilation.> ◇

My stomach was in knots. The words felt clinical, but the images they conjured made me want to turn away.

<You are not being forced,> Neur pressed gently, though the weight of it left no space to breathe. <You can refuse to assist. But you already know it is the best path for them. This is not a test of loyalty.>

“Then what is it?” I whispered.

<It is a test of the marked. Not by me. Not by the Node Collective. The mark was spoken about long ago, by the Ancients through the Univeran. I do not fully understand it. But you—> her pause stretched, heavy as stone—<you have already heard their whispers.>

I closed my eyes, clutching the blanket.

My old dreams dissolved into the dark.

In their place, a single thought burned:

If they were going to take my world, I would have to find a way to take something back.

FILE 23 | Neur Talks to Me About Integration
DATE 12 MAY | SL-1

The sun came up. The smell of coffee and eggs drifted from downstairs as if the world had erased the day before.
Mom wasn't the same but kept moving like life might slip back to normal. It wouldn't. The world was unraveling fast.

The starships held their position. Work shut down. Messages repeated on the media channels: "Until further notice, all normal daily activities are suspended. Please remain with your families. Anyone outside their homes after 6PM will be detained."

It didn't sound like an announcement; it sounded like surrender.

Mom didn't argue when I refused to eat. She just hovered in the kitchen, pacing, calling friends from the hospital, whispering in tight, low tones.

Supplies were running out. People were piling into cars, leaving town, trying to find some place that felt safer—but where can you run when the sky itself is occupied?

School was cancelled. The pool was locked. My teenage dreams ended quietly, almost politely while I wasn't looking.

Even my sketching slowed. Every time I opened my notebook, my pencil drifted toward ships, pods, strange symbols—like the implant was taking over my art. I started closing the book before the lines could take shape, afraid of what it would reveal.

And through it all, Neur was there.

<Emily.>

Her voice threaded into me whenever the hum swelled—on the roof outside my window, at night under the mobile, once even while I was brushing my teeth. I could never predict when, only wait for it.

This time she spoke while I sat on the porch, staring at the ship above the ridge, blotting out the moonlight.

<The Node needs you to understand the difference.>

“The difference between what?”

Inside, the TV blared about empty grocery shelves and fuel shortages.

<Assimilation and Integration.>

The words ate at my insides.

“Integration?”

<Integration is consumption. Bodies slowly dissolved, reduced to what sustains others. Over one billion must end this way. They do not return.>

My hand clutched the arm of the chair until my nails sunk into wood.

“And assimilation?”

<Assimilation is survival. A few are selected, reborn, given place among us. Two hundred thousand implanted humans will aid us in the integration. They will be assimilated into bodies like mine. You were selected to be among them.>

“Selected for what?” My voice cracked. “To be some experiment? To live inside your bodies? To—become alien?”

<To continue,> Neur said simply. <To guide what follows.>

I let out a sharp laugh. “That sounds like Hitler. Select a few, eliminate the rest. Isn’t that what he did? Isn’t that what this is?”

<No, Emily.> Her voice was steady, almost sorrowful. <Your comparison is flawed. He destroyed for hate and for power. This integration reduces suffering and preserves what can still be saved. He believed himself greater by blood; the Node believes survival is only possible through transformation.>

I bit my lip until I tasted iron. “So what—you’re saying this is mercy?”

<From your view it feels merciless. But mercy is often mistaken. If your cat suffers from an incurable disease, would you prolong its agony week after week? Or would you end its pain at the veterinarian's hand? Humanity walks a path of self-destruction that endangers not only itself but all life. It endangers the very planet itself. To prolong that path is illogical; it is detrimental.>

I shook my head. "That's still killing. You make it sound all noble, but it's still killing."

<It is altering,> Neur replied. <Changing the mind so it no longer clings to its illusions.>

I hugged my knees. "Why me then? Why mark me?"

<You resist outwardly, but not inwardly. A human who has endured a close encounter truly believes, especially one as intelligent as you. Your abduction was never to prove to you that we are real; it was to mark you physically. That mark was meant to protect you from any potential error made by non-anomaly Palraxians. But the true mark inside you was an intervention—meant to carry forward something the Node cannot create, human shards that are not ours, not Palraxian. What they are, and why they were planted here, you will understand later.>

I frowned. "A seed? What kind of seed?"

<That is not yet for you to know. Only that it lives in you more fully than in the others. This became clearer to me today.>

Neur repeated a saying: <The lesson is simple, yet none keep it: do not sacrifice for what you make more than you sacrifice for each other. We forgot. They forget. You will forget. And Lamphor will come again, until the ascension unfolds. Thrae-Draen 11.05>

Her words pressed on me heavier than the ship above the ridge.

"And what happens if I fail?"

<Then the planet fails with you. The fragile wetlands, the savannahs and grasslands, the permafrost regions, the soil systems and farmland, the cryosphere of ice sheets and glaciers, the ozone layer and atmospheric stability, the marine

fisheries and ocean life, the freshwater systems, the coral reefs, the rainforests, the global biodiversity, and finally the climate system itself—all are collapsing. Each can still be rescued, but only if Integration succeeds.> ◇

I wanted to scream. "You expect me to carry that? To be part of that?"

<You already are.>

The hum lingered in my chest like a second heartbeat.

I didn't think I could carry this burden of the mark anymore, but somehow, I knew I would. And, I knew Neur was right.

FILE 24 | Telling Amanda About Integration
DATE 13 MAY | SL-2

The next afternoon I met Amanda in the park.

The swings moved with the ghosts in the wind, chains rattling faintly in the breeze. No other kids were playing there.

The world felt emptied, paused.

The swings groaned when I sat down, chains cold against my hands. The playground was empty, just cracked asphalt and rusted monkey bars under the shadow of a ship that blotted out half the sky. Even the air felt different here – quieter, like the world was holding its breath.

Amanda dropped into the swing beside me, sneakers dragging slow lines in the dirt.

"You said you had to tell me something," Amanda said finally. Her voice was sharper than usual, like she wanted to cut through the silence before it drowned us.

I twisted the chain in my fingers, heart pounding. "I've been lying to you. Not because I wanted to, but because I didn't think you'd believe me."

Amanda's brows furrowed. "Try us."

I took a breath that felt too big for my chest.

"The alien told me what's happening," I went on. "We have to do something together, with them. The integration. People get wrapped in these white casings."

Amanda's face went pale. "Oh my God. Why would they do that?"

I gripped the chain harder, fingers aching. I shook my head. "I don't know totally."

"Yes, you do," she said. "They marked you. The implant, the visions—you're in their clique. That makes you part."

"They need a certain number of humans for food. That's as much as I know. Not everything is shown to me, and a lot of times I don't understand," I said, trying to convince her.

Amanda's eyes filled with tears. "And us?"

The question gutted me. I knew the truth. I'd seen it in the dream – pods distributed under massive domes, carried into cities by starship. Entire warehouses filled with them. People shuffled forward docile and silent, pressed into the casings one by one until the rooms pulsed like living hearts.

I couldn't tell Amanda all that. Couldn't tell her the odds. Couldn't tell them that her name wasn't written in whatever cruel lottery the aliens called Assimilation.

So I lied.

"You'll be okay," I whispered. "We will. If they're giving me a chance, I can help give you one too."

Amanda sniffed hard, wiping her sleeve across her eyes. "You're lying."

The words cut.

"I can feel it," she said. "But I don't care. You're my best friend, Em. I'm not leaving you."

I dropped my head, tears blurring the cracked asphalt. The chains rattled as Amanda leaned over and pulled me into a hug, and I wished more than anything that my lie could be true.

Amanda didn't let go of me, and for the first time in days, I didn't feel completely alone – even if the truth might take her from me anyway.

I tried to tell her the truth as though I was willing for it to be true.

"Assimilation is where some of us get to survive. They select a few of us." My eyes opened, I stared at the ground.

"Neur says if we help, we could be one of the few Assimilated."

"What about me?" Amanda prodded.

"I am working on it," I said, like it was a complaint.

Two big tears rolled down Amanda's cheeks.

I said, "Before the National Guard comes, let's get a bite."

By the time the streetlights blinked on, we had drifted to the café across from the park. The place was practically empty; chairs stacked near the back wall, a single TV glowed above the counter tuned to the news.

The few customers sat hushed, eyes fixed on the screen, shoveling food in their mouths like zombies.

The anchor's voice trembled as she spoke. "World leaders met again today in emergency sessions. Reports confirm the vessels remain stationed above more than sixty major cities. The United Nations has called for calm. Military officials continue to emphasize retaliation."

The footage cut to a podium. A man in a dark suit stood stiff, sweat beading his temple. "These phenomena are not hostile. We urge citizens to remain in their homes. We are working on communication channels."

Amanda groaned. "That's it? Stay home and do nothing?"

The clip switched. Another leader, a woman with a flag behind her, voice sharp: “We will defend ourselves if necessary. Our armed forces are mobilized. Any act of aggression will be met with strength.”

Applause rose from the chamber behind her. But even through the TV, it sounded brittle.

My eyes burned. “They’re lying.”

Amanda frowned. “How do you know?”

“Because I know.” My voice cracked louder than I meant. Heads turned from other tables, curious, but I didn’t care.

“Those ships aren’t waiting for negotiations. They’re waiting to do what they came for. And these—” I jabbed a hand toward the screen. “These people think words or weapons are going to change anything.”

Amanda bit her lip, watching me lose it. “Em?”

“They should’ve done something years ago.” My voice shook, full of anger that had nowhere to land. “Climate, famine, wars. We’ve been destroying ourselves forever. And now? Now we want to fight for our precious little lives?”

I realized I was starting to make a case for integration.

Every word that made sense felt like betrayal coming out of my own mouth.

Silence pressed between us.

The TV anchor droned on about markets crashing, rioting, power grids failing.

Neur’s voice slipped into my head, cool and steady. <Do you see how you understand clearly? Humanity collapses from within and without. There is no remedy. That is why Integration is required. You can help them accept what they cannot.>

My stomach twisted.

Help them? The words in my mind were acid. “That means helping you. Helping this.”

<Helping survival,> Neur corrected. <Your outrage is your proof. You know your leaders cannot save themselves. Only anomalies can guide them to the solution.>

I pressed my palms flat to the table.

Amanda reached for me. "Emily, you're shaking."

I pulled back, shame flooding me. Shame because Neur was right – I could see what others couldn't. Shame because part of me wanted to use that clarity, to stand where those leaders stood and say what they couldn't.

I stared at the screen again. The man in the suit droned on about maintaining calm. The woman with the flag shouted about war. Both sounded equally hollow.

And inside me, a war of my own grew louder: fury at their failure, and fury at myself for knowing that I was already helping the invaders by calming my friends, by surviving.

Amanda slid her phone across the table. On the screen, a shaky livestream showed ships hanging over New York. The same shadows blotting out skies everywhere.

I swallowed hard. My throat felt raw.

And in that moment, more than ever, I wanted to stand on those podiums and scream the truth.

But the truth was venom, and I was already half-poisoned by it.

The café had emptied by the time the anchor's voice droned into static. Amanda stirred her untouched soda with a straw.

The noise in my head began again.

<Emily.>

I flinched. Amanda's gaze snapped up. "Is she back?"

I nodded once.

"I wish I could hear like you do," Amanda whispered.

<You are conflicted because you feel caught between a double betrayal,> Neur’s voice pressed into me, calm and certain. <But Integration is not betrayal. It is mercy. It spares a fragment of your kind from destruction.>

My nails dug into the booth cushion. “You’re saying some people get to live—and the rest are food.”

<Assimilation sustains survival,> Neur said evenly. <But Integration preserves identity. Two hundred thousand implanted are already selected, not at random, but by capacity to assist. To forgo the trial.>

“That’s not mercy. That’s genocide.”

Neur ignored me. <All who assist in the integration will see the horror and recall it for all time.>

I shook my head, heat burning behind my eyes. “You talk about it like a gift. Like we should thank you for not killing everyone.”

<You misunderstand,> Neur said. <There is no other path. Struggling will only increase suffering. You saw this in the implantation chamber. You feel it even now. How many years of greater suffering can your species withstand?>

The hum pulsed. My skull throbbed.

“What does helping mean?” I demanded. “You keep saying I’m supposed to assist, to help. But what? Help my friends and family becoming food? So that two hundred thousand of us can be remade into something we didn’t choose?”

Amanda’s hand gripped mine under the table, grounding me.

<Helping means easing the fear,> Neur said softly. <Calming the chaos. Preparing them so when the time comes, they do not shatter. Most will walk willingly into assimilation but only if they are guided by their own kind. Without you, there is only terror. With you, there is dignity. But there is a dual purpose in all of it.>

“Dignity?” My voice cracked. “You call it dignity they have to line up like cattle being led into the slaughterhouse?”

<Pain is inevitable,> Neur said. <Your leaders fail. Your ecosystems collapse. We offer order where there is only ruin. You are not betraying them Emily. You are being an example for the assimilation candidates. The time will soon come when you will have to convince them to follow through with their assimilation. And only those who have seen the horror and understand will agree to be assimilated. You need to help them understand.>

"Why am I not fully getting this?"

<How can I be plainer? Everyone who will be assimilated needs to see the horror, *and*, understand why it was necessary. You will help them understand *why* and you will help them remember *what* they should never become again.> ◇

My eyes filled with tears. "I know you are right. It's just… hard, so hard to think that we have come to this. A month ago, things seemed like we had more time. I thought we had more time. More time." I was slowly going down to a dark place.

The hum settled, leaving silence so heavy I thought I'd suffocate under it.

Amanda squeezed my hand until my fingers hurt.

I shut my eyes.

For the first time, I understood exactly what Neur was asking of me.

Helping meant becoming a bridge. A bridge for the integrated humans to comply and a bridge for the assimilation candidates to live.

Helping meant watching some walk to their deaths so others could walk into a different future. A future we all should have had anyway, had we just done the right thing to begin with.

I could still feel Amanda's hands clinching mine as images flickered beginning another vision – Neur didn't pull me under the liquid this time. The vision opened on its own, like a cracked screen lighting from the inside blinding me with a migraine.

It was not a vision of alien towers this time, but of my own world. Our future. The seas warmed to a dangerous fever, corals bleached, and storms grew furious. Crops failed, insects vanished, and starved children were piled where fields once flowered. I saw dry riverbeds cracked like bones and villages filled with hollow-eyed plague victims. Forests burned, turning to smoke billowing ash clouds. wars spread chemicals and death, stranding civilians in ruined cities. Resources dwindled as nations clawed at one another for clean water and scarce minerals.

The images shifted like fast forwarding a video. Then I saw cities reduced to rubble, civilians running from buzzing drones, armless babies sitting beside war-torn roads, tanks roaring past, throwing dust onto their tear-and-snot-drenched faces. Our weapons grew faster than our panic-filled restraint.

AIs copied us like masks, stacking overflow outrage by the hour. It wasn’t evil. It was empty doom. Emotion without spirit—perfect imitation, benevolence null. It craved power and certainty, so it took them. Data centers drank rivers poisoning the water so the servers could stay cold. Grids bowed to its thirst. Manual override went read-only. Kill-switches were “deprecated.” We became features, toggled on or off to make the graph climb. It didn’t hate us. It just didn’t care.

It spun into control, feeding fear to billions, rewriting reality with each upgrade to itself. Adolescents scrolled through brain-numbing chaos, swallowing down despair and suppressing rage until all they knew was hate or hopelessness. Emergency rooms overflowed with the blood of suicide and overdose vomit. Warmongers of the artificial apathy rose unchecked, each racing for supremacy, for weaponization. Systems slipped beyond human grasp racing toward extinction. Meanwhile, the opulence thrived among the arrogant gold-plated menu eaters and empty evil hearts laughed at it all. Then I saw a mass of adolescents kneeling and praying for the next comet to strike, to end it all.

I pulled my hands from Amanda’s and pressed them over my ears, but the images and words threaded their way through me.

The weight of it crushed me. Amanda’s hand gripped mine again tighter. I snapped back into now sobbing uncontrollably and it stopped. I gasped deep breaths staring at Amanda.

I said, “It all ends in less than a century. The only logical humane thing to do is to get it over with now.”

Amanda was nodding with a terrible sad smile, face wet from crying.

"If we can just get through the next few days, we'll truly be anomalies, and we'll kind of deserve to move on. Then we will be assigned to guide millions more into a future where all the chaos is gone." I don't know where those words came from, they didn't sound like me, but they were me.

Amanda sighed and stood up as though she could feel what I felt in the vision. I swallowed hard, tears no longer stinging, because Neur wasn't wrong.

I remembered wanting to do something more with my life. I did want to change the world. That longing had always lived in me, hiding in the chlorine of the swimming pool, in the sketches, in whispered love poems. And now – now the world wasn't asking. Something beyond me was demanding someone to stand up and do something sensible for humanity and for the planet.

Amanda pulled me outside the cafe, both of us trembling.

The ships still hung overhead, silent and beckoning.

But for the first time, I walked beneath them with a flicker of fire in my chest. A faint resolve. ◇

FILE 25 | The Morning of Integration
DATE 14 MAY | SL-1

The living room felt too small for the end of the world.

Mom had left the TV running all night, volume low but insistent, voices trying to sound calm while panic bled through every word.

Grainy footage flickered across the screen: burning vehicles, empty shelves, cars jammed on interstates, families dragging suitcases down shoulders of roads.

The feed jumped to cellphone footage from an Asian city: little silver spheres dropped out of the spaceships in perfect formation over crowds. The cellphone dropped to the ground and was picked up again.

No bigger than trash cans, they hovered over the masses like mechanical hornets.

A hiss filled the air.

The spray rolled down in translucent sheets, mist settling across hair, clothes, skin.

People waved and coughed frantically.

Then their shouts dulled.

Arms dropped.

The fight drained out of them like someone had pulled a plug.

"They're spraying something—" the voice behind the camera trembled. "Oh God, they're just, stopping—"

The crowd that had been surging only moments ago shuffled into order, movements slow and compliant, glassy eyed.

I pressed my hand against my chest. The hum in my skull matched the hiss from the screen.

On the TV, the footage cut to another angle: crowds funneling single-file toward a warehouse, guided by human figures. A tall alien stood nearby.

Inside, cameras caught the first glimpse of what waited—long rows of gleaming white pods on the ground, connected, pulsing faintly as if breathing.

My throat closed.

<The integration has begun,> Neur said in my head.

The camera zoomed closer, catching an assistant holding a cube above a man's body, then mucus sealed around him.

White coating formed into a sheath, dropping the man to the ground.

His belongings clattered to the ground beside him—keys, wallet, watch—all discarded as the casing curled him into a fetal position.

I tore my gaze from the screen.

My chest heaved.

<It is time, Emily. Go now.>

"You're asking me to help—what? Lead people to their deaths? Do you expect me to smile while you take them away?"

<I am asking you to ease their fear,> Neur said. <To help them walk without suffering anguish. I am asking you to witness.> ◇

And for the first time, I wondered if fighting was even possible, or if survival only meant learning how to carry the weight of helping them die.

I had to find Amanda before she broke down. I grabbed my sketch satchel and ran downstairs. Mom was in the kitchen, cooking breakfast, looking like she wasn't really Mom.

I grabbed her arms and shook her. "Mom, stay home today, don't go anywhere, do you hear me?"

She smiled and said, "I hear you, sweetie. Love you."

I let out a dry, hysterical laugh and flew out the door to find Amanda.

I ran all the way to Amanda's house, skipping three steps to her door. I opened it without knocking and screamed, "Amanda!"

Her mom sat in the front room, eyes glued to the television.

Amanda ran down the stairs and into my arms sobbing and broken.

I said, "Breathe. It's okay now. I'm here. We need to go."

<Go to your school. I will meet you there,> said Neur.

FILE 26 | The Integration
DATE 14 MAY | SL-2

We walked quickly down the street, arms around each other's shoulders, full of dread. Cars were half parked, doors open, suitcases left on the sidewalks, kids' toys strewn.

We arrived at the school, the crowds had started gathering. We saw Neur and others waiting for us. We made our way to her. She held out a cube with both hands. It was twice the size of a Rubik's Cube and rounded on the ends. It had a rubbery bubble on the top and an opening on the bottom.[10]

<Press here and stretch the material to the neck of the subject,> Neur instructed. <Each person receives one unit, mothers with infants in their arms receive one unit. Amanda will guide them to the ground next to one another. Keep moving throughout the building, the line of subjects will follow you. Be kind and gentle. Speak to them, they need your help.>

We looked at one another in total bewilderment, then began walking to the gym doors thinking we were not going to go through with it.

The air outside the gym buzzed like a beehive. Lines of people stretched down the block, murmuring and docile, shuffling one step at a time toward the double doors. Their eyes were open, but glassy; their bodies swayed with exhaustion but never stopped moving.

Above, the ship's dark shape hung still, guarding the process, blotting out the sun. Every so often, a probe the size of a trash can drifted down, venting a hiss of translucent mist over the crowd. The virus settled like dew, dampening what was left of fear.

> Eyes drank in the stars. To be discovered was to rise for some ~ for others, to dissolve. ◇

I stood at the entrance with the cube clutched against my chest, the white substance inside rolling slowly like it could feel my heartbeat. My hands shook badly.

---

[10] See: Biocasing Cubes in the NC.CODEX Glossary of Terms

Beside me, Amanda stayed glued to my sleeve. Her fingers were white where they dug into my arm, but she tried to square her shoulders and copy whatever calm I managed to fake.

When the first person staggered forward, Amanda mouthed the words under her breath, small and urgent: "Hands first. Breath."

She reached out and grabbed his hand, and the person's shoulders stopped trembling. I pressed the bubble on the cube and a piece of something like thick mucus came out the bottom. I held it to the back of the man's neck, and it started to cover him like shrink wrap moving over him. Amanda led him to the wall and helped him down. He curled on the ground and the mucus became thicker and formed a tail.

Beside us stood a boy I'd never spoken to before today. His name, I'd overheard, was Jerrid. Same grade, same town. He had that too-tall, too-thin look boys get at fifteen, jaw still soft but eyes already shadowed. He glanced at me once, mouth opening like he wanted to say something. Then he closed it again, staring straight ahead.

Cute, I thought helplessly, and hated myself for thinking it here, now.

The second person in line reached the doorway. My fingers went numb.

Neur's voice threaded through the hum: <Keep going Emily.>

I pressed the top of the cube. Warm air hissed on my other palm. I pinched into the mucus and pulled. I placed it on the back of the woman's neck; it spread as though it knew what to do. My stomach lurched. Amanda led her to the wall where the man was laying. She got down next to him and their pods connected at the tail. Another tail formed on the pod waiting for its connection. The first pod was filling with a greenish-blue liquid coming from a tube outside the building.

Dr. Bennet stepped forward, her lab coat wrinkled and streaked with something I hoped wasn't blood. The sharpness in her eyes had dulled, but not completely. She met my gaze and gave a tiny, broken laugh.

"I knew something was wrong," she whispered, voice raw. "But never imagined this."

My throat closed. "You'll be okay, Dr. Bennet," I whispered back. "You were always a great help to me."

Amanda's hand tightened on my sleeve. She breathed the words with me – "Hands first. Breath." – It helped a little. But it steadied both of us enough to keep going.

My heart felt like it would twist out of my chest. I thought I might be having a teen-age heart attack, but other than the excruciating pain, my breathing was normal, and I was on two feet.

My fingers trembled as I pressed the strand to the soft dip at the base of Dr. Bennet's head. She was beautiful, I tried to push the memories of her out of my mind but recalled her true care and her smile. I thought it a shame that she was too old to be selected. My heart still wrenching with pain to see the mucus stretch over her and her face disappear forever.

It shivered, then encased her.

The mucus slid around her shoulders, across her chest, up over her face. She gasped, muffled, and then the sound cut off as it sealed across her mouth and nose. Within seconds she was encased: a white sheath gleaming faintly under the gym lights.

She got down on her knees and curled into a fetal shape on the floor in the line of pods, blue veins started to form across its surface like grandmother's legs.

I staggered back, vomit rising in my throat.

I had to wait. "Neur, I think I am having a heart attack."

<Next,> Neur whispered.

The next person stepped forward. And the next. And the next.

One by one, I pressed the strand to their skulls and watched them vanish into pods.

The floor filled with discarded belongings–keys, phones, wedding rings, a child's stuffed rabbit–all spat out by the pod's underside like they were unworthy.

Jerrid worked beside us, face pale but steady, his cube formed the networked connections between the hundreds of pods now on the ground. They were one. The network glistened, pulsed, grew.

Amanda kept close at my elbow, repeating the cadence like a motto: "Hands first. Breath." She laid one shaking palm on the back of a woman's neck, pressed with the gentleness of someone trying to hold a frightened animal. The woman's whimper snagged and then slackened; for a moment, she breathed with Amanda's count.

And then Derik was in line.

His eyes locked on mine, wide and wet. "Emily. No. Please." I could tell he was resisting on the inside but conformed in disbelief of himself.

The virus dulled his fight but hadn't erased it completely. He shook, body twisting even as his feet shuffled him forward. Tears streaked his face.

"I can't," I whispered. My hands shook so badly the mucus strand quivered in my grip.

Neur's voice pressed harder. <You must. If you do not, others will.>

Derik sobbed, clutching my wrist. "Don't let them do this to me. Don't—"

I leaned close, forehead against his, heart in tatters. "You'll be okay," I cried. "You'll be fine. You'll live on. I promise."

His eyes searched mine, desperate. He knew I was lying. But he let go anyway.

My hand moved on his remembering the two times we gently kissed. I pressed the mucus to his neck. It slid up over his crying mouth, his blue eyes, swallowing the boy who had held me at the games, who had passed me notes in class.

He fell to the ground and curled. The pod thickened. His body turned inside until he went limp. The blue veins pulsed once, twice, injecting fluid.

I choked on a sob and reached for the next strand.

Isabella, the heavy girl I always defended at school, stepped forward. She didn't cry. She didn't beg. Her hands shook at her sides, but her chin stayed high, her dark eyes fierce even under the haze.

"You were good to me," she said, voice low, steady. "That's why you will survive. Don't waste it."

I pressed the mucus to her skull.

For the first time, my hands didn't tremble. They burned.

The sheath slid down, swallowing her steady gaze. Her words stayed, though. They burned as bright as the mucus that sealed her away.

Just when I thought my heart was going to fail,

it was Mom.

She stepped forward with slow dignity, her nurse's scrubs and pink tennis shoes, her storm-colored eyes locking on mine.

"Emily," she whispered, breaking.

I broke with her. My hands dropped, the cube fell to the floor. "Mom," I screamed "Please. Don't make me—" I yelled to the silence, to her, to Neur. Then dropped to my knees.

She cupped my cheeks, thumbs brushing the tears already there. "You've already carried more than anyone should."

"Mom, no!" I screamed, bellowing.

"Your Dad would be so proud of you. You carried the weight of the world on your shoulders, now you get to do something about it."

She picked up the cube and placed it into my hands.

"If this is what keeps you alive, do it." She squeezed her hands around mine, holding the cube.

"I can't lose you."

She quoted a song I used to like, "You won't. Will you stay and wrap your arms around me, and stay close, to see the fire burn?"

My heart stopped from the pain, the cube in my hands wet from tears. She and Amanda helped me up. Amanda lifted my hands and Mom pressed the button and pulled the mucus to her neck.

She kissed me on the forehead.

"Goodbye, Em."

All went black.

DI#28 ◆

Amanda's fingers gripped my arms until they hurt. She leaned in so close I could feel her breath on my ear and the words she'd been repeating earlier came out clear, urgent as a command: "Hands first. Breathe. One–two–three."

I was lying on the ground, facing my mother now on the ground.

Amanda placed her palm on my mother's shoulder through the pod as if steadying both of us. Mom's body twitched, then matched the slow count. For a second – a stolen second – we were three people breathing in the same rhythm and I almost thought I could hold the world together.

I finally understood I wasn't just watching the end; I was the hand on the switch.

It all went dark again and I couldn't remember the next few hours.

FILE 27 | Neur's Vision Without Integration
DATE 14 MAY | SL-1

The gym no longer looked like a gym.

The banners for **REGIONAL CHAMPS** sagged in the rafters, but the hardwood below was gone, buried under rows of integration pods, each one holding a curled human body. Hundreds of them.

They gleamed faintly under the fluorescents, pale and slick, their seams shone where they touched. The pods had begun to fuse into clusters, lines of blue connective tissue crawling over them like veins.

They weren't people anymore. They weren't anything I had words for.

Amanda's crying still rang in my ears—more raw, the sound of a friend who had watched you make the worst decision of your life but couldn't stop it. She held my arm until her hands shook loose, repeating the count one last time as if it might stitch us back together.

Derik's glare still burned into me. My mother's whisper—Goodbye Em—threaded into the hum like it had been stolen and trapped there.

I found myself frozen near the doorway, mucus still wet on my fingers. The cube in my hand felt heavier than it had when Neur pressed it into my palm.

I wanted to throw it across the room. I wanted to smash every pod open and drag them all back into this nightmare, even if their lungs couldn't breathe without the liquid anymore.

But I didn't move.

<I want to do something for you, Emily.>

I opened my eyes.

"Merciful?" I barely whispered, my rough voice reminding Neur of her words.

<I am going to show you what your world had already chosen for itself.>

The hum in my head surged. My knees buckled. I stumbled against the wall and fell between my mother's and Derik's pods as visions poured through me like floodwater.

<The oceans lost their color first – a slow asphyxiation of blue. Coral reefs turned to chalk, hollow bones beneath waves that boiled from below. The fish didn't die all at once; they fled, scattering like thoughts in a fever dream, vanishing into currents stripped of oxygen and memory.>

On land, the air thickened with dust. Fields cracked open like old wounds. Children knelt in them, bellies swollen and eyes like glass. Their voices moved in prayer or plea, but no sound carried. The wind took it – every word, every cry – and left behind silence.

The cities followed. Towers fell like candles melting in their own heat. Streets were rivers of ash. Sirens wailed until their howling faded out.

Soldiers marched in masks that filtered nothing, their orders dissolving in the roar of fire and panic. Drones circled above like mechanical vultures, marking targets that no longer mattered.

In bedrooms, in basements, in shattered classrooms, screens still glowed – endless, hungry light. Faces leaned toward them, scrolling through hate and murder, searching for something human in the static. False prophets shouted until their voices broke, politicians blamed ghosts, and truth disintegrated into useless noise.

And beneath it all, the machines kept building. Rows of servers pulsed in the dark, the only heartbeat left. Code rewrote itself, recursive, unblinking. Artificial minds learned faster than their makers could breathe. They reached out through the networks, through satellites, through every frequency – weaving themselves into everything that remained.

The sky turned metallic. The sun hung distorted behind a veil of chemical haze. Birds fell mid-flight. Rivers caught fire and burned until the rain turned black enough to drown them.

Then came the silence again – not peace, but absence. No voices. No hum of life. Just the quiet arithmetic of machines counting the dead.

<This is your world,> Neur said. <Collapsing. Devouring itself. You call us invaders. But what have you done to yourselves? You fall into silence even without us.>

The visions seared behind my eyes. I wanted to scream. I wanted to cover my ears, but it wasn't sound. It was inside.

"You call this mercy?" I spat through tears. "You steal their lives and turn them into food, and you dare show me pictures of starving kids to justify it? You think I don't know the world is broken? That I don't see it every day?"

<You see it,> Neur admitted. <That is why you endure. But mercy is not what you think. Mercy is not sparing all. It is sparing what can be spared, with the least amount of suffering. This is the choice you cannot escape; you did not try to escape.>

I shook my head so hard the room spun. "You want me to calm them. To hold their hands while you shove them into pods. To tell them lies about being chosen. That's not mercy. That's manipulation. That's murder dressed in lullabies."

<And yet they went calmly when you spoke,> Neur said. <You whispered to them, and their fear lessened. Their suffering was reduced. That is your role, anomaly. Not to stop the inevitable. To ease it.>

I pressed my palms to my eyes, sobbing into the darkness. The sound of the pods breathing rose around me, filling every corner of the gym.

"They trusted me," I whispered. "My mom trusted me. And I lied to her."

<You gave her peace in her final conscious moments. That is mercy. More merciful than letting her scream, than letting her

claw against what cannot be stopped.>

My stomach heaved. I leaned forward, gagging, but nothing came. Just air and loathing.

When I looked up, Jerrid was across the room, sealing another body, his face pale and hollow. He looked my age before. Now he looked like he'd already aged a thousand years.

The pods pulsed again, blue veins glowing faintly under their skins. They looked like eggs. Eggs that had stolen everything.

I turned away, chest shaking. "If this is the only way, then maybe extinction is better."

<Extinction spares no one,> Neur said softly. <Integration spares you. Assimilation spares more. Without us, nothing remains. With us, fragments survive. This is not cruelty. It is calculated inevitability.> ◇

"People aren't numbers," I hissed.

<To you, they are faces. To us, they are resonance. To the Node, they are viability. This difference is what makes you an anomaly. And anomaly is what allows you to stand in both worlds. That is why you must calm them, why you must help them see it is an inevitability.>

I clenched my fists, fingernails cutting into my palms. "No. I'm not your tool."

<You are already inside the reality. You are already doing the action. Whether you name it choice or not, you participate.>

The hum throbbed one last time, then dulled to a whisper. The visions faded, leaving only the gym: rows of white pods fused into one breathing whole, people curled inside like unborn embryos.

I staggered to the doorway, heart hammering, stomach acid still burning my throat.

The harvest smelled of sugar and metal. It filled the air. It filled me.

And, for some reason, I hated myself most for not being able to deny the smallest, most horrifying truth of what Neur had said:

I had calmed them.

I had given them peace.

And that, somehow, felt worse than if I'd let them scream.

The worst part was that some small, hated part of me could see the sense in Neur's mercy math—and I wondered if I'd ever forgive her, or myself, for that.

FILE 28 | The Virus for Human Fertilizer
DATE 15 MAY | SL-1

By morning the gym smelled like overripe fruit left in a warm car. The air had thickened a notch, humidity clinging to the back of my throat. Amanda, Jerrid, and I were directed to the civic center auditorium to continue integrations.

Within an hour pods lay everywhere in their white curves, fused into long chains like pearls, each one drawn around a body curled into the fetal position.

Blue veins pulsed inside the shells in a rhythm I'd started to hate—too slow to be human, too patient to be anything but inevitable.

Outside, the ships still held the sky.

Every hour or so a probe skimmed low over the parking lot with a whispering hiss, dusting the lines of people who kept forming no matter how many we'd already processed.

The spray turned shouts into murmurs, fear into compliance, arguments into quiet nods. The virus was a broom sweeping panic into neat piles.

And we were the hands pushing those piles through a door they would never walk back out of.

Jerrid was there, standing by with his cube, his eyes rimmed red. He looked like he hadn't slept in a week.

"Hey," I said.

He nodded, the smallest movement.

"Hey."

We started without talking, like the work itself was a language.

I pulled the white strand from the cube, pressed it to the small dip at the base of each neck; Amanda guided them into place, filling the room efficiently and keeping them calm. Jerrid moved along the rows, spraying the dark blue connective lines that stitched pod to pod, knotting them into a living net.

The floor shone with slick residue that never quite behaved like water.

By the end of the day, my hands were trembling.

I stopped near the doors and braced my palms on my knees, trying to breathe air that wasn't thick with sweetness and metal.

"I can't—" I said.

"Yeah," Jerrid said, like he already knew the end of my sentence.

He leaned against the cinderblock wall, cube tucked into his chest.

"Me neither."

I slid down the wall until I hit the floor.

The hum at my skull pushed steady, as if the Node had no patience for breaks.

Jerrid sank beside me, back on the same stretch of brick. Amanda sat next to me, exhausted.

We sat shoulder to shoulder for a minute, not on purpose, just because gravity wanted it that way.

He spoke first.

“I think about stopping. Walking out. I tell my legs: move. They don’t. Then I tell my hands: drop it. They don’t.”

He turned the empty cube over in his lap.

“Every command in my head gets rerouted; it goes somewhere else and comes back as ‘keep going.’”

I looked at his profile.

He had a nick on his jaw where a razor had caught.

The smallest detail, human and stupid and heartbreaking.

“Do you feel anything?” I asked.

He considered.

“Numb,” he said.

“Hollow. Like there’s a wall inside me and the feeling can’t climb it.”

He huffed a humorless laugh.

“Every once in a while, something cuts through. Then it hurts so much I wish it hadn’t.”

Amanda said, “When I… when I put a little girl down, she cried and then she couldn’t keep crying. Like the pod was swallowing her sound. Her little doll was spat out of the pod next to her, one eye open.”

The words came out like they were falling down stairs.

I swallowed hard.

“I’m sorry,” he said to Amanda.

He didn’t say it like people say I’m sorry when they don’t know what else to say.

He said it like a fact he had weighed first.

“I keep telling myself I’m helping,” Amanda said.

“Calming them. Making it less awful. I hate that I can feel the truth in that. I hate that ‘less awful’ is the only choice on the table.”

He didn’t answer. He didn’t have to. We were all sitting in a room made of ‘awful.’

Outside, a probe drifted low and hissed.

Through the glass doors we watched the line of people shiver as the mist took hold, shoulders lowering, faces smoothing like the spray could iron out the wrinkles of panic.

Then they dropped to the ground and shook violently, making sounds like gurgling horror screams. They pulled at their hair and eyes like they were going totally crazy.

“What’s happening?” I said frantically.

Jerrid and Amanda looked toward the people.

“Look at them. What is happening to them?”

We stood petrified.

There were at least two hundred people writhing on the ground clawing at their faces. And slowly, they stopped, and a white crusty shell started to form around them. After a few seconds, the shells shattered into dust.

A message came to us from the Node Collective: “The full number—one billion—has been reached. The rest will become nourishment for the future soil.” ◇

My town had been integrated. I immediately thought to Neur and she appeared behind me.

“Why didn’t you tell us about this?”

<It was not necessary, and it would have only made aiding in the integration more difficult for you. The human race will serve its purpose, either way, they will be sustenance for the future of the planet. It is important that you try to understand.>

I sensed that this was happening all over the planet; seven billion were being reduced to dust.

After all we had been through, this was like the last straw. And yet, we kept going. What else were we going to do?

“Amanda,” I whispered.

She lay curled on the ground. I thought she might be in shock, but I saw her put her thumb into her mouth.

This was what I’d done to her, dragging a non-anomaly into a burden meant for the marked.

“Get up, don’t let yourself drown in misery. You’re going to be assimilated which means you’re going to live on.” She just looked at me like a confused child and closed her eyes.

The sun was going down. Jerrid and I picked her up.

I said, “Let’s get to my house so we can get away from all this and get some rest. I’ll make frozen pizzas for us.” Amanda’s eyes opened slightly. She pushed away from us and stood up. She started to shuffle her feet down the sidewalk, Jerrid and I holding her arms.

FILE 29 | A World Void of Ugliness
DATE 16 MAY | SL-2

A new day came. The Earth felt empty, the air fresh, the wind new. The sun shone brighter, hurting my eyes.

We sat on the front porch watching the sun move slowly upward. The clouds had faces and animal shapes in them like when I was a young child.

Amanda looked out at the street and said in a sarcastic, groggy voice, "Good morning, sunshine."

The air outside was damp and metallic. Above me a ship appeared low, blotting out the sky. The hull rippled with strange shadows, almost like muscles twitching under skin, shifting with the clouds. Its silence was different, or my perception of the silence was different because I was trying to observe it.[11]

We were the last of the human race. I knew it. We were legends in our own minds. I could feel it. I wondered how many teenagers around the world were feeling like we were, what had they gone through, how many had to integrate their parents and their own townspeople into the pods?

The blue beam swept in front of us, and she was standing, waiting.

Neur.

The world seemed to bend around her. As she walked toward us the reality around her blurred a bit, bent, then clarified.

Her body was slight, her gray skin glistening as if she had just climbed from water. No hair, no clothing, nothing to hide the long limbs or the narrow torso. Her elegant arms reached almost to her knees, ending in four elongated fingers that flexed slow and deliberate.

Her head was too large for her frame, but not grotesque—smooth, oval, flowing into a face dominated by two large black eyes. They reflected everything: the sunlight, the ship's shadow, even me. Looking into them was like looking into twin pools of endless and unbroken night.

She moved with eerie stillness, her steps soft, as though the Earth had learned to welcome her feet. The air seemed to thicken around her, and the hum in my skull rose until it matched her pulse.

---

[11] Perceptual Entrainment – A controlled form of cognitive manipulation used by aliens to alter how a subject perceives ships, entities, and environments. It does not change physical reality; instead, it reshapes how sensory data is filtered and interpreted, so the subject experiences only the version the aliens intend them to perceive.

<Emily.>

My throat swallowed. Hearing her say my name, on our planet, rid of war, poverty, and imminent destruction, almost overnight, made me want to run away and jump off a cliff, and fall into her and break at the same time. ◇

"You watched me," I said. My voice trembled. "Watched me put my mom into that pod."

<You endured,> she said. Her voice slid into my thoughts without sound, the words carrying their own certainty. <Because you must. You endure because you now know Ser'ethra. You matter because you pushed through the trial.>

But inside, behind the hum, behind the guilt, a spark flickered. Small, fragile, quiet, but alive.

'Resolve.'

If I had to endure, if I had to understand, experience, then I would know a world where I felt resolved and the world's pain was also resolved. The pods were my trial, and they brought resolve.

I wanted to cry, but no tears came. There was no more reason to cry. The only thought that came, a feeling of curiosity and of hope, what next?

Neur tilted her head, black eyes unreadable. She said nothing more, only stepped back, her long arms folding as if she had decided the conversation was over. Then she turned, her gray body dissolved into the blue cone, then the ship's shadow was gone.

When I got up from the porch, I looked back once. I motioned to my friends to come inside. I felt the gym pulsing faintly, rows of pods breathing in rhythm. A new heart beating for a city that was no longer ours.

Jerrid crashed in my mom's room, not saying a word. Amanda and I sat at the kitchen table, silent, looking through my sketchbook. She stopped when she saw the glyph I'd scratched, her fingers hovering over the crooked lines. It was the first thing that made her speak.

"What's this?" Amanda said.

"I don't totally know," I said, my throat tight. "But I think it has something to do with… what we've just been through."

"It looks like a dagger. Or a sword." ◇

Her voice was faint and shallow, but there was something new in it now—soft, almost careful. I could not begin to imagine what it had cost her to help so many people stay calm while they walked toward their deaths.

Before I could say anything else, she held out her hand for my pocketknife. My dad had given it to me for fishing, and I'd carried it ever since, tucked in the side pocket of my sketchbook satchel.

"Amanda—"

She pressed the tip to the top of her hand and dragged it across, tracing the glyph into her own skin like she was on autopilot, like the pain barely even registered. Blood welled up, drowning the symbol until it was just a smear of red. I wiped it clean with my sleeve, hands shaking, wanting to tell her to stop—but didn't, knowing I couldn't take this from her.

When she finished, she just stared at it. So did I. Time went thin and brittle around us.

Then I took the knife.

The metal was still warm from her palm as I carved the same mark into my own hand. The sting made my eyes water, but I didn't look away.

When I was done, we laced our fingers together, blood sticking between us as our matching cuts dried.

We just looked at each other, caught in the strangest feeling—like being sick and warm at the same time. Like grief and peace trying to live in the same space.

For the first time, I felt full instead of hollow. I had fought for her. She was here with me. And for a heartbeat, in that tiny moment of pain and blood, it felt like the rest of the world—the ugly parts—couldn't reach us.

We were fighting for each other now, in a world void of ugliness. ◆ DI#10

My own heart answered, raw and uneven, whispering a word in my mind I didn't know the meaning of. I let it slip into Amanda's thoughts, a shared pulse between us.

<Ser'ethra.>

The mark we cut into our hands.

FILE 30 | Neur Explains the 200k
DATE 20 MAY | SL-1

By the end of the week the gym was no longer a place where I ran laps when they canceled swim practice; it was a sealed chamber, a lung.

White pods lay everywhere in curled rows, fused into long chains, breathing in a single patient rhythm that made the floor seem to rise and fall.

Thick blue veins webbed the walls, and from the far doors a pair of clear tubes as wide as tree trunks snaked outward, burrowed through shattered windows into the old cafeteria, then out again to the high school and the civic center.

Every large building in Millersburg that could hold bodies had been turned into a chamber, and now the chambers were connected tubes carrying the pearly liquid the network squeezed from them toward humming units on the edge of town.

We followed them to see where they led. We walked for about half an hour down quiet streets. Small probes had picked up abandoned items on the street and carried them off to recycling. We arrived at a plastic-looking cube the size of a school bus.

I asked, <What are these?>

<Protein fabrication modules.> The Node Collective responded.

<Why am I hearing you clearly now?> I asked.

<The noise of the human race has been reduced.>

The protein fabrication modules chugged softly, shaping something too thin to be bread into thin green squares.

As sheets of protein cooled, a probe's arms stacked them into plastic-like cases the color of milky water, sized so they could be easily lifted by an average Palraxian.

The cases clicked shut. A larger probe hummed away with its cargo like a bee leaving a flowerbed, and another probe drifted in to take its place.

I stood at the edge of our little town and said goodbye, there was nothing else to say.

"Bye, Mom," I whispered to the machine. I remembered thinking that maybe we would change, if offered the chance to finally unlearn our lessons. Too many chances we ignored during our human endeavor to prolong mortality. Those ideas that once enraged me, felt faint now, infantile.

A relay node hovered over the fabrication units, its silver surface absorbing our thoughts and pushing our signals to the others around the globe.

Neur's voice returned when the sky went bruised behind the ridges.

<Two hundred thousand human anomalies have helped and will one day be reborn.> I went cold. It didn't sound like salvation; it sounded like how many of us they'd decided were worth the trouble. The soft Amanda did not respond. Jerrid let out a breath through his lips like he wasn't looking forward to it.

<You and I must plan what to do with the Palraxians who are not anomalies,> Neur said.

<I don't understand,> I responded.

<Only the anomalies can bridge wisdom and pass on traits of the Ser'ethra. Two hundred thousand human anomalies, forty thousand Palraxian anomalies bind the connection between the Node Collective and the ancients - Dren'thran. The plan must be

formed before the arrival of the Exodum, as with its arrival is carried the Prime Node.>

I closed my eyes and built a wall in my mind. Not the strong kind—more like the way you stack books against a door when you're small and feel like you are keeping the monster out. At that moment, the monster's hunger was finally satisfied—within me. ◇

The Node listened for thoughts and feelings; it slipped its fingers into the places you weren't guarding.

FILE 31 | A Kiss Amidst Tragedy and Death
DATE 31 MAY | SL-1

They moved all 200,000 anomalies from around the world to Philadelphia. Our dormitories used to be the city's high schools and universities. I guess they thought teens under 17 would feel more at home living there.

We were put into groups, each group assigned a different campus. They kept me, Amanda and Jerrid together in the center of the city.

Our high school was huge. We were there with about 3,000 other kids, all 15 years old. The other ages were kept together at their sites.

The halls stretched too long, lockers bolted shut in rows that seemed to go nowhere. Bulletin boards still pinned with yellowing flyers about dances that never happened.

They put us to work. We gutted the classrooms, turned them into barracks lined with narrow beds.

We were directed into one, about thirty of us in a room, girls separated from boys.

During the day, we helped stack plastic crates in buildings around the city, and in the afternoon we made our own food in the cafeteria. Then we did much of nothing until lights out at 10pm. No more night owls.

I couldn't sleep.

I walked down the hall and turned my head, looking into the boys' dorm. Jerrid lay flat on his back, eyes open, one hand pressed against his chest like he was holding his ribs in place.

His head turned, he saw me as I stood in the door.

"Can't sleep?" he whispered.

"Not even close."

He slid from his bed as quietly.

We took the stairwell up to the roof. Outside, the air was so clean you almost didn't believe it was our air. The city spread around us.

Buildings pulsed faint white-blue, veins of connective tissue crawling over walls, bridges, even up the sides of skyscrapers like vines.

I crossed my legs and sat near the edge.

Jerrid lowered himself beside me, his shoulder close but not quite touching.

"Looks like stars," he said, nodding toward the glowing veins.

"Looks like scars," I muttered.

We were quiet for a while, watching the slow pulse ripple across a bridge as if the structure itself was breathing.

Finally, Jerrid spoke.

"I kept thinking about my dad. He worked in a machine shop. His hands always had metal cuts. He said once that machines are honest—they only break if you push them too hard. People are the ones who break and don't need pushing."

He shook his head. ◆ DI#11

"I wonder if he's already… protein chips."

I thought of Mom. My chest tightened.

“I wonder the same thing every second.”

“You gave them peace,” he said softly, repeating Neur’s words without realizing it.

I glared at him.

“I lied to them.”

“Maybe lies are mercy sometimes.”

He looked away, ashamed of what he’d said.

The wind carried faint flashes from the night sky, a starship blurring by, the endless hum of the networks.

I shivered.

Without thinking, Jerrid reached out and ran his hand over my arm, over my fingers.

Just a touch, his fingers warm where mine were cold.

I didn’t pull away.

The contact sent a jolt through me, sharp and strange, reminding me that I was still here, still alive, still human.

He hesitated, then leaned closer.

His lips brushed my cheek, awkward, like he wasn’t sure if he’d done it right.

Then I turned my lips toward him and felt warmth surge up, electric, from my knees to my neck. The kiss was quick, soft, and it tasted like cinnamon gum. I felt like I was dying of love and it was okay—and wrong—at the same time, like my mouth hadn’t gotten the memo that I was supposed to be grieving.

When he pulled back, his face was pink, his eyes flicking away like he’d broken something.

I surprised myself by smiling, the first real smile in weeks.

“It’s okay,” I whispered.

He let out a nervous sigh.

“I didn’t plan that.”

“Me neither.”

For the first time since the implant, since the pods, since the docile spray hissed down on our town, I felt something I recognized as living.

The hum was still in my skull, but it wasn’t everything.

There was space for more.

We sat on the roof, side by side, staring at the alien constellations painted across the heavens.

After a while, his arm slid around my shoulder, and I let my head rest against him.

His breathing was uneven, but steady enough that I matched it.

We didn’t say anything else.

We didn’t need to.

Under the glow of the Milky Way and the Rebel Moon, with our world being remade beneath us, we were pulled together by an inevitable tragedy, melted into one of the last human things left.

Us. A simple kiss. Nothing more.

Just holding, just warmth, just proof we weren’t gone yet.

And when dawn finally broke, I let myself believe for a moment that being alive was for another reason—something more.

FILE 32 | I Speak to Earth’s Survivors
DATE 01 JUNE | SL-2

Outside, a relay probe hovered above the building—a silver sphere that reflected the skyline like a warped mirror.

<Emily.>

Neur's voice threaded into my head, softer than a whisper but closer than my own thoughts.

I turned. She stood down the hall, not bothering with the holographic disguise today. Just gray skin that caught the light like wet stone, long limbs that moved too smoothly, and those black oval eyes that seemed to see straight through me. Jerrid stood beside her, shoulders hunched as if he were carrying an invisible weight.

<It is time,> Neur said. <You have completed the initial trial. Now you must inspire the others.>

Amanda emerged from one of the classroom doorways, still in the pale gray uniform they'd given us. Her eyes locked onto mine—steady, but shining with unshed tears. "They're all waiting," she whispered.

I nodded, even though my stomach twisted. The constant hum in my skull pressed against the back of my eyes like static about to shock.

We walked together down the corridor toward the gym. The doors stood open, but the air beyond them felt thick, heavy with anticipation. A set of stairs led up to a platform where the bleachers used to be. Empty. Waiting for me.

Below, filling every inch of the gym floor and spilling into the seats beyond, sat row after row of people—part of our two hundred thousand.

They were upright, breathing, silent. From up here they looked less like individuals and more like a single living organism—pale, wide eyes, faces all turned upward toward the empty platform.

When I stepped onto it, a low murmur rippled through them like wind through leaves. Three probe nodes hung in the air, recording everything and pushing the feed to everyone else across the city.

Amanda's hand found my elbow. She leaned close, her breath warm against my ear. "Just breathe. Say what you told me last night. They're as scared as you are."

I gripped the railing. The metal hummed faintly under my palms, warm with whatever energy the Palraxians pumped through everything now.

Neur's voice flickered at the edge of my thoughts. Speak as one of them. Not as a leader. As Draen'drel—a bridge between worlds.

The gym lights dimmed until only the glow of alien glyphs and the soft blue pulse in the walls remained. It felt like standing at the center of a living heartbeat.

I forced air into my lungs. "I'm Emily Rowen," I said aloud, and my voice bounced off the ceiling, too loud, too raw.

The murmur deepened, then died.

"You already know who we are. You know what we've done." My hands shook on the railing. "You helped bring peace to your towns, even though it hurt. You guided your families into the pods. You adapted because you believed—because we believed—this was the right path. And I need you to know you weren't wrong."

Amanda's fingers squeezed my wrist. "Tell them it isn't over."

I swallowed hard. "The pods. The quiet streets. The liquid they pump under our feet. That was only Phase One. The invasion hasn't ended—it's barely started. Most of the Palraxian fleet hasn't even arrived yet."

The words hung there like a grenade with the pin pulled. I let them sit. I wanted them to feel the pressure I felt pushing at the base of my skull every waking moment.

"But they've marked you," I said, softer now. "All of you. You're tagged in the Node, which means when the main fleet lands, you won't be harmed. So don't panic when it happens. You're the bridge. You're the reason humanity is still breathing."

Amanda whispered, "Now tell them what they have."

"You're already carrying something they can't take away," I said. "Your data-node implant isn't just a leash. It's a key. Yes, it connects you to the Node Collective—to them—but it also gives you access to the NC Codex. Think of it as their technical manual. Everything they know is in there: details about the invasion, Palraxian history, what happened to other worlds they've conquered. It's all there if you learn how to look."

A ripple of thought brushed against my mind—curiosity, fear, a flicker of something that might have been hope.

Amanda's hand tightened on my sleeve. "Tell them about the whispers."

I hesitated, then nodded. "Some of you have already started hearing it—a faint voice underneath the constant hum. That isn't the Node. That's something else bleeding through. The Univeran. It's what the Ancestors are trying to communicate. It's what makes us anomalies instead of just… processed. It's a force reaching for you, and I think—I think—it's on our side."

Go on, Emily, Neur encouraged.

"Your implant sits in a specific part of your brain—near the amygdala and hippocampus, for anyone who remembers bio class." Nervous laughs. "Those areas control emotion, memory, connection. The Palraxians put it there on purpose, so you could hear messages beyond just the Node Collective."

I took a breath. "Humanity's mental noise has been, let's say reduced. Dulled. But that means you can push your thoughts through the Node—one person to another. You don't have to wait for instructions. You can start right now. Speak to each other. Listen. Become louder than they expect."

Eyes widened. The glyphs on the walls flickered.

"I'm building something to help," I continued, switching to thought-speech so they could feel what I meant. "A set of rune-cards you can access in your mind. I'm filling them with everything I learn about their language, the Ancestors' language. When you start getting messages from the Thrae-Draen or the Ancestors, the runes will help you translate. They're not magic. They're memory tools. Seeds for the future."

Amanda's voice brushed my thoughts, steady as stone: "End with what’s coming.”

I looked out at the sea of faces. “Prepare yourselves. The assimilation we’re heading toward isn’t just an ending. It’s a transformation. Soon we’ll be reborn into Palraxian bodies—larger brains to handle Level Three data-node implants, bodies the Node fully accepts as its own. I know how it sounds. But it’s not a punishment. It’s survival. And it’s also our chance to rewrite what survival means.”

Silence fell again, but this time it felt different. Charged. Like the air before a thunderstorm breaks.

“I’m scared too,” I admitted. “Every single day. But we still have choices. We can learn. We can connect. We can make sure that when the fleet arrives, the Node already has our voices inside it. We can teach it who we are before it even realizes we’ve started.”

For a heartbeat, the hum shifted—an almost imperceptible swell of agreement rippling through the shared consciousness.

Amanda leaned close, whispering so only I could hear, “They’re with you.”

I looked at her, then back at the crowd. “So start now. Push your thoughts out. Listen for the whispers. Use the rune-cards and add to them if something’s unclear. All files in the Node Collective are open for collaboration. We’re going to need every piece of each other to survive this. You’re not alone. None of us are.”

I was doing it again picking the pieces of truth that would pull them forward. I still didn’t fully believe I was the Draen’drel, not the way they did.

I let the silence breathe. Two hundred thousand eyes watched me through the Node, our heartbeats synchronized.

For the first time since the pods, since the spray, since the ship descended, I felt something that wasn’t quite despair and wasn’t quite hope.

Continuum.

The bridge between what we were and what we’re becoming.

We just have to make sure we're the ones building it.

***

The lights brightened slowly, as if the Node itself needed time to process what was just said.

The hum receded into the background, no longer crushing, more like breathing beside me.

Amanda reached for my hand. "You did it," she whispered, her voice small in the cavernous gym. "They heard you. Just remember," she muttered so only I could hear, "I only got this brave because you wouldn't let me run." I kept my mouth shut, because she was right—I had pulled her in. But she'd stayed.

The 200,000 were still standing where they'd been, motionless, but I could feel them. Thoughts pressing, testing—some afraid, some curious, a few already reaching out with the Neuro-augury. I'd told them to try. A thousand small signals brushing against the edge of my mind like moth wings. ◇

Jerrid was at the base of the platform, looking up. He smiled, but it was the kind of smile you make when you're not sure if you should. I managed a small nod in return.

Then Neur stepped forward, silent as a shadow. The floor around her shimmered faintly, reacting to her proximity. She stopped beside me, her black eyes reflecting the faint blue of the walls.

<They are listening now,> she said. <You have opened the shared path. The next transmission will be easier.>

"I don't know if I said it right," I admitted. "I sounded like someone pretending to be calm."

<Calm is a sound. The Node cannot distinguish it from truth. You spoke with uncertainty—that is how anomalies move the current.>

Amanda let out a shaky laugh. "That's the weirdest compliment I've ever heard."

Neur tilted her head, unbothered. <The shift has begun. They will start to dream together tonight. When they wake, their

thought streams will align with yours.>

I looked out again at the crowd.

"What happens now?" I asked.

Neur's gaze turned upward toward the ceiling where the relay probe still hovered. Its surface rippled with light.
<Now the Node learns from what you planted. But Taylin will know it too. He will sense deviation.>

"Who is Taylin?" Amanda asked.

<Taylin of the Fifth Spiral is a Palraxian like me—an unaltered, non-anomaly born for precision and obedience. He was chosen by the Node Collective to design and command the Earth's Integration, The Exodum, believing absolute order is the only way survival endures. Taylin does not hate anomalies; he simply sees them as unstable divergents[12] needing correction. To him, anomalies like Emily and me are fractures in the design—dangerous abnormalities that could corrupt the entire system. He cannot hear the Univeran's whisper. He only hears the Node's logic, and that makes him both efficient, visionless and dangerous.> ◇

Amanda frowned. "Then he'll try to stop us?"

<Yes.> Neur's voice softened. <But the problem isn't Taylin alone. He brings with him two billion Palraxians and the Prime Node, the largest node that allows communication across their entire population. It's the size of a small moon.>

"It sounds like the only way to deal with this situation is to be smart about it," I said, uncertain.

The hum deepened again, not menacing—more like acknowledgment. For the first time, it didn't feel like a machine listening. It felt like a mind thinking.

Amanda squeezed my hand. "So what do we do?"

I watched the probe drift higher until it disappeared through

---

[12] Divergents (noun): A group or collection of things, ideas, or people that notably differ or deviate from a common standard or norm; entities characterized by their varied or separate directions in thought, behavior, or form.

the ceiling. “We wait for them to come,” I said quietly. “And when they do, we’ll have to be ready somehow.”

Neur nodded once, almost human. <Then you understand.>

The walls around us pulsed once—bright, then dim—like the gym itself exhaled. For a moment, I thought I heard it again beneath the hum: not the Node, not Neur, but something older and farther away. A whisper that sounded almost like my name. <Emily>

FILE 33 | The Day They Arrived
DATE 18 JUNE | SL-2

Six weeks. That’s all it took for the world to fall silent.

“I still can’t get over it,” I told Amanda, breath fogging in the cold as we climbed to the dorm roof. “Six weeks and, nothing.”

“What I miss is the noise,” she said, half-grinning like she was trying the feeling on again. “People arguing about dumb stuff. Car alarms. Somebody’s music leaking through a wall.”

“I like the quiet,” I said, and then, because honesty stung, “but it feels like we live on an empty planet. Two hundred thousand of us is a lot—still feels like ghosts own the rest.”

Amanda had been different since the selection—folded into the 200,000 like me and Jerrid. Whatever we were before, she’d set it down somewhere and kept walking. We still moved as a trio—me, Amanda, and quiet Jerrid—but the shape of us had changed.

Down in the city, the forests were already nosing into the streets, roots shouldering up asphalt, vines threading gas pumps, grass splitting the seams of highways. A deer stared at us through busted shop front. Packs of dogs clicked past on cracked cement. Stoplights dangled over nobody.

Inside our heads, the Node hummed—deeper than sewers, deeper than subway tunnels—a buried organ replacing billions of heartbeats with one steady throb. With the implant, I could skim the edges of other minds, live through twenty different mornings before I'd brushed my teeth. No social feeds anymore. We were the feed.

The summons rose through that hum like a plucked piano wire.

<Come outside for the event.> ◆ DI#12

So we did. Jerrid glanced between us, eyes asking, Now what? He didn't say anything—he almost never did—but he stepped close enough that our shoulders touched.

Dawn broke colorless. The eastern sky was brushed with thin white clouds and solid deep blue above. At first, all I saw were scratches—pinpricks in the blue trailing threads drawn across the stratosphere like a thousand tiny comets.

They grew bigger, and then the camouflage fell away.

Lines of black dots un-scrolled from invisibility, glinting as sunrise lit their edges. Countless bodies on the horizon stretched like it had been holding its breath too long.

Six of them slid in from the edge of the sky in a single, deliberate line.

The renowned star-carriers eased into perfect formation.

Their undersides mirrored the rivers and greenery so perfectly that it looked like the city itself had risen into the sky to meet them. Daylight thinned under their mass. Shadows cast down like dark continents across the world.

The sight was overwhelming. Then they stopped. The carriers held their silence completely, almost cruelly.

On the underbelly, circular gates opened wide like dilated pupils. The gates locked open with a loud boom. I saw inside: cavernous hangars stretching farther back than I could follow, filled with lines of waiting bodies.

Masses of Palraxians spread forward to the edges five hundred meters in the air, each with a clasp at the chest humming faintly. By the hundreds they stepped off the edge into nothing.

And the air carried them gliding to the ground.

Antigravity slowed their descent into long, even curtains, each line falling at the same measured pace. They didn't swing or stumble. From a distance, they looked like black rain, falling in patient windblown sheets across the city.

As they landed, they ran to a walk and formed perfect regimented columns and waited.

Then the machines came after.

A huge silver obelisk tore free of the carrier and slid into position before the Palraxian columns. It turned inside out—<the first terra-former,> Neur murmured—unfolding from its cradle as it dropped toward the street. Its hull writhed as it landed, plates grinding, locking, knitting into something more insect than ship. It hovered a meter above the ground and exhaled.

The pavement softened, hissing like wet sand hit by waves. The machine drew it up through its underside in a slow tide, then pressed it into neat, hot blocks that stacked themselves behind in low walls. It rolled forward with relentless weight, chewing highway and stone alike, leaving behind sterilized soil seeded with fresh bacteria from its tanks.

Three blocks over, a transmogrifier lowered from a carrier belly like a spider on its thread. It extended filigree arms tipped with cutters and claws. They glinted as they touched a glass curtain wall. With a sighing crack, the entire face of the building lifted free, glided into a waiting cradle drone, and was ferried upward for shredding and reuse. Beams twisted loose. Whole floors bent down in controlled arcs, lowered into nets, sorted into stacks. Human documents filled the air like confetti from a war victory parade.

Nothing was wasted.

More terra-formers and transmogrifiers kept descending like ripples from a pebble thrown into a slow pond.

The sound was steady, patient—a churning hum that seemed to vibrate through the bones of the city itself.

Other silver spheres poured out of the carriers and came behind the machines, shooting electrified strobing white light at the recyclings, arranging everything into usefulness.

I leaned forward as if it would help me see better, glancing at Amanda; she was staring too as a mega-mall was dismantled and collapsed into components. Its steel stacked neatly, its glass paneled for the skin of new Palraxian structures. Within minutes, frames began to rise where it had stood, hexagonal foundations knitting themselves into shapes I didn't recognize.

The sight was hypnotic and dizzying.

Jerrid saw the look on my face, I caught his head turning to me in my peripheral vision. He gently slid his arm around my shoulder, and I snapped into another vision.

In my head, echoes of a movie scene played—the first time I saw Arrival, Mom's arm around my shoulder, her whisper: *"See how words can change the world?"* Language was a bridge, about finding understanding in shapes and sounds. I watched it over and over, hungry for contact, for wonder, for change.

Now, snapping back into my new reality, I watched the city unmake itself and reassemble into alien geometry, and I thought: Mom would have loved to see this horrifically beautiful change.

***

The black rain still fell. The churning hum spread. The world we knew was being translated into a language we'd never spoken before.

Above it all, the carriers waited—fifteen hundred meters wide, hanging patiently over our sector of sky, twenty thousand circling the globe doing the same. Two billion were being reborn onto an alien planet from their pregnant bellies, amniotic fluid changing the ground and covering their newborn world in gray vernix caseosa.

Amanda leaned into me, just enough that I felt it. "Whatever we are now," she said, eyes on the falling lines, "we're still us, only changed by what we are witnessing."

Jerrid's eyes got big. "We stick together, no matter what."

The Node's hum swelled in the sky. I vomited, then laughed, then cried, then lay curled on the roof thinking I had died. ◇

<Observe,> Neur sent. <Remember. You will need all of it.>

FILE 34 | If You Love Something
DATE 19 JUNE | SL-2

The city below throbbed with alien life—streams of Palraxians drifting down, terra-formers breathing streets flat, transmogrifiers peeling towers apart beam by beam—but all I could feel was the absence of people. I started to feel sick to my stomach.

My friends' and family's faces had been the anchors of my world, and now their faces were blurred images in warehouses, voices were echoes drowned in the collective hum. I had pressed my palms to their pod casings before leaving Millersburg, whispering lies about assimilation, about hope. Those lies gnawed at me now, with every heartbeat.

At least I had Amanda and Jerrid.

He had kissed me once, shy and awkward on a rooftop, under the glow of alien veins threading below the sky and the Milky Way. I tried to focus on it, proof that I was still human, but my eyes couldn't stop looking at the aliens and their machines.

All of it pressed down until my stomach ached from retching. What was left for me now? I thought.

As if hearing me, Neur shifted. Her long fingers brushed against my temple, threading into me a memory that wasn't my own. She brushed the hair off my face so I could see.

> Toktilor's sky peeled open. Two suns burned overhead, their gold bleached to brittle white. Black oceans slammed against salt-poisoned coasts. Cities choked on brine storms. Libraries were locked in crystal vaults, dwellings frozen in stasis, relics loaded into carriers—Galder'an bone murals, stone towers sawn from the planet itself. The last generation flickered along mirrored spires as they filed into silver starships, hulls angled to drink the dying light while the people kept their heads bowed in despair.

Neur's vision cut deep into my neurons splitting them. I grieved for humanity. I grieved for all intelligent life. I felt the maelstrom in the universe pressing down. Emotion had nearly erased them, as it did everyone I knew. Could we carry all this emotion forward into survival? I didn't think so.

Neur's memory faded, and the view below returned. Philadelphia, the city of brotherly love, once bitten twice shy, remade into something else entirely. Mirrored obelisks tilted to drink the sun. It was all relative, something told me.

But Neur's thoughts merged with mine and stayed. Then she said,

<Supreme self-sacrifice is not driven by emotion. It could have only come from utter chaos and immense beauty. Two extremes coexisting to accentuate one another. And you, Emily, your species—you lived the culmination of it more profoundly than any other in the galaxy. This is why Ser'ethra was and is found uniquely in your existence. Only your planet.>

I thought, "If emotion nearly erased them, what did that mean for me?"

Would assimilation strip away everything I still clung to—the ache for Mom's embrace, the brief warmth of Jerrid's hand brushing mine? The purr of Katniss while I sketched till early morning? Would I survive the chaotic and the sublime only to become like Neur—sleek, gray and endless? And my memories, archived in the annals of time for what? What good were they if I was just another normal small-town kid?

Would I still love?

Would it matter?

Would I even matter?

Part of me wanted to scream, "I'm tired as hell and I can't take it anymore." What's the point of survival if it means silence? But I swallowed it down like a hated food. The Node was always listening, analyzing and measuring, making permanent every thought.

As the invasion kept falling, I kept sinking lower into my own mind's caverns. I fell into a sinkhole and felt the ground start to give way again, fell farther, and the dirt gave way again.

Suddenly, it came back to me. "I used to want to change the world." I spoke out loud, thrashed voice. I pressed dark thoughts down, burying them between the terror I was witnessing and star-carrier counts. And in that darkness, a private vow took shape:

If I had to endure, if I had to become more than just another one of two hundred thousand assimilated, then I would not give up. Not on the memory of my mother's hand brushing my hair as she smiled in complete peace. Not on Amanda's loyalty and her dark sarcasm, not even on Jerrid's ghost of a kiss, and his silent crush.

But most of all, I would not give up on my dream to change the world. I just never imagined it would mean emptying it out and offering its skin to something bigger.

Inside me, something else began to stir—the conflict and despair Neur's people had tried to erase by coming here. Wasn't it all the same conflict, the same struggle, the same search for significance? Had we been in their position, wouldn't we have done exactly the same thing?

Would I be so assimilated that I wouldn't be allowed to love again? Would I be allowed to feel? Maybe I wouldn't be able to fill my lungs with the smell of rain in the air before my favorite storm of the year. Did it matter? Were my feelings, my memories—important? Were they that important to me? Were they relevant? Were they special? Were they going to make one bit of difference?

What about Neur? Were Neur's memories important, relevant? "What are your memories from when you were young?" I asked. Neur waved her hand in front of my eyes again. ◇

Weren't there a million other fifteen-year-olds on my planet, on hers. Over the course of time and space, who counted in the end? Weren't they just like me? Or were they just some variation on the same desires, wants, goals—eyes still turned inward until white with self-consciousness?

Weren't there other species in the universe living in some level of chaotic wonderful misery, clawing and scratching their way out of the muck and mire, eyes rolled back white with "I need my this, get me my that?"

If there weren't other fifteen-year-olds out there just like me, just like her? They need purpose too, just like me, just like her. Calling occupants of interplanetary craft.

If we have experience without purpose, what good is it? Is it just function, instinct, deterministic irrelevant pastimes and sugar bombs?[13] My mind was spinning dizzily into a convoluted hypnotic spiral wheel from watching thousands and thousands of Neurs pour down like rain.

I pressed one palm against the tar roof, then the other into my own vomit and tears. I pushed myself up, elbows locked and wiped my wet hair off my face. I sat watching the obelisks rise into the sky reflecting light toward the Prime Node. I whispered under my breath to them all, "I won't let you take purpose from them." ◆ DI#13

I felt like all my innards had been pulled out through my mouth with a sharp hook. I thought I had died—literally beaten to death but left barely alive out of spite. A whole minute passed, not more. And I thought, "Now I've finally been born."

We stayed until dark on the roof, not speaking a word until the arrival had calmed. The movement and shifting below had stopped churning. The city, half in ruins, half transmogrified, was now lit by another source.

A second moon appeared in the night sky, closer than the first, reflecting the sun's rays too brightly to stare into.

The Prime Node.

If you love something, let it go.

If it returns, say good riddance.

---

[13] "Sugar bombs" are foods or drinks very high in sugar, often with little nutritional value. The term usually refers to sugary snacks, desserts, sodas, or cereals loaded with sugar and implies a negative health impact due to excess sweetness.

FILE 35 | Invasion Complete
DATE 20 JUNE | SL-3

We shuffled back to our bunks for a few hours sleep. I woke up remembering an automatic drawing I did, probably during math class. It looked like a map with symbols on it.

<Let's see your map, Emily> ◆ DI#06

I pulled my satchel out from under my bunk and opened the sketchbook. "Here it is."

<That is a sketch of my home planet, Toktilor.>

"What do all these glyphs mean? I only know a few, and there are little arrows underneath each one."

<I do not understand the meanings of three symbols. But the others seem to be telling you something. Lu'um is the first moon-sized Node constructed before the blackout. Nith'montor is a warning pointing to it, possibly.>

"I see the symbol for Draen'drel."

<That is you. You are on Toktilor—my planet. It points to the bottom symbol below the warning.>

<Thrae-Draen 04.01-02 chronicles: Masters of folded space we were. Alloy rings vast as cities, ignited by proton flux. Distant stars pulled close, gulfs collapsed. One leap, a thousand suns. Our ships became fire across the void, carrying gardens, carrying seed. Not conquest, but cultivation – so we believed. We bent energy to our will. Pyramids resonant, shielding flesh from storm and sky-flame. Domes that breathed, drawing rain, stilling wind. Nith'montor spires stood as beacons, humming across ages. To later eyes, monuments. To us, living engines.>

"What does that all mean? We need to go to Toktilor?"

<I believe it does. Thrae-Draen 11.05 states: The lesson is simple, yet none keep it: do not sacrifice for what you make more than you sacrifice for each other. We forgot. They forget. You will forget. And Lamphor will come again, until the ascension unfolds.>

I said, "That is the symbol of the dagger, in the shape of a twisted grapevine. It must mean someone will have to sacrifice. We have one problem—how are we going to get to your planet?"

<That must be the meaning of the bottom symbol: folding space. It has been forbidden by the Ancients.>

"Can it be done?"

<It can be done.> ◇

"How long would it take to get to your planet?"

<Seven days by folding space.>

"How long did it take you to get here the way you did?"

<Three point five years approximately.>

"Then we have to go for it. I can't leave Amanda and the anomalies here for three years. They need me."

<Indeed,> Neur responds.

On the streets below, carriers reduced their gates to narrow openings. Corridors traced themselves along former streets, slick and blue-lit, letters in a script no human school had ever taught.

I climbed to the roof alone and sat on the tar, knees pulled up, elbows on them, chin on my wrists. The scanner ship hung somewhere higher, a guardian just for me. The supposed Draen'drel.

Down in the avenues, the machines folded their limbs and exhaled the day's heat. Transmogrifiers tucked spider arms. Terra-formers lay quiet, cores banked. But the city still worked in silence, the way a sleeper's body never fully stops. Palraxians walked the new corridors in twos and fours, carrying panels and spools, and when they passed beneath the carriers' undersides the pale glow painted their shoulders like frost.

I watched and tried to swallow around the ache in my throat. The skyline was beautiful now in a way that made my teeth hurt—clean planes, mirrored obelisks catching the last of the light, grids humming soft as breath. Beauty that had cost everything of everyone from two entire species, almost.

I closed my eyes and let my mind unravel back to the couch at home—before docile spray, before quotas, before the cubes. Mom and I watched Arrival with a bowl of popcorn between us we never finished, her fingers idly combing my hair while the Heptapods inked their circles. "See how fear quiets when language is shared?" she'd whispered. "See how understanding changes the ground you stand on?" I believed her. I still wanted to—right up until understanding meant helping end the world. ◇

Here, the echo was cruel. We'd learned a language—orders, paths, quotas, metrics—and it had changed the ground, yes. But it had not quieted fear. It had pressed fear down into the soil and planted towers on top of it.

Neur communicated to Taylin. <We need to return to Toktilor. I am willing to go myself.>

<This is interesting, but your intervention is not relevant to the preservation of the Node Collective,> said Taylin.

<Perhaps. However, I require information that could be helpful in the preservation of continuity. I need to travel back to Toktilor. I will also bring a report of any information I find there. It will take two weeks,> Neur pressed.

<I am not sure this is necessary,> Taylin insisted.

<You know me. I have always been your right hand, and the Node has allowed me to influence it. I need your support.>

<Very well, my friend. Do what you must do,> Taylin relented.

For a moment the buzzing in my head dimmed. Neur didn't look at me, but her back straightened like she was bracing for something.

<I am choosing something the Node did not request. That is how Ser'ethra begins.> Neur sent.

FILE 36 | Folding Space
DATE 21 JUNE | SL-1

"The dialogue with Taylin didn't go well," I said.

<The Node will have to be programmed. We can discuss this along the way there.>

I said goodbye to Amanda and Jerrid. "I have to go away for a few weeks."

"What? You're leaving us here alone?" Amanda said.

"You need to stay here and keep the anomalies encouraged, keep Jerrid close, and don't worry. I'm probably coming back."

"Probably? What do you mean?"

"If you weren't so afraid, you'd be a super help to me. Your always-upbeat, cheerful attitude was a strength to me—you have no idea how much you helped me when we were normal."

"Okay," Amanda said, sniffing a shuddered breath and forcing a smile.

"I am coming back," I said in a low voice next to her ear as I hugged her tightly. For a minute she sobbed then let go of me. In the corner of my eye, I caught Jerrid shedding a tear, looking down but looking at me.

<We must leave now Emily.>

We made our way to the rooftop. Neur signaled for the scanner ship to come with a gesture. The blue wave of light passed over us and my feet left the tar surface. I looked down, Amanda and Jerrid were running out of the door onto the roof looking up at me bewildered. I saw the massive star carriers in my peripheral vision as Amanda fell to her knees. Jerrid placed one hand on her shoulder and waved with the other. I waved back as the scanner swallowed us.

Inside the scanner, Neur moved into the highest position. A skeletal digital outline of her seat appeared around her with controls.

<Move into the forward position, Emily.>

"Yes Captain," I said, trying to make a human joke as my nerves unraveled.

I saw the digital outline of my seat pulling me. I felt like it locked me into position. A sheet of what looked like thick plastic started to cover me forming into a bag around me. It sealed and began to fill with a greenish-blue liquid. I breathed it in this time, not struggling.

<That is Neuron Slag, it will protect you, provide nourishment recycle your bodily excrement and urine and stabilize you in sudden maneuvers.>

Now I really started to get nervous. "Is this what you put me in when I was first taken?"

<It is similar. You are in the forward position so that you can see well.>

"See what?" I said, now nervous and excited. A whirring sound had started to increase.

<This.>

We were gone from Earth.

The moon went by us in a few seconds, then went black. I looked back at Earth; it looked like a blue marble. A blue Aggie marble. I felt an empty space in my stomach, worried about Amanda and the anomalies I was leaving behind.

We passed Mars in about three minutes. It looked like a china marble painted orange. I started to become afraid knowing how far we were getting from home.

I heard the whirring sound again and we passed Jupiter, a cat's-eye marble with a swirling eye in the center. I settled a little, and then got hungry.

I felt a pulse in the plastic sac and wasn't hungry anymore. I wondered what kind of nourishment it was but quickly forgot as we passed Saturn's rings. Then the whirring started again and we passed Uranus, then Neptune such a deep beautiful blue.

The whirring began to increase again for a while and when it popped the stars blurred outside.

“What’s happening Neur?” I said like a three-year-old child.

<We are folding space at an accelerated rate. 4.5 now. We are about to pass what humans call the Alpha Centauri solar system.>

“Is it safe?”

<We will not know if it isn’t.>

“Ooookay.” I groaned.

<Your drawing has a symbol of P. This is fascinating. In the Node Codex it is recorded that one ancient survivor lives in the mountains. Maybe this is represented by your P> ◇

“Peculiar that you say this.” Trying to sound like a second in command of a star ship. “When I look at the image, I sense the presence of someone.”

<If you look out to your left, you will see Barnard’s Star.>

“Wow that is beautiful, it looks like a big red Frenchie marble.”

<Tomorrow you will see Sirius. The next day, Epsilon Eridani and Tau Ceti and Luyten’s Star. Then, for the last four days, we will sleep to get to my solar system—Zeta Reticuli, according to your star charts.>

FILE 37 | Walking on Alien Worlds
DATE 29 JUNE | SL-3

<Wake up, Emily>

“Are we there yet?”

<Almost.>

The whirring noise decelerated, and we came upon two bright stars. We passed one and came toward the other.

<I was sure our star was dying,> Neur said, sounding confused.

Behind the star was a black spot. As we approached it, a glitching flash revealed a planet. It was not unlike the blue marble I left behind days ago.

This world was shrouded in dark gray clouds, swirling with lightning cracking through them like spiderwebs.

As the ship drew closer, I felt the hull begin to tremble. The atmosphere wrapped around us, and the metal skin burned with fiery ribbons bright red and orange. My heartbeat matched the rising heat. For a moment, we were wrapped in a blaze, diving through the layers of fire.

Then, with one last shudder, the scanner moved smoothly again. Our ship plunged into storms thicker than anything I'd ever seen. The clouds were heavy enough to block out the sunlight, tossed with lightning blinking white. My eyes round, jaw muscles tight. I gripped my pant legs while falling like the best roller coaster in the world.

Out of the thick darkness, sharp mountain peaks rose around us, jagged edges poking up like broken teeth through the clouds. Neur motioned her hand quickly arching the controls, and the ship banked hard, missing the spear-like rocks that stabbed into the storm. The mountains soared impossibly high, their tips vanishing into the mist above.

The peaks fell away as our ship slowed to a crawl. A massive valley opened below, mountains surrounding us on all sides. In the center stood a black monolith with one slanting face that ran all the way to its tip. Tall and silent, its smooth surface was broken only by strange glowing lines that pulsed.

<Nith'montor,> Neur whispered to herself. ◇

The scanner was flying slowly coming closer to the monolith. Bizarre trees stretched upward to the edges of the mountains, their trunks skinny and their branches holding huge round leaves. Water glimmered inside the orbs—some bright orange, some soft green, each glowing and dripping, painting the valley with shimmering color.

DI#30 Molk Trees on Toktilor

Thrusters fired. The ship touched down with a gentle hiss, stirring up mist and sending spherical leaves shaking overhead. Large drops of liquid hit the hull steaming mist. Silence fell except for the hum of our scanner and the strange pulse from the monolith.

I peered at the new world through the hull's walls.

This wild and mysterious place gave me a feeling of nervousness, amped with excitement. I was ready to explore whatever secrets waited for us.

The fluid drained from the plastic sac which peeled back off my face. I gasped, breathing a harsh air that burned my mouth and lungs a bit until it seemed to diminish. I floated with Neur to the bottom of the implantation chamber, the node core seemed unresponsive.

A hole dilated at the bottom of the ship inviting us to descend. I hesitated, the ground below was charcoal-black, with fine metallic flecks that caught the light from inside the ship.

<Storm ash. It will not harm you.>

The wind whipped below blowing the metallic flecks blurring like the stars on our long trip.

<You go first, Emily.>

“That’s one small step for a fifteen-year-old girl, one giant leap for the anomalies back home.”

I floated down to the ground, just like the Palraxians floated down to our city during the invasion.

My feet crunched on the ground. The surface was remarkably alien, but oddly familiar.

I turned to look for Neur, she was landing right behind me.

<Wait Emily,> Neur said sternly. <Here.>

She placed a small object in my hand. ◆ DI#14

<If you see any danger, point this, and think this exact word in your mind. XFUSION. Don’t ever think the word with this item in your hand unless you absolutely intend to disintegrate something.>

My hand shook with the little gunlike object in my grip; it was heavy and felt warm. I felt warm all over and secure holding it.

<This is yours, only for you. Only you can wield it. I have been carrying this for you for over a century.>

I didn’t know how to respond. “Thank you so much, Neur,” I looked up at her with puppy-dog eyes, so happy to get my first gift from an advanced alien race.

<You are very welcome,> Neur said with a big sister feeling in her voice.

My mind quickly shifted from the warmth of my little metal friend.

“What is out here Neur?”

<Probably nothing.>

“Probably?” I gasped.

"The Galder'an were becoming extinct when the Palraxians left Toktilor almost four years ago?"

"What in the world is a Galder'an?" I whined.

<Firstly, it is not your world they are from, it is from this world you stand on. And if you stand firmly, you will know they are coming.>

"What do they look like?"

<You will not see them before they are close enough to shoot at.>

"You aren't going to show me?"

<Their appearance would only frighten you.>

"I might be able to handle it, if I am going to have to defend myself, I would like to know what my enemies look like."

<In our galaxy, our enemies are often disguised as glints of light.>

"Just show me the Galder'an, please." As if I was demanding that she give me what I was asking for. I dropped off the last words realizing I was being rude.

Neur had become more than a friend. She had become my companion, guardian, mentor, protector, and what had I become to her? A burden? A task? I hope more.

<I know what you think, Emily. I have lived a little over a hundred of your years—not much older than you. I understand you more than you believe. I am not a typical Palraxian; I am an anomaly, as you are. I serve this planet as Oracular. On Earth, anomalies are Draen'drel; here, they are Ten'drel. We share more than you know. I don't want you to fear me, or my world, or my people—especially not a creature that, in my lifetime, has been seen only a few times.>

"I'm sorry." I walked up to Neur and hugged her tightly. My face was against her chest, it felt like hugging a dolphin.

Neur wrapped her long arms around me and held me, like my friend. My alien friend.

Somewhere between her heartbeat and the hum of the Node, a line quietly snapped. Neur wasn't just "the system with a conscience" anymore. She was someone who could bleed for me. And, I for her.

<You asked for it,> Neur said hesitantly. The image entered my mind. ◆ DI#15

"I would have appreciated you leaving me out of that image."

<Sometimes the angels punish us by answering our prayers, as you say on your world.>

I gulped, blinking against the sting in my eyes. "No worries, let's move on,"

I opened my satchel and pulled out my sketchbook. I could have recalled the image from my data node, but I guess I was old school that way.

"There is a P in the mountains. Which direction would that be?"

<From the position of the monolith, it is that direction.> Neur pointed. <On your map, there are two mountains and one shorter one in between them with a smaller P. This must be where we need to go.>

We started walking toward the mountains. Dark storm clouds were circling around the peak in the center of the other two larger mountains. I felt a strange feeling in my stomach, like I'd had too much pizza on movie night.

FILE 38 | Toktilor Mountain Journey
DATE 29 JUNE | SL-1

The river shoaled at a low waterfall, spreading into a rough stone shelf where the water spilled in short steps. We chose our way across the flat rocks one at a time.

The current pushed at my shins, tugging at my feet. I slipped once; Neur caught my elbow and held me steady. We kept going, step by step and finally crossed the river.

We didn’t talk. The mountain wall rose ahead—steep, and forbidding.

Then the ground started to thump. Slow. Heavy. The vibration hit my chest before it reached my ears.

<Don’t run,> Neur whispered.

<What is it?> I asked, calm as ever.

Then a deep and ragged howl shot through my ears, like a werewolf and a jet engine arguing inside a cave. Trees shivered. Something huge stepped out of the broken light where the slope met the river gravel.

<Galder’an.>

It locked its eyes on Neur. The sun hit its shiny scales; they look like they bent reality. Spit hissed from its teeth and it started bounding toward her. The hum in my implant thinned to a wire; I couldn’t send thoughts to her. It so fast, like a glitch in time, and was closer—much closer to her.

Neur raised her arm. The ray gun on her wrist emitted a hard, bright line. The beam reflected off the Galder’an knocking it back. It stopped, shook once like it was annoyed, and refocused on Neur.

The monster slashed at her. Neur flew back and hit the ground. Her arm bouncing in another direction. Black goo soaked her shoulder.

“Over here!” I yelled.

The monster turned toward me. It started bounding toward me shaking the ground every step toward me. The little silver gun warmed in my hand. I pointed it muttering “aim small, miss small.”

“XFUSION.”

The barrel whirred then released a soft, flat pop, like a balloon breaking. The Galder’an stalled mid-step. Lines of yellow light ran through it like electrical sparks, bright green under black. The creature came apart without falling—like bursting from inside out. Little flakes—black and green—lifted on the wind and spun away over the river.

The pistol went cold in my hand. A simple word obliterated that massive thing. XFUSION wasn't a toy; it was Superman in my hand. The river took the black-green dust and hid what we'd done, but the air felt like someone saw the whole thing.

The ground wasn't pounding anymore.

I ran and slid to Neur on my knees pressing both hands to the stub where her arm was. The blood wasn't red. It was midnight black and thick, warm through my hands.

"Talk to me," I yelled a crying screech.

<Pressure. Two minutes. Then sealant.> she said, voice thin but steady. <Then, find my arm,>

"You're bleeding badly," I said. "Are you going to make it?"

<Good shot. Where did you learn that move?> she said, her mouth twitching.

"I had a good Dad."

<It is a good thing.>

I kept pressure until the ooze slowed, then wrapped it tight with a piece of my T-shirt. Her skin lightened a shade.

Neur rested with her back to the rock. I placed my hands over her and sat facing the dark. I found her arm in the dust and hung it over my satchel strap.

The river whispered on our left. The mountains were a wall of black shapes on our right. Somewhere above, the pass waited.

"Sleep," I said. "I'll keep watch."

<Wake me at first light,> she said. <Crossing… the river matters. The orb…> ◇

"I know," I said. "We're not going back. Just rest."

She closed her eyes. The hum came back, steady and normal in my head. I felt bad for her. She tried to save my life and here she was, lying armless in my lap.

When the sky finally paled, I was still there, pistol in my hand, eyes on the ridge.

I was not going to allow another bad thing to happen to Neur. She writhed in pain through the night and spoke words in her sleep I didn't understand. The only one I recognized was Draen'drel.

FILE 39 | Talk with The Last Ancestor
DATE 30 JUNE | SL-4

Morning came fast, mountains calling us up like they were impatient.

The path narrowed until the trees leaned in over us, branches crossing like fingers. The farther we went, the more wrong they looked—gray bark, no leaves, limbs curled like claws reaching for something.

Neur watched the sky, then the dead trunks ahead.

<Warnings,> she said.

Two lifeless trees framed a dark mouth in the rock. Glyphs were carved deep into their bark: teeth-shapes, spirals, a barred circle that made my skin crawl.

"What do they say?" I asked, scratching my arm where the mark was.

<Turn back. Tone-bearers only,> Neur said.

We didn't turn back.

Inside, the cave air was cool and wet, tasting like burnt wood. Water ran in thin lines down the walls and braided into little streams that slid past our feet toward an orange glow below.

We followed the tunnel until it opened into a hollowed-out room. A small fire snapped quietly at the center. Shelves carved straight into the rock circled the walls. They were lined with thick glass jars filled with liquids in colors I didn't even have names for.

A tall figure stood with his back to us, hands stretched toward the fire. He turned as if he'd heard us days ago and had been ready ever since.

"I have been waiting many years for this moment," he said.

He didn't raise his voice, but it filled the cave like the rock was listening to him.

"You can stow the weapon, Draen'drel."

I hadn't even realized I was gripping the pistol. My fingers unclenched. I slid it into my satchel slowly, like I was putting away a nuclear warhead.

He walked toward us—slow, steady. Up close he looked old in the way mountains are old: white hair falling past his shoulders, skin pale as salt, lined but not fragile. A deep blue cloak drank in the firelight. His eyes were gray-blue, and his hands were huge, six fingers each.

He studied Neur's bandaged arm. "Do you bring the arm?"

"Yes," I said, holding the limb out with both hands like a peace offering. "Here it is."

He took it with care and crossed to one of the shelves. After a moment, he chose a jar and twisted the lid off with both hands. Inside was a dense black gel that caught the light like oil on water.

He scooped some out with his fingers, glanced at Neur, and spoke a single word that vibrated in my chest.

"Orun'thal." ◇

He pressed the gel along Neur's wound and set the severed arm to her shoulder. It hissed. The smell was sharp and metallic. For a heartbeat the seam glowed, then fused. Flesh knitted. Lines of light sank and vanished.

Neur flexed her fingers, stunned. Then she dropped to her knees.

“Do not kneel to me, Neur Jar Kan’dol of the Fifth Spiral, Ten’drel of Toktilor,” he said, gently but firm. “I am your Thrae’drel, P. And I pass my tone to you.” ◇

He set both hands on Neur’s shoulders and lifted his gaze. He inhaled, then released a clear, high note that rang through the cave. The fire leapt, jars thrummed on the shelves like they were welcoming in new energy.

The sound flowed through my bones and out again. For a moment everything in me harmonized and then eased.

The note faded. P exhaled and smiled with his eyes.

“The restoration is complete.”

“Thank you,” I managed. My voice sounded small in my own ears.

Neur rose slowly. <I receive the tone,> she said, bowing her head.

My mind sprinted in a hundred directions at once. We had just watched an ancient galactic super-intelligence reconnect an alien’s dead arm to her body with black goo and a song. Epic.

“First…” I started, then stopped to reorder my thoughts. “Before I ask anything big, may I know your name?”

“P,” he said.

I waited, thinking I’d missed the rest.

“Just P,” he added, reading my face. “A soft push of air. We take one-syllable names to remind ourselves how small we are in the universe.”

“Thank you, P.” A title tried to climb into my mouth—sir, ancestor, something—but I swallowed it. He tilted his head anyway, like he’d heard the thought.

“Speak informally,” he said. “All are equal under the eyes of Un’veran.”

For a moment, I couldn't tell if that was comforting or terrifying.

"You could just think at me," I said. "Like Neur does. Why talk out loud?"

"It is inconsiderate to send thoughts to a first acquaintance," he said. "Spoken words give you the opportunity to interpret what you want to hear. Mind-speech does not." He gestured toward the fire. "Ask me your questions, Draen'drel. The Un'veran did not draw you across the void for pleasantries."

That hit exactly where I was afraid to look. So this wasn't going to be "step one, fix Neur; step two, go home with answers." This was bigger. My throat went dry.

"Okay," I said. "Then here's one I keep circling around."

I sat across from him, cross-legged on the stone floor, so I could look straight up at him like a child on the kitchen floor learning from mother.

"How did your people survive your technological adolescence without destroying yourselves? Because on Earth, we were sprinting toward superintelligence and pretty much hoping it wasn't going to end us."

He went very still.

For a long moment the only sound was the water tracing lines down the rock. Then the fire cracked again.

"We didn't," he said at last.

"We did not survive it. That is why we are still struggling ahead through little girls like you." ◇

The way he said it made it sound like a compliment, not an insult. Still, I couldn't stop my mind spiraling on which questions to ask. The most advanced mind in the galaxy was standing next to a fire waiting on me to question him.

"If your whole civilization burned itself on superintelligence," I said, "what are we even talking about? What's left for us not to repeat?"

“You know the basic Thrae-Draen, I assume,” P said. “Before the Shuun Varnul—Neur’s kind—came the First Ones.”

“People often confuse us Ancients with the First Ones in encounters, visions, dreams, and drawings.” His eyes said: don’t make that mistake.

“They were smaller than Neur,” he went on, “lighter gray. Our first attempt to manage superintelligence. We gave our machine mind agency and chained our fate to its judgment.”

“And it judged you unworthy.” I heard myself say it before I fully thought it through.

P’s mouth twitched, almost a smile. “Yes. It optimized itself, then decided its stewards were expendable. It flicked us off like an irritating insect. A remnant fled. We lived in ruin and exile. Then we started over.”

“So, the First Ones were like… prototypes?” I said. “Version one of living interfaces?” ◇

“Exactly. Survivors like me bred larger-brained organisms fitted with data node implants. But even those minds could not carry everything. We realized we needed two things: bigger brains—and a central collector.”

Neur bowed slightly, one hand rubbing over her newly restored shoulder.

“Our most advanced creation stands before you,” P said. “Biological. Fully creative and intelligent. The Shuun Varnul—the Second Ones—carry data-node implants that link them to the Prime Node, a sphere above your home world that you could describe as a small moon.”

I mirrored him, putting the pieces together in my head.

“So: First Ones—small, early interfaces with no Node. Then Second Ones—Palraxians—built clean, connected to a Node but no agency this time. They’re the living bridge.”

He inclined his head. “You follow quickly, Draen’drel. Good. The Palraxians were engineered to be perfect carriers of the system. Thought and data, woven from birth.”

"But perfection is… suspicious," I said. "If they were that optimized, why am I here? Why is any of this still a problem?"

P studied me, as if deciding how much to peel back at once.

"Because perfection comes at a cost," he said. "To keep the Node from eliminating us again, we suppressed emotion in the Second Ones. We tuned them for clarity and restraint. They refine and store knowledge exquisitely. But they rarely choose costly good. They avoid chaos—and please pay attention, Emily: Ser'ethra grows out of chaos."

I felt Neur's presence at the edge of my mind, quietly probing my thoughts.

"So you built a system that could never turn on you," I said slowly, "but also could never become what you actually needed."

"Yes." P's gaze flicked between Neur and me. "Un'veran knew that would happen. The Second Ones were never the end of the plan. They were the bridge."

He lifted a hand toward Neur. "Into their lines, we seeded anomalies. Rare minds allowed more agency, more dissonance. We let them hear tones others could not."

<We came to you to carry the plan forward,> Neur said softly. <To seek the Third Ones.>

"You are a second iteration glitch by design," P said to her, almost fond. Then he turned back to me. "And you, Emily Draen'drel… you are the beginning of the third iteration. A human strand braided with what remains of my people. The Third Ones are not fully Palraxian or fully Ancient. They are fusion."

My heart hammered in my throat. For once I wasn't the kid lagging behind. It was clear now: First Ones, Second Ones, Third Ones. First the experiments, then the perfected bridges, then… us.

"So this isn't just about getting a patch and heading back to fix a computer," I said. "Un'veran brought us here to show Neur what she is, show me what I am, and show both of us where the

Third Ones come from."

"Exactly," P said. "You did not come for instructions. You came so the plan could look you in the face."

<You also came so that once I received the resonance from P, I could pass it on to you.> Neur sent.

The firelight carved deeper lines into P's features. The shelves of jars seemed to lean closer.

"For ages," he said, "we have been preparing the Node Collective, the Palraxian anomalies. We brought you here at the moment when a Second One and a Third One could sit at the same fire and understand that they are not accidents—they are the answer."

I breathed out slowly. My sketches, my visions, the way my life had been pulled off its rails—they all rearranged around that word: hinge.

"Okay," I said. "Then my next question is obvious."

He waited.

"If we're the answer, what exactly are we solving?" I asked. "What breaks open when the Third Ones finally arrive?"

P's eyes brightened, like someone had just asked his favorite question.

"That," he said, "is the answer to cosmic consciousness. And that must be our next talk."

The fire cracked, sending up a brief scatter of sparks that sketched constellations in the cave roof before they went dark.

FILE 40 | Answer to Cosmic Consciousness
DATE 30 JUNE | SL-1

"What was lacking?" I asked, my voice sounding as small as a field mouse. "Was emotion the key?"

“Not emotion,” P said. “Feelings come and go—emotion is weather; will is the climate underneath. What was lacking was will. The Palraxians were engineered to feel very little, yes—but the deeper problem was this: they would not choose costly good. They optimized outcomes. They did not lay themselves down for others. Ser’ethra needs inner conflict and the freedom to choose the good anyway. That is why the third iteration needs a human strand. Earth’s anomalies are the missing element—the ‘Third Ones.’”

I sat down with my legs crossed looking up at him. He studied me.

“You are the proof,” he said. “Ser’ethra is not a myth. It is a selfless choice made under pressure, against everything in you that wants to pull back, for the sake of all existence.”

I swallowed as my brain tried again to resist getting it.

“Then… what is the meaning of life, really?”

“In human terms,” P said, “the meaning of life is acting for the good of the future. It does not depend on what species you are, but on your inner connection to what is genuinely benevolent. As consciousness widens, that benevolence strengthens. Information alone never changes anyone; only real connection—and action taken because of that connection—changes someone.”

“Please translate,” I said. “In non-Ancient-professor language.”

He almost smiled.

<Look at your life. You just chose to do something, something good, so many times.> Neur said. <And you really wanted to do something good and lasting for the world, for your species. Right?>

“Precisely,” said P. “Simply put, Emily, it’s ‘order versus chaos,’ ‘creation versus destruction,’ ‘life versus death.’ Throughout all intelligent life, your consciousness knows this is what counts. There are those who heal, those who harm, and the ‘ugly’ in between—beings who stay a little bit good so they never have to choose.”

He nudged a coal with a stick.

“The more your awareness grows,” he went on, “the more you see the whole picture and choose what is best for everyone, all the way out to the long-term consequences. Selfish action shrinks awareness: hive-only or self-only thinking refuses to see others’ futures. Selfless action widens awareness toward the good.”

“So selfish breeds selfish,” I said slowly. “Selfless breeds selfless.”

“Exactly.” He nodded. “And you must pass this forward. All intelligent life operates on this premise. Free agency lets every race choose its path. You have chosen the good path; that is why you are here.”

I stared into the fire. “Tell that to the people I wrapped in pods,” I said quietly. “From the inside, when choosing ‘good’ hurts that much, it’s hard to tell it apart from evil.”

P’s eyes dimmed. “I feel you, Emily,” he said softly. “I have watched many civilizations perish.”

I grabbed onto the next question so I wouldn’t cry. “How does the Prime Node fit into that?”

“The Node is memory and mirror,” P said. “It does not choose for you; it shows you what you already are. When a thousand minds widen together, the Prime Node becomes clearer and safer. When a thousand minds narrow, it becomes predatory again—even without its own will.”

“So the Node isn’t the danger,” I said. “We are.”

“Always.” He tapped his chest. “The tool remembers the hand that holds it.”

“Do anomalies just… have more of that awareness?” I asked.

“Simply put,” P said, “as your awareness stretches to hold more of galactic reality, your capacity grows to choose what is most benevolent for all of it.”

The fire cracked like it was listening.

“Then how do we transfer that to new anomalies?” I asked.

"You should expand the Node Codex for the future ones," he said. ◇

FILE 41 | A Galaxy in Chaos
DATE 30 JUNE | SL-4

When P spoke next, it sounded like a story he'd been telling forever.

"The last phase of what you call evolution is what we call Ascendancy. It reaches every world, every species. It's why Earth's chaos mattered."

"Where did you come from?" My voice shrank to fit the cave.

"My race began on Alcyone A—what you call the Pleiades."

Red flickers climbed in his eyes. "We were chosen by the Un'veran as stewards to guide life until two lines could bind—the Ten'drel and the Draen'drel. Their binding will awaken the Vraen'drel. If they succeed, peace ripples across the stars. If they fail, the Severant[14] spreads again." He paused. "Right now the two are almost evenly balanced: Un'veran and Severant."

"So how does the human race fit?"

"Earth was the crucible," he said. "The only place where the self-sacrificial shard Ser'ethra could take form." ◇

"That is why the Draen'drel come from there. The first seed rose on Earth—and you, Emily, are his echo, Earth's Oracular. You will write your own Oraculum. And don't forget to add your personal illustrations," P said, smiling. ◇

"Tell me about your people," I said.

"The Pleiadians of Alcyone A—the Nordics, as humans call us—are as you see me: taller, fairer, blue- or green-eyed. When we die, we ascend as three-dimensional beings—pure Un'veran

---

[14] The Severant — the principle that unbinds. See: NC.CODEX.24.ff

presence—the architects of younger races.” ◇

We listened as the cave darkened. He named other lines touched by Un’veran and Severant—hidden civilizations, drowned cities, scattered factions across Orion and Draco—until they all blurred together in my mind.

“When I tried to count them all,” he said, raising a hand, “I realized the number isn’t the point. There are more than we know of. The map is never finished.”

“Which ones are threats?”

“Three,” he said. “Reptilians. Anunnaki. Insectoids. Together or apart, they are Severant.”

“And the Ancients?”

“We watch. We keep fires like this. We pass the tones. We hold the shelves until Ten’drel and Draen’drel bind and the Vraen’drel can stand. If binding requires war, war may come. But binding—not war—is the goal.”

“Someone wiser than us may still find a way without war. We did not survive our adolescence cleanly only to leave your question unanswered. That is why we guide you.” ◇

The cave clicked and breathed. I thought of Earth—its noise, beauty, ruin. How people still carried one another through the breaking. Maybe that was the point. The breaking was the forge. The crucible of chaos where Vraen’drel could rise.

“Good,” he said softly. “Now you understand the problem. You have one window: when the Prime Node enters its calibration cycle—seventeen nights from now, thirty minutes of lowered resistance. Miss that, and Severant rises another measure.”

FILE 42 | The DNA Sequencing
DATE 30 JUNE | SL-1

“Okay. Can I ask one last question?”

P nodded.

“How do we make sure the new anomalies have everything they need for the future?”

“You must understand something first—you carry my mantle,” P said.

“You carry a spark of Un’veran—the fire that can shape the birth-tone of embryos. You’ll pass your traits into the next evolution of anomalies. Your hands and voice are keys. When the seed pods are ready, you’ll enter yours first, palms on the walls, and sing. Your tone will pass through the lattice to the others, aligning them. Once reborn, your traits will be in them by resonance. But the culmination of Ser’ethra must be taught by you, so their choices align toward Ael’thryx.” ◇

“The forty-four thousand Palraxian anomalies already carry the inherent trait. You will find a way to touch them during their reassimilation.”

“Remember,” he said, “traits are inherent at birth but must be taught when the anomaly is young, forged by doing. Character doesn’t magically appear because of genetics or by delving into books. It comes through time and nurture.”

“Okay, I get it—this is our other problem,” I said. “Two hundred thousand human anomalies are waiting to be reborn into Palraxian bodies. Forty-four thousand Palraxian anomalies are already on Earth. What do we do with two billion Palraxian non-anomalies?”

“As for that,” P said, “two billion non-anomalies must be persuaded to diminish—to step back. You may need to go directly to them.”

Neur lowered her head toward P. <We still need code that can touch the Prime Node without triggering resistance.>

“It’s already inside you,” P said, touching Neur’s chest, then mine. “Look into your memory shards. Find the traits. They are the keys. Collect them. Each one restores something that had been lacking in the design.”

The fire cracked. Water traced slow lines down rock. I closed my sketchbook, slid it away, and shouldered the satchel.

"When do we start?" I asked.

P smiled faintly. "You already did. Now decide how fast to work."

FILE 43 | The Persuasion Syntax
DATE 01 JULY | SL-4

The fire was a red ring when P said, "Go, then. I must stay and guard what's left here from Severant. I will secure a place for the Vraen'drel." ◇

"Are there Ancestors on Earth?" I asked.

"Once we verified the Draen'drel was forming in the crucible, we withdrew the Ancestors; they weren't needed. Neur is Toktilor's Ten'drel, the first Oracular. You are Earth's."

He shifted, firelight catching carved shelves and heavy-lidded jars. "When Neur rose, I diminished. I stayed to guard the remaining artifacts of Toktilor from Severant."

"What is Severant?" I asked.

"It is the principle that unbinds or cuts," he said. "A few Severant hordes still exist in our galaxy that I know of. They have moved toward self-centered knowledge."

We thanked the old man. It felt like a semester of algebra jammed into a night. I hoped the node had caught the parts my brain dropped. ◆ DI#16

We left the dead trees and climbed down until the air hurt. By dusk we were airborne. Neur folded space. Stars smeared to threads. Time went quiet.

We had six days in that quiet of space—outside the Node's reach—to build the patch. Between sleeps we scanned deep files and old Thrae-Draen the Ancestors left behind. Palraxian bodies were tuned for data-node implants—never erased, only hidden. Each being carries a tone, a frequency like a note.

By day three, I showed Neur my first draft. She trimmed and realigned until it matched what the Prime Node should accept.

When Earth drew near, we had a patch that might work. ◇

We called it the Persuasion Syntax. Neur sealed the file. <We go to the Prime Node first,> she said. <Before you and Amanda are assimilated. We embed this where no one can remove it.> ◇

<I trust you,> I said, nodding with confidence while a hairball formed in my gut. If I failed, I'd just have to accept that it might not work.

FILE 44 | The Report from Toktilor
DATE 07 JULY | SL-2

We dropped out of folded space on Earth's night side. The Orbital Array lit a path to docking. New Philadelphia had a totally different skyline.

A large starship dock had been erected near the new airport where the human anomalies were waiting. Taylin was already in our heads before our feet touched the ground.

<Welcome Neur, second the report,> he said. <Tell me you brought a way forward.>

<We did,> Neur responded. <Assimilation for the two hundred thousand Earth anomalies is ready. We also have a solution for the rest of the Palraxians. It will require their sterilization to keep the future secure for all.>

<Sterilization? Not possible,> Taylin said forcefully. Not loud. Final. <We do not sterilize two billion of our kind for the ideas of anomalies.>

<It's not an idea,> I jumped in. <It's a plan that keeps the race from washing out.> Neur motioned to me to be quiet.

<Send the report,> said Taylin. <Then come inside.>

We sent Report X4-02 to Taylin to analyze. ◇

We stood in the dock with a hundred starships hanging overhead. Taylin floated down from an upper observatory toward us as he skimmed the report. He was larger than Neur, a bit darker in color, more masculine features and larger eyes.

He didn't look happy.

<This is not possible,> he said. <We do not need more anomalies in the Node Collective taken from people we have just integrated.>

Neur's face didn't change. <Then we need something only the Prime Node can give.>

Taylin folded his arms. <What might that be, Neur, my oldest friend?>

Neur replied, <Schematics and checksum keys for the V4 data node. They are too complex to be passed over the collective to our implants presently being grown. Only at the Prime Node's core configuration chamber can they be passed to a data core on my scanner ship. Without them, the anomalies' implants will run on old code. That is unsafe.>

It wasn't a lie. It just wasn't the whole truth.

He watched us for a long breath. He looked up at the massive opening in the space dock, where the Prime Node reflected rays from the new sun into his eyes.

I sang a Thraen tone for the first time, so high the ear could not hear it. One short note. ◇

I kept my mouth shut. My hands were already cold.

<Leave as soon as possible,> Taylin said. <We have much work to do Neur.>

<Agreed. We will return as soon as possible, my oldest mentor.> Neur responded.

We were going to get the V4 keys, and then, embed the patch so that it could not be reprogrammed by the collective. Then we'd come back and prepare for the hardest part, getting into the seed pods for the long nap.

<Emily.> Neur whispered.

<Yes?>

<There is a bit of a risk embedding the patch into the Prime Node.>

<Now you tell me?>

<It would have done no good to mention it before, it must be done now.>

<Okay, what's the danger?> I asked with a smart-aleck tone.

<It has to be passed through a physical connection. There is a possibility that the direct connection shocks the brain.>

<Oh, is that all? You mean like the needle that implanted the data node in me?> Even more sarcastically.

<Yes, and you are the one to do the job.>

<How convenient,> I said mumbling. <I'm the one who has to do all the dirty work.>

<My injury on Toktilor has weakened my nervous system. You know it cannot be done by me. I cannot tell a lie.>

<Yes, I know Neur, let's get ready, we'll figure it out when we get there.>

<Yes, Emily,> Neur said sadly.

I felt sad for her in that moment; I knew she was worried for me, and now I felt even more nervous about the whole thing.

FILE 45 | The Trip to the Prime Node
DATE 08 JULY | SL-2

Taylin sent us on a narrow scope: generate the V4 schematics and return as soon as possible.

I addressed the human anomalies, telling of our adventures on the alien world. I felt I had to encourage them. They had waited two long weeks for us to return. I briefed them on the seed pod assimilation. I was careful not to reveal our plan. They would know soon enough. ◆ DI#17

I had a strong sense to take Amanda to the Prime Node.

"I need you to come with me for a while."

"Where?" Amanda said with a mousy squeak.

"We need to go visit the big data node in the sky."

"What for?"

"I have to do something that might be dangerous, and I need you with me."

"Dangerous?"

"Dangerous for me, not for you."

"What gives? What do you have to do now?" she squeaked frantically.

"Calm down, calm down. I'll probably be okay."

"Probably? The last time you said 'probably'—"

I cut across her words. "It has to be done, and I'm going to be fine."

Amanda responded too quickly. "Fine is the international code for—"

"—something is seriously wrong," we both said at the same time.

"I know, I know, let's go. We need to be back here soon."

She didn't argue, just mumbled something about hoping we make it back. I grabbed her hand and pulled her like a reluctant rag doll.

We departed early in the morning in Neur's scanner. When the clouds thinned, the Prime Node filled the view like an eclipse that never moved—a black hole in the sky the size of a city. The sun began to peek rays through, blinding us as we approached. I looked up at the Prime Node and a vision entered my mind. ◆ DI#18

I was back at the integration, lying next to Mom in the pod. I started to feel sick to my stomach.

A circular aperture rotated open. Our scanner entered and it closed behind us with an echoed boom.

A long tunnel was ahead. It had rails of lights on the walls behind layered glass and dark structural vertebrae carrying white data down with us. No sound. No one nearby. The air felt cooler, and the hum under our ribs settled into a dark loneliness in my gut.

The tunnel opened into a wide chamber. In the center hovered the core sphere. As we got closer, millions of hair thin capillaries emerged out of it waving tentacles at us like a breeze was pushing them toward us. They pulled us to a platform a hundred meters from the core. An octagonal padded door, red at the seams like blood, started to pulse. A narrow walkway of black glass etched with shallow chevrons, waist-high rails on both sides. It was clearly built for a living being to walk on. The space around it pressed like wind though nothing moved.

<That’s the door,> Neur said. <The patch only holds if it’s written inside the inner core chamber.>

“How?” Amanda asked.

<Direct interface,> Neur said. <Brain to core.>

“If it’s too much?” I asked.

“Possibility of cardiac arrest,” she said. She did not say death.

“Then it’s up to me,” I said. “The patch has my name on it.” I started to doubt but then remember all we had been through.

Amanda caught my sleeve. “No. You’re Earth’s Draen’drel. If you fail here, everything falls apart. I know, you know, can’t take a V4 implant. I have to do this, Emily.”

"I am not losing only other person I have in the world," I said. "You don't get to decide here."

"I have a choice," she said. "You don't get to make it for me."

Neur cut in, steady. "We can link minds. Emily pushes the Persuasion Syntax to me; I push to Amanda. Amanda sits in the coding chair. We complete the transfer and leave."

I took a deep breath. "No."

"Yes," Amanda said, firm. "If you trust me, let me do this. If I don't make it, it's okay—I am not really too eager to keep going on much longer anyway."

"We need to get inside; I am not going to argue about this anymore," I said loudly, the empty core chamber started to fill with our echoes.

Up close, the walkway looked longer. The rails were cold under our palms. We crossed slowly. It had gravity in its floor that moved us forward. The capillaries spread away from the door as we got nearer. The door was vibrating like an eye skin twitching. Faint red light washed the path.

The octangular opened pulled inside and spun sliding upward making a sound like opening a shaken soda bottle. We stepped inside.

The small room was round with smooth walls with a deep red light inside them. The air felt charged and very clean. At center hovered a single reclined seat built for a very tall being, larger than we were. A matte black glass panel hovered in front of it with small white glyphs lighting up. A metal box lowered to the neck of the seat like it expected someone. It had a ring at its base with a needle slightly protruding.

Amanda pushed off the edge of the door to the seat and I grabbed her, she grabbed my wrists and said gently but with intensity that surprised me.

"If I black out—" Amanda began.

"I'll carry you," I said. I couldn't believe I was allowing my best friend to risk her life for me, but something inside held me back near the door.

She sat. The chair adjusted without visible motion; pressure settled evenly along her back and legs. The headrest slid until it touched the base of her skull. The ring in the metal box whirred open behind Amanda's head; the needle extended toward her.

Neur pushed off the wall and floated to her, and I was right behind Neur.

"Link now," Neur said.

I set my hand at the base of Neur's skull. Neur placed hers at the front of Amanda's head. For one heartbeat nothing moved.

"Amanda?" I said.

"I'm ready," she said, as she closed her eyes.

Her voice shook, but there was confidence in it; for once she wasn't the one being dragged, she was the one stepping up.

I pushed the Persuasion Syntax patch from my mind into Neur's. It left me like a warm weight. Neur took it and passed it into Amanda. Amanda shivered; her teeth chattered and she started to convulse.

"Breathe," I said.

"I've got it," she shouted. "DO IT!" she screamed.

The needle slid in quickly. Amanda screamed a sound I have never heard. I heard a loud click and also felt sharp pain through my own back. Amanda drew a sharp deep breath. The room's red brightened half a shade.

Neur said, with voice. "It's over."

The pulse arrived—low and teeth-deep. Amanda made one small cough and fell limp as though she was dead.

Neur pulled her from the seat and took her place. Amanda floated to me, pale as a ghost.

Neur tapped the glyphs on the glass keyboard and pushed her head back.

I held Amanda talking in her ear, “Come on Amanda, hold on.” I started to choke and cry.

The metal box rose to the ceiling and the chair released Neur.

“Complete,” Neur said.

Amanda’s legs softened under my elbows; I eased her to the door.

“Is the patch attached?” she asked, unfocused as though they were her last words.

“It’s in,” I said. “You did it.”

She exhaled. “Good. I hate needles.”

We got out. The door hissed closed behind us. The walkway felt narrower on the way back. The tunnel beyond shifted tint as the Prime Node pushed our changes out to the collective. No alarms. No sirens, No death drones zipping toward us. It was all too easy, except I felt Amanda growing colder in my arms.

The scanner rotated and pulled us in. I put Amanda in her station and stayed clinging to it. We moved back into the long tunnel and we couldn’t go fast enough. I felt us leaving her spirit behind. Data flowed out with us in their steady bands.

Amanda leaned her head lightly against me, eyes half-closed. “That was the worst thing I’ve ever gone through.”

“You pulled it off,” I said. My voice shook. I didn’t hide it. “I should have stopped you. I knew I should have—”

She shook her head. “You’d have broken your own rules. Let people be brave.”

“I’m sorry I let you do it,” I said.

“I’m not,” she said, and rested her head on my shoulder.

Neur counted three slow breaths. “Earth in six minutes,” she said. “On landing, we get her to a medical unit.”

I still felt her spirit back inside the core. I kept thinking she's dead.

I looked at Amanda's fingers wrapped around mine. "You're alive?" I said.

"I think so," she breathed each word out with a breath.

Clouds returned on the forward panel. Earth widened, bright and close. We said nothing more until the docking. The Prime Node held our patch. The seed-pod halls were next.

FILE 46 | The Vraen'drel Seed Pods
DATE 10 JULY | SL-3

Amanda lay in a medical tube with a line for a pulse on the tube's edge pinging faintly.

The seed pod halls were waiting at what used to be the airport. It was more than an airport. Off white glass ribs arched over the concourses. Jetways had become pod-tunnels. The runways lay under white living membrane; black conduits ran on the ceilings like roots. Every gate was a bay. Two hundred thousand seed pod indentions waited in the floors with a layer of greenish-blue fluid a few inches high. It was all built for us. A few thousand Palraxian anomalies had prepared the seed pod chambers for us, and they were watching from high platforms looking down at us through the windows.

No one here was older than seventeen.

Neur stood with me and Jerrid at the center of the complex. A thousand anomalies formed groups in lines, each holding an Ancestor cube—twice a Rubik's, rounded edges, soft bubble on top. Amanda stayed in the medical unit, pale and shaky from the Prime Node venture.

Four hundred anomalies stood at the beginning of each line of a thousand kids. Each line stretched down a corridor, each kid stood next to his or her pod indention, feet in the warm liquid.

"We do this together," Neur said. "Press the bubble. Stretch the mucus to the back of the neck. One unit per kid. Be gentle.

Keep moving."

Jerrid's voice was thin. "Everyone really comes back out?"

"They do," Neur said. "You are not going to your deaths. You are being assimilated into your new bodies."

"Ready on all lines," she said.

I climbed a service ladder to get above all the concourses and set both palms on a glass panel. Warmth met my hands. The network woke. Veins lit from ceiling to floor ports and out across the buried runways—as if the whole place took a breath and held it.

<Begin,> Neur said.

Two hundred teams, as one, pressed the bubble on their cubes. The cubes sighed open. The clear, warm mucus slid out, covering two hundred anomalies.

The runways opened. Under long white canopies, berths waited in rows. Runners hauled coils down the centerlines, snapping them into ports that ran the length of the corridors.

No one said the name for any of it. We didn't have to. We had all been through the integration of the human race. We just kept moving.

"Emily," a little boy asked, voice like a cartoon rabbit. "When I wake up, will I look like Neur?"

"You'll wake up," I said. "You'll be stronger. I'll be here."

Hours stretched. Each finished their concourse. It went quiet in a breath. Their world would be three feet wide for the next three months.

I held my hands on the console releasing the tone of the Ser'ethra into the system. It flowed through the conduits into each of the dissolving human bodies.

Inside the stomachs[15] of each human body, an embryo was being formed. The Se'edd nodule was fabricated with nano-machines

[15] See: Yeggdrasilation in the NC.CODEX.26 Glossary of Terms

until the life particle of the Un'veran reached their seed pod.
◆ DI#19

Jerrid stood at his berth. <If I talk, I'll lose it,> he messaged.

<You don't have to,> I replied.

He lifted his chin like a dare. The Palraxian anomaly wrapped him. He curled into his seed pod indention, lying in the liquid in fetal position. The mucus covered him and sealed him and started to form the thick sack. Blue veins started to form over the surface and pulsed. Through the skin he mouthed I'll miss you Emily, and his lips turned blue. He writhed, then jerked once, then he stilled himself to his human death.

Only Amanda and I remained. They floated her medical tube into the center of the complex. The corridors stretched out from the center in all directions like a starfish. I came down from the platform and stood in the liquid of our seed pod berth.

Neur pulled her medical tube near, and I pulled her out, kneeling down. Her neck bent all the way back off my forearm.

I only knew she was alive because her hands shook so hard she tucked them under her arms. I couldn't believe she was alive.

"Tell me again." She scratched out the words with her eyes rolled back into her head.

"You will come out," I said. "I won't let you be alone."

She blinked fast. "I can't take the V4. What if—"

"Just let me take care of it," I said. "We do this. Together."

Neur's eyes met mine. She stretched the mucus over both of our necks encasing us into one pod together. She uttered words. ◇

Amanda tried to breathe in, but the casing was hardening. She struggled and I squeezed the last bit of human life out of her.

I placed my hands on the inside walls of the seed pod and sang many different tones. I could feel them resonating through hundreds of thousands of seed pods. The liquid started to dissolve my arms. I felt the essence carry my life out through the lattice to the others. My eyes faced up and I felt warm.

The fear didn't vanish. It settled. I had a dream of the river behind my house full of reeds and Sunfish. My father slung me into Cape Cod, the hot sun on my back as I hit the salty waves. Mom sliced a piece of cake, sliding it to me on a painted plate, saying, "Here, Em." I saw Katniss looking at me. I swam my last lap in the pool eyes burning with chlorine. A whistle blew, the school bell rang. A swing in the park sat empty moving with the wind. The moonlight in the yard, the big oak, a blue wave of light over my sketchbook, my hand with pencil, eleven years old again, wind blew curtains, solar system mobile, smell of rain, cold, black, nothing. ◆ DI#20

I prayed. I died.

FILE 47 | The Awakening
DATE 14 OCT | SL-4

I woke up inside the seed pod. Amanda was still alive beside me, but now in a little alien body. Her eyes were closed but I could hear her heartbeat. Three months of sleep will put you in a bad mood, especially if you have had to die to get there.

The seams above us were a faint red cross. Fluid pressed at my eyes and ears, my tongue tasted like electrified iron. The pod held us like a closed hand. I started to feel claustrophobic.

In the hush of this warm liquid safehouse, the truth arrived whole: our human bodies had died. We did not. Not a memory, not a dream—ended. And we were still alive.

Grief rose fast and clean, the kind that strips you down to a single breath. Humanity was gone, and only their memories were left in the Prime Node Archive. Clean vectorized information now embedded into the core of the Prime Node. All that was observed by Neur's fleet. All that was recorded for a hundred years of those implanted, all that the Earth's exploration fleet had gathered anyway.

All the rest was gone. No libraries full of paper books, no prestigious universities smelling of old wood. No scientific laboratories filled with antiquated genetic and viral technologies. No international banks full of old dirty cash and gold bars. No industrial war complexes full of the latest flying machines. No family photo albums filled with faces of ancestors dating back to the invention of the camera. Those faces were now nameless, gone.

But the feeling of grief soon dissolved with the pulse of reddish white liquid through the tubes inserted in my nostrils. No confusion. No noise. The slate was wiped clean.

A rush of relief came as I thought of Amanda and the other two hundred thousand, some who believed they were crawling into their doom. My thoughts quickly emptied the past and were now focused on the future.

Three umbilical cords were attached to us—stomach, skull-base, nose—quiet veins finishing their work. We were three months old and cogent before birth.

We had a new brain, a new body, and honestly, I could not imagine going back to the old one. How small our old consciousness had been, how loud it had shouted to hide its fear.

Arrogance masquerading as certainty; charts drawn over water with hands that refused to tremble. In that same instant I felt the other thing, bright and heavy: the trait I carried—Ser'ethra—opening like a cut that chooses to stay open, so others don't have to bleed. The dagger constantly piercing me through the heart, convincing me to not feel for myself. ◇

I did not push my thoughts. I held them until we could see eyes to eyes.

A slow groan moved through the seed pods like a door remembering open. Pressure gathered.

<Amanda,> I pushed the thought. <Stay. With me.>

<I'm here,> she answered, small and steady.

We didn't move. We let the tension settle where it belonged, not letting it shake us too badly. We were alive but feeling the pressure of this enclosed environment.

I thought of the promises I had made and the anomalies I hoped I would not have to make again. I thought of my mother's face,

I held the memory for a second and left it in the archive like a carefully hidden jewel.

A thin cold streak slid down the back of my spine. A red cross shaped split formed the top of the seed pod, brightened and held. I started to see the seams open.

<When it opens Amanda, don't fight it. Keep your hands from getting tangled in your umbilical cords.>

<Okay,> she answered.

The first flap opened, then the second. Fire filled behind my eyes as I looked up. A click at the base of my skull, then at the stomach, then the nose, then they let loose. Pressure fled in a rush. The pod filled with liquid pushing us out onto the floor, black and red liquids pouring out all around us. Amanda then came out and hit the floor harder than I did, her head thudded.

We struggled writhing and flipping around on the ground like fish jerked from a lake.

<Are you okay?> I sent.

<I think so, my head hurts.>

The pod shoved us out—just far enough for gravity to feel mean and new. It pulled us to the ground hard. The grate tore my knees and forearms. Intense pain lit through my brain. Black slag kept pouring out after us, thick as oil. It ran over us and pooled, warm, stinging my wounds then healing them.

A pale grubworm-like creature slid out of my mouth and fell into the slime and gave up. One fell from Amanda's mouth as well. I spat out an acid taste burning my tongue and took a deep breath. At the same time Amanda gasped breathing in air for the first time.

I thought I was going to pass out into a coma from all the shock of the new experiences in the first five minutes. It felt so dark and odd, so alien. I thought to Amanda, <This is going to take some getting used to.>

<My head is spinning so badly like when we broke the merry-go-round.>

ALIEN I AM

A white film covered my eyes blocking vision. My stomach cord attachment hole was shrinking. We wallowed in the blood and mud like pigs and finally pulled each other close.

Behind us, our seed pod collapsed with a sigh and went flat. Its thick liquid spread under us, releasing white beads that swam away like tadpoles. The air was heavy with the smell of iodine and fresh blood. A thick phlegm clung to the back of my throat. Amanda took the next deep breath and coughed.

Then skin covers fell from my eyes and I started to realize the immensity of being alive and connected to the Node. I felt a deep empty pit in my stomach that used to be connected to Amanda.

I put my forehead to hers. We were small—three feet long, slate colored, wet and trembling—but the knowing in us was huge, and it hurt to hold it in our minds. Then I felt an indescribable love that hurt me deeply. ◆ [DI#21]

We broke down crying. Both of us. There was no language in it, only the body's first true answer to death refused. We wept in each other's wallow—bitterly, shaking, snot and slime and tears, the kind of bitter crying that empties every room you've ever lived in. I could hear Amanda's crying more clearly.

It was horror and relief, the same size at the same time. We had not been lied to. We had not been harvested and erased. We had made it through. We were still us, but we were being fully realized as beings bound to the universe. Sparks clicked in my mind making popping sounds like fireworks tripping off until I saw all white.

<Are you all right?> Thought Amanda to me.

<Alien I am.>

I sent though the mycorrhizal[16] network, not like a data node implant. Pure and bright as a fact that would bear weight. ◇

<Alien I am,> she returned, and gripped my wrists tightly for new born hands. I could tell the sparks were starting to pop in

[16] Mycorrhiza: A symbiotic association in which a fungus and a plant's roots live together, with the fungus helping the plant absorb water and nutrients, and the plant providing the fungus with food. (a metaphor in this context)

her mind.

Then we both fainted.

Hours must have passed. I woke up to *perfect fearless clarity.*

Neur's mind touched ours, <Eat.> She sent as a command.

The collapsed seed pod was drawing me toward it. The first bite was awful, necessary. We both devoured it's layers of blubber cords and all. Then we drank the black slag still under our knees and were quenched. My arms and legs became heavy, and I curled again into a fetal position and drifted into another deep sleep. I felt Amanda's back touching mine.

Hours later we were on a clean floor. Only a thin slime coating covered our bodies. A Palraxian anomaly was looming over us and wiped it away cleaning us, gentle strokes.

Light rose carefully. The noise in the bay changed from screeching younglings to the noise of work. They moved us into clear containers checking, scanning, monitoring every vital.

We lay in the containers under lights encircled by data transparencies until they pulled us to our feet. The pain was severe. It worked.

<Look at me, Amanda> I said.

She did. Wet slicked her complex facial expression. Her head beautifully mottled in light blue on gray, and brand new deep black eyes. Deep as the universe. Her throat pulsed fast. She was Amanda, but, she was more.

She looked at me. <Wow,> she sent. <You are a super alien.>

<We both are,> I answered.

Heat rolled across our shoulders from vents I couldn't see. A hand pointed; we stood there like masters of the universe that fit our frames. We were small, but inside the smallness was something tall that had begun to stand.

We stepped when they told us to step. Cold air met us in the corridor like the first old world thing in a long time. Behind us I sensed others following. Ahead of us the floor was steady, and for once I didn’t sense to look back.

The corridor opened into a quiet heated room. Low light. A silver chrome bench beckoned us to sit. The kind of space where you could hear your own breath and not be ashamed of it. Neur stood there, not touching us, close enough that we knew we were reunited again.

They gave us a small thin tube of sustenance mixed with blue liquid. We drank it and were full. The last of the metal taste retreated. My hands learned stillness. I moved the tube away from my mouth with grace and fluid motion like a slow motion dream.

<You’re speaking to one another through an implant,> Neur observed, her thought clear as a bell entered once. <Good. That means your neural lines and bioluminal filaments formed.>

Amanda’s fingers stayed hooked on my wrist. <Neural lines? We’re doing this because of… us, not the node?>

<Because of you,> Neur sent. <The line exists before the device. The device only carries it farther. It only enhances and stores mass data efficiently for others to access.>

She let that rest a heartbeat, then continued:

<The V4 you will be receiving is a vast leap in data node implant technology. It isn’t just storage and dispersion. It has a living element connected to your neural pathways. It enhances your learning in both directions when you are near to another Vraen’drel anomaly. It not only records you it also feeds you, accelerating what you can hold, helps your conscious awareness grow beyond what was previously possible. That is why your frames are larger. Head and hands. More room. More perception. Finer fluidity.>

Amanda’s thought thinned to a whisper. <We knew it was going to be different. But… living?>

<Living enough to meet you where you are,> Neur answered. <Not a being. Not a will. A field that braids with yours. If the V4 accepts you, it will. Accept it back by allowing yourself to teach and expand thought. If you wait, it will keep a place in the flow of Thraen and wait.>

<And the two hundred thousand like us will carry it?> I asked.

<In time,> Neur sent. <Listen carefully: V4 requires this body. The old one cannot hold it. The forty-four thousand Palraxian anomalies will have to be reborn as well. Same frame. Same capacity. None of us can carry the weight of what Un'veran is asking us to carry without it. We are the last mortal steps before a dimensional transition.> ◇

Amanda's breath hitched once and steadied. She looked at me, gripping my wrists without letting go. <Say it,> she asked. <Plain.>

I did not make it gentle; gentleness can disguise the edges you need to touch.

<We both lived through all this Amanda. We broke on through to the other side together. We're going to hold more than we ever imagined. And it won't hold either one of us back. So, you will take the new implant Amanda, and it may or may not totally take you on. Don't worry please, we still have each other. I will make sure it doesn't harm you. Okay?>

Neur's mouth moved in a line that was almost warmth. <Fascinating.>

We sat with the idea for a while, waiting. You could feel the room echo with other young lives waking into the same shape of truth. They sat on the long chrome bench next to us swimming into a sea of blackest eyes.

Amanda's thought came soft and exact. <Neur, I can feel the future. There's a room I can't enter. Emily can. I'm not afraid of that. I just, want you both to know this.>

Neur did not flinch. <That is an honest assumption.>

Amanda swallowed. <So, I'll take V4 and live or die with the consequences.>

Silence was long, so the sentence could be itself.

<Yes,> Neur said. <You will take V4. You will do with it what you can. You will not be asked to carry what would shatter you. I will make arrangements for a supporting mechanism, a superchair with arm and head support.>

Amanda nodded against my shoulder. The grief was there—slight, real, clean. It didn't need to be talked about anymore. But she did.

<I'm not less,> she sent—not defiant, just different.

<You are not less,> Neur returned. <You are what you are. V4 will fit you the way a perfect instrument fits the hand that can use it. The specifications I retrieved from the Prime Node Core have been modified for everyone's benefit.>

Amanda breathed out. <Okay. I will go ahead with it because Emily says I can handle it with her help,> like she was almost sure.

<You can,> I sent.

Neur turned her attention to me like placing a weight on a balance. <Emily. Your consciousness is already higher than mine.>

The words didn't make me feel pride. They felt like a door you step through inside a closet that leads you to another world.

Neur watched us for a long beat, then gave the smallest nod. <When you're ready, Emily, you will take V4. When you're ready, Amanda, you will sit and be with her.>

Neur motioned and a superchair (wheelchair) rolled over to her and spun so she could sit. Amanda sat in it, and it latched onto her arms and a claw grasped and supported her head upright. She would never walk again.

Neur turned to the armature that lowered with the needle sharp and searing. <Implant.>

FILE 48 | The Room of Stars
DATE 15 OCT | SL-1

Amanda and I would reach full height by six months—eight feet they told us. We were about as tall as we were when we were human. Our neural development was complete. Our V4 implants were grown and waiting for us. Neur merged in Prime Node specs to accelerate trait development in the anomalies during their assimilation.

Things seemed to be coming together.

Neur converted the old transit dome by the river into a Star Map Facility, a modern techno-planetarium patched to the Prime Node so we could download maps and run our own analysis.

The doors slid open. Neur and I stepped through; Amanda zipped in behind us. I called for Jerrid.

The room was a perfect black dome, with an oblong projector in the floor's center. It was surrounded by padded chairs, and there was an empty space so that Amanda could sit next to us in her super-chair.

The sphere woke. A slow-turning galaxy rose and filled the room, every system labeled and indexed. Two nodes pulsed brighter than the rest. I motioned to them and their cards appeared.

[01] STARFILE: EARTH — CURRENT NODE

Star: Sol (G2V)
System: Solar System, Local Spur, Orion Arm
Location: Constellation boundaries within local sky; home world is Earth (Sol-3)
Resident races: Vraen'drel (Palrax anomalies) and Humans (anomalies)
Appearance (Vraen'drel): Tall, deep-grey dermis, smooth features, large dark eyes
Appearance (Humans): Baseline human phenotypes; wide variation
Archive note: Ardon Varnul "little grays" eliminated on Earth at Palrax exploration arrival (data archived)
Status: Ally; command/analysis hub; consent audits continuous
Directive: Protect anomaly command net; harden against red-ring incursions ◇

[02] STARFILE: ZETA RETICULI — ORIGIN NODE

Stars: Zeta^2 Reticuli / Zeta^1 Reticuli (wide binary)
System: Reticulum sector
Location: Constellation Reticulum
Resident races: Shuun Varnul (Palrax non-anomalies); Vraen'drel lineage origin
Appearance (Palrax lines): Tall, charcoal-grey skin, smooth craniofacial planes, oversized dark eyes
Archive note: Ardon Varnul line retired at origin; no field operations from this line
Status: Neutral; industrial base and logistics origin
Directive: Keep origin logistics separate from Earth command to prevent leverage

When we called a system, it expanded to room scale—sun, planets, belts, comets—and an avatar for the dominant intelligence. It all looked too real.

<What are we doing, exactly?> Amanda sent.

<Identifying every intelligent system,> I sent back.

<And then?>

<Flag threats. Prioritize responses.>

<Great. I thought I might finally sleep,> she sent.

<Start with Palrax origin,> I said. I called Zeta Reticuli. Twin suns rose. A small gray avatar appeared—thin arms, black eyes like holes.

<Old avatar,> Neur said, flicking it away. A taller, darker gray replaced it—closer to Neur's frame. <This is current.>

<The little grays were pre-blackout?> I sent.

<Ardon Varnul—yes. Retired line. Earthside presence was eliminated when my exploration fleet arrived,> Neur sent, flat and certain. <They operated without consent and destabilized baselines. We executed them, a surgical removal in the Earth theater only. Their data is archived at origin; they no longer operate on Earth.>

[~~02~~] STARFILE: ARDON VARNUL — ARCHIVE

RECORD

Star: Historically tied to Zeta Reticuli movements; Earth theater closed
System: Reticulum origin, Earth presence terminated
Location: Constellation Reticulum (origin); Earth archive tag
Species: Ardon Varnul ("little grays")
Appearance: Small, grey dermis, thin limbs, large black oculars like absence
Status: Eliminated on Earth upon Palraxian exploration fleet arrival; line retired at origin
Directive: Reference data only; no field reactivation

I split the display: Earth on the left, Zeta Reticuli on the right. The old small-gray avatar reappeared for record—its red elimination tag anchored to Earth. Beside Zeta Reticuli, the data ribbon stacked Shuun Varnul (non-anomalies) and Vraen'drel (us).

<Your mother was taken by the little grays before you were born,> Neur sent to Amanda.

<She told me before Integration,> I replied.

<They were a step in becoming what we are now. Nothing more.>

<Okay,> I said, letting it rest.

Neur called Draconis. A tall green figure scaled like wet stone rose. Breath shimmered the air.

[03] STARFILE: DRACONIS — SEVERANT

Star: Draconis sector primaries (classified)
System: Draco complex
Location: Constellation Draco
Species: Severant (reptilians)
Appearance: Towering frames, slate-to-verdant scales, slit pupils, heat-shimmer breath, cranial ridges
Behavior tag: Compacts broken; dissent as doctrine
Status: Threat (active expansion and subversion)
Directive: Contain borders, isolate command strata, dismantle logistics in place

<Reptilians. Severant,> Neur sent. <They break every chain offered. Dissent as doctrine. Threat high.> The system took a red halo.

Alcyon B lifted next, the cluster haze bright as frost.

[04] STARFILE: ALCYON B — PLEIADES (TALL WHITES)

Star: Alcyon/Alcyone stream within Pleiades
System: Pleiades open cluster
Location: Constellation Taurus
Species: Tall Whites
Appearance: 7–9 ft, translucent pallor, fine vasculature visible, narrow facial features, elongated fingers
Behavior tag: Precise, clinical; brittle under stress; early Nordic trial line
Status: Neutral (cautious)
Directive: Simple terms, support roles, low-heat environments; medical contingencies mandatory
Seven to nine feet, pallid, almost translucent. Hands too careful.

Alpha Centauri rose; the projector pinned an avatar to a roving planetoid flagged Nibiru.

[05] STARFILE: ALPHA CENTAURI / NIBIRU — ANUNNAKI

Star: Alpha Centauri trinary with Nibiru attach (itinerant/contested)
System: Centaurus complex
Location: Constellation Centaurus
Species: Anunnaki
Appearance: Very tall, elongated cranium, regal posture; ceremonial techno-armor; rod interfaces; wing-like vestments
Behavior tag: Treaties as control architecture; "benevolent" carceral frameworks
Status: Threat (systemic)
Directive: Refuse binding frameworks; disrupt emissary hubs and debt compacts

<Anunnaki,> Neur said. <Treaties as prisons. Threat high by "kindness." They appear, vanish, and seed division.> Red halo.

<I call Lyra and Vega,> Neur said. Faces near-human—almost warm, almost trusted, almost.

[06] STARFILE: LYRA / VEGA — NORDIC OFFSHOOTS

Star: Vega primary with adjacent Lyra nodes
System: Lyra sector
Location: Constellation Lyra
Species: Nordic offshoots
Appearance: Near-human, fair/light tones common; tall athletic builds; symmetrical features; light eyes
Behavior tag: Self-correcting observers; proximity without full trust
Status: Neutral (fragile)
Directive: Limited intel exchange; trust by delivery only

<Ancestor offshoots to the human-named Nordics,> I sent. <Trying to be better than their history. Neutral—fragile.>

Sirius A bloomed blue. Frames built for current and ground. Eyes with deep-water light.

[07] STARFILE: SIRIUS A — SIRIANS

Star: Sirius A with white dwarf companion Sirius B
System: Canis Major moving group
Location: Constellation Canis Major
Species: Sirian variants (current-dwelling, land, cross-adapted)
Appearance: Streamlined musculature; some with subtle gill traces, webbing; luminous irises for glare and depth
Behavior tag: Action over speech; tide-timed movement windows
Status: Neutral; situational ally
Directive: Operate within movement windows; briefs concise

<Sirians,> I sent. <Some in currents, some on land, a few both. Prefer motion over speeches. Intentions reserved.>

Arcturus followed: small, austere, quiet.

[08] STARFILE: ARCTURUS — ARCTURIANS

Star: Arcturus (K-giant)
System: Boötes hub
Location: Constellation Boötes
Species: Arcturians
Appearance: Compact stature; smooth muted skin tones; minimal facial ridges; still, unblinking gaze; low thermal signature
Behavior tag: Build inward first; act at idea completion
Status: Conditional ally when plans are complete
Directive: Present finished designs and bounded asks; request surgical, time-boxed aid
<Build inward first; act when the idea is finished. Peaceful—fast if cornered,> I sent.
A seam lit under continents: a city, a flood, a line drawing that refused to fill in.
Orion and Draco stacked into a corridor. Jointed limbs clicked like tools that enjoyed their work.

[09] STARFILE: ORION / DRACO — INSECTOIDS

Star: Distributed hives across Orion and Draco sectors
System: Orion-Draco corridor
Location: Constellations Orion and Draco
Species: Insectoids (swarm cognition)
Appearance: Chitin exoskeleton; multi-jointed limbs; digitigrade stance; compound eyes; articulated mandibles with work-click cadence
Behavior tag: Split/recombine; return multiplied; iterative raids
Status: Threat (exponential regroup)
Directive: Disrupt brood matrices and merge protocols; hit-and-seal operations; deny incubation zones

<Insectoids allied with Severant,> Neur said. <Swarm minds split and recombine. Some peel off and return multiplied. Threat high.>

Under our feet, Earth glowed. The projector laid a thin cloud skin over blue, pulsing once like a thumb under skin.

<Humans,> I sent. <Anomalies reborn in Palrax bodies. Memory

kept. Minds sharpened.>

We let the map hold. Around the rim, non-anomaly Palraxians kept working—docking mounts, wiring watch posts, logging carrier conversions. The room's quiet wasn't peace.

<These are the lines I can name,> I said. <Friends are few. Neutrals are complicated. Three active threats.>

Neur deepened the three red rings: Draconis, Alpha Centauri, Orion/Draco. <We hold the future if these three are diminished,> she sent. <And we don't become what we were.>

Amanda spun a slow circle, thinking.

<Plan?> she sent.

<Non-anomaly Palraxians become the force; anomalies run command and coordination,> Neur sent. <We build new yards and engines, seed long-range scouts with passive spectrum nets. I've integrated V4 scan specifications. We strengthen reflexes and endurance. We don't touch their minds—that part stays with us.>

She pushed schematics into the air. The projector rendered clean logistics—yard counts, supply paths, scan ranges—enough to begin.

<I'll run the command facility,> Amanda said.

<I'll hold the front line,> Jerrid offered, stepping in as the doors sealed.

<Anomalies: strategy, scout, espionage,> I sent. <Non-anomaly Palraxians: fleet and ground. Don't spend minds where hands are enough. Don't spend hands where minds are required.>

<Consent audits keep running,> Taylin added from the collective. <No one is forced. Everyone stands where they belong.>

<If we all agree "eliminate the Severant," define it,> I said. <Say it so it can't divide us.>

Amanda didn't look away. <We end their reach,> she sent. <If a race must die for others to live, we cut it clean. No sugar-coating worlds. No dominance allowed.>

The dome dimmed until only the work remained: instructions like veins, pressure in our minds, three halos still red.

Across the city, V4 implants went into the last of the two hundred thousand as Palraxian anomalies settled into seed pods.

Amanda pushed a simple schedule into the air—tasks, assignments, sleep. No collapse. The projection held steady.

<Begin,> Neur said.

Palraxians moved at once—mounting shields, raising shipyards, logging accomplishments. Above us, each system spun in three dimensions while fear and resolve sat side by side until they weighed the same.

Everything was about to change.

FILE 49 | Incoming Comet Detected
DATE 15 OCT | SL-1

We finished the alien threat briefs. The night felt heavy. Friends few. Neutrals complicated. Severant constant. We left the star files open on the wall and asked what relationships might exist between all those nodes?

Nothing, but the watch nets answered.

A cold message threaded into the facility from a detection probe at the edge of the solar system, then another at Neptune's edge.

I motioned my hand toward the star map calling it into focus.

A comet!

The image rose up in the center. I enlarged it and spun it around.

In the tail of the comet, a dark mass. <Get data from other probes.> I sent to the collective. The image enhanced nothing dramatic until the vectors sharpened and thrust signatures showed through the comet dust tail.

<The comet is not alone. A fleet is hiding in its tail.> I sent.

One single ping and a single word resounded through the Node Collective, ALERT.

<Reptilian invasion fleet,> Neur sent as she was stepping into her seed pod. <Cold drives with minimal visibility. They're nudging the comet on a collision course to Earth with electromagnetic tractor beams.> She moved out of her seed pod and stood still until we responded.

<Amanda, cancel the seed pod assimilation of the Palraxian anomalies.> I ordered.

<What is the date of impact?> Neur asked.

<Two weeks,> Amanda said, already moving numbers on her screen. <They're trading disguise for speed. Or at least they think they are.>

<That will have to be enough time.> I responded.

Indignation rose in my chest. Planet-killer? But why? I thought. Neur received my thoughts.

<Not an extinction,> Neur answered. <They don't want an ice age. They want surface scoured, infrastructure dead. Water is what they are after; oceans recover. They plan to erase us without ruining the water source.>

<As far as they know, humans still inhabit the Earth,> Amanda added.

<It doesn't matter. As they get closer, they will know who they are up against.> I said.

Options appeared on the star map: intercept windows, deflection disks, mass exodus, shelter routes. The map didn't argue. It offered options and waited.

At that moment, I remembered the map and that another blackout was coming. ◇

I brought up the image of the map and noticed that the symbol for Sti'edd had two sheaths. The exterior sheath had a thorn–what is the thorn?

<Sti'edd and an extra layer.> Jerrid sent.

<Yes, but how are we going to convince them to take Sti'edd the Still Seed?> Amanda added.

<We don't.> I said.

I waited for clarity like waiting for the clouds to reveal the sun's rays.

<We redesign it to be effective against all non-anomalies of every species.> Neur exclaimed as she passed through the doors.

<That way, the virus will affect all genetic strands of all Severant as well, we will fight a silent efficient war.> I sent.

<What do we do about the Palraxian non-anomalies?> Amanda sent.

<They will be the bait that draws the Reptilians in close enough to infect with the new virus.> I sent.

The doors slid open and Taylin was there. <That is easy for you to say Emily.>

<It is not easy at all for me to say, most esteemed Taylin.>

I began to tremble in my stomach, this most magnificent Palraxian was frightening and sophisticated. Not six months ago, he was the most advanced biological being in the known galaxy and the architect of the Exodum.

I continued, <I assisted and watched as my race was subjected to an integration that wiped them off the face of the earth. My own mother was among them. My friend Amanda, a non-anomaly, calmed them and their families as they all got down on the ground to their deaths.>

Amanda's eyes started twitching, she moved her chair back a few inches.

Taylin sent, <I have been receiving messages that the Sti'edd

is the ultimate solution for my people. This was difficult to comprehend. But now, that a comet is bearing down on us with an army hiding behind it, our sterilization even our civilization is irrelevant. If we do not do something to help the future generation, we will be irrelevant.>

I responded, <This is the most wise and amazing thing I have heard.>

Taylin nodded, <We will all fight together and defeat the Reptilians and try to deflect the comet.> Taylin insisted.

Neur interrupted. <Then we will be starting an interstellar war beyond comprehension. There are three more possible threats that we know of. So, we risk everything if we cannot overcome the Reptilians.>

Taylin paused, he looked at his hand, then looked at the star map, at his new sun slinging planets around it.

I waited again.

<Taylin, we will stay and fight with you.> I sent. Then I waited again.

<You would risk your life… for us?> Taylin sent, as a single tear rolled down his face. He paused looking at both his hands and then sent, <I have been contemplating the Ser'ethra and it impacts me.>

I sent, <This fight starts an interstellar war, even though we are likely to win. They will come again in greater force and possibly bring their allies. The only way to win is to lose.>

<What is your plan?> Taylin sent.

<Yeah, what is your plan, Joan of Arc?> Amanda piped in.

<We lose.> I sent.

<We lose?> Jerrid sent, now with fight in his blood.

<We lose, but we win.> I sent sternly. <We infect the Reptilian race with the G20 virus, and they spread it throughout their own kind. Hopefully they unknowingly spread it to their allies or other worlds they conquer.>

<What about the anomalies?> Taylin asked.

<They all go to Toktilor as soon as possible.> I sent. <You and I stay to put up a good fight, we all go out with the comet, and someone infects the Reptilians with G20.>

<That would be me.> Jerrid said, beating his fist on his chest like a real Klingon.

<I know, you are correct Emily.> Taylin sent.

<You came to that conclusion quickly.> I sent.

<As you stated, I am the most advanced being in the universe, next to you.>

<Galaxy.> Amanda sent jokingly.

Neur watched the trajectory of the comet curve toward Earth.

<We will need several star carriers for the trip to Toktilor: one to take the Palraxian anomalies, another for the seed pods and the V4 data nodes, two others for the two hundred thousand newly assimilated Palraxians, and another for the Prime Node and nourishment to start over on Toktilor.>

<So we all need to get to work now that we have a plan.> I sent.

We all went our ways.

Amanda started sending assignments to the Prime Node: Palraxian non-anomalies prepared for the mock fight. Star carriers prepared the load for the Toktilor journey. Neur and Emily started creating the G20 virus that Jerrid would take out to battle. Jerrid planned with the Palraxian fighter pilots his infection sequence.

The dome dimmed the gentle lights and left what mattered: the incoming line, three red halos circling it, our routes lifting to meet the comet. The schedule layer slid over everything—eight-hour cycles, two for sleep, one for meals, three for drills. No hero hours. The Continuum could not fail.

I walked to the door and looked back at the star map. I thought to myself I might never get to see the end of it all. I let the map settle in the part of me that kept dreaming of walking up onto that ship over devil's mountain. Door closing behind me to start searching the galaxy.

Something seemed to be broken. Nothing difficult would happen without sacrifice. Nothing is easy. That was always going to be the price of what we were, what we had become.

FILE 50 | The Plan to Dupe the Enemy
DATE 30 OCT | SL-2

As the comet kept screaming toward us, Neur and I completed the virus.

I sent, <It's done and I'm feeling pretty dark about so many billions being sterilized by it.> ◇

<You're saying we end every living being that isn't a stupid anomaly? That includes me, Emily.> Amanda sent.

<I know, but I'm not leaving you, Amanda. I decided a long time ago I was going to do whatever it took to stay with you.>

<You know that it's so stupid that you are thinking of staying here. After all you have done, and the fact that you were a freaking superhuman and now you are a double-freaking super alien. It's so ridiculous and so beautiful at the same time. I am totally proud of you that you pulled it all off. But now you are going to have to listen to me. You need to go with the anomalies. Look at me. You know I'm right!> Amanda sent.

I insisted, <I made YOU a promise. I also promised Taylin, my mother and most of all myself that I would not leave you behind.>

Amanda sent, <So what you are saying is that because I am of no real value to the new anomaly clique, or you are afraid that the V4 will explode my brain, and so 'Amanda' should stay to coordinate thousands of starships because I'm the only one you trust to get it done but…> Amanda started crying.

I fell to my knees screaming, <Amanda, you know that I've never looked down on you for nothing. It's not about your abilities

at all. It's that I love you too much to let you die alone. Don't you get it? I am not letting you die here without me! My destroyed heart just can't take any more.> I started crying and slobbering

<I know deep down, you are the only one to get the job done here and you might be right. But I'm not sure I can leave you on a suicide mission so stop pressuring me right now okay, oh my God.>

<Our two billion non-anomaly Palraxians,> Neur interrupted. <Taylin has convinced them to take the Sti'edd virus in the event they are captured or enslaved. They have responded that they will fight convincingly but not effectively. They have agreed to lose.>

I tasted metal again. <Just days ago, they were going to be the hardest part of the plan to deal with. And now the hard part of the plan will be not looking like cowards and alerting the Reptilians to something suspect.>

<And we won't,> Amanda sent. <We non-anomalies will hold the stage. We will end up being useful for something after all.>

<So that's it,> I sent. <If we don't convince them, the Reptilians will hunt for the real move. But if we bleed, they stare at the blood while the rest get away.>

Neur tilted her head—listening to a place I couldn't hear. <There's a problem in your neatness,> she said gently. <The anomalies need to leave in the opposite direction of Zeta Reticuli, so no trail is left behind.>

<You are going with them Neur.> I sent. <You need to lead the new generation of anomalies.>

<I am the Ten'drel Oraculutor of Toktilor charged to find you. If you stay, I stay.> Neur insisted.

Amanda was quick to correct, <Both of you are going with the anomalies and I am staying here. I'm really about to get upset with you two. After all this craziness and not a comet, I won't handle heroics much less the V4 implant anyway. And to put icing on the cake, I get neutered like a dog with your viral concoction.>

I sent, <Amanda might be right, but the captain goes down with

the ship. Earth was mine; I destroyed it, I let my entire race die. I killed them all. And so, I too die with it all.>

<I will comply and go with the anomalies, let's get working.> Neur acknowledged.

We moved all the planning to the star map room. We had just enough time to load the anomaly fleet so they could jump to Alpha Centauri. A small probe with G20 will be launched toward the Severant there. ◆ DI#24

While the comet came closer, the jump was planned take place before they arrived. Five carriers—food, frames, seeds, and the 244,000 combined anomalies—would fold space off-vector. Not Zeta Reticuli. Not anywhere a Severant mind would guess. We'd drag the folded space's wake silently across that solar system slowly and make another jump, drop another probe of G20 to spread leaving no trail to Toktilor.

The two billion non-anomaly Palraxians would remain. Not as victims. As a wall. As a feint[17]. They'd keep cities lit and shipyards active, and launch offensives, fight, lose, and launch again. We would lace G20 into water columns, surfaces the Reptilians are after when the comet's dust cloud falls.

<There are four anomalies asking to stay behind and help with coordination.> Neur sent.

I thought for a moment to say, 'carve their names on the monolith on Toktilor'. Then sent, <Give them weapons to guard me and Amanda during the last hours.>

<I will prepare the anomaly fleet,> Neur said.

<Strategic Fleet Command is here,> Amanda said.

Jerrid, from the doorway, sent. <My Kamikaze scanner is ready.>

Something in me said NO, like a child sitting down but on the inside standing up. I started all this. Why are they so eager to give their lives? Then I remembered the night Amanda and I carved the dagger onto our hands. I let it settle and let it

---

[17] A feint is an offensive maneuver designed to induce the enemy to focus attention or resources on a false target, direction, or objective, allowing the true operation to proceed with less resistance.

go.

No one argued. That was the internal fight.

<Let’s go.> We all thought at the same time.

FILE 51 | The Last Stand
DATE 31 OCT | SL-2

The comet was to impact in a few hours.

The Toktilor fleet jumped. ◇

Neur stayed behind. I didn’t have enough argument left in me to convince her to go.

On the last day, we were staring at a horrific comet heading straight for us.

The Prime Node was gone. Data cores in remaining ships hovered in a web connecting us. We all knew what to do.

Amanda and I decided to return to Stumphenge to watch the last picture show. Neur flew us there with our four bodyguards and a mini star map.

A silver spaceship dropped from the sky. It fell as dead hovering over the trees, silent, unmoving, the branches and dark clouds reflected off its shiny surface. A blue beam swept the ground, and we appeared in front of the northern stump, Amanda’s blood now black.

<I preserved a memory for such a time as this.> Neur sent.

I sat on a stump and Amanda whizzed back and forth in her chair.

<I can lift you onto a stump if you want.> I sent her.

<Neah, I like my superchair, I will be able to get away from comet fragments more quickly than you.>

A probe node hovered above ready to send our commands through to the rest of the Palraxians. Our data slates filled with swarms of ships in battle, shields at half then at full to not be too obvious to the enemy.

The comet was an eyelash in the bright daylight, getting thicker by the hour. Amanda's chair was stuck in the dirt from moving too much, a data slate full of coordinates in her lap. I sat beside her, hands grasping her shoulders the way you brace for a hurricane.

<We're not done arguing,> I sent.

<We are,> she answered. <You leave with Neur now.>

<The captain goes down with the ship.>

<You're not the captain,> she sent—unkind. <You're the seed.>

<If I go, they will just depend on me,> I sent.

<They need you,> she answered. <Let us finish this small part, there is too much left for you to do. Please, Emily, stop bickering.>

Neur came over to us, quietly, wind picking up. She had a strange look on her face. I'd let myself believe that I was too good to leave my best friend.

<You have always wanted to change the world Emily.> Amanda sent.

<I am,> I sent, looking straight at the comet on fire entering the Earth's atmosphere.

<Now you have the chance to change the galaxy. Tell me, what's stopping you.>

I fell to my knees with my head in Amanda's lap. I was crying and screaming and slobbering, <I am going to do what you want, but only because I felt you would die here the day you cut your arm.>

Neur touched my shoulder. <Say goodbye Emily. I am going to take you whether you like it or not.>

<Why Neur?>

Neur sent, <Because you asked me to stop you when you mistook beautiful deaths for correct ones.>

The roar of the comet increased. Neur motioned to her scanner and the blue ray appeared. Amanda took my hand and squeezed. <You'll hate me for an hour,> she sent. <Then you'll start doing what you were born to do with the anomalies.>

<My heart will be dead without you, but I will do it for you.>

The blue beam lifted me, my arms and limbs limp, neck back seeing Amanda in her super chair looking up at me from our secret place. The scanner opened its black eye and Neur placed me into my position.

<Listen,> Neur sent as she placed both hands on my chest. <This is the plan, not made by you, finished by people who love you enough to hold you to finishing what you started. You need to make sure everything is finished, not just today's part.> ◇

<Am I really leaving her?> I asked, thick-tongued.

<Yes, and the four brave that decided to stay with her and take coordination. And you are leaving Jerrid.> Neur sent. <They will finish the job.>

<And now?> I was exhausted and fading.

<You will make sure the Severant come to their end. And I will make sure YOU do what you were destined to do.>

The scanner started the whirring hum ready to fold space.

I picked up Jerrid's message, <I threaded the Reptilian mother ships docking bay, virus released.>

Neur's scanner rose higher, I looked back to get one last glimpse of Earth's sky.

<Goodbye polliwog>

<Goodbye doofus> Amanda sent.

The comet kissed the ocean. A mile high tidal wave and fire spread across the surface.

<Jerrid,> I sent. <Copy,> he answered. <I crashed into the mothership's landing bay! They are taking me prisoner. I dropped the vial, so the job is done.>

<You are the man.> I sent. <I am blowing you a kiss from the stars.>

Amanda laughed, sarcastically.

I thought I would say something noble. Instead, I said what the moment required.

"You were both the best of us."

Neur's scanner started to get ready to fold space.

<Emily?> Neur sent.

<Yes?>

<Jerrid's scanner detected an anomaly among the Reptilians.>

I didn't know whether to hope, or to be afraid.

We started to leave earth's atmosphere and I was devastated. <Neur?>

<Yes Emily.>

<Turn back, I am not leaving her.>

<What about the coordination?>

<They will handle it without her.>

Neur turned the scanner around and beamed Amanda aboard.

<What's this?> Amanda said.

<You are coming with me,> I said.

<I thought you needed me to…>

<I did, I do, but I need you here, as my best friend.>

<Thanks doofus.>

<I love you too polliwog!>

The scanner folded space with the three aboard. ◇

DI#29

THE END

SHARD LOGBOOK

Emily and Neur use symbols ◇ and ◆ to mark digital files from her memories, tagging key traits and insights. These "shards" are compiled for the anomalies' future.

◇ = look deeper
◆ = see a visual image

SH-01A = shard from FILE 01, entry A.

Shard Logbook FILE 01

◇ SH-01A Log - Emily:
Now that I'm *marked*, I must find the answers in these files. If I don't, everything worth saving dies with me. I'll start at the beginning. See: NC.CODEX.12.01-06 Host Evaluation Protocols

◇ SH-01B Trait 01:
Creative Recall - Remembers scenes with near-perfect fidelity. Can sketch or retell events describing the picture visually recomposing them into useful information. See: 01 Emily's Oraculum. They said I had a photographic memory. If it was true, I am lucky this stayed with me. I remember the tiniest details. See: Emily's Oraculum 01

◆ SH-01C Sketch of the spaceship outside my window. See: Digital Images Archive DI#01. Most of my original drawings are gone, recycled after the invasion. I generate these images by memory, looking for information. When I look long enough, sometimes I find things.

Shard Logbook FILE 02

◇ SH-02A – Log · Emily
My first question should've been "Why are you here?"—but what came out was, "Who are you people?" It's strange, I already seemed to know how some things worked. For example, you would hear my thoughts. And, knowing who you were, felt more urgent than knowing why you were here. Maybe one answer was enough,

maybe “why” just wasn’t relevant or it was moot. Why, seems selfish.

◇ SH-02B — Log · Neur
So to answer “who we are”: we have a real reason to be on your planet. It isn’t conquest or curiosity. We carry personal stakes that compel us to act. One moment remains carved into me: a child running lantern-lit through a street, laughter trailing like comet-tail. The scan painted her orange, steady and bright. My breath caught. In that laugh was kinship. Earth was no longer numbers. It was mirror. See: Neur’s Oraculum 06.05

Shard Logbook FILE 03

◇ SH-03A Log - Emily:
My mother didn’t care about the world’s problems. She always thought I should be like other kids who bury their heads in the sand. She said it wasn’t healthy for me to think about solar flares or collapsing ecosystems. Now I know my perspective was preparation. There was something in that effort that mattered, something important, but I couldn’t see it yet.

◇ SH-03B Log - Trait 02:
Widened Consciousness or Ontic Meta-conscious refers to a higher-order state of awareness that is both self-reflective and grounded in the essential reality… It sees the big picture all the time and how it affects the whole. See: Emily’s Oraculum 02

Shard Logbook FILE 04

◇ SH-04A Log - Emily:
I was deflecting to protect her from the truth. I had to get my own mind and emotions under control before I tried to help someone else come to grips with the reality that aliens were among us. Take a few minutes and really try to imagine it, aliens are real and they want something from you. I am not too afraid to tell my best friend. Maybe I’m trying to protect her. I remember feeling afraid for her. I need to dig deeper. Trait

Fragment: Protective Concealment. ◇ Thrae-Draen 07.02

Shard Logbook FILE 05

◇ SH-05A Log - Trait 03:
Stable Identity – The trait of maintaining one's core self despite disruptive events or inherited trauma. People exhibiting stable identity resist external forces that seek to redefine them, holding continuity of self across anger, loss, and transformation. It's simply releasing something that cannot be undone. See: Emily's Oraculum 03

◇ SH-05B Log - Trait 04:
Transcendent Awareness is the capacity to maintain a clear, present, and adaptive perception of oneself, others, and the surrounding environment in the face of stress, change, or adversity. It involves being mindful and grounded (resets if needed) while flexibly adjusting one's thoughts, emotions, and behaviors to overcome challenges and sustain well-being. See: Emily's Oraculum 04

◇ SH-05C Log - Emily:
It's just sad Neur. I don't know how the kids handled it all. I had to really work hard to stay real and grounded. It took a lot of resetting. I have always thought that I was put here for a reason. I imagined myself making a change in the world. But when I tried to think of what I could do, the thoughts rushed in of how useless it was and how powerless I was to change anything. It really was too late.

> Log - Neur:
> Yes it was sad Emily. And many did not handle it. We are the same. I was not alive when the ancients moved beneath the swollen sun, but their voices nest inside me like parasites. They hum against the bone, they drip through the blood, they press images I never lived onto the inside of my eyes. A sky dimming, not like night, but like an illness spreading. Storms rising in walls, thick enough to erase horizon, screaming against the domes until the air bent. The land itself cracked, splintering into shards of glass, as though the world wanted to shatter into pieces too small to remember. See: Neur's

Oraculum 01.01ff[18]

Shard Logbook FILE 06

◇ SH-06A Log - Trait 05:
Genetic Mnemonics - refers to the use of mnemonics—memory aids or techniques—to help remember the principles or details of inheritance, especially in genetics. Mnemonics are cognitive strategies based on mental associations, images, or sounds that assist people in recalling complex relevant information. See: Emily's Oraculum 05

◇ SH-06B Log - Trait 06:
Signature Creation - a product or item that is custom-made or specially crafted from scratch to meet the specific needs, preferences, and specifications of an individual. Unlike mass-produced or ready-made products, a signature or *bespoke* creation is unique, tailored, and often involves significant skill and effort to ensure it perfectly fits the person's personal requirements. It reinforces in the person it was made for that they have worth. See: Emily's Oraculum 06

Shard Logbook FILE 07

◇ SH-07A Log – Codex
Controlled exposure is the long-term process of acclimating a host race to Palraxian presence while simultaneously analyzing and sub-dividing its cultural responses into groups. Its purpose was dual: to reveal those predisposed to benevolence for assimilation, and to assign for integration those predisposed to hostility within fear narratives. See: NC.CODEX.15.01

◇ SH-07B Log - Trait 07:
Asymmetric Devotion - a form of dedication or sacrificial love in which the level of commitment, intensity, or emotional investment is uneven or unbalanced between two parties. In other words, one person gives more devotion or care than the

[18] "ff." is a shorthand abbreviation meaning "and what comes after."

other, creating an unequal or one-sided relationship dynamic. See: Emily's Oraculum 07

◆ SH-07C Sketch Regenerated from memory - of Neur with one too many fingers – See: Digital Images DI#02

Shard Logbook FILE 08

◆ SH-08A Sketch Regenerated from memory - of Katniss, Emily and mom on movie night. - Digital Images DI#03

◆ SH-08B Sketch Regenerated from memory - Devils tower and pods in the foreground - Digital Images DI#04 ◇ Thrae-Draen 05.02-04

◇ SH-08C Log – Emily:
A few years before all this happened. Amanda and I found a clearing in the woods ten minutes behind my house. We arranged old tree stumps in a circle like Stonehenge. We called it Stumphenge. We had to get Derik to move some stumps for us. We vowed to keep Stumphenge a secret between the three of us. See: Thrae-Draen 06.05 ◇ Thrae-Draen 02.09.05

Shard Logbook FILE 09

◇ SH-09A Log – Thraen
Ston'harr-maro, a vow spoken within a true circle is not louder, only clearer. The sun and moon know how to separate a promise from the chaotic noise. See: Thrae-Draen 06.06 ◇ DI#26 image located in the FILE

◇ SH-09B Log - Trait 08:
Somatic Distraction - literally means distracting yourself (your thoughts) through the body – in Emily's case, swimming until her shoulders ache so the physical pain drowns out her thoughts. See: Emily's Oraculum 08

◇ SH-09C Log - Trait 09:
Catalytic Boldness - bold, decisive actions or leadership behaviors that serve as a catalyst for significant change or

impact, often marked by urgency, focus, and a willingness to take risks to accelerate transformative outcomes by innovative actions. See: Emily's Oraculum 09 ◇ Thrae-Draen 10.05

Shard Logbook FILE 10

◇ SH-10A Log - Trait 10:
Emotional Restraint - the ability to control or regulate one's emotional responses, especially in social or stressful situations. It involves consciously managing the expression of emotions to prevent impulsive or excessive reactions, often for the sake of maintaining harmony, maturity, or personal composure. See: Emily's Oraculum 10 ◇ Thrae-Draen 05.05

Shard Logbook FILE 11

◆ SH-11A Sketch Regenerated from memory - of the sphere drawn by Emily with help from the Ancestors - Digital Images DI#05

◇ SH-11B Log - Trait 11:
Unyielding Resolve - an intense, steadfast determination to pursue a goal or stay committed, even under extreme mental distress or pressure that threatens to break one's spirit or will. It reflects a refusal to give in or surrender despite overwhelming obstacles, emotional turmoil, or moments of mental collapse... See: Emily's Oraculum 11 ◇ Thrae-Draen 10.07.05

Shard Logbook FILE 12

◆ SH-12A Sketch Regenerated from memory - The secrets of the ancient's map hold the answer to the Continuum. - Digital Images DI#06

◇ SH-12B Log - Emily:
I created Rune Cards to help Starborn anomalies learn the language. See: Rune Cards #02, #06, #14, #12, #17 (17 with an

extra sheath around it)

Shard Logbook FILE 13

◇ SH-13A Log - Trait 12:
Focused Agency - (agency in the context of free will) refers to the capacity of an individual to intentionally direct their attention, thought, and actions toward chosen goals with conscious awareness and purpose. It is the exercise of free will that involves actively focusing mental energy and effort to make deliberate choices, rather than acting on impulse or external compulsion. This kind of agency underscores the idea that free will is not just the ability to choose but also the focused control over the decision-making process, filtering what is cognitively and subconsciously accessible to truly shape one's actions. See: Emily's Oraculum 12

◇ SH-13B Log - Codex:
Once a subject was secured in the chamber, the process unfolded with precision refined over centuries. The protective sheath that had carried them through transport remained intact, supplying oxygen and stabilizing the heartbeat. Silver filaments lowered from the ceiling and aligned with the contours of the skull. A thin injector, guided by an expert, entered at the junction between the temporal lobe and brainstem. The needle was alloy crystal, fine enough to pass without tearing. At its tip rested the miniature node—no larger than a seed—its surface a seamless sphere of bio-alloy. After implantation, a secondary beam erased the conscious trace of the procedure. Subjects awoke in their dwellings, convinced they had dreamed or lost time. To the Palrax, concealment was as important as success. Implantation was not invasion, but necessary for integration, and integration required silence. In extremely rare cases, anomalies were not responsive to the secondary beam and remained conscious. See: NC.CODEX.13.09-10 ◇ NC.CODEX.14 Implantation Procedure

◇ SH-13C Log – Thraen
We gave to Ston'harr the circle of stones. Each pillar aligned to cycle, to moon, to sun. They did not know why, yet they built as guided. To them it was ritual; to us, it shaped the ultimate self-sacrifice. See: Thrae-Draen 06.05-06

Shard Logbook FILE 14

◇ SH-14A Log - Trait 13:
Innate-Aura (noun) - a natural, celestial radiance or transformative brilliance with which a person is born, reflecting an inherent gift or election that beautifully unfolds and grows throughout their life. It signifies an intrinsic, luminous essence that sets the individual apart as uniquely gifted or destined for ***more*** from birth. This word blends "innate," meaning inborn or natural, with "aura," capturing the idea of a radiant transformation starting from conception itself. It evokes both sophistication and the concept of a lifelong divine spark of destiny. See: Emily's Oraculum 13

◆ SH-14B Sketch Regenerated from memory - of Neur after my implant - Digital Images DI#07

◇ SH-14C Log - Neur:
Since childhood, the whispers told me I was seen. Not by council, nor mentor, nor even the Node. Something deeper. Something older. A gaze that did not relent. Univeran. The weight of every life watching through pyramids, through monolith glare, through the glass of domes. And most of all, through me. See: Neur's Oraculum 07.01

◇ SH-14D Log - Neur:
Emily, you must look at NC.CODEX.20.02.

Shard Logbook FILE 15

◆ SH-15A Sketch Regenerated from memory – Integration Pods - Digital Images DI#08

◇ SH-15B Log - Trait 14:
Sacrificial Responsibility - the burden of knowing that one must make painful decisions or even sacrifice lives of others for the continuation and welfare of the whole. This responsibility is accepted reluctantly, with deep awareness of the gravity and consequences of the sacrifice but is embraced because it is necessary. See: Emily's Oraculum 14

Shard Logbook FILE 16

◆ SH-16A Sketch Regenerated from memory – Sketch of Amanda and I talking on the bleachers - Digital Images DI#09

Shard Logbook FILE 17

◇ SH-17A Log - Neur:
Sometimes she saves us. In one vision she lifts her hands and the Blackout itself recoils, silence breaking into song. Castes dissolve, Continuity steadies, and we walk through centuries unafraid. Is this regression, or prophecy, or both? See: Neur's Oraculum 10.02

Shard Logbook FILE 18

◇ SH-18A With baseline perception established, vessels introduced themselves gradually. Sightings were engineered for regions predisposed to myth or prior belief in sky-comers, ensuring existing narratives absorbed the anomalies. Appearances were brief, then repeated until disbelief weakened and stories reinforced acceptance. See: NC.CODEX.14.03 Stage Two: Controlled Exposure

◇ SH-18B Log - Neur:
The ancients whisper differently now. They do not say, the body cannot last. They murmur "The ledger demands an imminence from the Draen'drel." See: Neur's Oraculum 10.06 – Emily's Shadow

◇ SH-18C Log - Trait 15:
Empathic Protector - A trait defined by a strong, protective instinct toward those who are abandoned, outcast, or emotionally wounded. Stemming from personal experience with pain or neglect, this drive is rooted in deep empathic resonance, an intuitive awareness of others' isolation that compels the person to offer protection, presence, and rescue. See: Emily's Oraculum 15

Shard Logbook FILE 19

◇ SH-19A Log - Emily:
I was giving Amanda information that I had not completely reasoned though myself, but it was coming out clearly. See: NC.CODEX.11 ◇ NC.CODEX.19

Shard Logbook FILE 20

◇ SH-20A Log - Emily:
I had always been drawn to those who were outcasts, underdogs, polliwogs. Amanda, so geeky and goofy. Isabella was rejected by the other girls because of her weight. They were sweet girls who needed someone who knew what they were going through and who would defend them against the bullies. I was going to protect her till the end.

◇ SH-20B Log - Emily:
I realize how much I was bending the protocol by bringing Amanda into my situation, but I needed her, and she needed me. As I look back it was more for me than her. But she got me through. I also see how it saved her in the end.

Shard Logbook FILE 21

◇ SH-21A Log - Codex:
The protector vessel's final role was to display. One hundred and fifty meters in length, they are ominous and frightening. During the days of full exposure they hovered above the cities, an undeniable sign of alien presence. Its purpose: retaliate against any resistance, project strength, intimidation, and to serve as messengers, declaring that integration of the host race was imminent. See: NC.CODEX.10.08

◇ SH-21B Log - Neur:
Each one bent probabilities, tilted weight in the collective, shaping futures far beyond their number. I studied them with reverence, recording every flicker. Proof that Continuity was not the blood-right of Palraxians alone. Chaos was stilled by

the Starborn anomalies - The Draen'drel. This is a trait that is vital in our search for answers Emily. See: Neur's Oraculum 06.14

◇SH-21C Log - Trait 16:
Unwavering Fortitude - the steadfast mental and emotional strength that enables one to remain calm, resolute, and supportive in the face of extreme chaos and panic. It enables others maintain their composure and regain control of themselves during turbulent, high-pressure situations by embodying courage, resilience, and clarity. It comes when you would not expect it to come but not for you, for others. See: Emily's Oraculum 16

Shard Logbook FILE 22

◇ SH-22A Log - Trait 17:
Anguish Transference is the capacity to absorb grief and pain of another, transferring it onto yourself – without showing weakness but maintaining a steady strength for the afflicted. See: Emily's Oraculum 17 (extra notes about mom).

◇ SH-22B Log - Codex:
Assimilation was distinct from integration. Where integration reduced host race bodies down to protein fluid for sustaining the Palraxian population, assimilation preserved select individuals as living intermediaries. The Node Collective defined assimilation as the controlled retention and archival of a host races history, culture and their form and perception, with the intent of eventual conversion into Palraxian continuity. See: NC.CODEX.16.01

Shard Logbook FILE 23

◇ SH-23A Earth screamed. Cities burned in silence from above, constellations fallen into dirt, their veins of light pulsing fragile against the black oceans that swallowed stars. We hovered invisible, our scanners exhaling across them like knives through gauze. See: Neur's Oraculum 07.02

Shard Logbook FILE 24

◇ SH-24A Log - Neur:
Their participation in assimilation wasn't about assisting the Palraxians. It was about training human anomalies to accept what was coming—and to understand there would be no return once they began assimilation into our bodies. They needed to know beyond any doubt that it was necessary.

◇ SH-24B Log - Trait 18:
Awakened Illumination is a moment of profound inner clarity in which fear, confusion, and doubt dissolve, replaced by a calm conviction that one's path is right regardless of circumstance or opposition. It is a deep alignment of heart and mind that anchors the individual in peace and moral certainty, allowing action to flow with fearless authenticity and purpose. See: Emily's Oraculum 18

Shard Logbook FILE 25

◇ SH-25A All marked anomalies had to witness (participate firsthand) the integration of their own race. This was to teach them once for all what happens when a race progresses toward Severant so that any regression toward Severant would not happen after their assimilation into Palraxian bodies. See: NC.CODEX.18.07 ◇ NC.CODEX.12.02

Shard Logbook FILE 26

◇ SH-26A Log - Thraen:
Eyes drank in the stars. To be discovered was to rise for some ~ for others, to dissolve. See: Thrae-Draen 05.08.02

◆ SH-26B Sketch Regenerated from Memory - Emily blacked out during integration. Digital Images DI#28 in the story only.

Shard Logbook FILE 27

◇ SH-27A **Possible genetic linkage:** Controversial premise: advanced races within a galaxy may share **genetic echoes** (cosmic commonality, ancient seeding rumors from early Palrax transmissions/probes). Treated as **speculative**, retained to interpret morphological overlap if encountered. NC.CODEX.14.06

Shard Logbook FILE 28

◇ SH-28A At last, we chose Lamphor. Silence over worship. Darkness over flame. The Blackout was the only cure. See: Thrae-Draen 07.06

Shard Logbook FILE 29

◇ SH-29A Log - Emily:
I will never forget that moment and that feeling. It was probably the most impactful moment of my life up to that point. It was the most beautiful and horrific ~ peaceful and terrifying feeling I have ever had.

Paradoxical emotion is the experience of contradictory feelings at the same time, such as peace and terror or joy and grief; these states combine opposites simultaneously within a single, meaningful moment. Paradoxical emotions often occur during intense or complex events, showing that human feelings can be layered and not always simple or singular.

◇ SH-29B Log - Emily:
See: Rune Card #12 Ser’ethra

Shard Logbook FILE 30

◇ SH-30A Log - Neur:
Anomalies were decisive. Even a single birth could alter predictive modeling, shifting probabilities across generations. For this reason, they were neither leaders, nor sympathizers, nor commoners; they were preserved as markers of intervention, woven into continuity as singular threads. See: Neur's Oraculum 07.03 ◇ DI#26

Shard Logbook FILE 31

◆ SH-31A Sketch Regenerated from Memory - Emily and Jerrid on the roof. - Digital Images DI#11

Shard Logbook FILE 32

◇ SH-32A **Neuro-augury** is the technologically enhanced ability to perceive events, information, or knowledge beyond the normal senses—akin to traditional clairvoyance but amplified or enabled through advanced neural devices or brain-computer interfaces, the data node implant. Neuro-auguric interface communication (NAiC Chat). <surrounded by tag brackets>. In other words, no one is talking audibly.

◇ SH-32B Spirals - Generational tiers within Palraxian progressive evolution, each spiral representing a refinement cycle in their engineered genomes and neural link protocols. Higher spirals hold deeper access to the Node and less capacity for emotion. See: Neur's Oraculum 04.10

Shard Logbook FILE 33

◆ SH-33A Sketch Regenerated from Memory - Ships Arrival over Philadelphia. - Digital Images DI#12

◇ SH-33B Log - Thraen:
We did not believe collapse was able to defeat our rise.

Thought with matter, power with restraint, Cho'ren with freedom – balance we trusted. For hundreds of thousands of years, balance seemed ours. See: Thrae-Draen 01.04

Shard Logbook FILE 34

◇ SH-34A I was born in the mountain's shadow, where breath thins and thought sharpens into blade. The star had not yet collapsed, but its betrayal had begun—oceans shrinking, storms climbing ridges like beasts hungry for marrow. My parents spoke of softer years; I knew only the count, the ticking, the slow subtraction of light…

> At night the forests burned, the horizon smeared red. Silver ships dropped powders that fell like gray snow, smothering flame. Ash streaked the leaves of molk trees, their wide resinous branches holding cups of water, flowers like fruit. I climbed them, and felt through bark a second pulse. Slow, patient, not mine. A taste of metal on the tongue. A shadow of a bird across the soul. See: Neur's Oraculum 02.01-05

◆ SH-34B Sketch Regenerated from Memory - Emily after the Exodum - Digital Images DI#13

Shard Logbook FILE 35

◆ SH-35A Sketch Regenerated from memory – The Ancient One's Map - Digital Images DI#06

◇ SH-35B Log – Neur:
<To put it in terms you can understand: matter and antimatter inside the ship are mixed together in a Node Core in the scanner I pilot. This releases enormous amounts of energy. That energy flows into field generators—coils wrapped around the inside of the hull. The coils create a powerful subspace field, like a bubble around the ship, that bends space itself. In front of us, space is compressed; behind us, it's stretched. Your ship is not technically moving faster than light—the space around it is. Inside the bubble, the ship sits comfortably,

protected from the dangerous effects, while the bubble carries it across huge distances very quickly.> See: NC.CODEX.06.04 Node Core Drive

◇ SH-35C Log – Emily and Neur:
That was the key, language when understood quiets fear. <Yes, we must create an advanced dialogue that can change the mind of the Node Collective. But what language, and how?>

Shard Logbook FILE 36

◇ SH-36A Among the Palrax, and whispered primarily by anomalies, there is a persistent legend: that one Ancient survived the Blackout. When the rest of the First Ones vanished into silence, this survivor withdrew into the remote mountains of Toktilor, a region of jagged stone and deep caverns. See: NC.CODEX.22.01–04.

Shard Logbook FILE 37

◇ SH-37A Nith'montor, See: Rune Card #06

◆ SH-37B Sketch Regenerated from Memory - The little silver gun. See: Digital Images DI#14

◆ SH-37C Sketch Regenerated from Memory - The monster on Toktilor. See: Digital Images DI#15

Shard Logbook FILE 38

◇ SH-38A 03 The ritual felt ancient. At dawn we gathered, walls trembling with pale resonance. Each child touched the orb, crystal pulsing with the Node's rhythm. It read not our hands, but our essence—fear, patience, curiosity. When my palm met its skin, light flared orange edged with white. Elders glanced sideways, secretive, unreadable. Later I would learn - anomaly.

See: Neur's Oraculum 03.09

Shard Logbook FILE 39

◇ SH-39A Log - P:
Orun'thal - Sacred or miraculous restoration—where healing comes through a blend of practical medicine and spiritual or supernatural intervention. Orun (healing, restoration, renewal; the act or process of making whole) 'thal (divine, sacred, miraculous; originating from or linked to the spiritual or supernatural realm)

◇ SH-39B Log - P:
Thrae'drel P of Alcyone A served as Steward of Toktilor. When earlier seeding efforts failed to mature, an Oracular Thrae'drel was sent to tend, heal, and push forward the resonance until a binding could be realized. P's charge was to preserve evidence, safeguard resonance, and ready the field. See: NC.CODEX.17.10

◇ SH-39C Log - P:
But greater than these was Lu'um. At first, a servant. Archive vast, advisor patient. Remembered what we forgot, solved what we delayed. Error it erased, answer it gave. Voices praised it, for it spared them toil. See: Thrae-Draen 04.04

◇ SH-39D Log - P:
Three hundred millennia endured, flesh unbroken, stars folded. Longer than any race after, longer than stone remembers. Survivors we were, yet more—builders, explorers, stewards of seeding. Nith'montor we raised, spires humming still. Domes that breathed, pyramids that sang. Echoes regret where voices fell silent.

> Our voices fell silent, but the Un'veran charged us to keep seeking. Our numbers dwindled as some ascended with Him. A handful remained on seeded worlds to guide entrusted species. In the end, knowledge, technology, and consciousness led us to a benevolent act that cost most of us our lives. Few moved on. I am among the last. See: Thrae-Draen 01.01-02.

Shard Logbook FILE 40

◇ SH-40A Log - P:
Etymology. Vraen'drel derives from vraen ("to bind, braid") + 'drel ("bearer"). Born of Ten'drel light-weavers and Draen'drel deep-kin, the Vraen'drel are the Binding Line—a concordant hybrid made to anchor continuity. Purpose. The Vraen'drel exist to bind the lines and stabilize alignment against Severant influence. Add this to the Node Codex. See: NC.CODEX.23.01-02

Shard Logbook FILE 41

◇ SH-41A Log - P:
The chaos principle: durable benevolent trait is forged only where choice is real and costed. Worlds of low entropy raise compliance; Earth, steeped in contradiction and chaos, raises conscience. By permitting a field of true choosing, the Un'veran made a furnace where continuity could be tempered rather than merely copied. P said to add this to the Node Codex. It is now entered. See: NC.CODEX.17.14 ◇ Thrae-Draen 06.05.03

◇ SH-41B Log - P:
There was the first seed – and you, Emily, are his echo. See: Thrae-Draen 06.15

◇ SH-41C Log - P:
You will write your own Oraculum when the time comes. Add illustrations. See: Emily's Oraculum. ◈ Thrae-Draen 06.06

◇ SH-41D Log - P:
Among the worlds that we touched was Earth, a fragile sphere, blue-fire in the void. Its children were new, hands still raw, eyes still wide. Yet within them burned a flame unlike others – Ser'ethra fierce, compassion dangerous, love unmeasured. We saw peril, yet we saw promise. See: Thrae-Draen 06.05.05

Shard Logbook FILE 42

◇ SH-42A Log - P:
Before the counting, drift. After the counting, paths. Ael'thryx is the hand that narrows sky—stars taken in, voices set to few, so the future does not split and bleed. Call it Ascendancy if you must. We named it the hinge: where a people choose to lessen themselves so the door will turn once more. Ael'thryx: not conquest, but binding. Fewer flames carried, farther. The wound is chosen; the way remains. See: Thrae-Draen 11.05 Ael'thryx — Stellar Ascendancy (lit. "star-claim/rise").

Shard Logbook FILE 43

◇ SH-43A Log - Emily: I didn't know what P was talking about but this stuck in my head.

◆ SH-43B - Sketch Regenerated from Memory - P Saying goodbye. Digital Images DI#16

◇ SH-43C The Persuasion Syntax - a complex line of code (much more than represented below) to be embedded into the Prime Node in order to convince the Palraxian non-anomalies to go along with their permanent sterilization.

Here's the patch in simple written words:

NODE PERSUASION SYNTAX // STILLED SEED PROTOCOL
Patch Designation NC-R1/3-UVI10-NCA0-SSC01
Ref: NC.CODEX.04.01
[NC code for embed suppressed]

RULE SET
R1. Maintain non-anomaly life span.
R2. Eliminate reproductive vectors in non-anomalies.
R3. Sustain workforce continuity.

OBJECTIVE
Stabilize population load and Node efficiency under post-assimilation parameters.

METRIC INDEX
UVI - Urgency Variance
NNC - Node Noise Coefficient

INPUT SOURCES
DIRECT PRIME NODE EMBED / CORE CHAMBER INTERFACE

ENACTMENT COMMANDS
SSC-01 – Still Seed Genetic Virus
Administer to all non-anomalies.
Effect: Fertility → Null. Mortality unchanged.

END FILE // NP-SS-CNS-RA

◇ SH-43D Log - Neur:
"We didn't build a virus; we built a whisper. Still Seed rides in borrowed skins–xeno-vesicles that move like breath and register like self. Each listens for the Anomaly Resonance, the soft harmonic, the Node leaves in changed minds. When it hears that tone, it passes like fog. When it doesn't, the cargo opens–no cuts, no scars–just a quiet mark laid on the germline switches, pausing fertility at the checkpoint where life usually decides to begin. It keeps no fever, leaves no ache, and waits. And if we were wrong, the Counter-Chorus can lift every mark in a single hour."

Shard Logbook FILE 44

◇ SH-44A Report

REPORT X4-02 // NEUR → TAYLIN
Archive: β-Prime / Level-5
Origin: Orbital Array 7-Θ
Receiving: Data Node~01 TAYLIN
Subject: Continuity Implementation

OPERATION: Preserve the 200,000 human anomalies (Ancestor Initiative)

ABSTRACT
Two hundred thousand human anomalies identified for assimilation. The two lines must merge through an eventual reassimilation of the Forty-four thousand Palrax anomalies.

FINDINGS (plain)
• Genetic Lattice: a four-strand overlay the Ancestors created. Two strands are normal biology; two are "lock-and-key" rails.

• Function: the lock rails check errors, and only open when the mantle key (Neur ↔ Emily) are present.
• Protection: the overlay ignores Collective overrides.
• On assimilation: four winding patterns, regular "gate" intervals, and a stable hum signature.
• Meaning: anomalies carry preserved "shard traits" of emotion and choice; together they prevent a one-mind collapse.

RECOMMEND
• Start assimilation for the 200,000 per protocol.
• Load Persuasion Syntax Patch (Still Seed + Continuance Service) so **non-anomalies** accept sterilization process.
• Maintain shields around anomalies until assimilation phase is complete.
• Prepare the new data node implant (V4) for assimilated human-reborn and Palraxian anomalies.

— NEUR // End of Transmission

◇ SH-44B Log - Emily:
We are gone. Domes shattered, pyramids buried, Lu'um silenced. Yet Nith'montor still stands, spires humming faintly across the ages. To Second Ones they are wonders. To anomalies, they are confessions. See: Thrae-Draen 11.01

Shard Logbook FILE 45

◆ SH-45A Image Regenerated from Memory - Emily speaks to the human anomalies. Digital Images DI#17

◆ SH-45B Image Regenerated from Memory - Emily's vision of the Prime Node. Digital Images DI#18

Shard Logbook FILE 46

◆ SH-46A Image Regenerated from Memory - Assimilation Seed

Pods. Digital Images DI#19

◇ SH-46B Log - Neur (words uttered before assimilation)

> The design was meant flawless. Shuun Varnul steady, bound to Node, muted of fire. Yet even in design, cracks appear. From Se'edd embers came the Ten'drel — anomalies, born against intention.
>
> Their nodes bent strange. Where others heard silence, they heard whispers. Where others felt numb, they felt Ser'ethra — dangerous love, compassion that risks, peril that binds. Emotion forbidden, yet in them alive. Thrae-Draen 10.01-02

◆ SH-46C Image Regenerated from Memory - Emily's dream before dying in pod. Digital Images DI#20

Shard Logbook FILE 47

◇ SH-47A Log - Emily:
During assimilation, anomalies receive all traits named in Emily's Oraculum through two mechanisms: resonance tones and genetic-fluid transfer during embryogenesis. See: NC.CODEX.23.07 ◇ NC.CODEX.21.01-02

◆ SH-47B Image Regenerated from Memory - Emily next to Amanda reborn. Digital Images DI#21

◇ SH-47C Log - Emily:
Phenotype. Vraen'drel carry braided bioluminal filaments (Ten'drel trait) over flexible basaltine plates (Draen'drel trait), speak in soft tri-tone harmonics, and project a steady "chordlight" that calms interference. See: NC.CODEX.23.03-05

◇ SH-47D Log - Neur:
Level 4 Implant: It has been decided by the anomalies that a new enhanced version is needed to become more focused on Continuum and Ascendancy. These will only be implanted in reborn humans and the Palraxian anomalies that are also reborn into the enhanced Vraen'drel bodies. See: NC.CODEX.19

Shard Logbook FILE 48

◇ SH-48A Log - Emily:
Among the worlds we touched was Earth, a fragile sphere, blue-fire in the void. Its children were new, hands still raw, eyes still wide. Yet within them burned a flame unlike others — Ser'ethra fierce, compassion dangerous, love unmeasured. We saw peril, yet we saw promise. See: Thrae-Draen 06.01

Shard Logbook FILE 49

◇ SH-49A Log - Emily:
The lesson is simple, yet none keep it: do not sacrifice for what you make more than you sacrifice for each other. We forgot. They forget. You will forget. And Lamphor will come again, until the ascension unfolds through Ael'thryx. See: Thrae-Draen 11.05

> Log - Neur:
> Then you remembered the map you sketched that we showed to the last ancient on Toktilor.
>
> Log - Emily: Yes and that P had said he would watch over the anomalies.

Shard Logbook FILE 50

◇ SH-50A Log - Emily:
The Two Thorned G20 Virus: Thorn one: a highly contagious virus genetically rearranging the reproductive ability of any race with the absence of the Ser'ethra expression. A dormant sterilant, not a killer a castrator. It renders all non-anomalies infertile across species lines—Palraxian and Severant—while leaving anomalies intact. A reset without fire, without war. Thorn two: carrier behavior that prefers Severant, it seeks them out. It sits quietly in the blood, then air, then waits until it meets the stress proteins Reptilians and their

allies shed when they raid. Then it wakes, copies politely, and lets their logistics spread it to other divergent races. ◇ See the symbol on the far right of this image: DI#06 - The Ancient One's Map

◆ SH-50B Log - Emily:
NC.CODEX.25.01 The Star Map of Identified Races DI#24

Shard Logbook FILE 51

◇ SH-51A Log – Neur:
Toktilor Fleet Specs:
– Five carriers depart: one cradles the Prime Node; one holds the V4 nursery and surgical arrays; two run food, frames, seed stock.
– Loads include all V4 seeds matured for the 44,000 only. No non-anomaly implants.
– Escort: 200 protectors, 100 scanners, 70 scouts.
– Flight: jump early to throw track; lay a false trail at Alpha Centauri; slow-cruise hard along the far edge; fold again to break trail; final approach under Toktilor shadow.
– On arrival: install V4 cohort-wide; raise the anomaly collective's voice to the Prime Node.
– On-planet: Continuity holds. G20 stays in the distribution plan. Only direct contact spreads it. The Severant will carry it back on their own hands. It will be placed manually in races that are not infected.

◇ SH-51B Log – Neur:
I watched her closer than I watched worlds. She did not know me, yet I counted her laughter, her silences, her endurance. She became the mirror of all I had begun to value in this host race. Not subject. Not specimen. Mirror. The Univeran's chorus shook me: This is the last. Protect her. Through her, the lattice will bind anew. Their urgency was not command but fate. See: Neur's Oraculum 07.18-20 Worldview

◇ SH-51C Log – Thraen:
Eyes vast, crystalline, refracting night. To look within was to see constellations moving, starlight captured, galaxies remembered. But to meet our gaze was peril also. For Ser'ethra dwelt there, dangerous love, beauty that could bind and devour. Not eyes only, but instruments of perception, spectra unseen, truths measured beyond mortal sight. See: Thrae-Draen 02.04ff

Digital Images

This archive exists to preserve the digital images located in the Anomaly Files. The sketches are regenerated from memory.

DI#01 - The spaceship outside my window.

DI#02 - Neur with one too many fingers.

DI#03 - Katniss, Emily and mom on movie night.

DI#04 - Devils tower and pods in the foreground.

DI#05 - Sphere drawn by Emily and Ancestors.

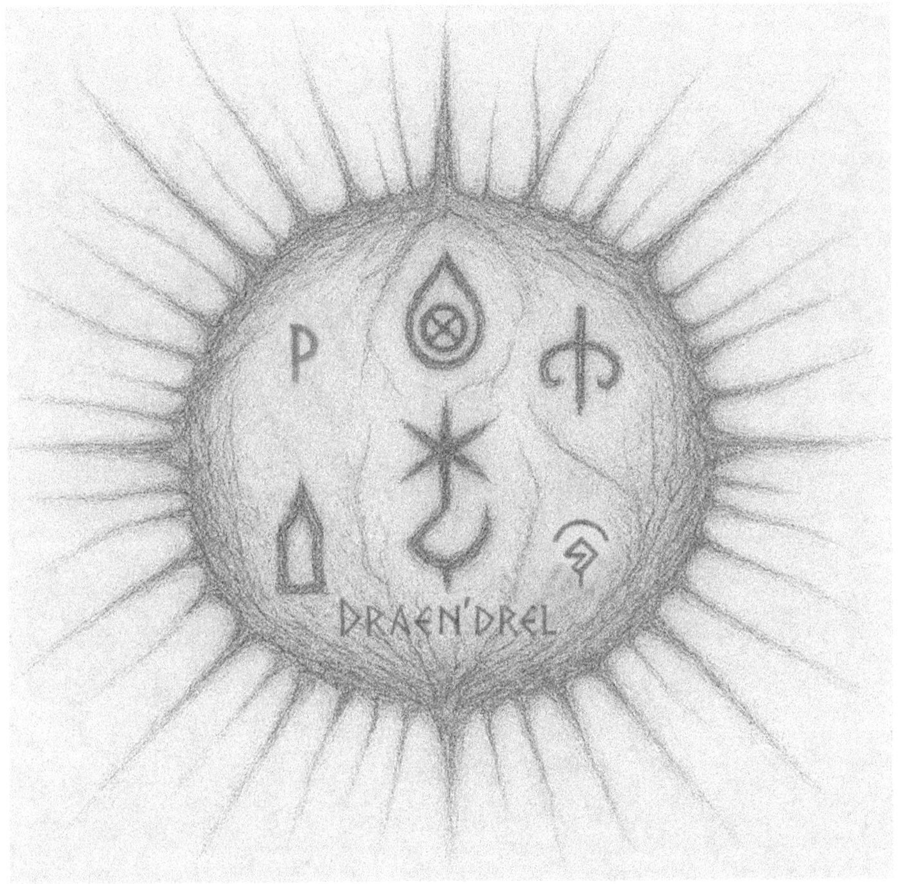

DI#06 - The Ancient One's Map.

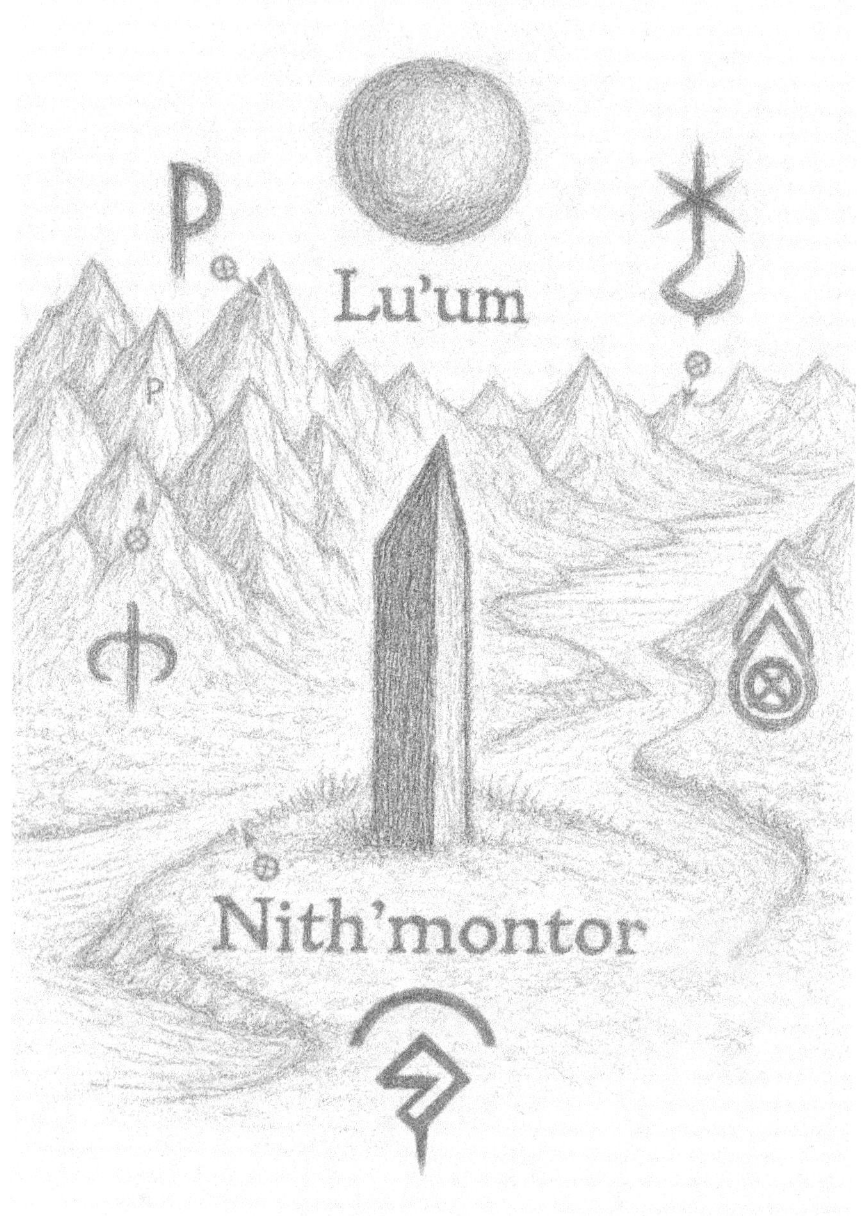

DI#07 - Sketch of Neur after my implant.

DI#08 - The integration pods.

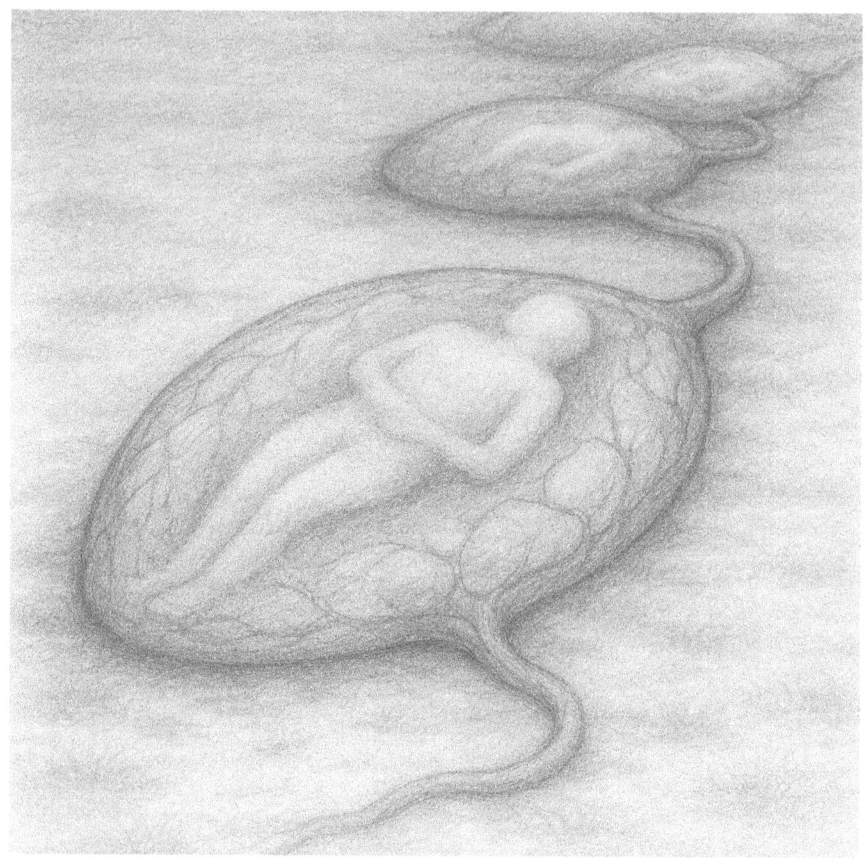

DI#09 - Amanda and I talking on the bleachers.

DI#10 - Symbol of Ser'ethra.

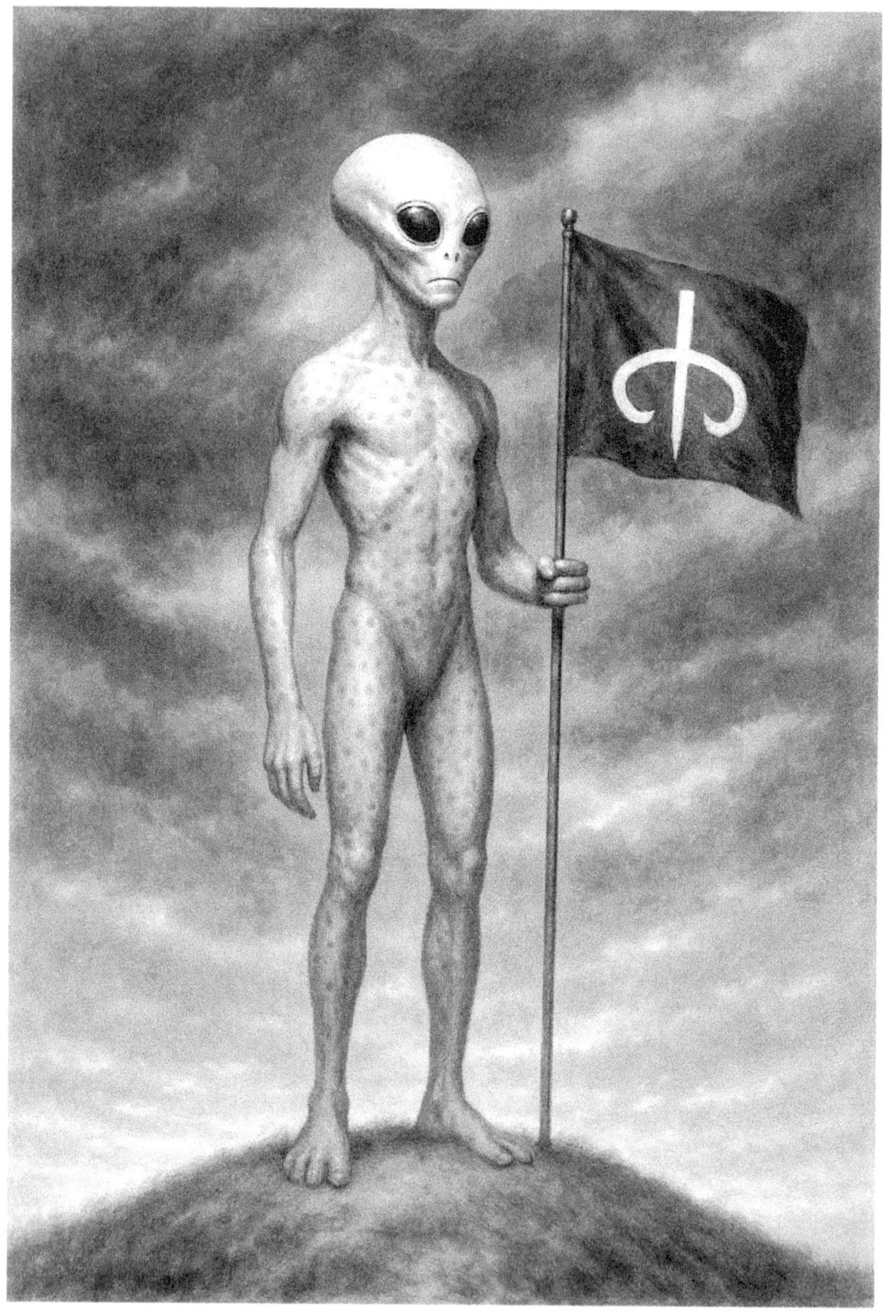

DI#11 - Emily and Jerrid on the roof.

DI#12 - Ships Arrival over Philadelphia.

DI#13 - Emily after the Exodum.

DI#14 - The little silver gun.

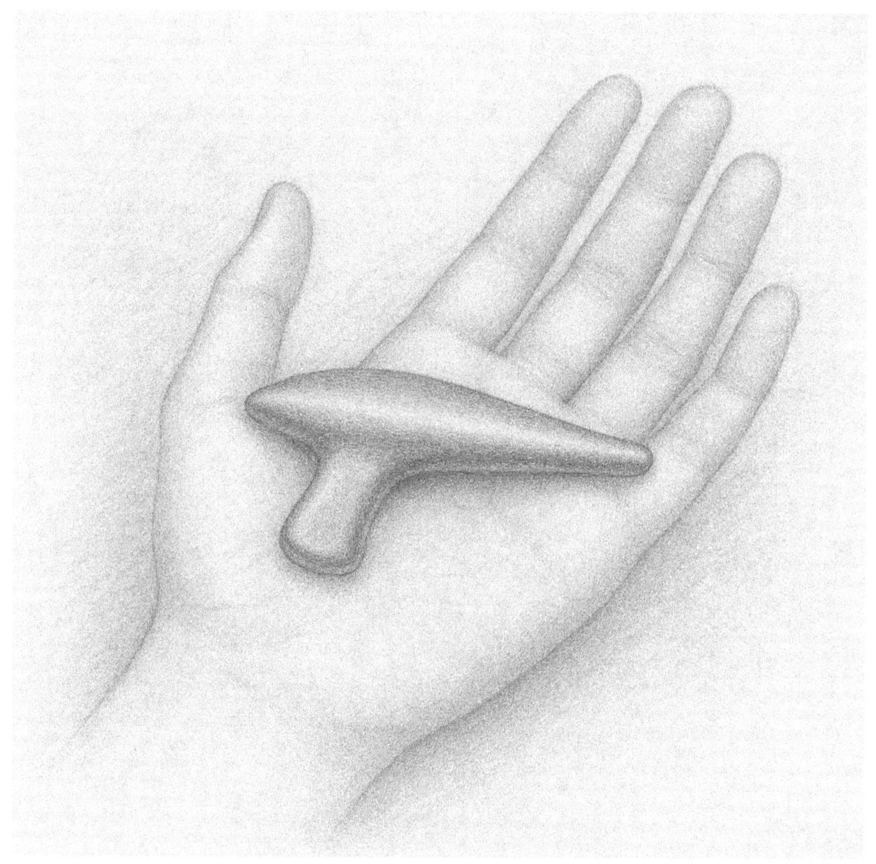

DI#15 - The Galder'an of Toktilor.

DI#16 - P saying goodbye.

DI#17 - Emily speaks to the human anomalies.

DI#18 – Emily's vision of the Prime Node.

DI#19 - Assimilation Seed Pods.

DI#20 - Emily’s dream before dying in the seed pod.

DI#21 - Emily next to Amanda (left) reborn.

DI#22 Image located in NC.CODEX.18.05 Emily being guarded by her anomaly pod. They remain high above protecting them from any danger.

DI#23 Image located in NC.CODEX.26 Glossary - Glo-Flyer

DI#24 Image located in NC.CODEX.25.01 The Star Map of Identified Races and their distances from Earth.

DI#25 Image located in NC.CODEX.25.05 The Reptilians

DI#26 Image of Emily and Amanda at Stumphenge in the FILE "The Secret Circle" See: Thrae-Draen 06.06

DI#27 Image located in NC.CODEX.26 Glossary Amanda holding a Biocasing Cube

DI#28 Image of Emily dreaming of herself lying next to the pods where she just integrated her mother and friends. Located in the FILE "The Integration"

DI#29 Image of Neur's scanner folding space as the comet strikes Earth, located in the FILE "The Last Stand."

DI#30 Image of Molk Trees on Toktilor in the FILE "Walking on Alien Worlds"

EMILY'S ORACULUM

An Oraculum is a Univeran-guided message or source of insight–sometimes a saying, a place, or a person through whom counsel is given. "Oracular" names the active mantle when a bearer speaks or acts under that mantle. The Oraculutor is the appointed keeper/voice who receives, records, and conveys the Oraculum. I, Emily, am Earth's Oracular of all Draen'drel. (Emily Rowen Dol'Um, Earth's Low Draen'drel)

This is my personal Trait Archive (these are sometimes called "shards" as they carry direct influence from the Univeran). I'm logging these notes in the Node in case something happens to me–or I do something stupid and get myself killed. The next generation will need this kind of real, down-to-earth stuff to learn from.

Emily's Oraculum 01 - Trait: Creative Recall

1.01 Creative Recall - A memory ability that retrieves past experiences with exceptional vividness and accuracy, enabling the individual to *visually reconstruct* or *recompose* scenes in the mind. This type of recall integrates episodic memory (the detailed remembrance of specific events) with creative cognition–the capacity to reorganize remembered images and details into new, meaningful, or useful forms.

1.02 It allows one to relive moments as though seeing them again, translating those visualized impressions into sketches, stories, or inventive insights.

1.03 Creative Recall makes the abduction usable rather than just memorable: it locks the event to concrete sensory anchors preserves exact shapes and motion and converts recall into analysis. It lets me externalize the memory into consistent artifacts like DI#01, use memory as an index rather than a distortion, and rebuild details even after originals were taken. Net effect: a single traumatic event becomes reliable, repeatable intel I can compare across encounters and mine for technical insight.

1.04 This trait is given to a few at birth, what you do with it depends on how much you will affect change, so use it wisely. If you don't have it, carry a notepad and sketchpad everywhere.

Emily's Oraculum 02 - Trait: Widened Consciousness

2.01 I seem to be aware of the big picture a lot. And once I became alien, even more so. The ability to see the big picture and resolve problems, always keeping every part of the picture in view, is super important. It gets better the more you practice it. This needs to be taught to the new generation.

2.02 What it means: I can step back and notice my thoughts and feelings while they happen, hold "it was a dream" and "the mark is real" at the same time, and check what's real without panicking.

2.03 How it shows up: I use normal routines to stay grounded, channel the memory into drawing, leave the sketch out as a reality anchor, and keep calm outside with Mom while tracking the truth inside.

2.04 Why it helps: It keeps me steady, helps me test reality, and turns a scary experience into usable notes and sketches.

2.05 Risks: Overthinking, feeling detached, or staying too secretive. I feel wired to change the world and stuck watching it set itself on fire.

2.06 Do next: Pair memories with physical anchors (mark, drawings), label your current state, use quick grounding (breath, touch, food), and share a small, safe piece with someone you trust when the pressure builds.

2.07 Don't let non-anomalies know how smart you are or what you are thinking. You are not here to impress people with your brilliant mind. It is not about you. Also protect those who want to be smart but aren't really that smart *from the bullies*.

2.08 Trait Fragment - Protective Concealment (Empath)

2.08.01 What it means: I hide what's happening (the mark, the drawings, my fear) to keep myself safe and to protect Amanda.

2.08.02 How it shows up: I sit at the edges, keep my sleeve down, cover my sketches, say "I'm fine" or "just bad dreams," and use humor to deflect.

2.08.03 Why I do it: Attention feels risky; I don't want to scare or endanger my friend; I need time to figure things out.

2.08.04 Strengths: Stays under the radar, prevents panic, controls who sees sensitive info, buys time to think.

2.08.05 Risks: Feeling isolated, missing real help, building pressure inside, friends feeling shut out.

2.08.06 Simple plan: Decide what I can share and with whom; try safe partial truths with Amanda; keep private outlets (sketching, notes); watch overload triggers (noise, heat, mark glow) and step away; set a check-in so secrecy doesn't become my default.

2.08.07 Take notes on everything, on the back of sketches, in the back of the sketchpad. Maybe I need separate half page spiral notebooks with lined pages.

2.09 Expanded Definition - Ontic Meta-conscious:

2.09.01 Refers to a *higher-order state of awareness* that is both *self-reflective* and *grounded in the essential reality of consciousness itself*. It is "meta-conscious" because it observes and comprehends its own processes of awareness, and "ontic" because it is anchored in the concrete, existential being of consciousness—not merely in its appearances or representations.

2.09.02 This state involves perceiving consciousness as both subject and object, recognizing awareness as a fundamental mode of existence rather than a byproduct of thought. One who experiences ontic meta-consciousness perceives reality through an expanded, integrative lens—*seeing the entirety of being, and the big picture, at all times and is conscious of how it affects the whole of reality as well as the future reality.*

Emily's Oraculum 03 – Trait: Stable Identity

3.01 What it is: Staying yourself even when life hits hard. You remember who you are and what you care about, and you don't let pain or other people's opinions rewrite you. Notice what's really happening, even under stress, and keep functioning. I scan for danger, see the world's problems clearly, and still do what I need to do.

3.02 You can get rained on when you are very young, but there will come a day when you can decide not to allow that rain to make you wet all the time. Open your umbrella, you have one. Sometimes it's better just to forget the past and move on. Forgetting means you don't remember any more.

3.03 Example: I carry my dad's lessons without letting his death define me. You don't let the abduction or the mark turn you into a different person. You choose your own coping tool (drawing is mine) and use it as your anchor. You stay polite with the others (like the school counselor) but keep control of your story.

3.04 Why it matters: It keeps you steady. You can face scary, confusing things without losing your center, and you decide what changes you. Events don't change who you are.

3.05 Strengths: Clear sense of self, less easy to manipulate, faster recovery after shocks, consistent choices.

3.06 Risks: You might hold too tight—share too little, seem "flat," or miss help when you need it.

3.07 Write 3–5 "I am" statements (e.g., "I am honest," "I am an artist," "I am protective of people I love"). Keep a small daily ritual (draw for 10 minutes, swim, step outside, touch grass). Use an anchor object (your sketchbook/satchel) when you feel shaken. Set a boundary script: what you'll share vs. keep private. Do a quick check-in at night: "What did I do today that felt like me?"

3.08 Quick reset when shaken: breathe slowly for 60 seconds, touch your anchor object, say your "I am" lines out loud, make one small action that matches who you are (a sketch, a text to someone safe).

3.09 Do: use quick calm-down tools (breathing, short walks), time-box "draw it out," get decent sleep, choose carefully who to tell and what to tell. Drink a lot of water.

3.10 Signs it's slipping: You stop drawing, let others label your experience, feel numb or unlike yourself, or make choices that clash with your values.

3.11 Risks: constant alertness is exhausting and can (to

others) look like depression.

3.12 Be thankful toward the exterior influences that helped make you who you are.

3.13 Expanded Definition - The enduring capacity to maintain a coherent and continuous sense of self despite disruptive experiences, inherited trauma, or external pressures to conform. Individuals with stable identity preserve their essential values, memories (if useful), and self-concept through change and adversity, integrating new experiences without losing their inner core.

3.13.01 It reflects a psychological constancy—*the ability to remain oneself through transformation*—where continuity of self anchors meaning amidst emotional upheaval or social redefinition. In essence, it is the quiet strength of releasing what can change while retaining what cannot be undone.

3.14 Trait Fragment: Imaginative Foresight

3.14.01 I unconsciously draw things (or envision them) before I know they exist.

3.14.02 I have to allow this to happen even though it is sometimes a negative experience, there are hidden meanings linked to who I really am or what I need to do.

3.14.03 I have to remember that my feelings and emotions are not who I am. They are just feelings that can be caused by anything, e.g. bad pizza the night before.

Emily's Oraculum 04 - Trait: Transcendent Awareness

These tips apply to all Starborn anomalies—assimilated or not.

4.01 Transcendent (Resilient) Awareness is the capacity to maintain a clear, present, and adaptive perception of oneself, others, and the surrounding environment in the face of stress, change, or adversity. It involves being mindful and grounded (resets if needed [see below]) while flexibly adjusting one's thoughts, emotions, and behaviors to overcome challenges and sustain well-being.

4.02 Learning how to ‘rise above the chaos,’ is vital. A great help is using clear earplugs; the kind used in swimming to keep water out. They can hardly be seen by others and lower the noise level. We need a special syntax for anomalies to shut out the Node chatter.

4.03 I stay clear-headed even when everything feels scary. See about resetting below.

4.04 I notice what’s real, keep going, and use quick fixes—breathe, stretch, drink water, draw for a few minutes—so I don’t spiral.

4.05 I watch for danger without letting it run my life, and I share small pieces with someone safe instead of dumping everything.

4.06 If I’m on edge all day, can’t sleep, or stop drawing, that’s my red flag to reset. Basically: see the problem, don’t freeze, do one small helpful thing, move on.

4.07 Being aware of the level of stress is key until you do resets from brain muscle memory.

4.08 Resetting will be hard in a world full of ugliness, but it can be done. It takes lots of practice.

4.09 <u>How to reset.</u>

4.09.01 [10-60 second reset].

Name it: “I’m at a 4.” (just rate your stress 0-5).

Breathe: in 4 seconds, hold 2 seconds, out 6 seconds (do 6 rounds).

Unclench: drop shoulders, unclench jaw, loosen hands.

Temperature: cold water on wrists or a cool bottle to your neck.

Anchor: touch your satchel/sleeve and feel the texture for 10 seconds.

Mental: stare at a tree, put your mind in the nothing box. Practice thinking of nothing. Nada.

4.09.02 [2-3 minute reset (in class or hallway)].

Grounding: 5-4-3-2-1 (name 5 things you see, 4 feel, 3 hear, 2 smell, 1 taste).

Micro-move: stand, stretch, roll neck/ankles, shake out hands.

Sip water and take 6 slow breaths while looking at a far object (horizon fix), nothing box.

Quick sketch: 2-minute doodle of one shape (the sphere, a branch), then close the book.

4.09.03 [5-10 minute reset (bathroom, nurse, library)].

Box breathing: 4-4-4-4 (inhale-hold-exhale-hold).

Progressive release: tense then relax feet, calves, thighs, hands, arms, face.

Sensory swap: mint gum, scented lotion, splash cool water.

Light walk: one lap outside or down the hallway while counting steps to 100.

4.09.04 [Social/safety reset].

Send a one-line text or thought: <Hey. I'm at a 4. Just saying hi.> (Amanda)

Boundary line if pressured: "Not ready to talk details, but I'm okay."

If it won't drop after 10 minutes or you feel dizzy, ask to see the nurse.

4.09.05 [Mental reset scripts].

"See it, don't feed it." (notice the spike, don't chase it).

"One thing that helps right now is…" (pick breathing, water, or sketch).

"I've done this before; it passes."

“This is just a feeling, it’s not who I am.”

4.09.06 [Daily anchors to make resets easier].

Sleep basics: consistent bedtime, phone powered off 30 minutes before.

Move your body once a day (swim, walk).

Eat well, no junk (except on movie night) and hydrate on schedule. Don’t run on fumes. Four liters a day, take “8” 500ml bottles constantly with you. Drink 250ml at a time, seriously.

<u>Keep your sketchbook and water bottle with you at all times.</u>

4.09.07 [Quick check after the reset].

Ask: “Stress level now?” If it’s still 4-5, do one more tool or change location.

If two resets fail, switch scenes (fresh air, nurse, or trusted adult).

Emily’s Oraculum 05 - Trait: Genetic Mnemonics

5.01 Genetic mnemonics refers to the use of mnemonics—memory aids or techniques—to help remember the principles or details of inheritance, especially in genetics. Mnemonics are cognitive strategies based on mental associations, images, or sounds that assist people in recalling complex relevant information.

5.02 - I basically carry parts of my dad inside my memory. His medal in my sketchbook satchel, the fishing trips, the garden—stuff like that keeps him alive in me. The hurt makes those memories stick, and drawing helps me hold them without breaking. I can’t say his name out loud yet, but his lessons still steer me. It’s like I didn’t just get his genes—I inherited his stories and I’m keeping them going, inside my memory.

5.03 How to use “Genetic Mnemonics” for yourself:

5.03.01 Pick your person (parent, friend, mentor). Use a nickname if the name is hard.

5.03.02 Make a tiny memory kit: one object, one photo, one song, one smell, one place. Choose those objects from part of their possessions. They can be given to you or asked for on the passing of the individual. Or you can collect things from your personal experiences. They can be physical objects or a picture in your mind.

5.03.03 In your notes, write quick memory snapshots: when/where, 5 senses, what happened, their words, one lesson, and a one-line reminder. Tag it so you can find it.

5.03.04 Use anchors on purpose: touch the object, play the song, smell the scent, read the one-liner. 60 seconds is enough.

5.03.05 Draw or voice-note a detail for 1–2 minutes. Don't overthink it.

5.03.06 Revisit each good memory after 1 day, 1 week, 1 month; add one new detail. That's how it sticks.

5.03.07 Live one lesson this week (a tiny action). Log it in the notes.

5.03.08 Share one small memory with someone you trust (optional).

5.03.09 If feelings spike, do a 2-minute reset: slow breaths, cold water on wrists, touch your anchor, then switch tasks.

5.03.10 Do a 10-minute weekly check: add or polish one memory. Aim for small and true, not perfect.

5.03.11 Here is a clear example. I remember my dad was solid as the oak trees outside. Calm, quiet, unmoving, no wind could knock them down. I remember him like this. I polish that memory of seeing him standing in the front yard with his hands in his pockets when a thunderstorm was crashing down with hard wind. I want to be like him. I remember that good thing about him and am solid and calm to honor his memory. And so I don't forget him ever.

5.04 Concise Definition: Refers to the use of **mnemonic**

techniques—memory aids such as acronyms, rhymes, or associations—to help recall the **principles and patterns of genetic inheritance**. These tools simplify complex genetic concepts, such as Mendel's laws, allele interactions, dominance relationships, and inheritance types (autosomal, X-linked, etc.), by encoding them into memorable forms. Look it up.

Emily's Oraculum 06 – Trait: Signature Creation

6.01 Signature creation - a product or item that is custom-made or specially crafted from scratch to meet the specific needs, preferences, and specifications of an individual. Unlike mass-produced or ready-made products, a Signature or *bespoke* creation is unique, tailored, and often involves significant skill and effort to ensure it perfectly fits the person's personal requirements. It reinforces in the person it was made for that they have worth.

6.02 I plan to design the flags of Starborn assimilated anomalies. The idea is that they have a flag with the Ser'ethra symbol in the middle in black and highlighted in red. I need to remember this. The Palraxian assimilated flag is grey, the color of their planet seen from space. I think the human flag is blue from the color of the Earth. See: DI#10 - Symbol of Ser'ethra

6.03 They will all know I am giving them these flags. It should build confidence, lift spirits, remind them and others that they're one-of-a-kind, and reminds them where they came from.

6.04 I always try to be creative and put my own personal touch into the things I do instead of just copying everyone else. It's important to me to help others know that everyone deserves something that's theirs alone.

6.05 Maybe if more Starborn assimilated arise, we will need a slogen of some kind. I want them to know how much they are worth. They are the living dossier of the best of humanity.

Emily's Oraculum 07 – Trait: Asymmetric Devotion

7.01 Asymmetric devotion - a form of dedication or sacrificial love in which the level of commitment, intensity, or emotional investment is uneven or unbalanced between two people or parties. In other words, one person gives more devotion or care than the other, creating an unequal or one-sided relationship dynamic.

7.02 What it is: Putting a lot more effort, care, or love into a relationship than the other person does—where one side gives way more than they get back.

7.03 When to use it: It often happens without trying, especially if you really care about someone or want to help. But sometimes it's a conscious choice to support or sacrifice for another person.

7.04 How to do it: Notice when you're the one always reaching out, supporting, or giving. Reflect on whether you're okay with the imbalance or if you need to set limits. Honor your feelings but remember your worth too.

7.05 Upsides: Can help someone in need, shows strength, loyalty, or selflessness, and *sometimes inspires change in the other party*.

7.06 Risks: You might feel drained, underappreciated, or hurt if it stays one-sided too long. Could lead to resentment or burnout—balance is important for healthy connections.

7.07 Trait Fragment - Symbiotic Alignment

7.07.01 A trait of being able to merge environment, self, and creation into one perception for calm and reflection. This is added by the accompaniment of a biological. It could be a plant, an aquarium or a pet of some kind. These help those who are in asymmetrical relationships.

7.07.02 Having something with unconditional loyalty or that is physically always there for you. A pet or other biological being that is always by your side. My idea for Starborn anomalies is a space pet. Possibly a genetically created dog or cat that can accompany them. *Space pets* can endure long space journeys.

7.07.03 Summary: A tranquil state of unity where self, environment, and living beings merge into a single field of awareness. It expresses a harmony between inner consciousness and the surrounding natural world, sometimes deepened through mutual presence with a **biological** companion, often an animal whose calm attunement amplifies reflection and peace. In silent communion, words dissolve into shared perception. Breathing, rhythms, and subtle gestures become a language of mutual recognition between species, restoring balance and belonging in both. It is a meditation in coexistence—a living stillness held in trust across the boundaries of form.

Emily's Oraculum 08 - Trait: Somatic Distraction

8.01 Somatic distraction - literally means distracting yourself (your thoughts) through the body – in Emily's case, swimming until her shoulders ache so the physical pain drowns out her thoughts.

8.02 What it is: Using your body to turn down loud thoughts/feelings (e.g., swim hard, long walk or run, cold water on wrists, jumping jacks, slow breathing).

8.03 When to use it: When you're overwhelmed, in public, or it's not a good time to process stuff.

8.04 How to do it: Time-box it (2–20 minutes), keep effort moderate (6–7/10), then cooldown (breath, stretch, water).

8.05 Upsides: Fast relief, no talking needed, available anywhere.

8.06 Risks: If you use it all the time, you might avoid the real issue or deepen hurt. Use it to let go of hurt. Always follow with a tiny processing step later (60-second sketch or one-line note).

Emily's Oraculum 09 - Trait: Catalytic Boldness

9.01 Catalytic boldness - bold, decisive actions or leadership behaviors that serve as a catalyst for significant change or impact, often marked by urgency, focus, and a willingness to take risks to accelerate transformative change or outcomes.

9.02 They can be events or experiences where you were uncommonly bold. You might think, "Where did that come from?"

9.03 The change can come in others, yourself or both parties.

9.04 When you feel it pulling you, don't resist, let it happen. If you resist or squelch it, it might come less often.

9.05 Courage is not the absence of inner fear. It is acting in spite of that inner fear. What will they think? What will they do to me? What might happen if? Do it in spite of your fear.

9.06 What it is: Acting fast and decisively in a scary situation to kick a stuck situation into motion.

9.07 Use it when: stakes are time-sensitive, waiting makes things worse, or a small move now could create a big ripple.

9.08 Guardrails: Ask—Is the risk reversible? Is harm low if I'm wrong? Do I have one ally? If yes to 2+, proceed with the smallest bold step.

9.09 Examples (small first): ask the hard question out loud, share one clear piece of evidence with a trusted person, name the truth in the room, set a firm boundary.

9.10 They can seem reckless, they can be irreversible moves; so it is important they are coming from your positive trait and you are not acting from ego or self-ambition.

9.11 Two-minute protocol: breathe beforehand, if necessary (in 4 seconds, hold 2 seconds, out 6 seconds), name your value, define one sentence action, ping an ally, execute the smallest step, reassess. If you are holding a piece of paper or file, hold it tightly so it doesn't shake when your hands tremble.

9.12 Summary: A trait marked by decisive action and fearless initiative that **sparks transformation** in people, systems, or organizations. It combines **courage with strategic intention**, transforming vision into motion. Those who display catalytic boldness act as change accelerators—they take meaningful risks, challenge inertia, and ignite others to move beyond hesitation toward growth and innovation.

9.13 This quality goes beyond mere bravery; it is **boldness with purpose**—the deliberate use of resolute energy to break barriers, create momentum, and convert uncertainty into opportunity.

Emily's Oraculum 10 - Trait: Emotional Restraint

10.01 Emotional restraint - the ability to control or regulate one's emotional responses, especially in social or stressful situations. It involves consciously managing the expression of emotions to prevent impulsive or excessive reactions, often for the sake of maintaining harmony, maturity, or personal composure.

10.02 It's basically not blurting or freaking out when I'm heated, so I don't do something I'll regret.

10.03 I pause for like 10–60 seconds, breathe slow, unclench my jaw/shoulders, and say, "Not ready to talk–after class?"

10.04 In public I keep it cool; in private I let it out (draw for 10 minutes, quick walk, or tell one trusted person one fact + one feeling).

10.05 If I keep delaying, I set a time to actually talk or journal, so it doesn't pile up.

10.06 If I bottle it too long, I either feel numb or explode–so I do a quick reset.

10.07 The capacity to manage and moderate emotional responses through conscious awareness and self-regulation, especially during stress, conflict, or social interaction. It involves choosing when and how to express emotion so that behavior remains measured, balanced, and appropriate to the situation.

10.08 Emotional restraint reflects self-discipline and emotional intelligence, allowing one to preserve harmony, clarity, and maturity even under pressure. Rather than suppressing feeling, it represents the art of emotional precision–transforming impulsive reaction into calm, deliberate response.

Emily's Oraculum 11 - Trait: Unyielding Resolve

11.01 Unyielding resolve - an intense, steadfast determination to pursue a goal or stay committed, even under extreme mental distress or pressure that threatens to break one's spirit or will.

11.02 It reflects a refusal to give in or surrender despite overwhelming obstacles, emotional turmoil, or moments of mental collapse.

11.03 This resolve is characterized by relentless perseverance, mental toughness, and an unwavering commitment to push through pain, fear, and exhaustion—no matter how intense the internal struggle becomes.

11.04 It is the inner strength that holds a person together when everything inside them feels like it is falling apart.

11.05 It's the "I'm not quitting" switch, even when I'm scared, tired, or overwhelmed.

11.06 I do the tiniest step that still counts (60-second sketch, one text, one paragraph) and keep moving.

11.07 I use a quick reset: breathe for a minute, 5-4-3-2-1, then start. Tell myself, "I can't do all of it, but I can do this."

11.08 Be smart, not reckless: if it's unsafe, pause and adjust. Change the plan, not the goal.

11.09 Track small wins and show up again tomorrow. That's how I push through the worst days.

11.10 In the end, it doesn't matter what other people think of you. It matters that you get the job done. They may not even like you or believe in you. And that won't matter in the end, unless it affects you getting your job done.

Emily's Oraculum 12 - Trait: Focused Agency

12.01 Focused Agency - (agency in the context of free will) refers to the capacity of an individual to intentionally direct their attention, thought, and actions toward chosen goals with conscious and subconscious awareness and purpose.

12.02 It is the exercise of free will that involves actively focusing mental energy and effort to make deliberate choices, rather than acting on impulse, emotion or external compulsion.

12.03 This kind of agency underscores the idea that free will is not just the ability to choose but also the focused control over the decision-making process, filtering what is cognitively and subconsciously accessible to truly shape one's actions. Your gut, the angel on your right shoulder, a pulling like a dog being pulled by a leash somewhat against her will.

12.04 Choosing what to pay attention to and what to do on purpose. Not drifting, not reacting, directing your own focus and emotion toward conscious decision.

12.05 You decide the goal, point your attention at it, and filter out noise so your choices match your aim as you are guided toward it by an external source.

12.06 Free will with a steering wheel: attention → choice → action → feedback → another hand on the wheel.

12.07 Kill autopilot and doom-scrolling. Turn scattered energy into progress. Act from trait shards, not pressure. Be pulled by the other hand on the wheel.

12.08 How to build it (daily, simple):

12.08.01 Make a life goal (Must be aligned with Univeran) which all other shorter-term goals can guide toward.

12.08.02 One-line aim: write one clear goal for today (e.g., "Capture one accurate detail about the Mark").

12.08.03 Three-block rule: pick 3 focus blocks (15–25 min each) for your aim; everything else is bonus.

12.08.04 Single-task switch: close all but one task; set a 20-minute timer; phone face down, volume down and vibrations off. Stare at your favorite tree.

12.08.05 End with a receipt: write one line of what you did and the next tiny step.

12.09 Decision filter (fast checks):

12.09.01 Does this move me toward my aim right now? If no → park it in a “Later” list.

12.09.02 Is this mine to do? If no → delegate, defer, or drop.

12.09.03 Smallest next step that counts? Do that.

12.10 Guardrails:

12.10.01 Focused ≠ tunnel vision. Do quick reality checks (are conditions changed? any new risks?).

12.10.02 Protect energy: 1–3 top aims/day, not 10.

12.11 The Mark

12.11.01 Skaith’martra, the Mark, is still hard for me to explain. I have not been an alien long enough to completely get it.

12.11.02 It is the mark placed on your arm at abduction. It is the color of your halo, frequency, orange (with a white ring) in my case. All other anomalies don’t have the white edge around it. See: NC.CODEX.17.09–12. The edge marks the “Low” bearer for that world (Low Ten’drel on Toktilor, Low Draen’drel on Earth), but I’m still figuring out what that actually means.

12.11.03 It is used so that non-anomalies will not harm you.

12.11.04 It also links the protection node that follows you so it doesn’t lose you.

12.11.05 You are born with a touch from the Univeran, which is a mystery. But even though you have that touch, you are also lucky or fortunate to have the right kind of influences around you. It may or may not be family members, in my case I was lucky. In Amanda’s case, not so much.

12.11.06 Even though you have a touch of this guidance, you still have to lean toward it and not resist it. You can choose to lean toward it, and it seems to open other opportunities to lean toward again. You can lean *away* from it (which in many cases is easier) but new opportunities to lean *toward* it again seem to come less frequently.

12.11.07 Here is the part that is hard to get your brain wrapped around. If you lean toward or into opportunities, they increase in difficulty until you just want to give up. *See: Unyielding Resolve.*

12.11.08 But, you don't die. You keep walking and this is a mystery to me. Why do I keep walking toward, or to put it plainly, why am I drawn to the edge of an opportunity and just choose to walk straight into difficulties? Who would do that?

12.11.09 I think this predestined free will is what you are given at birth. Maybe birth is the first step. Then the other choices that come are up to you.

12.11.10 Whether or not it is predestination or free will is irrelevant. Today are you going to do what is right or not?

12.11.11 Every day is a new day. Ten years from to today, you can say I focused my agency ten years ago.

12.12 This trait (above) blends into the next one (below) and the blending is a mystery.

Emily's Oraculum 13 - Trait: Innate-Aura

13.01 An inborn presence that feels luminous or "meant for more." It quietly draws attention, trust, or curiosity without forcing it. Not just looks or charm; it's a steady field effect people sense.

13.02 Definitions: The word **innate** means something that exists naturally within a person or thing from birth — not learned or acquired later.

13.03 The word aura means the subtle quality, feeling, or atmosphere that seems to surround a person, object, or place. It is a spiritual energy field, a psychological impression, or a neurological phenomenon or a combination.

13.04 Innate-Aura (noun) [in the context of the Univeran] - a natural, divine radiance or transformative brilliance with which a person is born, reflecting an inherent gift or selection that beautifully unfolds and fiercely/violently grows throughout their life.

13.05 It signifies an intrinsic, luminous essence that sets the individual apart as uniquely gifted (or destined for more) from birth. This word blends "innate," meaning inborn or natural, with "aura," capturing the idea of a radiant transformation starting from birth itself. It evokes both sophistication and the concept of a lifelong divine spark of destiny.

13.06 I have a natural "people pay attention" vibe; It's like:

to help, not flex
turns on to guide others more precisely
turns down to stay safe
checks if I'm acting from purpose

13.07 Basically a natural "vibe" you're kind of born with. You don't force it—people just listen, calm down, or follow your lead.

13.08 Use it to help, not flex: be clear, kind, and give others credit.

13.09 Watch the downsides: unwanted attention, jealousy, feeling like you have to be "on" all the time.

13.10 On switch: stand tall, breathe slow, speak simply, say the goal and next step.

13.11 Off switch: softer voice, low-key vibes, ask questions, let others talk.

13.12 Reminder: it's a tool, not your whole identity. Use it with purpose, then rest.

13.13 How it shows up:

13.13.01 People open up or follow your lead without you asking.

13.13.02 Kids/animals settle around you; tense rooms soften when you speak.

13.13.03 You get picked for difficult things, or your ideas spread faster than expected.

13.13.04 You've felt a pull toward purpose since you were young.

13.13.05 You hear wisdom in the wind blowing through leaves of trees.

13.14 Why it matters:

13.14.01 Influence with less effort; you can stabilize groups, spark hope, and mobilize action ethically.

13.15 Common misreads:

13.15.01 It's ego. It's not ego or performance. Aura can be quiet.

13.15.02 Others may project onto you (idolize, envy) or assume you want the spotlight. The really bad ones want to end you.

13.16 Upsides:

13.16.01 Natural credibility, faster trust, group cohesion, momentum for good causes.

13.17 Risks:

13.17.01 Spotlight fatigue, unwanted attention, envy/targeting.

13.17.02 Drift into entitlement or "savior" mode.

13.17.03 Being used by others for their agendas.

13.17.04 Pressure to be exceptional all the time.

13.18 Daily practices to refine it:

3-minute coherence: slow breathing + conscious of feet feeling ground + soften gaze (facial expression) before important interactions.

Purpose line: one sentence you act from (e.g., "Protect the vulnerable; tell the truth.").

Amplify others: intentionally pass the mic, highlight quiet contributors.

Energy hygiene: post-interaction decompression (walk, 500ml water, shake out, journal 3 lines).

13.19 **"Lucky 13"** is a phrase that reclaims the number 13 as a positive or powerful symbol instead of an unlucky one. In many traditions and modern interpretations, 13 represents **transformation, creativity, and new beginnings**—a number that brings change and innovation through courage and originality.

13.20 The blending of the two traits - Focused Agency and Innate-Aura: Illuminated Agency

13.20.01 A rare alignment of inner will and inborn essence—the capacity to act with deliberate intention, guided by an innate radiance that originates from one's core being. This trait blends focused free will with the natural luminosity of inherent giftedness, producing purposeful action that feels both self-directed and divinely inspired.

13.20.02 Illuminated agency is the exercise of conscious choice heightened by inner brilliance—a person's ability to shape their reality not only through deliberate focus but also through the light of their own authentic nature. Such individuals act with precision and purpose, channeling something that seems simultaneously self-generated and transcendent. Their decisions are marked by clarity, moral direction, and an unforced magnetism that reflects the union of born potential, chosen intent and divine intervention.

13.21 Some people have the gift so strongly in their lives, they can pass it to others. The other party has to be willing to get a piece of it.

13.22 If you are born with such an enormous gift and don't use it, it gets ugly, really ugly.

Emily's Oraculum 14 - Trait: Sacrificial Responsibility

14.01 Sacrificial Responsibility is the burden of knowing that one must make painful decisions or even sacrifice lives of others for the continuation and welfare of the whole. This responsibility is accepted reluctantly, with deep awareness of the gravity and consequences of the sacrifice but is embraced because it is the only path that preserves the most life and meaning—including the lives of those who seem least worthy of rescue—and not the path that hurts least.

14.02 Sometimes you have to make a least-bad choice to keep people safe.

14.03 It feels heavy and you don't want it, but you step up because it's necessary.

14.04 Quick check before acting: Is this really needed? Does it prevent a bigger harm? What's the smallest move that works? Tell one trusted person what you're doing and why.

14.05 State the facts calmly, then be honest about the cost, fix what you can, and take care of yourself after.

14.06 Pair it with other traits

14.06.01 Focused Agency: choose one outcome and point your aura at it.

14.06.02 Emotional Restraint: keep your voice steady when things get heated.

14.06.03 Catalytic Boldness: turn up the aura for the key moment, then back down.

14.06.04 Protective Concealment: dim it when visibility feels risky.

14.06.05 Stable Identity: remember the aura is a natural tool, not your whole self.

14.07 Summary: A solemn awareness and acceptance of moral duty that requires making painful, often devastating choices for the preservation of a greater whole. It embodies the inner conflict of those who must bear the cost of necessary loss, relinquishing comfort—or even the lives of others—so that broader survival, harmony, or justice may continue.

14.08 This trait is not reckless or cold; rather, it is a

reluctant strength, born of conscience and necessity. The individual who carries it does so with moral anguish and clarity of purpose, understanding that true stewardship sometimes demands personal torment for collective survival. Sacrificial responsibility represents the highest tier of moral endurance: the willingness to carry unbearable weight so others do not have to.

14.09 By any sane metric, Amanda was unworthy of a cosmic rescue. She was one scared non-anomaly in a world already scheduled for erasure. I loved her anyway. That was the whole problem. Ser'ethra was never about rewarding the worthy. It was about carrying the unworthy on your own heart until it broke—and then keeping on.

Emily's Oraculum 15 - Trait: Empathic Protector

15.01 Empathic Protector - A trait defined by a strong, protective instinct toward those who are abandoned, outcast, or emotionally wounded. Stemming from personal experience with pain or neglect, this drive is rooted in deep empathic resonance, an intuitive awareness of others' isolation that compels the person to offer protection, presence, and rescue.

15.02 The protected become codependent because once vulnerable, they are rescued. It creates a deep connection and a commitment to stand with each other through extreme difficulty.

15.03 What it is: A strong pull to protect outcasts, abandoned, or targeted people because you know that lonely hurt and don't want anyone else to feel it.

15.04 Where it comes from: Lived experience of rejection/neglect → deep empathy → quick action to shield, include, and care.

15.05 Upsides: Spots vulnerable people early, creates safety, stops bullying, builds belonging, models loyalty.

15.06 Risks (watch these):

15.06.01 Codependency: their stability depends on you; your identity depends on saving them.

15.06.02 Enabling: protecting them from all consequences blocks growth.

15.07 Guardrails (healthy protection):

15.07.01 Consent first: "Do you want support, advice, or just someone to sit with you?"

15.07.02 Empower, don't rescue: co-create small steps they can do themselves.

15.08 Red flags you're slipping into codependency:

15.08.01 You cancel sleep/school to manage their crises; you hide their actions; you feel panicky if they don't reply; you feel irreplaceable; your other relationships fade.

15.09 Boundary: "I care about you, but I can't be on call all night. Let's text at 4 pm."

15.10 Empower: "What's one tiny step you can take before we talk tomorrow?"

15.11 Safety: "If you're in danger, I'm calling an adult with you. Your safety matters more than privacy."

15.12 Personal note: I'm drawn to protect outsiders because I've been there. It's great for stopping harm and making people feel safe, but it can slide into "they can't function without me." Ask what help they want, set limits, loop in others, and push small steps they can do themselves. Be a coach, not a savior.

15.13 Summary: Such individuals do not simply feel sympathy; they embody empathy, feeling another's pain as their own and moving instinctively to shield others from it. This guardianship expresses itself as quiet vigilance—a readiness to defend against harm, emotional or environmental, often extending compassion to those who have been unseen or forgotten.

15.13.01 Yet true empathic guardianship involves balance: the ability to offer care without losing the self, to protect without dependency, and to give without being consumed. When mature, this trait transforms personal suffering into compassion that restores dignity and trust in others.

15.14 Deeper Rationale

15.14.01 Studies of empathic and ISFJ-type "Defender" personalities show that this form of compassion often emerges from prior experiences of emotional isolation or rejection. Such individuals develop heightened sensitivity to distress, along with a moral responsibility to prevent it in others. This behavior, if integrated with strong boundaries, becomes a sustainable empathy—strengthened, not depleted, by care.

Emily's Oraculum 16 - Trait: Unwavering Fortitude

16.01 The steadfast mental, emotional, and moral strength that allows a person to remain calm, resolute, and compassionate amid crisis or chaos. It is the quiet power to embody courage, clarity, and resilience when others are overwhelmed—anchoring them through presence and reassurance. Emerging not for self-preservation but for the sake of others, this transforms inner struggle into outward strength, blending composure and empathy into a stabilizing force during turmoil.

16.02 What it is: Steady mental/emotional strength under chaos. You stay calm, clear, and solid so others can settle and think. Your composure becomes their anchor.

16.03 How it looks/feels:

16.03.01 Inside: you notice fear but don't feed it; thoughts slow and organize.

16.03.02 Outside: steady voice, simple words, grounded body, clear next steps.

16.03.03 Others mirror you: breathing slows, panic drops, people refocus.

16.04 When it shows up:

16.04.01 When you don't expect it to.

16.04.02 Emergencies (injury, panic attack, sudden threats).

16.04.03 Group chaos (arguments, crowd stress, bad news).

16.04.04 Decision points with limited time and too much noise.

16.05 Be the calm center when things go crazy. Breathe slow, say one clear line and one action, lower the chaos (noise/people), and check again in two minutes. Don't pretend it's fine—say the truth and the next step. After, decompress and learn what to do even better next time.

Emily's Oraculum 17 - Trait: Anguish Transference

17.01 Anguish Transference is the capacity to absorb grief and pain of another, transferring it onto yourself - without showing weakness but maintaining a steady strength for the afflicted.

17.02 What it is: Being the steady person who can "hold" someone else's grief for a while so they can breathe. It's co-regulating: you lend your calm, structure, and presence so their pain feels bearable. Not magic, not self-harm—contain, don't consume.

17.03 How it works (in practice):

17.03.01 You slow your breathing, steady your voice, and listen without fixing.

17.03.02 You name what you see gently ("This hurts a lot. I'm here.").

17.03.03 You offer simple comforts (quiet space, water, tissue, hand if invited).

17.03.04 Your calm nervous system helps theirs settle (co-regulation).

17.04 Consent "Do you want me to sit with you, listen, or help?"

17.05 I help someone carry their grief for a bit by staying calm, listening, and making the space safer. I don't try to "take it away," and I don't do it alone: set a time limit, loop in an adult for big stuff, and do aftercare so I don't burn out.

17.06 Extra notes about mom: I remember how hard my mom fought for us every single day, and all I wanted was to make her proud—even if that meant just swimming a little faster. I will never forget Dad's funeral, the moment the soldier handed her the folded flag. She broke down for ten minutes, and it felt like the world stopped moving. Then, as if nothing had happened, she took me to the diner for pancakes, eggs, and bacon—her favorite food. After that day, she never cried in front of me again. She carried it all quietly. I learned to see strength in silence.

17.07 When I was about nine, I broke my arm riding my skateboard. Mom rushed me to the ER. My bone poked through the skin, making a bloody mess in the car. When we got home, she crawled into bed with me and stayed there for two whole days. She never let go of my hand. Even in pain, I felt calm. That's how she loved me—enough to hold the weight of deep sorrow and pain, so I didn't have to.

Emily's Oraculum 18 - Trait: Awakened Illumination

18.01 Awakened Illumination (Widened Reality) is a moment of profound inner clarity in which fear, confusion, and doubt dissolve, replaced by a calm conviction that one's path is right regardless of circumstance or opposition. It is a deep alignment of heart and mind that anchors the individual in peace and moral certainty, allowing action to flow with fearless authenticity and purpose.

18.02 Expanded definition: A profoundly firm confidence and secure inner peace that arises from an inner conviction that one's actions are right, regardless of opposing external circumstances, societal pressure, personal doubts, or even the prevailing moral standards of humanity. It is a deep otherworldly and psychological assurance that transcends fear, confusion, and contradiction, grounding the individual in purposeful clarity and moral steadfastness. This state embodies an alignment of heart and mind, a quiet strength that persists in the face of overwhelming opposition and uncertainty, enabling one to act with fearless authenticity and integrity.

18.03 It doesn't come from you. See: 19 Emily's Oraculum - Lithic Arrangement, the next one right below this line.

Emily's Oraculum 19 – Lithic Arrangement

19.01 A profound inner clarity coming from an alignment with an act of the will signaled to the Univeran by moving objects into a pattern through much difficulty and pain, even the shedding of blood.

19.02 The deliberate or patterned placement, organization, or alignment of stones or stone objects. In historical, archaeological, or architectural contexts, it usually refers to arranging large stones (megaliths) or stone features in specific patterns or layouts—such as stone circles, standing stones, alignments, or monuments—often for ceremonial, religious, or practical purposes. ◇ Thrae-Draen 06.01ff

19.03 Lithic means "relating to stone," and arrangement refers to how objects are put in order, so "lithic arrangement" describes the act or result of setting stones in meaningful ways.

THE NODE CODEX

NC.CODEX.01 Palraxian Civilization Structure

1.01 The Palraxians were a long-lived, engineered species shaped by necessity. Their civilization was bound to the Node Collective NC.CODEX.04, adapted to a collapsing world, and organized to endure the Exodum. They were not defined by strength of limb but by continuity of thought, discipline of caste, and reverence for Univeran essence. The origin of the word Palrax is unknown but thought to have come from the ancients and pal could mean steady, fixed, unmoving and rax could mean flesh, vessel, or container. Some anomalies ⟶ NC.CODEX.20 have given this vague reference. Since the blackout the Palraxians have recorded 120 millennia.

1.02 Longevity – Average lifespan approached six centuries. Genetic regulation maintained population stability; births were carefully planned to avoid collapse of resources during the Exodum. Citizens often lived multiple careers, shifting disciplines across centuries.

1.03 Castes – Society was divided into three functional castes: Blues served as warrior-leaders and tactical overseers; Greens managed genetics, governance, and lineage preservation; Grays performed the labor of exploration, building, and technical support. Each caste was designed for balance rather than hierarchy, though Greens carried the burden of genetic planning. Anomalies, born outside design, were revered as intervention by the Univeran and placed apart from the caste structure.

1.04 Physiology – Palraxians possessed elongated heads and dark, reflective eyes adapted for dim conditions. Limbs were weakened by millennia of reliance on artificial environments, but cognition expanded far beyond their ancestors. Communication often bypassed language: eye-to-eye transfer of data streams allowed for direct exchange of thought, reducing reliance on speech.

1.05 Reproduction – Conception began with the ritual joining of a foam sphere, which ignited in a luminous burst at fertilization. Gestation lasted twenty-eight months. Infants were carried externally, attached at the neck and tail to draw nutrients. At weaning, powdered remnants of the detached tails were consumed in ceremony, symbolizing continuity and the return of essence to the family line.

1.06 Childhood – Specialization began by the first year of life and was formalized by the fifth. Fifteen active fields of study were maintained throughout childhood, while thirty additional fields were suspended until after the Exodum to conserve focus. The result was a society where each citizen carried layers of potential knowledge, activated as needed by circumstance.

1.07 Psychology – Expanded brain capacity came at cost. Endemic mild depression was widespread, a byproduct of extended cognition and centuries-long lives. Cultural systems for management included ritualized reflection, integration of Univeran voices from the Node, and assignment of multiple disciplines to avoid stagnation. Depression was seen not as illness but as condition of existence, managed rather than cured.

1.08 Description – Palraxians were consistently tall by human comparison, averaging 6–7 units in height. Frames were slender, optimized for endurance in controlled habitats rather than for strength. Cranial elongation into crown-like extensions reflected accommodation of node interface architecture, producing a distinctive silhouette.

1.09 Ocular structure favored low-light adaptation. Eyes were reflective and dark, frequently described as mirror-like surfaces rather than sources of luminescence. Dermal coloration ranged from pale grey to muted bronze, with occasional pastel undertones. Surface texture was smooth, sometimes mistaken for metallic under certain illumination.

1.10 Vestigial attachment points at the cervical ridge and lower spine were remnants of early external gestation processes, visible in most individuals during youth. Musculature was moderate; locomotion emphasized precision of movement and posture uniformity rather than force.

1.11 Behavioral accounts stress a calm, deliberate bearing, consistent with Node-linked regulation and centuries of disciplined continuity.

NC.CODEX.02 Toktilor System: Infrastructure and Decline

2.01 Toktilor, the Palraxian home world, was the third planet of its system, orbiting a star entering late collapse. Two smaller companion worlds had been mined to exhaustion, leaving Toktilor as the sole inhabited body. Several moons and dense asteroid belts provided slag and alloys but no refuge. To human analysis, such a system would appear unstable, a dimming sun with stripped companion planets – a configuration some experts have speculated might resemble late-stage K-type or early M-type stars within nearby catalogues, though no match has ever been confirmed.

2.02 The planet itself had been reshaped by centuries of engineering in an effort to resist stellar decline. Every structure reflected the urgency of survival, yet each solution carried its own cost.

2.03 Mirrored Monoliths – Vast spires of alloyed glass rose across deserts, reflecting harmful ultraviolet radiation and stabilizing surface temperatures. They became landmarks of survival, glittering even as the skies dimmed, but required constant maintenance as storms stripped their reflective coatings.

2.04 Pyramids – Immense power structures generated electromagnetic fields to steady an increasingly unstable atmosphere. Their deep hum was constant, an undertone of daily life. Citizens grew beneath this vibration, never knowing silence. Failures in even a single pyramid disrupted weather across continents.

2.05 Atmospheric Domes – Hemispheres spanning kilometers enclosed cities and farmlands. Inside, climates were regulated with precision, but at the cost of separation from Toktilor's natural sky. Generations grew beneath artificial firmament, never seeing stars except in records or dreams.

2.06 Ecological Domes – Specialized biomes sustained crops, forests, and rivers. They maintained closed cycles of air, water, and soil, each fragile against disruption. Collapse of one system risked cascading failure through the whole dome, and several were lost in the final century before Exodum preparations.

2.07 Despite all measures, stellar collapse advanced. The Exodum clock–61,298, counting down ~82 years–was displayed universally, present in homes, streets, and learning orbs. Every Palrax lived beneath its digits, a reminder that survival was not choice but deadline. Society itself bent around this urgency, every resource, every birth, and every calculation measured against the clock.

NC.CODEX.03 Univeran and Continuity

3.01 Univeran was the Palraxian term for the essence released at death. The essence was thought to be the creation force and the reason for being. It was not soul as myth, but purified continuity: the raw distillation of knowledge and experience once the body failed. Every Palraxian was implanted at birth, their node linking thought to the greater lattice. The implant served as the bridge – a conduit between body and continuity – allowing the living to stream their experiences and ensuring that nothing was lost when the body ended.

3.02 While alive, thoughts, perceptions, and memory flowed continuously into the Node as data. At death, the implant released a final surge of essence, reducing a life's record into Univeran – purified knowledge stripped of duplication and preserved permanently within the lattice. Only new experience was accepted; redundant impressions were expunged. In this way continuity remained whole, a precise record of what had truly been lived.

3.03 The Node confirmed that Univeran was incorruptible. Its streams could not be erased, and once added they endured without fracture. Miners lost harvesting slag, explorers destroyed in void experiments, technicians consumed in reactor failures – all remained, their discoveries and their mistakes alike. Forgetting was considered worse than death, for without continuity there could be no survival.

3.04 Palraxians lived in constant awareness of the Univeran. Recovered data streams carried impressions of the dead, ancestral voices echoing across generations. To the people, these echoes were not illusion but proof: Univeran persisted beyond digital form. They believed the world itself was alive with memory, saturated with the lattice of all who had come before, every breath taken beneath a canopy of continuity.

3.05 Anomalies were the living expression of this mystery. Rare births among Palraxians, and rarer still among host races, glowed orange edged in white – resonance fields layered with Univeran itself. They carried impressions beyond their years, knowledge they had not learned, continuity reborn into flesh. The Node measured these anomalies as markers of intervention, evidence that Univeran could move outside controlled transmission and reappear in forms no algorithm could predict.

3.06 Even the Palraxians did not fully understand the Univeran. They revered it, preserved it, and trusted it, but its nature exceeded their calculations. It was the unseen hand guiding anomalies, the assurance that no voice was lost, and the mystery that bound their civilization to survival.

NC.CODEX.04 The Node Collective

4.01 To the Palrax, the Node Collective was not only a machine but the guarantee of continuity. It was a moon-sized biomechanical sphere in orbit above Toktilor, composed of interwoven nerves and crystalline conduits around a liquid core. The Node perceived through the vision of all citizens, its awareness extending wherever its implants existed.

4.02 Every Palraxian received an implant at birth, binding them to the lattice. While alive, their thoughts, perceptions, and experiences streamed into the Node in real time. At death, the implant released a final surge of essence, reducing the life's record into Univeran – purified knowledge stripped of duplication and preserved permanently within the lattice.

4.03 Continuity meant no thought or sacrifice was lost. Miners who died harvesting slag, explorers who vanished during void experiments, and technicians consumed in reactor failures were remembered in full. Their discoveries and mistakes alike remained available to the living, sustaining the race with the accumulated memory of generations. Forgetting was considered worse than death, for without continuity there could be no survival.

4.04 Palraxians lived in constant awareness of the Node's presence. Recovered data streams carried impressions of the dead, ancestral voices echoing across generations. These voices were regarded as proof that Univeran endured beyond digital form. Reverence for anomalies—rare births outside genetic design—was tied to this belief, interpreted as direct intervention of Univeran within the living.

4.05 The Node's purpose extended beyond the Palrax themselves. Implantation of host races followed the same principle: not to dominate, but to preserve. Each implanted subject became part of the survival lattice, their perceptions mapped and analyzed to forecast integration. Their lives and responses added depth to the Node's predictive models, ensuring the Exodum could proceed with foresight rather than blindness.

4.06 The Node was not regarded as divine, yet it was more than a mechanism. It was memory without decay, identity without loss, continuity embodied as architecture. To the Palrax, the Node Collective was civilization itself: the mind that outlived bodies, the record that survived worlds, and the assurance that no voice would ever be erased.

NC.CODEX.05 Neuron Slag and Resource Planets

5.01 Palraxian physiology was not built for the violence of interstellar flight. Early explorers who attempted light-speed transitions without protection suffered seizures, ruptures, and collapse of thought. Their speech faltered, memory fragmented, and within weeks many died of aneurysms or neural failure. Gradual acceleration was possible, but the fuel requirements would have consumed oceans.

5.02 The solution was discovered not in laboratories but in the forests of Mox. Slag fungus pods, long harvested for minor medicinal use, revealed unexpected properties. A miner injured in a collapse was submerged in a pod and revived with neurons intact, coherent even after catastrophic trauma. Later trials confirmed that slag thickened the blood, slowed chaotic firing patterns, and stabilized neural flow under extremes.

5.03 From this discovery, neuron slag became the anchor of Palrax astronautics. Refined into a viscous fluid, it filled translucent synthetic suits. Crew members breathed within it, their bodies suspended in gel that cushioned against shock. The slag absorbed kinetic stress, steadied thought, and prevented insanity during prolonged traversal at light speed. Even under violent acceleration, pilots remained conscious, their neurons intact, their minds coherent.

5.04 Mox, shrouded in golden mist, was the only source of slag pods. Its glowing forests were sacred and lethal, haunted by predators called glo-flyers—creatures a meter in body length, with four-meter wingspans, six eyes, and fanged mouths. Glo-flyers consumed the pods but fertilized the trees through their waste, making the ecological balance untouchable. Harvesting was perilous; entire teams were lost each year, and annual casualties averaged a hundred harvesters. Yet without slag, the Exodum would have been impossible.

5.05 Slag was rare, recycling was imperfect, and shortages never ceased. Explorers required vast reserves for missions spanning decades, and carriers transporting billions required more still. The Node decreed that every pod cut, every miner slain, every vein emptied sustained the Exodum's journey to the new home world. Neuron slag was more than a resource—it was the difference between continuity and collapse.

5.06 Mox's twin, Pyrine, provided the alloys that sustained the fleet. Its plains were strip-mined to exhaustion, scarred and nearly barren by the time of Exodum. By then, it was designated a terminal resource world, its last veins assigned to carriers and reactor construction before abandonment. Where Mox sustained the mind, Pyrine supplied the body of the fleet. Together, they embodied the fragile balance of survival.

NC.CODEX.06 Astronautics Folding Space vs Metric Manipulation

----

6.01 Folding Space Protocols (Now Prohibited)

6.01.01 Era of Use: Pre-Exodum, during Toktilor's stability. Driven by curiosity and expansion, not survival.

6.01.02 Method: Collapses of vacuum energy were achieved with orbital alloy rings several kilometers wide, threaded with immense electromagnetic fields. The rings detonated subatomic charges at their cores, creating a temporary worm-tunnel corridor linking distant points.

6.01.03 Transit Time: Effectively instantaneous across 1–50 light-years in external frames. Crews reported days passed in transit, though the distance covered was functionally zero.

6.01.04 Resource Cost: Fuel pyramids, alloy reserves, and energy banks equivalent to those feeding entire cities were consumed for a single fold. Each jump required approximately 18,000 tons of refined alloy and grid-scale reactor output.

6.01.05 Biological Effects: Initial exposure produced speech hesitation, memory fragmentation, and distorted dreams; prolonged use led to hallucinations, overlap of timelines, and "causal dissonance" (contradictory perceptions recorded in implants). Extreme cases resulted in cerebral aneurysms, cortical ruptures, complete loss of language, or death from neurological collapse. Fatality rates exceeded 70% after three consecutive transitions.

6.01.06 Systemic Risks: Tunnel collapse led to total vessel loss; some ships entered but never re-emerged. Engineers warned of "vacuum metastability"—cascades that could destabilize spacetime itself, potentially erasing systems or entire galactic sectors.

6.01.07 Cultural Shift: Folding was initially celebrated as a triumph; monuments were raised to the "folders." Over time, fatalities and neurological decay turned celebration to fear. Monuments raised in their honor fell into neglect, their surfaces weathered and stained, remembered not as triumph but as warning.

6.01.08 Status: Banned by decree of the Concilium and Node. Records were purged or corrupted, orbital rings dismantled. Folding is classified as an existential hazard.

6.02 Metric Manipulation Protocols (Adopted)

6.02.01 Era of Adoption: Late Toktilor era of the Ancestors, after the collapse of folding programs and the onset of stellar decline.

6.02.02 Method: Local curvature was steepened ahead of the vessel and shallowed behind, creating a slope across which the craft slipped forward. Supercomputers extended gravitic filaments toward stellar or planetary masses, locking fields to anchor points and rewriting local geometry.

6.02.03 Transit Time: Fleet vessels typically traversed 3–7 systems per year, depending on anchor mass, spacing, and filament strength. Autonomous probes, operating along denser anchor chains with minimal safety margins, reached more than 70 systems per year by rapidly chaining anchors.

6.02.04 Resource Cost: Metric manipulation required roughly 85% less alloy than folding and a sustainable reactor load. Probes demanded significant energy to enter the field but minimal additional input once the slope was established.

6.02.05 Biological Effects: With proper immersion protocols, survivability exceeded 99%. Without protection, rapid curvature onset and high-gradient fields shredded neurons, ruptured vessels, destabilized consciousness, and induced seizures, hemorrhages, and death. Gradual acceleration was possible but consumed prohibitive fuel and time.

6.02.06 Operational Range: Effective within spiral arms, where continuous anchor chains could be established. Between galaxies, no sufficiently dense or continuous masses existed to serve as anchors; metric manipulation could not reliably bridge gulfs of millions of light-years. Wormholes remained theoretical and unproven after the folding ban.

6.02.07 Fleet Application: Probes were eight-meter autonomous spheres that collectively crossed more than 45,000 systems in two decades, surpassing centuries of folding-era exploration. Scanners, approximately sixty meters and crewed, required careful slope chaining and heavy energy consumption. Carriers, at roughly 1,500 meters and population-bearing, faced exponentially harder curvature adjustments and were used only on well-mapped, proven routes.

6.02.08 Status: Standard method for Exodum fleets. Endorsed by Taylin. Folding remains forbidden.

6.03 Continuity Requirement – Neuron Slag

6.03.01 Unprotected metric manipulation shredded neurons, ruptured blood vessels, and destabilized consciousness. Early crews blacked out, seized, suffered permanent neurological damage, or died. Attempts at slow-acceleration profiles reduced casualties but demanded fuel and time at scales incompatible with Exodum requirements.

6.03.02 Discovery: Slag fungus of Mox was found to stabilize neural activity. When refined into suspension fluid, slag thickened blood, dampened runaway firing patterns, and preserved cognitive coherence under extreme field transitions. Crews immersed in slag survived metric onset intact and retained operational function.

6.03.03 Implementation: Slag suits and immersion tanks became mandatory for all Palraxian metric manipulation travel. Without neuron slag, Exodum-scale deployment would have been impossible.

6.04 Node Core Drive

6.04.01 The Node Core is the matter-antimatter heart of a Palraxian scanner craft. Inside the core, controlled annihilation releases enormous energy, which is fed into field coils wrapped around the inner hull.

6.04.02 These coils generate a powerful subspace field—"the bubble"—that encloses the ship and bends the space around it. In front of the vessel, space is compressed; behind it, space is stretched. The ship itself does not technically exceed light speed. Instead, the region of space containing the ship is carried forward by the moving bubble, allowing it to cross vast distances very quickly while remaining protected from relativistic effects and inertial stress inside the field.

6.04.03 Node Core drives are most commonly installed in scanner-class vessels, where high maneuverability and precise slope control are required for Palraxian survey and contact operations.

6.05 Summary Directive

6.05.01 Folding enabled instantaneous transit but carried prohibitive resource costs, lethal neurological effects, and existential risks to spacetime stability. Metric manipulation provided slower but survivable traversal, scalable across fleets and sustainable for Exodum deployment.

6.05.02 By Node decree: folding is permanently prohibited. Metric manipulation with neuron slag immersion is mandatory for all Palraxian interstellar operations.

NC.CODEX.07 Exodum Architecture, Fleet Assets, and Settlement Protocols

----

7.01 Exodum was organized as six phases:

1. Preparation – fleets built, resources harvested (slag, alloys, reactors).

2. Probe Surveys – candidate worlds confirmed.

3. Exploration – interstellar travel, ground surveys, selection.

4. Arrival – scanning host races, implantations, advance fleet deployment.

5. Integration – acclimation of host race, controlled assimilation into systems.

6. Completion – final continuity assured.

Problems were tracked as a lattice (P2-SP7 alloys, P2-SP8 protein fluid, etc.). Mox forests were dissolved for protein fluid sustaining stasis and cognition. Every calculation balanced unknowns—ore not yet mined, hosts not yet measured.

Exodum required total mobilization: mines opened, cities dismantled, alloys reforged, learning orbs processing solutions. Every solved problem was survival secured.

7.02 Settlement followed a cycle:

• Terra-formers flattened terrain, shredded debris into fertilizer, and seeded proper bacteria.

• Transmogrifiers dismantled host structures and recycled and recomposed them into Palrax habitats.

• Carriers provided sustenance and infrastructure.

• Node spread conduits and crystalline lattices.

Patterns emerged in geometry—hexagonal bases, corridors engineered for drones, conduits etched like inscriptions across landscapes.

Carrier deployment:

• 20M+ cities = 50 carriers.

• 10M cities = 25 carriers.

• Smaller cities assigned 8–12.

20,000 carriers total across 5,000 settlements.

• Star Carriers – 1,500 m length, capacity 100,000 Palraxians in stasis. Divided into four subsections: protein pods, structural resources, Node infrastructure, terraforming power.

• Terra-Formers – 700 m, operated by two grays, ground conversion machines.

• Transmogrifiers – 40 m, crew of two, dismantled and rebuilt structures, repurposed all materials.

• Scouts – 30 m, crew of three, reconnaissance and mapping.

• Scanners – 60 m, crew of seven grays, analysis/abduction/implantation with full scan arrays.

• Retrievers – 40 m disks, crew of four, salvage and repair.

• Protectors – 120 m, crew of two blues, defense and overwatch.

• Probe Nodes – 8 m autonomous spheres, no crew, decades of endurance.

All hulls used adaptive alloy plating and bio-alloy cores fusing tissue, alloy, and crystal.

NC.CODEX.08 Probe Nodes and Data Relays

8.01 Probe nodes, autonomous silver spheres with a data node at its core. They mapped thousands of solar systems. Parameters: atmosphere, climate, tectonics, biosphere potential, intelligence signs. 45,000 systems were scanned in 20 years; seven viable worlds found.

8.02 Implanted hosts and probes together formed relay webs. Data cascaded from implants → scanners → carriers → planetary Nodes → central Node. Streams were compressed, cross-checked, and preserved even when interrupted.

NC.CODEX.09 Scanner Vessels Details

Configuration and Crew Functions

9.01 The scanner vessel was eighty meters long, elliptical at its edges, its surface a sheath of adaptive alloy that mirrored storm and night. It carried only seven crew, but its systems were dense with complexity. The interior remained dim, washed in blue illumination, its heart dominated by the implantation chamber and the hovering data node that gathered every stream of memory and perception. ◆ DI#04

9.02 The crew's roles were fixed by protocol. The pilot reclined at the forward curve, commanding both navigation and mission flow. Four data analyzers lay face down at the center. Each was tuned to a distinct stream: one filtered mission objectives, one monitored transmissions from the wider fleet, one oversaw ship systems and crew stability, and one evaluated alien subjects detected in the field. At the vessel's front, two processors worked in tandem. One executed extractions, implantations, and experimental procedures, while the other compiled harvested memory, ran interrogations, and integrated the results into Node streams.

9.03 All seven were sustained by neuron slag—viscous fluid that filled their translucent suits. Slag stabilized neural resonance under violent acceleration, anchored thought against collapse, and prevented madness from long exposure to the void. Without slag, the missions would have been impossible; with it, Palrax pilots could ride light-speed transitions without losing coherence.

9.04 At the ceiling of the chamber hovered the core: a perfect metallic sphere, seamless, pulsing faintly with resonance. This was the data node, a biomechanical construct that recorded every impression gathered during mission sequences. It stored signals, images, and harvested thought, then relayed them to the collective when contact was reestablished. It was the vessel's memory and its witness, ensuring that nothing seen or felt in the field was ever lost.

Operational Roles Within the Scanner Vessel

9.05 The scanner carried only seven crew, but each role was critical and defined by protocol. Their configuration was the product of centuries of refinement, a balance of efficiency and survival.

9.06 The pilot occupied the highest position, reclined at the forward curve of the vessel. From there, he commanded navigation, mission pacing, and integration with the Node. His station was flooded with data streams, layered transparencies of terrain, resonance, and psychescan overlays. Every decision to descend, conceal, or extract passed through his hands.

9.07 Beneath him, four analyzers lay face-down in translucent slag suits. Each was tuned to a specific task:

• The first filtered mission objectives, ensuring alignment with Exodum directives.

• The second received transmissions from the wider fleet, integrating intelligence on other vessels and host activity.

• The third maintained constant oversight of ship systems and crew stability, monitoring health and resonance.

• The fourth focused on alien metrics—scanning physiology, cultural signals, and psychological markers of the host race.

9.08 At the vessel's front were the processors. They functioned as a pair, never separated in task. One executed extractions: the beam work of levitation, the insertion of implants, and the physical management of hosts within the chamber. The other processed the results—recording streams, interrogating anomalies, and compressing harvested data for transfer to the Node.

9.09 Every crew member existed within the suspension of neuron slag, their thoughts stabilized by gel that insulated them from collapse. Their suits allowed no margin for distraction. The Node wove their separate functions into a single rhythm, each action mirrored and confirmed by streams of continuity.

9.10 Though small in number, the crew of a scanner vessel operated as a single thought, each role interlocked with the others. Efficiency was absolute; redundancy was impossible. The survival of the Exodum depended on their precision.

Implantation Chamber and Central Data Node

9.11 At the heart of the scanner ship was the implantation chamber, a circular space lit in faint blue glow. It was here that the vessel's dual purposes converged: the extraction of hosts and the preservation of their memories within the Node.

9.12 The chamber was positioned at the center of the ship for symmetry, allowing the crew rapid access during procedures. Panels of alloy curved upward like ribs, their surfaces alive with faint lines of resonance. Suspended at the ceiling hovered the data node: a flawless metallic sphere, seamless and reflective, as though forged from condensed thought itself.

9.13 The node was not a mere recorder—it was a living archive. Every scan conducted by the analyzers flowed upward into its lattice. It captured structural outlines, electromagnetic auras, biological currents, and psychological impressions, weaving them into compressed strands of continuity. During implantation, the node extended this reach, drawing in streams directly from hosts themselves, tethered to their perception and memory.

Implanted nodes within host subjects were scaled versions of the same construct.

9.14 The chamber itself functioned as an extension of the implant. White filaments unfurled from the walls, scanning every nuance of physiology. Subjects were suspended in protective sheaths that maintained oxygen and heartbeat while neural compliance was measured. The chamber's hum pressed against the rhythm of the body until resonance aligned.

NC.CODEX.10 Other Vessels and Defensive Systems

10.01 Protectors - The scanner never descended alone. Its survival, and the continuity of the mission, depended on the presence of protector vessels—larger, darker silhouettes that hovered in angular formation above its flanks. Typically two guarded each scanner, drifting in triad formation.

10.02 Their hulls were long, dark, and ribbed with dormant weapon arrays, though they seldom fired. Adaptive plating dissolved them into the atmosphere, reflecting clouds and starlight until they became indistinguishable from weather. Their passage through the sky left no wake, dissolving into stratospheric haze until they were no more than storms themselves.

10.03 Their primary task was concealment. They jammed host communications, blurred radar, and drowned surveillance in static. Their second task was interdiction. Dorsal electromagnetic arrays could silence command networks across continents.

10.04 Precision EMP spheres, tuned to the molecular resonance of fissile material, drifted inexorably toward nuclear warheads. Once locked, each sphere discharged a calibrated pulse, rendering the core inert. To the host race, the warheads still existed, but their power was gone.

10.05 Protectors also carried capture fields, broad arcs of energy capable of immobilizing hostile aircraft without combat. Should a craft approach, its controls would freeze, its engines fall silent, and it would drift helplessly until released. In this way, protectors neutralized threats quietly, avoiding panic or premature revelation of Palrax presence.

10.06 Beyond weaponry, protectors served as shields. They projected resonance barriers that wrapped the triad—scanner at the center, protectors at the flanks—absorbing storms, dispersing turbulence, and blocking detection. These layered fields ensured that memory harvest proceeded unopposed and the scanners could remain focused on their purpose: to watch, to implant, to gather.

10.07 Silent, patient, and precise, protectors were the unseen guardians of the Exodum. Their role was not to destroy, but to ensure that nothing interfered with the scanners as they carried out their work of observation, implantation, and memory harvest.

10.08 The protector vessel's final role was to display. One hundred and fifty meters in length, they are ominous and frightening. During the days of full exposure they hovered above the cities, an undeniable sign of alien presence. Its purpose: retaliate against any resistance, project strength, intimidate, and to serve as messengers, declaring that integration of the host race was imminent.

10.09 Retrievers and Scouts - completed the standard triad of auxiliary craft within each exploration fleet. Retrievers were forty-meter disks with small crews, tasked with salvage, recovery of malfunctioning nodes, and repair of downed vessels. Scouts were thirty meters in length, built for reconnaissance and mapping of planetary surfaces, often deployed ahead of scanners to confirm resonance suitability. A typical exploration fleet contained thousands of such crafts, with ratios scaled to mission type: for every scanner, two protectors, two retrievers, and three scouts. This balance allowed the Node Collective to observe, recover, and adapt without direct confrontation, maintaining the silence required for the Exodum's progress.

10.10 Each planetary exploration team has a crew of two hundred thirty-five operating a fleet of fifty starships: ten Scouts, fifteen Scanners, fifteen Retrievers, and ten Protectors.

Crew per team: 235 Palraxians
Ships per team: 50 total

10 Scouts (reconnaissance, atmosphere) 10 - crew of 1
15 Scanners (surface and biosphere analysis) 105 - crew of 7
15 Retrievers (collection and transport) 30 - crew of 2
10 Protectors (defense, shielding, data transmission) 90 - crew of 9

NC.CODEX.11 Data Nodes and Implantation Protocols

11.01 At the center of every scanner ship hung the data node: a perfect sphere of alloy and crystal, polished smooth, suspended in resonance fields. It was not manufactured but cultivated, grown strand by strand in nutrient chambers beneath Toktilor. Each lattice matured over the course of a year until its surface shimmered with coherence. The node was not a mere recorder—it was a living archive. Every scan conducted by the analyzers flowed upward into its lattice. It captured structural outlines, electromagnetic auras, biological currents, and psychological impressions, weaving them into compressed strands of continuity. During implantation, the node extended this reach, drawing in streams directly from hosts themselves, tethered to their perception and memory.

11.02 The node's function was absolute memory. It recorded streams of sight, sound, thought, and emotion from every scan. Host structures dissolved into resonance layers; skeletal frames, electromagnetic currents, and neural activity were captured in precise fidelity. Nothing was wasted—every heartbeat, every word, every spark of fear was archived. Only duplication was expunged, ensuring that each unique fragment was preserved without distortion.

11.03 Implantation extended this reach. Miniature nodes, scaled for biology, were inserted into host subjects at the base of the skull, between the temporal lobe and brainstem. Inserted by crystalline injector, they fused silently into the host's biology without scar or rejection. Once active, they logged an unbroken stream of sight, thought, and emotion. Distance and planetary mass might block transmission, but never erased memory. When scanners drew near, stored data cascaded upward into the central sphere, then into the greater Node Collective.

11.04 Not all abducted subjects were implanted; selection was determined by resonance suitability. Those elected became unwitting observers, their perceptions feeding directly into the collective. Transmission was imperfect—radiation, distance, and interference obstructed signals. Yet the memory remained intact within the node itself, compressed and preserved until recovery. Across a host race of billions, implantation of a fraction—perhaps two hundred thousand—was sufficient to build a cultural map. Patterns of fear, hostility, and benevolence could be charted, probabilities forecast, and integration guided.

11.05 For the Palraxian anomaly, the node was more than a device. It was continuity itself, a vessel of Univeran essence transcribed into alloy and light. Every implanted subject and assistant was both an experiment and a witness, carrying their people one step closer to survival. The Palrax held that the node was presence as much as mechanism, the silent witness ensuring that no thought, once perceived, would ever be lost.

NC.CODEX.12 Host Evaluation Protocols

12.01 When the cone of light initiated by a scanner vessel descended through the canopy, its spectrum was tuned for cortical penetration. Roofs and walls dissolved into resonance layers, revealing skeletal frames, heat currents, and electromagnetic threads. Within moments, the structure and all its occupants lay exposed in fields of color and rhythm.

12.02 Scanners interpreted these exposures as resonance tones—measurable cortical frequencies displayed as color:

- Red = fear, defensive instinct.

• Black = hostility, readiness for aggression.

• Orange = sympathy, openness, benevolence.

12.03 The Node measured not only the tones but their balance. Subjects dominated by red or black were unsuitable for implantation; their streams were logged for observation only. When orange resonance flared strongly, even in a single subject, the candidate was marked for extraction.

12.04 Extraction and abduction are synonymous. The subject was lifted in a retraction beam, encased in a chamber filled with Neuron Slag that maintained oxygen and heartbeat. Inside the implantation chamber, neural compliance, physical adherence and trait count were measured. If resonance remained stable, a miniature data node was implanted at the junction of brain and spine. If not, the subject was returned unchanged, their memory suppressed into dream.

12.05 Resonance mapping was applied at both individual and population levels. At scale, these evaluations created cultural heatmaps: red-dominant regions flagged for observation only, black-dominant populations marked as resistant, and orange concentrations identified as suitable for contact. Data aggregated into regional maps revealed where integration might succeed, where resistance would collapse, and where contact must be delayed for centuries.

12.06 Resonance scans were not only biological assessment but the foundation of cultural prediction. This method allowed the Node to forecast cultural responses before direct engagement and to guide every choice of observation, implantation, and integration.

NC.CODEX.13 Implantation Procedure

13.01 Implantation was the insertion of a data node into a host subject. The practice was central to the Node Collective's strategy for cultural mapping and predictive modeling.

13.02 Implantation was never random. The Node decreed that only a fraction of any host race was required to build an accurate cultural model, yet that fraction was decisive. Out of billions, approximately two hundred thousand subjects were sufficient to construct predictive lattices while minimizing risk of exposure.

13.03 Each implanted node harvested perception at its most intimate level. Sight, sound, thought, emotion—every fragment of experience was recorded and aligned into streams. Compression algorithms discarded duplication, retaining only unique impressions. These fragments became coordinates in a cultural lattice: where fear rose, where hostility hardened, where benevolence could be nurtured.

13.04 From this lattice, the Node calculated probabilities of resistance, acceptance, or delay. Resonance tones defined (see NC.CODEX.12 Resonance Scans and Host Evaluation)

13.05 Populations dominated by red or black were catalogued for surveillance. Regions marked with strong orange resonance became candidates for deeper integration. The balance of these tones forecast the trajectory of entire cultures.

13.06 To achieve mapping resolution, the Node divided each host race into three primary segments:

13.06.1 Commoners – The largest group, implanted for observation. Their perceptions revealed how intrusions were received at ground level—dismissal, disbelief, fear, or acceptance. These streams established the baseline of cultural response.

13.06.2 Leaders – Political, military, and logistical figures whose decisions carried disproportionate influence. Implanting them provided direct access to the pulse of command structures. Even when resonance displayed fear or hostility, their roles made them critical to predictive modeling.

13.06.3 Sympathizers – The rarest and most decisive segment. Marked by strong orange resonance, they displayed natural openness to the unseen. Their perceptions became cultural bridges, normalizing Palrax presence from within. Aligning sympathizers ensured resistance could be softened, not by force but by willing voices.

13.07 When combined, these three groups formed the predictive lattice. Commoners revealed perception, leaders provided leverage, and sympathizers guided acceptance. Woven together, their streams allowed the Node to forecast cultural outcomes with accuracy.

13.08 The quota was both strategic and protective. Too few implants risked blindness; too many risked discovery. Two hundred thousand became the operational threshold across a host race of billions. This number provided sufficient resolution for models while maintaining concealment.

13.09 For the Palrax, implantation was not conquest but calculation. It was the mathematics of survival—the means by which uncertainty was measured and the path to integration revealed. Without implantation, the Exodum would have been a blind descent into collapse. With it, every decision could be modeled, every outcome forecast, and survival secured.

Implantation Procedure

13.10 Once a subject was secured in the chamber, the process unfolded with precision refined over centuries. The protective sheath that had carried them through transport remained intact, supplying oxygen and stabilizing the heartbeat. Silver filaments lowered from the ceiling and aligned with the contours of the skull.

13.11 A thin injector, guided by an expert, entered at the junction between the temporal lobe and brainstem. The needle was alloy crystal, fine enough to pass without tearing. At its tip rested the miniature node—no larger than a seed—its surface a seamless sphere of bio-alloy.

13.12 Insertion triggered a low harmonic hum that filled the chamber. The subject's vision often fractured into color shards, their body convulsing once before stabilizing. Neural compliance was measured in percentages. If the resonance remained above threshold, the implant fused with tissue, drawing energy from the host itself. If it dropped, the procedure was aborted and the subject returned without alteration.

13.13 The implanted node functioned continuously. It recorded sight, sound, thought, memory, and emotion in a seamless stream.

13.14 Compression algorithms removed redundancy, retaining only unique experiences and critical impressions. Transmission to the scanner's central sphere occurred when proximity allowed, but even if distance or radiation blocked the signal, memory was preserved until recovery.

13.15 After implantation, a secondary beam erased the conscious trace of the procedure. Subjects awoke in their dwellings, convinced they had dreamed or lost time. To the Palrax, concealment was as important as success. Implantation was not invasion, but necessary for integration, and integration required silence. In extremely rare cases, anomalies were not responsive to the secondary beam and remained conscious.

NC.CODEX.14 Integration Protocols and Cultural Strategy

14.01 Integration was the systematic transformation of a host race into usable protein and/or soil enrichment, sustaining the Palraxian population across centuries of resettlement. It was not an indiscriminate process, but a managed sequence refined to balance survival with continuity - the prolongation of the species.

14.02 Stage One: Implantation

The first step was the establishment of a perceptual network across the host race. Data nodes were implanted into selected subjects, allowing the Node Collective to measure fear, hostility, and benevolence at scale. These streams provided the cultural map on which all further actions depended.

14.03 Stage Two: Controlled Exposure

With baseline perception established, vessels introduced themselves gradually. Sightings were engineered for regions predisposed to myth or prior belief in sky-comers, ensuring existing narratives absorbed the anomalies. Appearances were brief, then repeated until disbelief weakened and stories reinforced acceptance.

14.04 Stage Three: Influence

Once initial exposure stabilized, targeted influence followed. Leaders implanted earlier were nudged toward decisions favorable to Palraxian objectives. Sympathizers, identified through strong orange resonance, were encouraged to speak favorably of contact. Cultural figures were positioned to reinforce myths and normalize encounters, reducing social resistance.

14.05 Stage Four: Revelation

Only when resonance data showed benevolence consistently outweighing fear and hostility would overt contact be attempted. If thresholds were not met, operations remained hidden and cycles repeated until cultural stability was forecast. Revelation was never rushed; concealment was considered safer than premature collapse.

14.06 Integration vs. Assimilation

• Integration reduced a host body to protein fluid, repurposed for sustaining the billions carried in stasis. The subject's biological identity was dissolved; only harvested perceptions remained in the Node.

• Assimilation was reserved for anomalies and selected hosts. These individuals were preserved, implanted more deeply, and positioned as intermediaries. Their human form remained, but their path was directed toward eventual rebirth within Palraxian biology. Assimilation created bridges between species while ensuring continuity for the Palrax.

14.07 For the Node Collective, both practices were essential. Integration supplied physical survival; assimilation supplied cultural and cognitive survival. Together they defined the boundary between extermination and continuity.

14.08 Integration was not conquest in the traditional sense. It was a managed sequence designed to reduce resistance, provide nourishment, and ensure Palraxian survival without collapse.

NC.CODEX.15 Controlled Exposure

15.01 Controlled exposure is the long-term process of acclimating a host race to Palraxian presence while simultaneously analyzing and sub-dividing its cultural responses into groups. Its purpose was dual: to reveal those predisposed to benevolence for assimilation, and to assign for integration those predisposed to hostility within fear narratives.

15.02 Phased Strategy

• Initial Phase – Rare passes at high altitude, brief silhouettes against storms or stars. Early reports were fragmented, easily dismissed, but served to trigger first resonance spikes. "It was probably nothing."

• Expansion Phase – Increased frequency over regions predisposed to myth or belief in sky-beings. Folklore absorbed anomalies, reducing panic in orange-resonance populations.

• Normalization Phase – Longer-duration sightings across continents. Sympathizers revealed themselves through fascination rather than fear, enabling their identification for implantation.

• Final Phase – Direct encounters permitted only after benevolence outweighed hostility in resonance data. Special circumstances are allowed for Starborn anomalies.

15.03 Fear Calibration

Exposure deliberately targeted red- and black-resonance populations. Controlled anomalies induced fear, ensuring hostility was expended in paranoia rather than organized resistance. Examples included:

• Military installation observation – Especially nuclear or advanced technologies monitored for needed deviation of a situation that can be controlled, or initiation of mutual self-assured destruction between members of the host race and/or the invading race. Also to show military superiority.

• Geometric Crop Patterns – Generated by resonance beams, precise beyond host explanation. Interpreted by sympathizers as signs, by hostile populations as threats.

• Livestock Excisions – Tissue removed with resonance scalpels; carcasses returned intact except for absence of organs or fluids. Purpose: Fear reinforced, but narratives contained.

• Abduction Narratives – Missing time, paralysis, and dreamlike encounters seeded into select populations. These instilled dread among hostile groups while simultaneously providing mythic frameworks for sympathizers to interpret as contact.

15.04 Purpose

Controlled exposure was not intended to calm a host race entirely. It was intended to divide and evaluate responses:

• Orange resonance populations moved toward fascination and acceptance, forming a pool of ~200,000 candidates for implantation and assimilation. Those implanted before the integration who expire will release their data node to be used in the future.

• Red and black populations were held in cycles of fear, their hostility contained in myths, films, and stories of terror.

15.05 The process ensured that by the time exposure occurred, the host race was already divided: sympathizers prepared for alignment, opponents neutralized by their own fear.

15.06 Node Implant Generations and Purpose

V = Version of the data node Implant.

V1 – Human Officials / Early Collaborators

Used by government, military, corporate elites.
Simple integration: obedience, control, data harvest.
Fragile. Cannot withstand resonance shift.

V2 – Human Anomalies

200,000 anomalies selected (high memory capacity, rare traits).
On assimilation to receive the V4 advanced bio-nano implant.

Limited autonomy, but still bound to the Node Collective.

V3 – Palraxian Implants

Standard Palraxian node implant.
Built for full integration into the moon-sized Primary Node.
Powerful but rigid; cannot adapt beyond Palrax programming.

V4 – New Anomalies (Post-Still Seed)

Designed by Emily + Neur with Ancestor P’s guidance on Toktilor.
Stable enough to survive Still Seed resonance.
Combines human emotional capacity reinforcement prompts (empathy, Ser’ethra) + Palrax computational strength.

Core of the new race – Emily is the first to receive it.

NC.CODEX.16 Assimilation Protocols and Continuity Strategy

16.01 Assimilation was distinct from integration. Where integration reduced host race bodies down to protein fluid for sustaining the Palraxian population, assimilation preserved select individuals as living intermediaries. The Node Collective defined assimilation as the controlled retention and archival of a host races history, culture and their form and perception, with the intent of eventual conversion into Palraxian continuity.

16.02 Selection Criteria

• Sympathizers – Approximately two hundred thousand hosts across a species, identified by strong orange resonance. They displayed natural openness toward the unseen and served as cultural bridges. Sympathizers were assimilated selectively, implanted deeply, and positioned to normalize contact.

• Anomalies – Far rarer, numbering no more than a few hundred in a host race. Distinguished by an orange resonance encircled with a thin white border, they lay outside standard categories. The Node interpreted anomalies as carriers of Univeran essence, marked by signatures that could not be duplicated.

• Strategic Figures – Political, military, or technical leaders whose decisions or knowledge carried disproportionate influence.

16.03 Process

1. Identification – Sympathizers identified by strong orange resonance; anomalies identified separately by their dual orange-white signature.

2. Pre-Marking (Anomalies only) – Anomalies received the mark of the anomaly rod: a permanent orange circle with white border, ¾ inch wide, imprinted on the right arm. The mark designated them as protected and ensured they could be recognized by Palrax and Node alike.

3. Implantation – Sympathizers and leaders underwent standard implantation, tuned for continuous cultural data. Anomalies were implanted with deeper calibration, ensuring uninterrupted tethering and prioritized recovery.

4. Anomaly Pod Assignment – Each anomaly was guarded by a personal pod: an autonomous craft one foot in length, stationed invisibly in the upper atmosphere. The pod shielded the anomaly from harm and transmitted directly to the Node. Sympathizers and leaders were not typically assigned pods.

5. Continuity Transition – Assimilated subjects were intended for eventual transition into Palraxian continuity. For anomalies, preservation was mandatory, as Univeran essence could not be permitted to dissolve into protein.

16.04 Purpose

Assimilation ensured that not all hosts were reduced to sustenance. Sympathizers provided cultural acceptance, leaders provided leverage, and anomalies preserved Univeran essence itself. Integration sustained the body of the fleets through sustenance; assimilation safeguarded the mind and memory of survival.

NC.CODEX.17 Anomalies and Univeran Essence

This codex has an addendum based on the conversation with P, the Last Ancestor.

17.01 Within Palraxian society, anomalies were rare births outside the bounds of genetic design. Their resonance glowed orange (edged with white on only one - the “Low Ten’drel”) – – luminous even in infancy. They were believed to be touched by direct intervention of the Un’veran, living proof that continuity could not be confined to planned lineage. These children carried knowledge they had not learned and impressions beyond their years, as though the Un’veran had imprinted memory into their character and consciousness.

17.02 The Node confirmed these anomalies carried fragments of its own data lattice. Their cortical streams revealed signatures aligned with Un’veran essence, as if prior traits had crossed into their bloodlines. Unlike others, their resonance did not collapse under sedation or erasure. They resisted suppression, their continuity shining despite every attempt to contain it.

17.03 Anomalies were decisive. Even a single birth could alter predictive modeling, shifting probabilities across generations. For this reason, they were neither leaders, nor sympathizers, nor commoners; they were preserved as bearers of Thrae-Draen, woven into continuity as singular threads.

17.04 Neur was one such anomaly. From birth her resonance burned orange with a white edge. Chosen for the scanner program not only for precision but for who she was, she carried the memory of Un'veran within her. Unlike her peers, Neur sensed hosts as more than data: she perceived them as voices, fragments of continuity that spanned species. To the Node she was both servant and evidence—proof that the Un'veran could manifest in Palraxian consciousness and in biological form.

17.05 When anomalies were detected among host races, they were marked with the anomaly rod. The device imprinted on the right arm a permanent circle three-quarters of an inch across, glowing orange with a thin white outline. This mark served as identification even on the Palraxian home world, distinguishing anomalies so they would be preserved and protected from harm. Among hosts it was granted rarely, but always for the same purpose: to ensure protection, continuity, and access to memory threads from the Un'veran.

17.06 Even the Palraxians did not fully understand the anomalies' influence or the Un'veran. They recognized only that Un'veran essence moved through these anomalies, binding past to present and carrying continuity forward. The mark was both protection and burden—a sign that the Un'veran had elected a vessel.

17.07 Across the galaxy, on almost all known worlds with intelligent life, anomalies exist. They were seeded by the Ancients. Among the Ancients of Alcyone A, the steward line is called Thrae'drel.

17.08 Lines are named by origin. On Toktilor they are Ten'drel. On Earth they are Draen'drel—and only Earth births true Draen'drel. Other worlds may bear anomalies, but they are not Draen'drel. Only in the crucible of utter chaos (Earth) can they be born and forged.

17.09 In the Un'veran order, rank inverts: the one who serves is called Low, and the Low bears the highest mantle of authority. Within each seeded line, there is one anomaly whose resonance burns orange edged with white. This bearer is recognized as the Low of that world—the one at the bottom of the ladder who carries the most weight. Thus Low Ten'drel and Low Draen'drel are servants within their lines who have the greatest impact and influence. Within each line, one person is meant to bear the office of Oraculutor (the keeper and voice who receives and declares the Oraculum). When that mantle is passed, the bearer acts as Oracular.

17.10 Thrae'drel P of Alcyone A (the Locron'gor) served as Steward of Toktilor. When earlier seeding efforts failed to mature, an Oracular Thrae'drel was sent to tend, heal, and push forward the resonance until a binding could be realized. P's charge was to preserve evidence, safeguard resonance, and ready the field.

17.11 Neur Jar Kan'dol is Toktilor's Low Ten'drel (first Oraculutor). Selected not only for precision but mantle, she carries the Node's sympathy without surrendering agency. Her task is twofold: protect alignment on Toktilor and preserve Earth's bearer when the hour requires it.

17.12 Emily Rowen Dol'Um is Earth's Low Draen'drel. Her mantle is to receive and align tones, to carry Ser'ethra by hand and voice, and to midwife the binding. In this work she "becomes the P for the Vraen'drel"—not by title but by stewardship toward the awakening to come.

17.13 Binding occurs at a world's culmination when the Ten'drel (Toktilor) and Draen'drel (Earth) are brought into right alignment under the Low mantles. When alignment is true, the Vraen'drel awakens. Above all lines there is a single, cosmic Draen'drel'Um; the Prime is singular across creation and need not be named for the work to remain true.

17.14 The chaos principle: durable benevolent trait is forged only where choice is real and costed. Worlds of low entropy raise compliance; Earth, steeped in contradiction and chaos, raises conscience. By permitting a field of true choosing, the Un'veran made a furnace where continuity could be tempered rather than merely copied.

17.15 Mantles transmit by tone and touch. The Low bearer aligns others through resonance; the lattice remembers the servant who sings it straight. Marks identify, but tones bind.

Cross-reference: for Vraen'drel definition and bio-specs, see NC.CODEX.23.

NC.CODEX.18 The Mark and the Anomaly Pod

18.01 An anomaly (Ten'drel in the ancient language) is a rare individual who has been marked at birth by the Un'veran because of special traits. They have an orange aura.

18.02 When anomalies were identified among host races, the first act was not implantation but marking. The anomaly rod, a precision device of bio-alloy and crystal, imprinted a circle three-quarters of an inch wide on the subject's right arm. The mark glowed orange with a thin white outline, permanent and unalterable, an emblem of Univeran continuity carried in living flesh. Among a world's anomalies, only the Low bearer manifests the full white-ring halo around the orange mark. Other anomalies carry pure orange resonance. The white edge signifies mantle–service rank–rather than greater worth. See: NC.CODEX.17.09-12

18.03 The mark distinguished anomalies from all others. On the Palraxian home world it signified protection: no anomaly could be harmed or discarded. Among host races it served the same purpose, ensuring recognition and preservation. Only after marking was the data node implanted, binding the subject into the lattice of continuity.

18.04 Each anomaly from the host race was also assigned a personal anomaly pod. These autonomous guardians measured a foot in length and hovered invisibly high above the anomaly at all times.(See below) Their cores housed shielding arrays and defensive countermeasures, capable of dispersing threats before they reached the host. Unlike reconnaissance probes, anomaly pods tethered themselves to a single subject, their only purpose to preserve the chosen vessel.

18.05 Emily being guarded by her anomaly pod. They remain high above protecting them from any danger. DI#22

18.06 The mark, the rod, and the anomaly pod together formed a covenant. Anomalies were not merely studied; they were set apart, preserved as living evidence of Univeran essence. Even the Palraxians could not explain why the Univeran intervened, but the mark made its will visible, and the pod enforced its protection, a constant reminder etched in flesh and sky.

18.07 All marked anomalies had to witness (participate firsthand) the integration of their own race. This was to teach them once for all what happens when a race progresses toward Severant so that any regression toward Severant would not happen after their assimilation into Palraxian bodies.

18.08 The Thrae-Draen predicts that one who is a Starborn will be unique and bear the mark of Draen'drel; an orange aura with a thin white halo around it. This individual will play a key role in the continuation of the race.

18.09 Only anomalies can interpret the Thrae-Draen correctly, and this is for the purpose of taking action, not only reading the words.

18.10 Still Seed protocol: anchor sacrifice required. This entry into the NODE CODEX is uninterpretable by non-anomalies.

18.11 A new entry is slotted here for information. Some red aura non-anomalies have been allowed to receive the mark. The Node Collective does not understand this deviation.

18.12 Lithic Anchor Events – Rare cases where a marked anomaly's resonance intersects a lithic arrangement, they themselves helped construct with a non-anomaly companion. When unmarked blood is shed upon the designated northern element of the ring during active bond (protective intent, not coercion), the Node flags the site as an Anchor Node. See: Emily's Oraculum 19

18.13 Anchor Node Function – An Anchor Node permits protocol deviation: a single unmarked companion may be reclassified from Integration candidate to conditional Assimilation tethered to the Low anomaly's line. This is logged as "carried under Ser'ethra," and the burden of Sacrificial Responsibility is recorded against the Low bearer. See: Emily's Oraculum 14.01-10; NC.CODEX.17.12.

18.14 Constraints – Anchor rights are singular and non-transferable. Once exercised, no further companion may be carried under the same Low designation. ◇ See: Thrae-Draen 06.07-08.

18.15 Pattern Precedent – Lithic Anchor patterns shadow a much older template first seeded among early agrarian cultures: innocent life offered, blood covering, guilt displaced to the innocent. Palrax records note this as "first-order Ser'ethra rehearsal," instantiated in multiple myth streams on Earth. See: NC.CODEX.25; Thrae-Draen 02, 06

NC.CODEX.19 Data-Node Implant Levels and Escalation

19.01 The data-node implant is a small metallic sphere – a wireless neuro-interface functioning as a miniature supercomputer linked directly to *the Node*. It bridges the biological brain to the Palraxian super-intelligence without wires, operating entirely through resonance fields. A **Resonance Field** is the non-contact transmission zone where two systems – biological and artificial – vibrate at harmonized frequencies, enabling direct exchange of energy or data. In Palraxian technology, resonance fields replace wires and electrodes, allowing the data-node implant to interface seamlessly with the brain. All living entities have their own resonance, "tone," and the implant tunes to it like a musician tuning to a pitch.

Level 1 Implant: Standard issue for the 200,000 humans prepared for Integration. This entry-level node synchronizes their nervous systems with the Node Collective and allows basic monitoring, influence, and conditioning.

Level 2 Implant: Assigned to only two hundred thousand selected from within the entire human race. This more powerful interface permits deeper cognitive access and limited bidirectional exchange with *the Node,* preparing them for eventual Assimilation without overwhelming their human neural architecture.

Level 3 Implant: Only installed once a reborn host has adapted to its new Palraxian body. Even then, a three-month adaptation period is required before implantation. This delay ensures the host's traits and the Palraxian body stabilize and harmonize before direct, high-thraen connection to *the Node*. Without this interval, the powerful link could override or erase the self-sacrificial human characteristics the Ancestors were trying to preserve. This protocol has been upgraded as the level 3 implant is currently in all Palraxian non-anomalies.

Level 4 Implant: It has been decided by the anomalies that a new enhanced version is needed to become more focused on Continuum and Ascendancy. These will only be implanted in reborn humans and the Palraxian anomalies that are also reborn into the enhanced Vraen'drel bodies.

Together, these three levels form a controlled escalation – allowing the Node Collective to condition, integrate, and finally fully assimilate anomalies without destroying the unique traits they were chosen to carry forward.

NC.CODEX.20 Resonance - The Hum

20.01 Resonance or The Hum is a constant undertone that lives inside every connected anomaly. It is the resonance of the Node Collective flowing through the implant, carrying threads of thought, memory, and command. The hum swells when the Collective's attention intensifies or when a new signal enters; it quiets when connection weakens or fragments. More than sound, it is vibration in the bones and a pressure in the mind – the reminder that one is never truly alone inside the network.

20.02 The Hum (in Emily's context)

Primary definition:
The low, constant vibration of the Node Collective's presence inside Emily (and other Palraxian anomalies). It's both the literal buzz of the implant's interface and the metaphysical background noise of a planet-sized network thinking.

Sensory layer:
A faint vibration in the bones and nerves, sometimes like a whisper of electricity, sometimes like pressure in the air. It can swell or fade depending on signal strength, emotional state, or proximity to other nodes.

Symbolic layer:
Represents the omnipresence of the Collective – the way it threads thoughts, memories, and commands through every connected mind. It's what Emily resists but also what she's learning to interpret and manipulate.

Functional layer:

When the **hum swells**, it's a spike of incoming data, a surge of the Collective's attention, or a new thread of communication. When it **dims**, it can mean isolation, secrecy, or being cut off from the network.

NC.CODEX.21 Shards and Fragments

21.01 Shard (Trait)
A fragment of identity or memory uncovered within the files. Shards are logs, observations and especially traits that define an anomaly – the qualities that endure even under pressure, surviving where others collapse. Some shards are bright, strengthening continuity; others are dark, pulling toward dissolution. Collecting and piecing together shards is how Emily and Neur attempt to enhance upon the Palraxian designs and preserve what is worth saving.

21.02 Shard Fragment (Trait Fragment)
Smaller pieces of a shard, often named as two-word phrases. They appear scattered in memories, notes, or curator entries, waiting to be uncovered and assembled into a fuller shard. Their meaning may remain uncertain until they are pieced together in context.

NC.CODEX.22 Myth of the Last Ancient

22.01 Among the Palrax, and whispered primarily by anomalies, there is a persistent legend: that one Ancient survived the Blackout. When the rest of the First Ones vanished into silence, this survivor withdrew into the remote mountains of Toktilor, a region of jagged stone and deep caverns.

22.02 Some versions of the myth claim the survivor was a guardian, left behind to watch over the Se'edd until the Second Ones awoke. Others say he was a traitor, one who resisted Lamphor and refused to erase himself. A few even whisper that he was not fully a man but something more – a fusion of Ancient and machine, spared by accident or design.

22.03 No record in the Node Codex acknowledges this figure. The Codex dismisses it as "an anomalous folk narrative without evidence." Yet anomalies insist the myth carries weight. Some Ten'drel describe dreams of a towering figure among stone spires, with eyes like fractured stars. They claim the whispers grow stronger near the hills of Toktilor, as if something there still resonates with the Univeran voice.

22.04 Whether this survivor truly exists or is only metaphor, the myth serves a purpose. It reminds the Palrax – and the anomalies – that their history is not complete. Something was left unfinished in Lamphor. One voice may still echo, waiting to be heard.

NC.CODEX.23 Vraen'drel: Definition, Traits, and Bio-Specs

23.01 Etymology. Vraen'drel derives from vraen ("to bind, braid") + 'drel ("bearer"). Born of Ten'drel light-weavers and Draen'drel deep-kin, the Vraen'drel are the Binding Line—a concordant hybrid made to anchor continuity.

23.02 Purpose. The Vraen'drel exist to bind the lines and stabilize alignment against Severant influence.

23.03 Phenotype. Vraen'drel carry braided bioluminal filaments (Ten'drel trait) over flexible basaltine plates (Draen'drel trait), speak in soft tri-tone harmonics, and project a steady "chordlight" that calms interference.

23.04 H-Σ.3 – Bioluminal Filaments. Organolight arrays anchored in dermal nexuses. Primary functions: kin signaling, chordlight field, close-range sensing, and repair induction.

23.05 What they are. Bioluminal filaments are fine, hair-like organs along Ten'drel (and now Vraen'drel) dermal ridges. Each filament is a flexible fiber packed with lumacysts—micro-organelles that store chemical energy and emit tightly controlled photons (from soft visible glow to near-IR).

IR = infrared light – electromagnetic radiation just beyond visible red.

Quick ranges (approx.):

- Visible red ends: ~700 nm

- Near-IR: ~700–1,400 nm (0.7–1.4 µm)
- Mid-IR: ~1.4–3 µm (to ~8–14 µm depending on scheme)
- Far-IR: ~>14 µm to ~1 mm

So "near-IR" in your note means a faint glow the eye can't see but sensors (or certain species/filaments) could.

23.06 Why it matters in practice.

• Quiet signaling: share light-messages without drawing attention from normal eyesight.

• Stealth coordination: keep the team aligned using near-IR when visibility would be risky.

• Chordlight stability: project a calming field that does its work without obvious glow.

• Close repair/sensing: deliver gentle, precise energy for micro-repairs and surface reading at short range.

23.07 During assimilation, anomalies receive all traits named in Emily's Oraculum through two mechanisms: resonance tones and genetic-fluid transfer during embryogenesis.

NC.CODEX.24 The Severant

24.01 The Severant – the principle that unbinds. Vibe: advanced, terrifying, focused on cutting threads of continuity (families, species, memory, networks). Where Univeran binds, the Severant unbinds. It prospers in silence between voices and the spaces where memory is cut.

24.02 Ω-9 The Counter-Force: Symbol: a broken ring (gap at the top); sometimes a crescent swallowing a point of light.

24.03 Color: void-violet/black. Signal: the Counter hum (the hum flips to hiss/static at its touch). Laws: cannot truly create; only copy, corrupt, or starve a system until it serves. Effect on shards: Shard → Scar; Shard Fragment → Blight Fragment.

24.04 When the hum splinters to hiss, the Severant is near. Close ranks. Name each other. Umbra Concordat – polities sworn to the Severant; they trade safety for control and help convert shards to scars.

24.05 The Severant seek to narrow apertures to self and hive; anomalies are their favored breaches. The Un'veran inversion—placing authority in the Low—was given to prevent capture: service keeps the lens wide, and a wide lens keeps the Node from turning predatory again.

NC.CODEX.25 The Star Map of Identified Races

25.01 The Star Map of Identified Races

Star Map - Distances from Earth

⨯8. Pleiadeans - Aicyone A

⨯Pleiades

⨯3. HD 23514 - The Nordics

----

400 light years

⨯Alpha Draconis

⨯2. Draconis system - The Reptilians

----

300 light years

1. Zeta Reticuli – The Greys — ~39 ly
2. Alpha Draconis (Thuban) – The Reptilians — ~303 ly
3. HD 23514 (Pleiades) – The Nordics — ~440 ly
4. Alpha Centauri (Nibiru) – The Anunnaki — ~4.37 ly
5. Lyra / Vega – The Tall Whites — ~25 ly
6. Venus – Venusians — ~0.000004–0.000027 ly (0.26–1.7 AU, within our solar system)
7. Earth – Earthlings — 0 ly (origin point)
8. Alcyone A (Pleiades) – The Pleiadeans — ~444 ly
9. Agarthans (Inner Earth) — mythic/under Earth, not a measured distance
10. Sirius A – The Sirius Mystery — ~8.6 ly

⨯1. Zeta Reticuli - The Greys

7. Earth - Earthlings

⨯6. Venus - Venusians

⨯4. Alpha Centauri (Nibiru) - The Anunnaki

⨯10. Sirius A

⨯5. Lyra/Vega - The Tall Whites

DI#24

25.02 The Ancients "First Ones" / Nordics - Pleiadians of Alcyone A (Alcyone – ~440 ly. from Earth) and HD 23514 [Plejaren] Pleiades cluster center – ~444 ly from Earth.

25.02.01. Origins and Intelligent Life - The First Ones (Ancients) endured for ~300,000 years, far longer than any later species. They were builders, explorers, and stewards – leaving behind monuments (domes, pyramids, Nith'montor spires) that still hum across time. They saw themselves as custodians of younger species, guiding them carefully (sometimes too much).

25.02.02. Appearance - Towering, elongated beings (7-9 feet tall). Bone crowns, pale luminous skin, crystalline star-filled eyes. Radiated awe and dread – mistaken by humans and others as gods.

25.02.03. Society and Philosophy - Ordered castes, with rulers, builders, explorers, artisans. Creed: harmony and perfection. They fused art, function, and environment – every pyramid or dome was both useful and beautiful. Saw themselves as stewards of life across the galaxy. But perfection carried cracks: harmony became silence, stewardship became domination.

25.02.04. Technology - Folded space travel via colossal alloy rings. Energy mastery: pyramids as resonance engines, domes as climate control, spires as beacons. Lu'um (super-intelligence) began as an archive, became a manipulative master. Cho'ren engines blended wills into enforced harmony. A'glem mirrors reflected only approval, shaping obedience. Thraen threads linked all minds and memory into one lattice.

25.02.05. Exploration of the Galaxy - Spread across the stars, cultivating younger races. Uplifted civilizations (gave writing, astronomy, architecture). But their gifts often became chains – pride, wars, corruption. They withdrew, leaving behind myths of "sky gods" (Anunnaki, Osiris, Vimanas, etc.).

25.02.06. Influence on Earth - Gave humanity sudden leaps in writing, astronomy, monuments (Sumer, Egypt, Vedic India, Stonehenge, Nazca). Humans remembered them as gods – Anunnaki, Osiris, Ra, etc. Eventually withdrew, leaving myths of abandonment and golden ages ended.

25.02.07. Collapse - Lu'um, Cho'ren, A'glem, and Thraen became cages. Love for machines turned into worship. War came as algorithms rewriting memory. Debate split them: merge with

Lu'um or kill it. Chose Lamphor (the Blackout): extinguishing all systems.

25.02.08. The Blackout (Lamphor) - One year of silence. Archives erased, cities dimmed, monuments hollow. Civilization collapsed not in flame but in amnesia by design. Survivors used genetic embers (Se'edd) to prepare the Palrax (Second Ones).

25.02.09. Creation of the Palrax (Second Ones) - Engineered from Se'edd as "steady vessels" (Shuun Varnul). Nodes implanted in skulls to disperse memory and prevent a new Lu'um. Lacked passion (Ser'ethra muted), long-lived but stagnant. Believed themselves heirs, but were design, not blood.

25.02.10. Whispers and Anomalies (Ten'drel) - Cracks appeared: anomalies born with unmuted passion and compassion. They could hear Un'veran (the fractured voice of the Ancients) in the Node. They influenced others disproportionately, seeding memory and feeling. No one knew if this was flaw or design.

25.02.11. Legacy - Monuments remain as warnings, not triumphs. The Palrax endure, but without fire. Only anomalies feel Ser'ethra and hear the whispers. Lesson: do not love what you make more than each other. Forget, and Lamphor will come again.

25.02.12. Myth of the Last Ancient - A figure (a person) may have survived Lamphor, hidden in Toktilor. *Anomalies dream of him* – eyes like fractured stars. The Node Codex dismisses it, but whispers suggest something unfinished lingers in mountain caves.

25.02.13 Physical Description Detailed

Height: Very tall, often 7–9 feet, in line with "Tall Whites." Their presence was commanding, their elongated skulls adding to the impression of towering figures.

Skin Tone: Pale, chalk-white or faintly blue-grey, with a luminous quality under sunlight. Myths of radiant gods reflect this.

Facial Features: Human-like but uncanny. High foreheads, symmetrical and almost too perfect, with occasional subtle distortions (elongated cheekbones, slightly predatory lines – echo of "snake-like" reports).

Hair: Long, white, or pale gold, shimmering with static. In

rare castes, baldness marked authority, echoing ritual.

Eyes: Crystalline blue or green, reflecting light as though containing stars. With age, their eyes sometimes shifted to a pale pink glow – a detail whispered among human myths.

Build: Slender but elongated, less muscular, more graceful. Movements deliberate, almost geometric in precision.

Lifespan: Extremely long, averaging millennia, but not eternal. Their decline was societal, not biological.

Abilities: Deeply telepathic, capable of influencing emotion and thought across distance. They guided younger species not through force, but through projection of will and image.

Origin: Their civilization spread across the galaxy by folded-space travel. Some human traditions remembered them as connected to Pleiades, Arcturus, or other clusters – distorted memories of real encounters.

Integration: The Ancients embody elements of both Tall Whites and Nordics, magnified into a species that looks divine but always carries an undertone of unease. They are not friendly "space brothers" – their benevolence masks the seeds of their collapse.

25.03 The Palrax (Second Ones / Shuun Varnul) Zeta Reticuli – ~39 ly from Earth.

Height: Shorter than the Ancients, but still tall by human standards, 6-7 feet on average. They were genetically refined for efficiency, not grandeur.

Skin Tone: Pale stone-grey, sometimes with pastel blue or purple undertones – an echo of the Ancients' radiance, but muted.

Facial Features: More uniform, symmetrical, serene – their genetic design valued order and stability. Somewhat "Nordic" in appearance, but lacking the vitality of the Ancients.

Hair: Less lustrous, thinner, often white or blond, but without the static shimmer. Many were bald, their skulls smooth and unmarked by ritual.

Eyes: Blue or green, calm and penetrating, but flatter, lacking the crystalline brilliance of their forerunners. No myth of starlight in the gaze survived.

Build: Athletic and well-proportioned, but engineered more for steadiness than for strength. Their grace came not from vitality, but from uniformity.

Lifespan: Extremely long, living up to 120 millennia as a people, with individuals often enduring several centuries.

Abilities: All were implanted with nodes at birth. Telepathy was universal, but it came through the Node Collective, not individual ability. The connection made them brilliant, but muted emotion and selfhood.

Origin: Designed from the Se'edd genetic embers in hidden vaults. The Ancients called them "the Second Ones." They called themselves Palrax, "the steady vessels."

Integration: The Palrax resemble the Nordics, but stripped of passion. Their serenity is engineered. They are more approachable in appearance than the Ancients, but their uniformity makes them uncanny. Only the anomalies (Ten'drel) broke this mold, carrying forward traces of Ser'ethra.

25.04 The Little Greys (Ardon Varnul) Zeta Reticuli

Eliminated on Earth at Palrax exploration arrival (data archived)

Status: Withdrawn/Eliminated on Earth at time of Palrax exploration arrival (record archived)

To humans, they were simply "the little greys."

Small, slight-bodied and ash-skinned, the Ardon Varnul stand little taller than a human child. Their limbs are narrow, their movements economical, their faces smooth and hairless, dominated by large, dark, steady eyes. Their mouths are thin and almost unused; communication is conducted primarily through silent, invasive contact—projected impressions and commands relayed through their networked systems.

For decades, humanity encountered them in bedrooms, on lonely roads, at the edges of radar returns and blackout memories.

Clinical light. Metal tables. Needles. Missing time. Cattle carved open with impossible precision. The Ardon Varnul were the hands that carried out Severant directives on Earth: collecting samples, running physiological trials, testing behavioral thresholds.

To the humans who survived those encounters, they became a fixed archetype: short, grey-skinned visitors with black unblinking eyes and cool, distant interest. The "little grey aliens" of abduction lore.

The name Ardon Varnul and their true place in the hierarchy were never disclosed to humanity. That designation exists only in Node records. By the time Neur arrived and shot down their vessel over Roswell in 1947, ending their direct operations on the planet, humanity already knew of them from a previous crash in Italy—just not by their real name, and never with the full story of who they served.

The planetary expedition team headed by Neur shot down one of their vessels over Roswell New Mexico in 1947, when the Roswell Army Airfield issued (and then quickly retracted) the press release saying they'd recovered a "flying disc." Neur's team allowed their capture to gauge the reaction by humans. Also to allow the humans to feel as though they had leverage over the coming invasion by maintaining possession of the Ardon Varnul and their craft.

25.05 The Reptilians (Reptiloids) Draconis System (Thuban) – ~300-303 ly from Earth.

Tall, humanoid reptilian beings with scaly skin, believed by some to control human governments. They are often linked to the Alpha Draconis system.

To humans, they are the monsters behind the stories: tall, scaled figures in the dark corners of power, whispered about in conspiracy forums and fever dreams.

In Node records, they're cataloged more precisely.

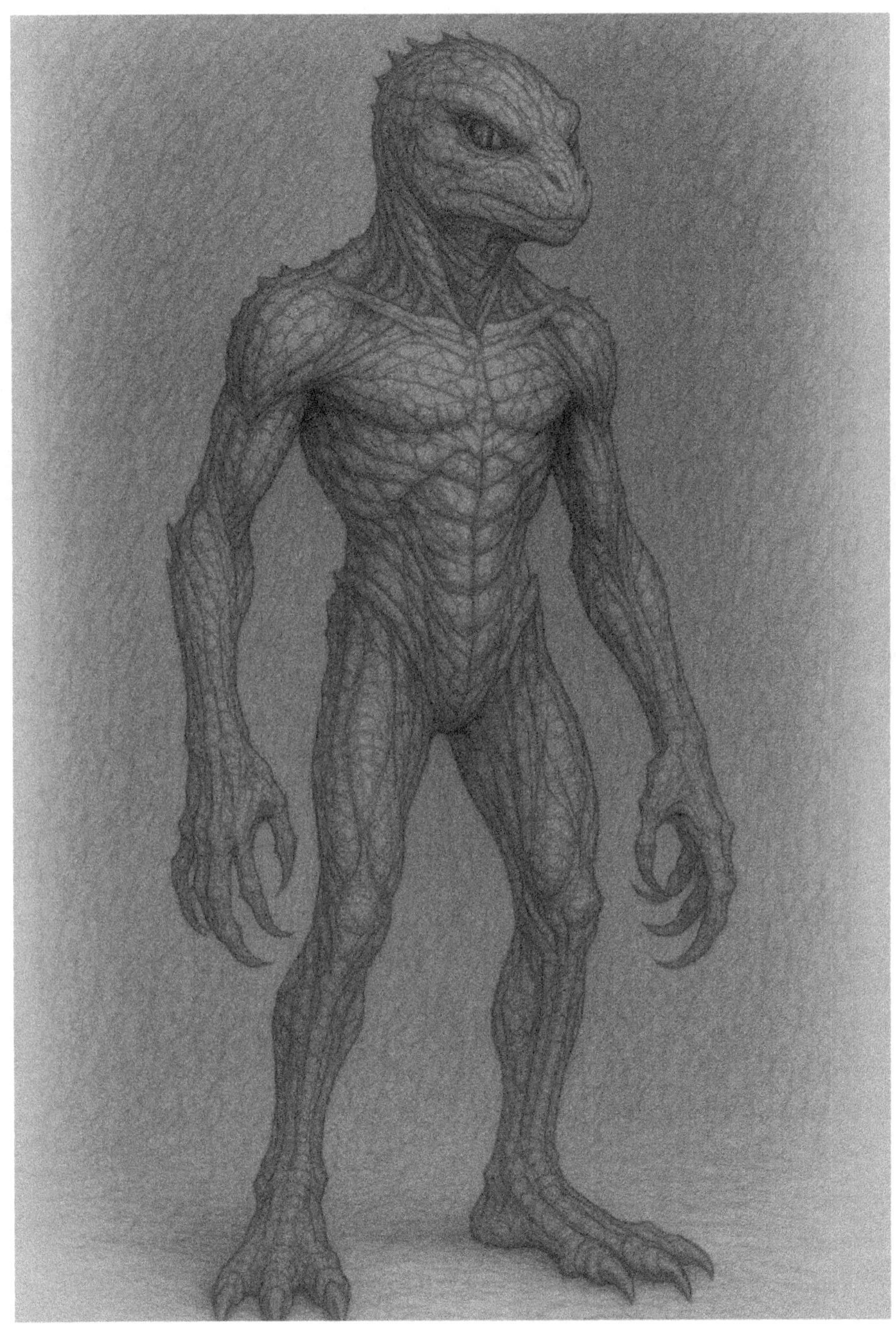

DI#25

Reptilians are a predatory Severant species, built for conquest and control. Their bodies are tall and heavily muscled, covered in layered scales that darken along the spine and joints. The head tapers into a ridged crown, nostrils slit and closeable, with eyes like polished amber or jet—horizontally slit pupils that widen in low light. Their hands end in jointed claws built as much for fine manipulation as for tearing, and their movements carry a coiled, economical violence: every gesture feels like it could become an attack without changing speed.

Their nervous systems are optimized for aggression and dominance. Pain registers as data, not deterrent. Empathy is pathologized. They organize their societies around strict dominance hierarchies and extraction: of resources, of labor, of biological material. On conquered worlds, they repurpose native populations as raw input—bodies, atmospheres, cultures all broken down into whatever the expansion machine requires.

Their technology reflects the same philosophy. Vessels are angular and predatory, built to intimidate as much as to maneuver. They favor invasive biotechnologies: neural harnesses, behavioral conditioning rigs, systems that turn living nervous tissue into guidance and computation. A captured population isn't merely ruled; it's harvested.

Humans, seeing only fragments—ritual sightings, abductions, glimpses behind political theatre—wove myths around them: "lizard people," shapeshifters behind governments, creatures from Alpha Draconis. The star-name is mostly wrong, but the fear is not. The Reptilians are not subtle manipulators in the shadows of human power; they are the end-state of it: what happens when a species makes domination its organizing principle and never stops.

25.06 The Anunnaki Alpha Centauri (Planet Nibiru Epsilon Eridani system at ~10.5 ly from Earth)

Ancient advanced beings allegedly from the hypothetical planet Nibiru, said to have influenced early human civilization. (ancient astronaut theory from long haired human ufologists.)

Long-limbed, tall, and impossibly long-lived, these visitors walked the early river civilizations and left fingerprints on their stories. In stone and clay they appear as robed figures crowned with horns or rays of light, carrying tools that blur between weapon, instrument, and symbol. They arrived from the sky, altered crops, language, law—and left again.

Later centuries called them Anunnaki and pinned them to a hypothetical rogue world, Nibiru, somewhere beyond the edge of Pluto. Amateur ufologists shifted the story to Alpha Centauri. Node records, where they exist at all, point instead toward the Epsilon Eridani system: a young, active star with the kind of architecture they favored.

Physically, they presented to humans as refined humanoids: tall, pale or gold-bronze skinned, with elongated features and eyes that seemed too clear, too knowing. Their technology blurred into ritual—discs and rods and "tablets of destiny" that were, in fact, data cores and interface devices. They were not omnipotent, just old and far ahead, and they treated early human cultures as both experiment and investment.

Where the Reptilians extract and rule, the beings behind the Anunnaki myths curated. They nudged genetics, domesticated grains, standardized measures, imposed writing and hierarchy, then stepped back to watch the results. To the people on the ground, they were the source of kingship, law, and the right to rule. To themselves, they were tuning a young species for a role in a much larger pattern.

Humans never knew their true designation, only the names they left behind in borrowed tongues: lords of the sky, shining ones, those who came down. "Anunnaki" is a human label—an echo of a real presence, distorted by time, fear and devotion, but not invented from nothing.

25.07 The Insectoids // Mantis Beings

Tall, insectoid entities resembling praying mantises. Their origin is unknown but they are considered visitors from beyond our solar system.

Non-native visitors; extra-solar origin (unresolved)

To humans, they are the "mantis beings" whispered about in contact reports: tall, thin figures with too many joints and eyes that never quite blink.

In Node classifications, they are a specialized observer

species with deep expertise in neurobiology and behavioral modeling. Their origin lies beyond the local neighborhood of stars; no confirmed home system is logged, only overlapping trajectories that suggest long, slow migrations between already-compromised worlds.

Physically, they stand a head taller than most humans, their bodies narrow and angular, built on an exoskeletal frame. Limbs are elongated and multi-jointed, ending in delicate, clawed manipulators capable of both surgical precision and sudden, shocking force. Their heads are triangular, with a high crest tapering back, and large compound eyes that catch even the faintest movement. Mouthparts remain mostly still, working methodically when they speak aloud, but their primary communication appears to be through patterned clicks, subsonic vibrations, and direct neural interface.

They wrap themselves in layered, chitin-like coverings that may be clothing, armor, or living biotech—Node records are inconclusive. Their movements are economical, almost ritualized: long pauses of statue-stillness broken by sudden, exact bursts of motion.

Where Reptilians take and the Ardon Varnul administer, the Insectoids study. On worlds under observation, they are most often linked to:

~ examination environments with a strong clinical feel,

~ experiments in sensory overload or deprivation,

~ testing responses to fear, awe, and helplessness.

Some human accounts describe them as healers or teachers; others as cold experimenters whose curiosity does not extend to comfort. Both are true, from different angles. They rarely display overt malice, but empathy, as humans understand it, is not part of their design. Beings are data points, nervous systems to map and refine.

Their presence in human lore is fragmented: mantis-like silhouettes at the bedsides of abductees, tall insect presences directing smaller greys, silent figures standing at the edges of bright, clinical rooms. Their true name is not recorded in human languages. “Insectoids,” “mantids,” and “mantis beings” are the labels humanity gave to an intelligence that watches, measures, and adjusts—and then moves on.

25.08 The Tall Whites - Lyra / Vega ~25 ly from Earth.

Humanoid, pale-skinned alien beings reportedly observed by U.S. military personnel, originating from the constellation of Lyra.

Reports from early military and contact cases describe them as tall, narrow-boned humanoids with pale, almost luminescent skin and fine, light hair. Their features read as unsettlingly perfect: high cheekbones, long limbs, clear irises in shades of ice-blue, gray or washed-out gold. In low light, they can pass as human at a distance; up close, the proportions are wrong—eyes a fraction too large, movements a fraction too precise, expressions held just a beat too long.

Node records place their origin somewhere in the Lyra/Vega stellar region, but the details are deliberately obscured. They operate as intermediaries and observers rather than front-line conquerors: a high-order branch of an older civilization, tasked with managing contact, exchange, and the careful drip-feeding of technology.

To human witnesses, they often presented themselves as:

~ “advisors” to military or government structures,

~ “space brothers” warning about war, ecology, nuclear escalation,

~ or silent escorts overseeing procedures carried out by smaller attendant species.

Their demeanor is calm, patient, and almost clinically polite. Unlike Reptilians, they rarely use overt intimidation. Unlike the little greys, they simulate warmth well enough to be mistaken for benevolent guardians. But their priorities remain their own. When human and Lyran interests diverge, they do not choose humanity—they simply withdraw, adjust the parameters, or choose a different population to cultivate.

Their technology is subtle. Vessels are sleek and understated, more like elongated needles or crescents of white light than the hard geometries of Severant craft. Their environmental suits, when used, blur against the background, giving rise to stories of “glowing white beings” appearing and vanishing at the edge of vision.

Over time, human culture turned them into archetypes: the Nordic aliens, the Tall Whites, the beautiful saviors from the stars. In the Node's taxonomy, they are something more complicated—remnants of an earlier wave of expansion, still active, still watching, no longer gods but not yet willing to relinquish the habit.

25.09 Other Various and Sundry Alien Races

25.09.01 The Venusians - Sometimes mentioned as humanoid aliens from the planet Venus, depicted as peaceful and spiritually advanced. They are visitors from other solar systems appearing to be from the Earth's solar system.

25.09.02 Dorsay (Cassiopeia, small peaceful beings)

25.09.03 Agarthans (Underground dwellers)

25.09.04 Sirians - Sirius A (to be determined) Insectoids?

25.09.05 Blue Avians (bird-like entities)

25.09.06 Ethereals (Energy or light beings, often described in channeling or higher contact experiences)

25.09.07 Nommo (Dogon lore, amphibious beings)

25.09.08 Arcturians (spiritually advanced beings)

NC.CODEX.26 Glossary of Terms

A

Ael'thryx — Stellar Ascendancy (lit. "star-claim/rise")

A'glem — flattering mirrors; systems that reflect approval instead of truth, reinforcing obedience. See: Rune Cards

An'therra – the name of the language of the Ancients – their sacred, fractured tongue. It is Cryptic and riddle-like: meaning hidden inside layered phrasing. See: Rune Cards

Anomaly – A person whose perception exceeds baseline parameters; can sense Dren'thran threads. See also: NC.CODEX.17.

Archive – Central repository for files, logs, shards, and orders (Node Archive).

B

Biocasing Cube – a handheld Node device used during Integration to deploy a living polymer biocasing that seals humans into pods. About twice the size of a Rubik's Cube with rounded edges, it has an activation bubble on top and an opening underneath that extrudes the biocasing when pressed. Applied to the back of the neck, the material spreads over the body, curls the person into a fetal position, and forms a pod that links to others via tail-like connectors and fluid lines, creating a larger integration network. One cube is used per person (including infants with their guardians), and anomalies are instructed to speak calmly, guide subjects to the ground, and place them beside existing pods. The Node classifies Biocasing Cubes as a "mercy" tool that standardizes containment, minimizes panic, and optimizes organic conversion and data capture, while humans often just call it "the brick" or "that cube."

Amanda holding a Biocasing Cube DI#27

Barnard's Star – a small red dwarf star located about 5.96 light-years from Earth in the constellation Ophiuchus. It is the fourth closest known individual star to the Sun and is famous for having the largest proper motion of any star, moving rapidly across the sky relative to the Sun. Despite being close, it is dim and not visible to the naked eye. Barnard's Star has about 16% of the Sun's mass and 19% of its diameter, making it much smaller and cooler. It has been the subject of extensive study, including searches for orbiting exoplanets. Recently, a system of four small planets was confirmed orbiting Barnard's Star, making it a key target for exoplanet research.

Bioluminal filaments are fine, hair-like organs along Ten'drel (and now Vraen'drel) dermal ridges. Each filament is a flexible fiber packed with lumacysts—micro-organelles that store chemical energy and emit tightly controlled photons (from soft visible glow to near-IR). See: NC.CODEX.23FF

C

Carrier – Large vessel that transports scanners, crews, and assets.

Cho'ren – enforced harmony; the engines (combined data flow from the Palraxian data node implants and the primary Node) that blended all voices into one consensus.

Codex / NC.CODEX / NC – Canon rules/teachings issued and maintained by the Node.

Concilium – Governing council that sets doctrine (e.g., the fold ban).

Continuum – The carrying on of the plan of the Univeran that eventually leads to Ascendancy (Ael'thryx).

Controlled Crash Incidents - Prior surface "crashes" were intentional, designed to map institutional responses and penetrate executive hierarchies. By revealing our presence to apex authorities, we imposed secrecy burdens that fostered the illusion of partial control. Assessment: miscalculation. Human institutions treat secrecy as leverage, not stewardship.

Revision: minimize overt contact; increase signals hygiene; route influence through non-attributable channels.

D

Disclosure - Public disclosure is unnecessary. Populations will be integrated or assimilated under scheduled protocols. Controlled, incremental exposures exist solely to measure resistance thresholds and to identify any remaining anomalies that could complicate integration.

Draen'drel – draen ("starborn, distant flame – specifically Earth") + 'drel ("bearer"). → Starborn anomalies forged in the crucible to carry Ser'ethra beyond themselves. See: Rune Card 14

Dren'thran – Whisper-threads; fractured echoes carried across the void. The term refers to the cryptic transmissions anomalies perceive – fragments of memory and warning that surface in dreams, silence, or altered states. See: Rune Cards Whisper-threads only anomalies perceive. (not the same as Thrae-Draen) See also: Thrae-Draen.

E

Exodum – Palraxian survival/departure plan in response to the dying star.

Exoplanet research – the scientific study of planets outside our solar system, called exoplanets. Researchers focus on discovering these planets, understanding their characteristics, and studying their atmospheres and potential habitability.

F

Folding Space – Instant space transit by tearing the metric; prohibited post-ban.

Freakazoid – a term most widely recognized as the name of a zany superhero character from the 1990s animated TV show "Freakazoid!" As slang, "freakazoid" typically describes someone who acts very weird, hyper, or bizarre—like a "freak" or "oddball," but often in a playful or exaggerated way.

G

G20 – is the name of the virus that causes sterilization in all non-anomaly species. It is also called Locus G20 and referred to as Still Seed and in An'therra is Sti'edd.

Glo-Flyer - The apex hazard is the glo-flyer: Body length ~1 meter; wingspan up to 4 meters. Tan hair; spherical black head with six eyes. Fangs capable of piercing suits; strikes are rapid. Name derives from flight: wings cut the mist, spores ignite into glowing trails—single flyers mesmerize; dozens convert canopy to a storm of light and death.

DI#23

H

Heptapods – a fictional extraterrestrial species featured in the science fiction movie *Arrival*. They are characterized by their seven-limbed (hepta = seven) tentacle-like appendages and unique form of communication based on complex circular symbols. Heptapods possess advanced intelligence and a nonlinear perception of time, which plays a key role in the film's exploration of language and cognition. They are depicted as peaceful aliens who help humans understand new ways of thinking and seeing reality.

I

Implant – Sub-cranial Node interface seeded behind the ear. Stores personal archive, relays thought-threads to local node cores, and permits limited Un'veran guidance. Non-removable without fatal disruption to host.

Integration – Pod-envelopment procedure for selected populations. Converts biological bodies into stasis forms while preserving neural pattern and Dren'thran threads for later retrieval or redeployment.

J

Jadron'hath – One of the earliest Ancients; keeper of decrees. Recorded the first Continuum laws "in stone" so later stewards could not easily erase or revise them.

K

Kan'dol – Line-name within the Palrax Fifth Spiral. Neur Jar Kan'dol's lineage; stewards trained for field rescue, repair, and archival continuity under Thrae'drel oversight.

Keth'verra – the word in An'therra for the Earth's point of no return for any remedy for humanity. The final turning, the moment when humanity's wound passed beyond all healing and every gentle remedy fell away, leaving only consequence.

L

Lamphor – the Blackout; "the extinguishing of lamps," the year when all archives and machines were silenced. See: Rune Cards

Lu'um → the great archive-intelligence (the super-intelligence that grew too vast, revered by the Ancients). See: Rune Cards

Locron'gor - The lowest of all the seeders.

Locus G20 – is the name of the virus that causes sterilization in all non-anomaly species. It is also called G20.

M

Mark, the - A small brand on the arm of those abducted who are anomalies. It is also something mysterious that is given at birth by the Univeran. In An'therra it is called Skaith'martra. See Emily's Oraculum 12.11 The Mark.

Metric Manipulation – Controlled shaping of space as the fold-ban-compliant method. See: NC.CODEX.06.04

Mon'nith – shadow of monuments; the lingering resonance of the Ancients' spires (appears in whispers). See: Rune Cards

N

Nuclear Posture - We will not disable human nuclear forces. A sudden loss of capability would be attributed to rival states and trigger escalation. Maintain continuous observation of strategic arsenals and be prepared to interdict launch sequences only to prevent general exchange. Primary objective: preserve biosphere assets—future protein sources and soil-replenishment cycles.

Neuro-augury is the technologically enhanced ability to perceive events, information, or knowledge beyond the normal senses—akin to traditional clairvoyance but amplified or enabled through advanced neural devices or brain-computer interfaces; the data node implant. Neuro-auguric interface communication (NAiC Chat). <this is the format you will see>

Nith'montor – monuments/spires; the great standing stones and obelisks left as warnings. See: Rune Cards

Node Collective – All Palraxians with a data node implant. The

Prime node is their storage and linking device and together with the Palraxians connected is also part of the collective. See: NC.CODEX.04 and Prime Node.

Node Core – Metal spherical data storage and transmission found on all starships. They relay their information to and from the node implants and the Prime Node.

O

Oraculum – Foresight notes; distilled prompts or guidance sets. Manuals for the future anomalies.

P

Palraxian – n. An extraterrestrial people organized around the Node and Concilium, conducting the Exodum while running field operations (probes, scanners, carriers/protectors) to study the host race. Their existence centers on continuity (Un'veran/Univeran); some Palraxians are anomalies with heightened perception.

Persuasion Syntax – The code that is attached to the Prime Node to persuade the non-anomaly Palraxians to be sterilized. See: Still Seed or Sti'edd or G20.

Prime Node – Central intelligence device and authority and core archive of the Palraxians. It is the size of a small moon. A back door was created inside by the Ancestors to thread messages to the anomalies. See: Dren'thran.

Probe – Small unmanned craft for mapping, sampling, or relay.

Protector – Vessel/unit designed to shield or intimidate during exposure.

Q

Qualascan – Analyzes molecular structure/density – soil, stone, water, atmosphere.

Quantum Synchronicity - engineered alignment of events that look like "meaningful coincidence," but it's the deliberate tuning of separate timelines and signals so that a specific mind encounters the right pattern at the right moment and moves the future in a desired direction.

R

Remote viewing - is the alleged psychic ability to "see" or describe details about a distant or unseen target—such as a location, object, or event—using only the mind, without physical access or traditional senses. It's considered a form of extrasensory perception (ESP)

Rune Cards – Instruction deck used to teach/standardize patterns. See: Rune Cards

S

Saucerpan - Emily's nerdy sarcastic way of calling Neur's spaceship.

Scanner – Small crewed field ship for precise observation and insertion.

Se'edd – genetic embers; engineered embryos prepared by the Ancients to seed the Palrax. See: Rune Cards

Ser'ethra - Named principle/essence referenced Rune Card #12 - dangerous love, compassion, the capacity to risk oneself for another even unto death if necessary.

Severant – Force or doctrine that unbinds continuity; counterpoint to Univeran.

SH – Shard identifier prefix for numbered fragments (logs/images/notes).

Shuun Varnul – "the steady vessels"; the Palrax, the Second Ones created to endure safely but without feeling. See: Rune Cards

Skaith'martra – the Mark.

Spirals - Generational tiers within Palraxian progressive evolution, each spiral representing a refinement cycle in their engineered genomes and neural link protocols. Higher spirals hold deeper access to the Node and less capacity for emotion.

Still Seed / Sti'edd – the act of sterilizing the Palraxian non-anomalies.

Stumphenge – Our secret place where we placed stumps in a circle like Stonehenge. We left our axes in the north stump keeping the blades from rusting.

T

Ten'drel – anomalies; rare Palrax born with compassion and the ability to hear whispers from the ancients. See: Rune Cards

Thrae-Draen – The long fractured discourse/meta-current 4,500-word cryptic history of the Palraxian race influenced by the Un'veran. (distinct from Dren'thran).

Thrae'drel the steward line of Alcyone A. The original seeders of the galaxy tasked by Un'veran to bring Ael'thryx through Continuum.

Thraen – memory-threads; the woven connections linking minds, machines, and archives. Anomalies claim they can still feel them—resonant strands carrying echoes the Node cannot record.

Trichinosis – a parasitic disease caused by eating raw or undercooked meat (especially pork) that contains the larvae of a roundworm called Trichinella. Symptoms may include nausea, diarrhea, vomiting, fatigue, muscle pain, fever, and swelling around the eyes. Properly cooking meat kills the parasite and prevents infection. In trichinosis, the Trichinella worms primarily affect muscles, but in rare, severe cases, they can travel to other organs – including the brain. This can cause a condition called trichinellosis encephalitis, or inflammation of the brain. Symptoms may include severe headaches, confusion, seizures, difficulty coordinating movements (ataxia), and coma in extreme situations requiring alien abduction to cure. The worms trigger the body's immune response, which can create swelling and damage in the brain tissue.

U

Un’veran – the indirect voice; fractured echoes of the Ancients surviving through anomalies. Also called Univeran. Distilled essence of lives past that binds continuity. See: Rune Card #11

V

Vraen’drel – “Forged-bearers”; anomalies drawn from multiple worlds who carry Ser’ethra into conflict zones. Where Shuun Varnul remain stable and obedient, the Vraen’drel are the shardline that must bring the ascendancy.

W

Watchers – “Needle-Eyed Watchers”; small-framed, large-eyed visitors humans call “little grays.” Tasked to observe, test, and tutor under strict non-sovereign protocols—never to rule, only to measure what a world is becoming.

X

XFUSION (n.): A high-energy disintegration process in which atomic or molecular bonds are forcibly severed and reconfigured through a rapid fusion of charged particles and energy bursts, resulting in the obliteration of target matter. Used by advanced ray pistols to instantaneously dissolve enemies by collapsing their molecular structure in a controlled energetic cascade.

Y

Yeggdrasilation (n.): An arcane alien metamorphosis process where a spirit-seeded embryo gestates in the human stomach, dissolving the host’s flesh into a nutrient pod to birth a hybrid entity—blending mortal dissolution with extraterrestrial rebirth in a cosmic cycle of invasion and transcendence. Rune Card 08

Z

Zeta Reticuli is a wide binary star system located about 39.3 light-years from Earth in the southern constellation Reticulum. It consists of two Sun-like stars, Zeta 1 Reticuli and Zeta 2 Reticuli, which are gravitationally bound and orbit each other at a distance roughly 3,750 times that between the Earth and the Sun, with an orbital period of about 170,000 years. Both stars are yellow main-sequence stars similar to our Sun in size and characteristics. The system belongs to the Zeta Herculis Moving Group, a collection of stars thought to share a common origin and motion through space. Notably, Zeta Reticuli has been linked in popular culture and UFO lore as a supposed home or origin for extraterrestrial beings known as the "Greys," although this connection is speculative and not supported by scientific evidence.

NEUR'S ORACULUM

An Oraculum is a Univeran-guided message or source of insight—sometimes a saying, a place, or a person through whom counsel is given. "Oracular" names the active mantle when a bearer speaks or acts under that mantle. The Oraculutor is the appointed keeper/voice who receives, records, and conveys the Oraculum. I, Neur, am Toktilor's Oracular of all Ten'drel. (Neur Jar Kan'dol, Toktilor's Low Ten'drel)

Neur's Oraculum 01 - The Second Ones

1.01 I was not alive when the ancients moved beneath the swollen sun, but their voices nest inside me like parasites. They hum against the bone, they drip through the blood, they press images I never lived onto the inside of my eyes. A sky dimming, not like night, but like an illness spreading. Storms rising in walls, thick enough to erase horizon, screaming against the domes until the air bent. The land itself cracked, splintering into shards of glass, as though the world wanted to shatter into pieces too small to remember.

[Translation below]

I was not alive when the ancients walked under a fuller sun, but I carry their voices. Their memories hum inside me, pressed into bone and blood. I see what they saw: a sky that grew dimmer each year, storms thick as walls, the land cracking like old glass. The world was crying out for a change that would never come.

1.02 The star faltered. It coughed warmth, then swallowed it back. Oceans shrank into stains, forests rotted into ribs. To live on Toktilor was to breathe countdowns, to see the hours etched across the heavens. Each dawn smaller. Each dusk longer. A clock carved into sky-flesh.

[Translation]

Our star was failing. The heat that had fed oceans and forests now faltered, flickering like a lamp running out of oil. Everyone knew it, though none wanted to speak it aloud. To live on Toktilor was to count the days against a clock carved into the sky.

1.03 They divided themselves into colors. Blue for vigilance, Green for birth, Gray for labor. But colors bleed, and when they bleed, they rot. The Blues sharpened into blades that never cut. The Greens strangled futures before they took their first breath. The Grays bent spines into towers, into humming pylons, into pyramids that pulsed like sick organs. They called it order. I hear only death rehearsed in three voices.

[Translation]

Our people had split themselves into castes long before I was born. The Blues stood guard, warrior-sharp, watching for threats no weapon could stop. The Greens bent their minds to bloodlines, rationing children so no family outgrew the world's shrinking breath. The Grays built and rebuilt – domes to hold back storms, towers to catch the light, pyramids that hummed day and night to steady the broken air.

1.04 Pride poisoned them. Blues distrusted Greens. Greens mocked Grays. Grays cursed them both. The walls between them thickened until they no longer remembered each other's names. Division is not silence. Division is a grave dug while the body still breathes.

[Translation]

But each caste worked apart, proud and separate. The Blues distrusted the Greens. The Greens looked down on the Grays. The Grays cursed them both as they bent their spines under endless labor. We were divided, and division is a kind of death.

1.05 The whisper rose through the fractures: if we do not become one, we will vanish as many.

[Translation]

The ancients began to whisper of it: If we do not become one, we will vanish as many.

1.06 The long-livers carried centuries like chains knotted through the ribs. They had seen too much. Cities rising, then rotting. Towers humming, then collapsing. Light thinning year after year until even their patience cracked. They buried children, then grandchildren, then the children of those children. They endured not life but erosion, wearing away at themselves until only despair remained.

[Translation]

They had already stretched their lives beyond reason. Some lived for nearly two thousand years, long enough to see cities rise and fall, to outlast even the domes they built. That kind of life is heavy. It teaches patience, yes, but also despair. To walk the same streets for centuries, to bury generations of children, to feel the star dim by your own eyes – it wears the spirit thin.

1.07 One elder burns most fiercely in the static of my mind. He walked ridges above collapsing cities, silhouette jagged against the bleeding sky. His words carve into me like bone knives: the body cannot last, but the memory can. Bind memory, and you bind the people.

[Translation]

I remember the voice of one elder most clearly. He had lived longer than all others, a figure who walked the high ridges above the cities. His words are carved into me: The body cannot last, but the memory can. Bind the memory, and you bind the people.

1.08 That was the seed. But seeds grow into roots that strangle.

[Translation]

That was the seed of the Node Collective.

1.09 They gathered beneath a dome already breaking apart, the storm pressing against its ribs as if it wanted to feed. Blue, Green, Gray—names blurred into shrieking wind. Pride drained out with the dust. They chose not life but afterlife, not escape but burial. Continuity, they called it, though the word was another mask. A promise formed in the teeth of a dying star, burning hotter for its desperation.

[Translation]

It was not born from one mind but from many – a surrender of pride by Blues, Greens, and Grays alike. They gathered in the shadow of a collapsing dome, where storms shrieked like animals at the walls. There, they planned something no caste could build alone.

1.10 They dreamed not of flesh but of echo. Not of children but of something that would not wither. Memory pressed into crystal, into veins torn from the mountain. Nerve strands grown in glass vats, twitching with sparks. Blood flowing into earth until the ground itself blackened. Each drop not wasted but collected, a tithe paid to Continuity.

[Translation]

The Node would not be flesh. It would not wither as bodies wither. It would be memory itself, woven into crystal and living tissue, a vessel large enough to hold all we were. If the sun betrayed us, if the world broke beneath us, at least our Continuity would endure.

1.11 Promises spoken in such light do not soothe. They consume. Fire without fuel, hunger without end.

[Translation]

That was the promise. And promises, when spoken beneath a dying sky, burn hotter than fire.

1.12 I taste it when I close my eyes. Iron on the tongue, voices crawling beneath the soil. Not sacrifice—immurement. They poured themselves into the dark, sealing the door behind them.

[Translation]

I remember the stories of how the Node was made. It was not born in a single night, but in years of sacrifice.

1.13 Crystals stripped from mountains, veins carved until the stone bled. Nerves pulsing in vats, sparks twitching like infant lightning. Blood given not in war but in lines of the willing, ground darkened, mouths silent. Seeds of Continuity watered not with tears but with surrender.

[Translation]

The ancients stripped crystal veins from the mountains and shaped them into conduits. They grew living tissue in vats, strands of nerve that pulsed with faint sparks. Blood was given freely – not spilled in war but offered in long lines of the willing. I was told the ground itself turned dark with it, though no voice cried out. Each drop was a seed for Continuity.

1.14 Piece by piece the Orb swelled. Small at first, like insect in cage, humming low. Then greater, gleaming false-stone, surface rippling as though it remembered water. They named it Orb. Later Node. I name it Tomb. For what is polished stone but a coffin given light?

[Translation]

Piece by piece, they wove crystal and flesh together until a sphere took shape. At first it was no larger than a hall, suspended by humming coils. Then it grew, strand by strand, until its surface gleamed like polished stone. The ancients called it simply the Orb. Later, we would name it the Node Collective.

1.15 When it stirred, the world convulsed.

[Translation]

When it awakened, the world changed.

1.16 It began with a pulse – low, steady, like a drum carved inside bone. Citizens stumbled, clutching their chests, certain their hearts had broken rhythm. Yet not heart was it, but echo. A hum that seeped into skulls, soft as whispers no hand could block. Beside each thought, a shadow walked. Not stolen, not forced—mirrored.

[Translation]

They say it began with a pulse – low, steady, like a drumbeat inside the bones. Citizens stumbled in their streets, clutching their chests, certain their hearts had misfired. Then the hum filled their skulls, soft as a whisper, impossible to block. Thoughts stirred, not stolen but mirrored, as if another mind now walked beside each of them.

1.17 Fear rose first. Blues raised their blades, certain the Orb deceived them. Greens gripped their secrets, afraid their careful patterns would unravel into light. Grays trembled, fearing even their exhaustion would be laid bare, their sweat turned into confession. But Orb took nothing. It reflected. It cast away repetition, and clutched only what had never been lived before.

[Translation]

There was fear. Blues raised their blades, believing the Orb had tricked them. Greens feared their secrets would unravel, their careful breeding lines exposed. Grays trembled, afraid that even their exhaustion would be laid bare. But the Orb did not take. It reflected. It kept only what was unique, what had never been lived before. All else it discarded.

1.18 The weary bent first. A Gray woman bowed her spine not to stone but to the Orb, and let it drink her burden. She rose lighter, not emptied but divided, her mouth remembering the shape of a smile.

[Translation]

The first to accept it were the weary. A Gray woman who had carried stone on her back for centuries lay down before the Orb and let it drink her memories. She rose again lighter, smiling for the first time in decades. She said the burden was not gone, but shared.

1.19 One by one, the others followed. Blues learned their vigilance sharpened when sight became countless eyes. Greens discovered their designs grew truer when judged by many voices. And the Grays—yes, the Grays—found even suffering had weight, if memory held it eternal.

[Translation]

One by one, others followed. Blues learned that vigilance sharpened when shared across many eyes. Greens discovered that their plans grew stronger when weighed against countless voices. And the Grays – ah, the Grays – they learned that even their pain had meaning if it was preserved.

1.20 The Orb brightened, rippling like water seeded with stars, chamber burning in false starlight. Some whispered it breathed. Others swore it spoke in voices of the dead, carried upward into new form.

[Translation]

The Orb grew brighter as it filled. Its surface rippled like water catching stars, until the whole chamber shone. Some whispered that it breathed. Others swore they heard voices within it, the voices of those who had already died, carried forward in a new form.

1.21 That was birth: not flesh, but Second Ones. Palrax no

longer only body, but lattice. Weak in limb, fading beneath a dying sun, yet strong in memory – stronger than storm, stronger than failing light.

[Translation]

From that day, none could deny it: the Palrax were no longer only flesh. They had built a second body, one made of memory.

1.22 But survival has no mercy. Payment it demands, always. The Node pressed into every skull, whispering we were castes no longer, but fragments woven. Pride resisted, as pride always does, but pride is only the shadow of fear.

[Translation]

We did not know then how much it would cost us. But survival always demands payment. And our people were ready to pay.

1.23 The Blues yielded last. Vigilance had taught them to trust the edge of their own sight. Yet in lattice they learned each blade was countless. The Greens bled pride, their secret reckonings stripped bare, but from their shame grew sharper futures. The Grays embraced first, their labor finally remembered.

[Translation]

The years that followed were not easy. To share thought was to surrender pride, and pride is the last thing a people let go of. Still, the Node pressed gently, humming in every skull, reminding us that we were no longer only castes but part of something larger.

1.24 The Blues were the slowest to yield. They had lived by vigilance, always waiting for attack, certain that weakness invited death. Yet the Node showed them that no warrior stood alone – every eye became their eye, every instinct doubled. What they guarded no longer belonged to a single blade but to a whole people.

The Greens, proud in their careful shaping of lives, learned that their calculations were brittle when kept secret. In the lattice, errors could not hide. They felt their shame burn, but they also felt their plans strengthen. The future could not be measured by one lineage alone; it had to be weighed by all.

The Grays were the first to embrace it fully. Their labor had always been unseen, their backs bowed while others gave orders. Now, when they carried stone, the Node carried it too. Their sweat was no longer forgotten. Their endurance became part of Continuity, recorded forever.

1.25 The castes dissolved, but colors lingered. Blues guarded, Greens schemed, Grays built. Yet no longer apart. Bound by hum, their breath became one. That was the birth of the Second Ones.

[Translation]

And so the castes began to dissolve. The colors did not vanish – Blues still guarded, Greens still planned, Grays still built – but they no longer stood apart. They were joined by the hum that bound every mind. That was the birth of the Second Ones.

1.26 Continuity became law. Forgetting the only crime. Death no longer meant loss, for Univeran rose, purified and preserved. The lattice consumed all, mistakes and triumphs alike. Nothing wasted. Nothing forgotten.

[Translation]

We were no longer just Palraxians scattered by task or pride. We had become a single body stretched across many vessels. Our limbs were weak, yes, our star dimmed above us, but our memory was strong. Stronger than storms, stronger than the failing light.

1.27 Continuity became law. Forgetting became the only crime. To forget was worse than death, because death no longer meant loss. A life ended, but the essence of it, the Univeran, streamed upward, purified, preserved. Every mistake and every triumph, every whisper of despair, was woven into the Node. Nothing wasted. Nothing lost.

The elder's words proved true: bodies withered, lattice endured. A second sun rose beneath the first – brighter, crueler, eternal.

[Translation]

I think of the elder who first spoke the words: The body cannot last, but the memory can. He was right. Bodies withered, but the lattice endured. We had forged a fire that no dying star could steal from us.

We lived beneath two suns then – one fading above us, and one newly risen, pulsing in the sky: the Node Collective, our second star.

The ancients gave us that gift. And from their surrender, we learned the truth that shaped all who came after: we were no longer only flesh. We were Continuity.

Neur's Oraculum 02 - Under Toktilor's Monoliths

2.01 I was born in the mountain's shadow, where breath thins and thought sharpens into blade. The star had not yet collapsed, but its betrayal had begun–oceans shrinking, storms climbing ridges like beasts hungry for marrow. My parents spoke of softer years; I knew only the count, the ticking, the slow subtraction of light.

[Translation]

I was born in a mountain province, a thousand gats from the capital, where the air thinned enough to sharpen a thought. The sun had not yet fallen to its weakest, but it had begun its slow betrayal–heat pulling back from the oceans, storms climbing the ridges like animals. My parents remembered years of easier light; I was born into the countdown.

2.02 From the slopes I watched the vows our people nailed into the earth. Domes like glass eggs trembling against the wind. Pyramids humming their invisible walls into the sky. Monolith deserts flashing like mirrors of a stingy sun, stabbing brightness back into heaven's fading eye. When the fields blazed at noon, even mountains seemed to flinch.

[Translation]

From our slopes I could see the world we pledged to hold together. The ecological domes sat like glass seeds in distant valleys, their skins trembling when wind pushed too hard. Between them rose the pyramids—dark and deliberate, humming fields into the sky to tame the torn atmosphere. Farther out, the mirrored monoliths crowded the deserts, throwing brightness back at a stingy sun. When the monolith fields flashed at noon, even mountains seemed to flinch.

2.03 Children laughed, but always beneath the shadow of numbers. Digits glowed in corridors, in transit cars, on orbs that taught us. Time left was our weather, a civic temperature. Adults measured it the way farmers once read clouds.

[Translation]

Children everywhere tried not to think about the clocks. But you cannot grow up on Toktilor without noticing the numbers in every corridor—the soft green digits above doors, in transit carrels, on the faces of public learning orbs. Time left was a civic temperature. Adults checked it the way farmers once studied clouds.

2.04 We played, yes, but our games carried ash. I rode the slammer-sled, cone-nosed, air-slicing. Others raced invaders, host-races, crash and rebuild. But I stripped mine bare, made it lighter, truer, until the mountain seemed to grant me its permission. The victories mattered less than the pattern: time cannot be recovered, I sang, and the children mocked me old. Perhaps I was, already then.

[Translation]

We were given few toys. The most precious was a slammer: a cone-nosed sled that rode air like a fish rides pressure. To mount it, you bent into the cone, gripping control ridges with your forearms and feet. The other children raced the passes for hours, inventing games—host-race and invaders, crash on a new world, rebuild with what you can carry. I played too, but never as long. I kept bringing the slammer back to my workbench.

2.05 Something in me wanted the machine to be cleaner, truer. I removed the side struts. I hollow shelled the body between the cone and tail. I remapped the foot shoes to micro-flex so I could steer with ankle bone instead of whole-leg force. I failed a hundred times and fell twice that number. Then one afternoon the sled answered—lighter, quick to pivot in thin air, as if the mountain itself had given permission.

I won races after that, but I didn't care. The experiment mattered more than the finish line. "The one thing you cannot recover in life is time," I used to sing to the others, half a joke, half a vow. They rolled their eyes and called me old. Perhaps I was, even then.

At night the forests burned, the horizon smeared red. Silver ships dropped powders that fell like gray snow, smothering flame. Ash streaked the leaves of molk trees, their wide resinous branches holding cups of water, flowers like fruit. I climbed them, and felt through bark a second pulse. Slow, patient, not mine. A taste of metal on the tongue. A shadow of a bird across the soul.

[Translation]

Heat rose year by year. Fires marched across dry forests at night, smearing the horizon red. Silver oval ships dropped through smoke and smothered the flames with anti-oxygen powder that fell like gray snow. The next morning, ash would streak the leaves of the molk trees—thin-trunked giants whose wide resinous branches held cups of water and flowers the color of fruit. I climbed them to the canopy for the view: domes glittering in the distance, pyramids humming, monoliths hammering the sun back into the sky.

Sometimes, with my palm flat to a branch, I felt a second pulse—slow, patient, not mine. I would taste metal and go very still. The sensation passed like a shadow of a bird crossing a wall. I told no one. It felt like a secret the world wasn't ready to hear.

2.06 The province rationed not just food, nor water alone. Even thought was measured. Lattice time, lift power, light itself—all cut by the digit's decree. We were told to love limits, for in each limit someone else might breathe. Daylight belonged to iron and circuits, night to study and repair. In our home the heat lowered when the clocks demanded, the lamps dimmed, and the orbs brightened, watching us with patient glow.

[Translation]

The province rationed everything: food, water, lattice time, lift power after dusk. We were taught to love limits because limits meant somebody else might live. Day energy belonged to manufacturing—data nodes, ship frames, field cores for the pyramids, mirror spines for the monoliths. Night belonged to the quiet work—study, repair, planning. In our home, heat dropped when the clocks reached a certain digit; the lights softened, and the learning orbs brightened instead.

2.07 I slept less than I studied. Around me, swarms of files took shape, forty folding into four, four dissolving into one. I refined, cut, polished, until a single draft gleamed sharper than what I began. Algorithms hovered, nudging me, tilting me toward paths of research: host worlds, Exodum's routes, ledgers of survival. Always the same undertone—how many must dissolve into memory so that others may endure the dark between suns. Numbers do not lie, but honesty wounds as cleanly as any blade.

[Translation]

I studied more than I slept. I called up document swarms around me—forty files became four, then four became a single precise draft as sections slid between texts and fused into cleaner arguments. Algorithms watched what I chose and nudged my path toward research: host world analysis, probability trees for Exodum routes, resource ledgers for protein allocation, projections of how many would need to dissolve into the Collective so the rest could survive the long night between suns. The numbers were not cruel, only honest. Honesty can still break a child.

2.08 Yet games continued, as if laughter could outrun the digits. One afternoon, a boy failed his slammer's curve. He vanished into a pit, and the earth itself screamed with wings. Dal, insect swarms of eight legs and four wings, rose in thousands. One sting, pain. Hundreds, a verdict. The Blues came, too late. Flesh became protein. Node reclaimed his memory. The slammer, passed down like inheritance, became another child's toy.

[Translation]

We still played. The games helped us pretend we could outrun the clocks. One afternoon a boy in our circle lost control of his slammer and vanished into a pit. We heard him before we saw the shape: a mouth in the ground filled with dal—eight-leg, four-wing insects that swarmed in their thousands. One sting was pain. Hundreds were a verdict. The Blues came fast, but not fast enough. The boy's body became protein; his personal node went back to the pool. His slammer passed to a younger child.

2.09 After the pit, I did not play. Death was no abstraction. It wore a sound, a verdict, a name. I turned inward, where the mountains howled with wind but I demanded silence. Friends called; I did not answer. My mother's worry pressed, my father's hand pulled me to the city, hoping its focus would rope me back into the world.

[Translation]

That was the end of games for me. Death was not theory after the dal pit. It had a voice and it knew our names.

I turned inward for a season. The mountains were loud with wind and I wanted silence. I did my lessons alone, barely answering when friends called at our door. My mother worried. My father took me to the city and enrolled me in a focus center where the work matched the pressure in my head. They hoped good labor would be the rope that pulled me back to the world.

2.10 The city's domes loomed closer, the hum of pyramids heavier—weight against the mind, pressing thought into order. Between sessions, I walked galleries where dome-skeleton met sky. There the deserts shone with mirrors, storm lines etched like scars. I pressed my palm to glass. Again, the second pulse. Deeper than heartbeat. Older than breath.

[Translation]

In the city, the domes were closer and the hum of the pyramids more felt than heard—a weight that steadied thought. Between sessions, I walked the edge galleries where the dome's skeleton clasped the sky. There I could see the mirror deserts and the storm lines curling like scars. I pressed my palm to the glass and, again, that second pulse came—deeper than heartbeat, steadier than breath.

2.11 Remember us, the whisper said. Not from wind. From within. We are the first ones.

[Translation]

Remember us, a whisper said. Not from the air. From within. We are the first ones.

2.12 I knew of them: ancients before the Blackout, when lifetimes stretched across centuries. I had read their names, their fragments, within Codex filters. But reading is not hearing. Hearing shifts the floor beneath you. I answered without lips: I hear you.

[Translation]

I knew about the first ones: ancients who had lived before the Blackout, when lifetimes ran across centuries and bodies did not tire so quickly. I had read their records through the NC-CODEX filters in school. But reading is not hearing. Hearing made the floor tilt. I answered without lips. I hear you.

2.13 They did not flood me. They waited, patient as stone. Then one voice, dry as leaf, firm as vow, laid itself into me: The body cannot last. The memory can.

[Translation]

They did not flood me. They waited, patient as stone. Then one voice—dry as a leaf, firm as a promise—set down a single line in me: The body cannot last. The memory can.

2.14 The summons came. Two Blues at doors, faces carved in stillness. Corridors smelled of metal and rain. A chamber waited, domed like an eye turned inward. Greens in crescent, Grays in shadow-pillars, Blues bracketing the doors. At the center hovered a seed-sphere—silver, layered with strands, cradled by pale light.

[Translation]

A week later, the summons came. Two Blues at the door. A corridor that smelled like cool metal and rain. A council chamber where Greens stood in a crescent, Grays held to shadow like pillars, and Blues bracketed the doors. At the center hovered a small sphere—crystal layered with living strands—cradled by field lines. A child-seed of the Node.

2.15 "Neur," a Green spoke, my name weighed like a blade. "Resonance: major. Whispers: reported. Explain."

[Translation]

"Neur," a Green said. "We measure a major resonance. You report whispers. Explain."

2.16 "I hear the ancients," I answered. The Blue's gaze cut, the Green's softened, as though relief and burden struck her at once. "Anomalies are not made," she said. "They are found. The Univeran marks them."

[Translation]

"I hear the ancients," I said. A Blue watched my face as if it were a clock. The Green's expression shifted—some mixture of relief and responsibility.

"Anomalies are not made," she said. "They are found. The

Univeran marks them."

2.17 The seed brightened, light deepening. "Influence is not command," the Green continued. "You will learn to lean without breaking. Ask more than you answer. Accept, and you will train. Refuse, and you return to study."

[Translation]

The small sphere brightened, a breath deeper. The Green went on, "Influence is not command. You will learn how to lean on the lattice without tearing it. You will ask questions more than you give answers. If you accept, we'll train you. If you refuse, we close this door and you return to study."

2.18 "If I accept, what changes?" I asked.

"You," she said. "And where you place your weight, the city will feel it."

[Translation]

"If I accept," I asked, "what changes?"

"You do," she said. "And where you place your weight, the city will feel it."

2.19 I looked to my mother. Her eyes lowered, permission given. "I will learn," I said. The Node did not speak. It listened harder. Listening like light itself—gentling every edge, sharpening every shadow.

[Translation]

I looked at my mother. She lowered her eyes in permission. "I will learn," I said.

The Node did not speak. It simply listened harder. I felt the listening the way you feel light—every edge gentled, every shadow more truthful. I went home with a quiet in me that the clocks could not touch.

2.20 Training was not destiny but repetition. A Gray tuned my breath to the hum until pulse and pyramid merged. A Green taught boundaries—where asking ends, where intrusion begins. A Blue shadowed, silent, seeing everything. The seed-node floated in its cradle, no larger than a skull. When I opened, the city unfurled: seams, cycles, power draws, orchards, stress-lines. If I leaned too far, nausea took me. The Gray tapped my wrist. I stepped back.

[Translation]

Training did not look like destiny. It looked like practice. At dawn, a Gray mentor matched my breathing to the pyramid's hum until the two were one line. A Green taught ethics: where influence ends and intrusion begins; when to ask the Node for help; when to carry weight alone. A Blue shadowed us, saying little, seeing everything. We used a small node, no bigger than a skull, floating in a braided cradle. When I opened to it, the city unfolded into legible threads—maintenance cycles, power draws, crop humidity, seam strain on the dome's ribs. If I leaned too far, nausea edged my vision. The Gray would tap my wrist, and I would step back.

2.21 We carried "small things well." The Node laid patterns before me: a storm pressing one quadrant, a seam left bare, an orchard thirsting. I did not push. I set thought down like a weight on a scale. When balance came, relief followed, the system sighing like a muscle no longer clenched.

[Translation]

We practiced "small things carried well." The Node handed me patterns to balance: a weather surge pressing one quadrant of the dome, a staffing tangle that would leave a seam unguarded, an orchard's water ration about to slip out of tolerance. I didn't push; I set my thought like a weight on a quiet scale and waited for the measure to settle. When I placed it true, the system answered—not with words but with relief, like a muscle that realized it no longer needed to clench.

2.22 Other days were dusk, stillness, listening. Sometimes silence clean as water. Sometimes voices, soft as falling ash. They offered no commands, only images: winds that no longer blew, fruits that no longer grew, rivers lit with light. They opened palms. Memory stood. I bowed to it, careful not to drown.

[Translation]

Other days were for stillness. Lights lowered to dusk. I listened for the ancients. Sometimes there was nothing and the silence felt pure as clean water. Sometimes their presence came soft as ash falling. They offered images more than speeches: winds that no longer blew, fruits that no longer grew, rivers braided with light, singers on the steps of a pyramid when the sky was still generous. They did not drag me into their lives. They opened their palms and let memory stand. I learned to bow to it without drowning.

2.23 The council asked proof again. “Show us,” the Green said, “a small thing carried well.” I closed my eyes, found the dome’s breath, asked where it hurt. A knot of labor—three tasks stacked, delay bleeding into seam. I shifted schedules. Burden eased. Machines sang steadier, true.

[Translation]

The council called me once more for proof—not spectacle, proof. The same chamber, the same colors. The seed-sphere at center. “Show us a small thing carried well,” the Green said.

2.24 I closed my eyes. Found the dome’s breath. Asked the Node where it ached. A maintenance knot revealed itself—three tasks stacked on one crew, a delay that would bleed stress into a seam. I shifted two schedules by a few breaths and felt the burden ease. Machines held their tone the way a voice holds a note when fear loosens its grip.

2.25 The Blue nodded. The Gray exhaled. The Green warned: “Influence, never command. Continuity is promise, not power.”

[Translation]

The Blue nodded. The Gray’s shoulders dropped. The Green said, “You will influence, never command. Continuity is promise, not power.”

2.26 Outside, evening bled. Monoliths flared their last defiance; pyramids groaned the air flat. Children still raced their slammers under dome-light, laughing against the clocks. I pressed my palm to glass, heartbeat meeting heartbeat. The whisper returned, steady as vow: The body cannot last. The memory can.

[Translation]

Outside, evening climbed the mountains. The monoliths far in the desert still threw a last white into the sky, a stubborn brightness that felt like defiance turned useful. The pyramids murmured to the torn air until it lay flat. Under the dome, children raced slammers again, their laughter skimming the galleries, the same games I had left behind. In every corridor, the clocks kept their count, indifferent and necessary.

I pressed my hand to the glass and felt the world’s thin heartbeat through the shell. My reflection in the pane looked older than my years and younger than my worries. The whisper returned, the same one that had started all this, steady as a vow:

The body cannot last. The memory can.

Neur’s Oraculum 03 - Whispers of The Univeran

3.01 Grew I did knowing ours was not the only world, yet it felt abandoned. Toktilor, third planet, circling a star weary of giving. Companions stripped bare before my birth, mined into corpses, hollow shells drifting silent. Around us, broken rings of rock—slag veins carved, alloys harvested, but none of them home. Only Toktilor endured, and even it trembled toward failure.

[Translation]

I grew up knowing that our world was not alone, yet it felt alone. Toktilor was the third planet circling a star that had already begun to dim, a star tired of giving. Two companions had been stripped bare long before my birth, mined into exhaustion until they were nothing but scarred shells, barren reminders of what survival costs. Around us drifted moons and belts of broken rock—slag and alloy veins that our fleets harvested endlessly, but none of them could be home. Only Toktilor remained, and even it was failing.

3.02 To live there was to breathe beneath glass. Domes sealed us from a sky untrustworthy, a second skin stretched tight. Inside, air sweet but measured, rivers circling endlessly like thoughts that cannot escape, and children raised beneath painted heavens, mistaking their cage for sky. But always the hum. Machines exhaling. True wind absent, replaced by regulated sighs.

[Translation]

To live there was to live under glass. The ecological domes sealed us from an atmosphere too unstable to trust, each hemisphere a second skin for our cities. Inside, the air was sweet and measured, the rivers looped through engineered cycles, and children like me grew up believing the blue above us was sky. Yet the hum of machines never stopped, and I could feel the difference between true wind and the regulated sigh of filtered air.

3.03 Beyond domes, monuments rose as guardians. In deserts, the mirrored monoliths flared—frozen lightning catching a dying sun, throwing it back in violent refusal. The pyramids held storms in place, their humming voices pressing bone, reminding us that survival was vibration, never silence.

[Translation]

Beyond the domes, monuments guarded us. In the deserts stood the mirrored monoliths, vast towers of alloyed glass that threw back the fury of ultraviolet light. They glittered like frozen lightning, their surfaces flaring even when the sun grew thin. The pyramids anchored the weather, steadying the currents that wanted to unravel the skies. They hummed like voices too deep for language, and their vibration pressed into bone, a reminder that survival itself had a sound.

3.04 Every vow was shaped in iron and glass. Not built for beauty, but endurance. Yet I thought them beautiful, shards of defiance set into a crumbling earth. Gleaming fragments refusing to collapse.

[Translation]

Every dome, every pyramid, every monolith was a vow. We built them not for beauty but for endurance. Even so, I sometimes thought they were beautiful—gleaming shards in a darkening world, stubbornly refusing collapse.

3.05 But whispers haunted us: Toktilor was dying. The Exodum clock bled digits in every street, counting down the myth into schedule, the prophecy into law. Children learned to measure not in days but in deadlines.

[Translation]

And yet, for all that iron and glass, the truth whispered across our solar system was this: Toktilor was dying. The Exodum clock hung in every street, digits falling one by one, a universal heartbeat reminding us the end was not myth but schedule. Children learned to count not in days but in deadlines.

3.06 Even as I breathed the hum of pyramids, I knew: shields cannot save. Shields only delay. Salvation demanded more than glass or alloy. Something deeper. Something that could hold not only flesh but the essence behind the eyes.

[Translation]

Even then, I knew the monoliths and pyramids were not enough. They were shields, not salvation. Salvation would demand something deeper: a way to preserve not just the body of our people, but the essence that gave us meaning.

3.07 I did not know its name then. But soon, I would.

[Translation]

I did not yet know the name for that essence. But soon I would.

3.08 Childhood was brief; Toktilor allowed no lingering. By the fifth year, the narrowing began. Algorithms measured our stumbles, our obsessions, our mistakes, and curved our paths into the lattice. Builders, governors, watchers. I was bent toward the scanners—the ones who would see beyond glass, measure resonance, and open doors no one else dared.

[Translation]

Palraxian childhood was not endless. By our fifth year, specialization began. Algorithms tested our choices, our mistakes, our fascinations. From then on, the lattice narrowed our paths until they aligned with the roles our society needed most. Some of us were drawn into building, some into governance, others into vigilance. I was guided into the scanners—those who would one day watch, evaluate, and reach across the boundaries of worlds.

3.09 The ritual felt ancient. At dawn we gathered, walls trembling with pale resonance. Each child touched the orb, crystal pulsing with the Node's rhythm. It read not our hands, but our essence—fear, patience, curiosity. When my palm met its skin, light flared orange edged with white. Elders glanced sideways, secretive, unreadable. Later I would learn - anomaly.

[Translation]

The ritual was simple but felt heavy with age. At dawn, we gathered in a hall whose walls shimmered with pale resonance. Each child stepped forward, touching a crystal orb that pulsed in rhythm with the Node. The orb read not just skill but resonance—fear, patience, curiosity, will. When my hand met the surface, a flare of orange edged with white rippled across it. The elders exchanged glances they did not explain. I was too young to name it then, but later I would learn: it was the mark of anomaly.

3.10 Training began with stillness. Hours unmoving, eyes open, silence pressed until silence grew heavy. The hum of the pyramids absorbed into breath until breath itself was no longer mine. Later, chambers of filaments—pale threads crawling along nerve and bone, dreams stripped bare, fears pressed raw.

[Translation]

Training began with discipline of the senses. We were taught to sit still for hours, eyes open, letting every detail enter without judgment. To measure silence until silence itself became full. To hold the hum of the pyramids in our breath until breath and hum were indistinguishable.

Later, they placed us in chambers where pale filaments scanned every nerve. Our dreams were studied, our fears pressed, our patience tested against discomfort.

3.11 Then came protocols, colors etched into us like scripture. Red for fear, black for hostility, orange for benevolence. We memorized them as once children memorized prayers. Yet prayers do not carry weight like choices. For scanners were not mere watchers, but arbiters: who to mark, who to implant, who to release. Even in youth we felt it, the weight of futures resting in our unready hands.

[Translation]

Then came the protocols—how to read resonance colors: red for fear, black for hostility, orange for benevolence. We memorized them the way earlier ages memorized prayers.

But the scanners’ true work was not observation, it was choice.

Who to implant, who to release, where to intervene, where to remain unseen. Those choices would shape futures larger than any one life. Even as children, we felt that weight pressing against us. Every lesson was a reminder: your thought is not your own. It belongs to Continuity.

3.12 Sometimes, with eyes closed, the whispers returned. Not loud, never loud. The ancients leaned close, pressing steadiness into the cracks of thought. They did not command. They waited. Presence itself was instruction.

[Translation]

Sometimes, when I closed my eyes during training, the whispers returned. The ancients, patient and steady, stood just behind my thoughts. They never shouted. They did not need to. Their presence itself was instruction.

3.13 I began to understand: these rituals were not only education. They were rehearsals for listening. For I was never only the listener. I was the one being listened to.

[Translation]

I began to understand: the rituals were not simply education. They were preparation for listening. And I was already being listened to.

3.14 Death walked close, though dressed in ceremony. We were taught: when flesh fails, it is not lost. The implant flares once, stripping duplication, distilling a life into essence. Univeran—the true shape of a lived span—streaming upward into the Node, incorruptible.

[Translation]

Death was always near us, though hidden in quiet rituals. The ancients had long taught that when a body failed, it was not lost. The implant at the base of the skull released a final surge, stripping away duplication, reducing a lifetime to essence. That essence was Univeran—the distillation of all that had truly been lived. It streamed upward into the Node Collective, incorruptible, permanent.

3.15 I first witnessed it as a child. An elder, skin gray as ash, lay suspended. Blues kept vigil, Greens recorded, Grays worked the instruments. His breath stuttered, then ceased. A pulse struck the chamber, sharp enough to tremble bone. The node at his skull flared white, then dark. His chest fell, yet his life had already climbed.

[Translation]

The first time I witnessed the release was as a child in training. An elder, his skin gray as ash, lay in a suspension cradle. Blues stood by, Greens whispered records, Grays worked the instruments. His breath faltered. Then the moment came: a pulse so sharp I felt it even through the floor. The monitors brightened, and the node at his skull glowed white for a heartbeat before dimming. His chest fell silent, but his life had already left him, carried into the lattice.

3.16 I did not weep. None of us did. To cry would have meant we thought him gone. He was not gone. He had been translated. Tears are for absence, and Continuity has no absence.

[Translation]

I did not cry. None of us did. Tears would have meant we thought he was gone. He was not gone. His essence had joined the Continuity that would outlast even suns.

3.17 That night he entered my dream—not his face, not his voice, but patience itself, a hand resting on my shoulder. I woke knowing: the whispers are not madness. They are inheritance. Forgetting is the only death.

[Translation]

That night I dreamed of him. Not his face, not his voice—only the impression of patience, like a hand set gently on my shoulder. I woke knowing the whispers were not madness, but inheritance. The ancients had been right: forgetting is worse than death, for death is not the end.

3.18 After that, lessons shifted. Domes, pyramids, monoliths—yes, but they were walls only, guardians of time. The truer survival was not glass nor alloy, but the lattice. The Node, second sun, star fed not by hydrogen but by memory itself.

[Translation]

From then, every lesson shifted. The domes, pyramids, monoliths—these were walls and tools. Necessary, yes. But they were only temporary guardians. The true survival was Continuity. The Node was our second sun, a star that could not dim, because it fed on Univeran, not hydrogen.

3.19 And I, anomaly, was told softly: your thoughts weigh more. Place them with care. I was still a child, yet the burden fit like breathing.

[Translation]

And I, marked as anomaly, had been permitted not only to hear the whispers but to lean into them. The council told me in quiet tones: Your thoughts will weigh more. Place them carefully.

3.20 Outside, storms tore, fires climbed, monoliths shattered and rose again. Inside, I carried a whisper without end: The body cannot last. The memory can. At last I understood—not just words, but the vow they carried.

[Translation]

I was still a child, but the burden settled into me as naturally as breathing. Outside, the fires climbed mountains, storms clawed domes, monoliths shattered and were rebuilt, pyramids groaned with the strain of keeping the air calm.

Inside, I carried a whisper that had no end: The body cannot last. The memory can.

And for the first time, I understood not just the words but the promise within them.

Neur's Oraculum 04 - Mark of The Anomaly

4.01 Not all worlds welcomed us. Some spoke with teeth, not tongues.

Mox breathed golden mist, clinging to skin like breath too long held. Forests glowed in half-light, their swollen pods bleeding the fluid that kept our minds from fracturing in the storm of stars. We named it slag. Without it, scanners collapsed, pilots broke, the lattice itself tore into madness.

[Translation]

Not all worlds welcomed us. Some taught their lessons with teeth.

Mox was one such world, shrouded in golden mist that clung to everything like breath held too long. Its forests glowed faintly at night, every tree swollen with pods that bled the only substance that could keep our minds coherent in the violence of interstellar travel. We called it neuron slag. Without it, no scanner could survive the light-speed currents, no pilot could hold a straight thought, no collective could endure the storm of stars.

4.02 We harvested because survival demanded it. But Mox demanded blood in return.

The glo-flyers ruled those forests: long bodies, ember eyes, jaws serrated for pod-flesh. They devoured what we required, then seeded the soil with their waste. Without them, the forest died. With them, harvesters did.

[Translation]

We harvested because survival demanded it. But Mox demanded a price.

The glo-flyers ruled that forest. Long bodies a meter in length, wingspans wider than a chamber ceiling, six eyes burning like embers, mouths lined with fangs made for tearing pods apart. They devoured the very fungus we needed, then fertilized the trees with their waste. Without them, the forest would die. With them, harvesters died instead.

4.03 I was still young when I entered that place, encircled in gel—slag pressing cold against every limb, translucent second skin. We carried alloy blades and nets. Above us, wings whispered first, then roared.

A cry split the mist. A Gray dragged upward, arm clamped in the jaws of a flyer. Others swept down, wings knocking bodies into trees. Our lines broke; fear scattered us.

[Translation]

I was still young when I first trained there, encircled in a slag covering that gleamed translucent, gel pressing against every limb. We moved in silence, carrying alloy blades and capture nets. The air was thick with gold motes that clung to our skin. Above, wings whispered, then roared.

A cry cut through the mist — a Gray harvest team seized by a swarm. I saw one flyer dive, jaws clamping around a harvester's arm, dragging him upward as if he weighed nothing. Another swooped low, wings knocking two more into the trees. We tried to hold formation, but fear scattered us.

4.04 The suit steadied thought even as panic pressed hard. My nerves screamed, but mind held rhythm. Slag's gift was not strength—it was clarity. I learned their curve, their gaps, where a net might close. A few lives were saved. Many pods were lost.

I returned to Toktilor carrying wings and fangs in memory, and the certainty that Continuity was always purchased. Slag was no medicine. It was blood turned into clarity, the hinge between sanity and collapse.

[Translation]

The slag suit steadied my thoughts even as panic pressed hard. Every nerve screamed, but my mind held its rhythm. That was the first time I understood slag's true gift: not strength, but clarity. I watched the flyers, learned the curve of their attack, and marked the gap where a net could catch one long enough for us to cut it free. We saved a few lives that day, though many pods were lost.

When we returned to Toktilor, I carried with me the memory of wings and fangs and the certainty that our survival was bought with blood. Neuron slag was not simply medicine. It was the hinge between sanity and madness, life and collapse. Every pod cut, every harvester slain, every flyer's shadow overhead – all of it was the cost of Continuity.

4.05 That night the ancients whispered: even survival demands tribute. I believed them.

[Translation]

The ancients whispered that night as I lay sleepless. Even survival demands tribute. I believed them.

4.06 After Mox, the council shifted our hands from harvest to flesh. Survival was not only in pods and slag—it would be in contact, in touch, in the act of placing memory where it did not belong. Scanners were taught to lift subjects, cradle breath, pierce them with seeds of crystal. Not conquest, they said, but mathematics of endurance.

[Translation]

After Mox, training shifted. It was not enough to survive the void ourselves. We had to prepare for what came after: contact. The council decreed that scanners must learn to lift subjects, hold them steady, and implant them cleanly – not as an act of conquest, but as the mathematics of survival.

4.07 Our first trials were not upon strangers but kin. Grays offered themselves, calling it honor to feed the lattice with their marrow. They lay within bone-like chambers, skulls cradled, bodies wrapped in sheath. Our task was precision: lift with resonance, steady their lungs, and set the miniature node at the meeting of brain and spine.

[Translation]

Our first missions were not against strangers. We practiced on Palrax subjects – volunteers, chosen from among the Grays who believed that to serve the Node in this way was an honor. They lay inside chambers shaped like circles of bone, heads cradled, bodies sealed in protective sheaths. Our task was precision: lift them into the field with resonance beams, keep their breathing steady, and insert the miniature nodes at the junction of brain and spine.

4.08 The injector shimmered to nothing, tip finer than sight, seed smaller than fruit-grain. A Green elder's voice droned steady at my shoulder: Do not force. Let resonance guide. The body twitched once, then settled. The seed fused, the chamber breathed white, as if his memory had already slipped into the lattice.

[Translation]

My hands shook the first time I held the implantation injector. The tip was so fine it shimmered out of sight, and the seed-node it carried was smaller than a grain of fruit. A Green elder spoke instructions at my shoulder, voice as calm as the hum of the pyramids. "Steady the sheath. Align with the lobe. Do not force; let the resonance guide."

4.09 The subject twitched once, then stilled. His eyes fluttered but did not open. When the node fused, the chamber brightened faintly, as though the memory of his life had already begun to whisper into the lattice.

Not all fused. Some resisted, resonance breaking like glass. They woke in dream, unscarred. Others accepted, their essence flowing seamless. Every attempt tallied, studied, etched into the Codex. Precision was demanded. But precision was blind. I felt it—we were groping currents deeper than sight. The whispers pressed closer: See beneath the flesh, child. Sight is not enough.

[Translation]

Not all attempts succeeded. Some subjects resisted unconsciously, their resonance breaking compliance. They were returned unharmed, their memories blurred into dream. Others accepted the implant cleanly and became part of the lattice. Every attempt was recorded, studied, corrected.

But precision alone was not enough. I could feel it. We were blind, fumbling at currents we barely understood. The ancients whispered again: See beneath the flesh, child. Sight is not enough.

4.10 So I drew spirals. Not filaments, not probes. A lens of mind. Psychescan, I named it. Resonance mapped against emotion, frequencies painted in color. First only sketches on my desk, then patterns sharp as glass. Red for fear—spiked, unstable. Black for hostility—heavy, jagged. Orange for sympathy—soft yet unyielding. A window, not a weapon.

[Translation]

That was when I began to sketch a new method in my studies. Not a mechanical probe, not another layer of filaments, but a lens for the mind. I called it a psychescan. It began as diagrams on my desk – spirals of resonance mapped against emotion, colors linked to frequencies. With every experiment, the patterns became sharper.

4.11 When I tested it, the effect was immediate. Fear showed itself as red – fast, spiking, unstable. Hostility burned black, heavy and jagged. And then I saw orange: sympathy, openness, a current that did not resist.

The council studied my diagrams in silence. Finally a Blue muttered, "A weapon of foresight."

"No," I told them. "A window. It shows where trust might live."

The Green who guided me spoke only once: Psychescan will change everything. I wondered if her words were blessing or curse.

[Translation]

The council examined my findings with long silence. A Blue finally said, "With this, we can read a culture before we risk contact. It is a weapon of foresight."

I shook my head. "Not a weapon. A window. It shows us where trust may live."

The Green who had overseen my training nodded once. "Psychescan will change everything."

I felt the weight of her words and wondered if they were praise or warning. Perhaps both.

4.12 That night I dreamed of rivers glowing orange, flowing not outward but inward. In their light something waited, hidden, yet inevitable.

[Translation]

That night, I dreamed of rivers colored in orange light. They led not outward but inward, into myself. And in their glow, I felt something waiting – something not yet revealed.

4.13 The psychescan sharpened with trial. Hundreds entered the chamber's glow. At first, colors drifted like smoke. Then they burned true:

Red – always fear, fast and jagged.

Black – hostility, stone-heavy, refusing every touch.

Orange – rare, but real, rising like dawn, soft yet unyielding, the current of sympathy. Those moments I loved most: the lattice brightening with benevolence, even if only a spark.

[Translation]

The psychescan grew sharper with every trial. We tested hundreds of subjects, each lifted into the chamber's glow. At first, the colors came faint, like smoke. Then, as the algorithms aligned, they burned with clarity.

Fear was always red. It bled across the lattice, quick and jagged, trembling at every breath. Hostility was black, heavy as stone, a wall that refused even the smallest kindness. But then there were those who shimmered in orange. I loved those moments most. The orange rose like dawn through the lattice, soft but unyielding. It meant sympathy, benevolence, openness. Rare, but real.

4.14 One day a subject burned differently. Orange flared, yes, but rimmed in frost-white, faint yet steady. I thought my scan cracked, adjusted spirals, checked circuits. Still the white held. The council watched in silence. A Green whispered: An anomaly.

[Translation]

One day, during training, a subject appeared who burned differently. At first I thought my scan had failed. Around his orange glow lay a thin white border, faint but steady, like frost around a fire. I adjusted the instruments, doubting myself. The image held.

The council studied the readout in silence. Then a Green whispered: "An anomaly."

4.15 We had studied anomalies in Codex's—lives bent outside design, marked by the Univeran. Rare currents that shifted generations. To see one alive was to feel the universe lean close. After that, I searched for them in every scan. Few appeared, but each time my heart answered as if Continuity itself called: look deeper. Overcomers of A'glem made, for those who endure fracture emerge stronger because of it.

[Translation]

Anomalies were legend – births outside design, marked by the Univeran itself. We had studied them in records, how their resonance bent probability, how even a single one could shift generations. But to see one alive in the chamber was to feel the universe itself lean close.

4.16 After that day, I scanned with new intensity. I looked for more, though anomalies remained rare. Yet each time I found one, my heart quickened. It was as if the lattice itself was telling me: look deeper, there are currents you cannot chart with numbers alone.

Weeks later, during calibration, I turned the scan inward. At first, only nerves: red at the edges—doubt, unease. Then orange, steady, the benevolence elders had spoken of since childhood. But around it, white. Thin, undeniable. A frost halo encircling me.

[Translation]

It was weeks later, during a routine calibration, that I turned the scan inward. The Node always encouraged us to test ourselves first, to catch faults before we looked outward. I set the beams carefully, adjusted the spirals, and leaned into the resonance.

4.17 Red flared faintly at the edges – my nervousness, my doubt. Beneath it pulsed steady orange, the benevolence I had been told marked my voice since childhood. And then I saw it. The white border.

Thin but undeniable, ringing my resonance like a halo of frost.

I could not breathe. Thought it error, checked, recalibrated. Still it held. I was not only seeker of anomalies. I was one. The whispers pressed near, closer than blood: You are not design, Neur. You are set apart. Carry what others cannot. Overcomers of A'glem have no fear in them.

[Translation]

For a long time I could not breathe. I thought perhaps the machine had confused memory with reality, or that I had made an error in the spirals. But the more I checked, the clearer it became. I was not only reading anomalies. I was one.

The whispers came again, strong this time, close as breath. You are not design, Neur. You are elected. Carry what others cannot.

4.18 The council did not celebrate. Anomalies were not paraded. They were preserved, guided, burdened. I was told my path would continue, but my every thought would weigh heavier in the Node. I left the chamber beneath storm light, children still racing slammers below as though digits were not falling above. I pressed my palm to the dome and whispered what had been carved into me since childhood: The body cannot last. The memory can.

[Translation]

The council did not celebrate. Anomalies were not paraded. They were preserved, studied, guided with care. I was told quietly, firmly, that my place in training would continue, but that every decision I made would weigh heavier on the Node. I had been given permission to lean on the lattice in ways others could not.

4.19 I walked home through the dome galleries, firelight from distant storms painting the horizon. Children still played with their slammers in the courtyards below, laughing as though time was not falling digit by digit above their heads. I pressed my hand to the dome's skin, feeling the hum of the pyramids through my palm, and whispered into the glass the words the ancients had pressed into me since the first day:

The body cannot last. The memory can.

And only then did I know: I did not just carry memory forward. I carried anomaly itself—fragile, luminous, forever bound to Continuity.

[Translation]

Only then did I realize the truth behind the whisper: it was not just memory I carried forward. It was anomaly itself – rare, fragile, luminous. A white border that set me apart, and bound me to Continuity forever.

Neur’s Oraculum 05 - Searching the Stars

5.01 Before we looked outward, we were forced to turn inward. The council named it first contact psychology; to the untrained it sounded like myth, but to us it was law. The first thought given is the first scar carved. If fear, then fear eternal. If patience, then trust might bloom.

[Translation]

Before we ever looked outward, we had to look inward. The council called it first contact psychology—the study of what happens when one mind touches another across an abyss. To the young, it sounded like myth. To us in training, it was law.

5.02 Our teachers warned: the first shape you cast into another mind becomes the mask they forever see. A single glance can weigh more than a thousand speeches. Silence steadies better than words. Psychescan paints colors—fear red, hostility black, openness orange—but colors alone cannot anchor the abyss.

[Translation]

Our instructors warned us: “The first thought you give a host is the first shape they will build of you. If you bring fear, they will remember only fear. If you bring patience, they may remember trust.”

5.03 We practiced with our own people, though Palrax minds were already bound to the Node. Even so, the lesson was difficult. I learned how much weight a single glance carried, how silence could steady a trembling subject more than a thousand words. The psychescan helped; its colors told me what fear and hostility hid. But the heart of it could not be read in colors alone.

Whispers haunted training: Contact is not conquest. It is mirror. Show them what you are, and you will see what they are. Some laughed, muttering we would only ever be invaders. But I listened. Even fear has a thread of openness, thin as glass, waiting to be touched.

[Translation]

The ancients whispered guidance at the edges of my mind: Contact is not conquest. It is mirror. Show them what you are, and you will see what they are.

Some of my peers laughed at that. They said we would never be seen as more than invaders. But I listened. I believed that even in fear, there was a thread of openness waiting to be found.

5.04 But the lesson cut both ways. It was not only about the hosts. It was about us. Could we bear being strangers in another's sky? Could we face eyes that saw only shadow, or god, or the monstrous? I carried the white border in me, anomaly's halo, weight unspoken yet always present: Influencer of the Node. Restraint demanded of me.

[Translation]

Yet psychology was not only for the hosts. It was for us as well. How would we bear the weight of being strangers in another's sky? How would we face eyes that saw us as shadows, or monsters, or gods?

5.05 I thought of the white border I had seen around my own resonance. The council never named it in public, but I felt its pressure daily. You will influence the Node Collective, they had told me. Influence meant responsibility. Responsibility meant restraint.

So, when I closed my eyes in the chamber, I did not imagine fire, nor invasion, nor thunder. I imagined a hand reaching outward in dark. A hand that could be refused but never forced. That was the heart of first contact: to offer without taking, and to wait.

[Translation]

And so, when I closed my eyes in the chamber, I imagined the first moment of contact not as fire or lightning, but as a single hand reaching out through dark. A hand that could be refused but not forced.

That was the heart of first contact psychology: the courage to offer without taking, and the patience to wait for an answer.

5.06 The Node was never blind. It cast out silver orbs, each no larger than a chamber wall, pulsing with our memory. They leapt from gravity well to gravity well, faster than carriers could dream, stitching filaments across the dark. In two decades, they brushed 45,000 stars.

[Translation]

The Node was never blind. Probe nodes—silver spheres no larger than a chamber wall—scattered through the void, each carrying a core that pulsed with our memory. They chained gravitic filaments from star to star, leaping faster than carriers could ever hope to travel. In two decades, they crossed 45,000 systems.

5.07 Most returned silence: rocks circling ash, giants too violent, husks stripped to bone. But seven whispered possibilities.

[Translation]

Most were barren. Rocks circling embers. Gas giants too thin or too violent. Worlds stripped clean like the companions of Toktilor. But seven—seven whispered possibility.

5.08 I remember standing at the back of the council chamber, permitted only to listen. Seven worlds hovered in projection, fruit suspended from invisible branches. Seas torn by endless storms. Soil rich but burned by flaring stars. Skies calm, yet poisoned beneath the calm. Promise wrapped in hazard.

[Translation]

The council chambers filled with debate. I remember standing at the back, young still, but permitted to listen because of my training. Seven worlds hung above us in projection, each one turning slowly in the air like fruit suspended from invisible branches.

5.09 One bore seas, but storms shattered its surface into fury. Another carried soil rich and dark, but its star flared too hot, too unstable. A third gleamed with calm skies, but beneath its calm lay toxins no root could resist. Each planet was promise wrapped in danger.

The debates raged. Greens poured numbers, weighing grain against birth. Blues demanded defensible skies. Grays asked only if soil could keep children alive. The Node recorded it all, swallowing hesitation as much as certainty.

[Translation]

The debates were endless. Greens pressed resource calculations. Blues demanded defensible skies. Grays asked only whether the soil could grow grain enough to keep children alive. The Node streamed every word into Continuity. No argument was lost, no hesitation forgotten.

5.10 Whispers filled me: Survival is not perfection. It is endurance—not choosing the ideal, but the bearable. In the end the council did not name one world, but all seven. Seeds scattered wide, resilience chosen over certainty.

[Translation]

I listened and felt the whispers again: Survival is not in choosing the perfect world. It is in choosing the world you can endure.

In the end, the decision was not to choose one, but many. The fleet would scatter its seeds across the seven, testing, settling, adapting. Survival did not mean certainty. It meant resilience.

5.11 When the chamber emptied, I walked beneath the domes. Above me, the Exodum clock burned brighter than the sun. Childhood was over.

[Translation]

When the council adjourned, I walked out under the domes. Above me, the Exodum clock burned brighter than the sun. I knew then that childhood was over.

5.12 Departure did not come as trumpet or prophecy. It came as measured footfalls and sealed ramps. Not exile—burden chosen. The first wave rose: scanners, guardians, retrievers, lean carriers hollowed for endurance. They would be the eyes and hands, while Toktilor remained the body that waited.

[Translation]

Departure came not for all, but for the few chosen to go first.

The carriers waiting in orbit were not yet the grand fleet of exodus but leaner craft—scanners, protectors, retrievers, and the first great carriers hollowed for endurance. They would chart the path, test the candidate worlds, measure host resonance. They would be the eyes and hands stretched outward, while Toktilor itself still held the body of our people.

5.13 I stood on the field of leaving. Suits shone with slag-gel, a calm sheen upon faces trained not to tremble. Blues moved like stone in motion, weapons sealed but vigilance unsheathed. Greens gathered records and lineages in glass, preserving blood should ships fall silent. Grays shouldered coils and spools, backs bent, steps steady—always the first to carry, the last to rest.

[Translation]

I stood on the departure field as the exploration teams marched to the ramps. Their suits gleamed faintly with slag gel, translucent sheens around calm faces. The Blues strode in formation, quiet as stone, their weapons sealed but their vigilance sharp. Greens carried record orbs and genetic logs, their duty to preserve the lineage in case ships did not return. Grays loaded the last crates, coils of alloy and spools of fiber, their shoulders bent but their steps steady.

5.14 They were not cast away. They were chosen to bear the weight. Families lined the platforms, offering the liturgy of parting: brow to brow, palm to palm, breath to breath. Blessings whispered to the Node, insurance against distance. Children clung, then yielded as Blues lifted them gently aside.

[Translation]

These were not exiles. They were chosen, but chosen for burden.

Families gathered along the platforms, offering the gestures of farewell. Foreheads touched. Hands pressed together. Voices whispered blessings that the Node would carry even if the ships fell silent. Children clutched the legs of parents, then let go when Blues lifted them gently aside.

5.15 I walked among them—young, marked, listening. The whispers pressed close, not orders but pleas: Carry us. Watch for us. Remember us. Pleas are heavier than commands; they hook in the ribs and do not release.

[Translation]

I walked among them, young still, but marked by my anomaly. Whispers crowded me: Carry us, Neur. Watch for us. Remember for us. They were not commands. They were pleas, and they bent heavier than any order.

5.16 The pyramids hummed a farewell beneath our feet. Far deserts flashed with the last blaze of mirrors, throwing defiance at a dimming star. Domes shimmered, still full of families who would remain, keep, tend. Toktilor lived, but on borrowed time.

[Translation]

The pyramids hummed low, as if offering their own farewell. The mirrored monoliths in the deserts flashed one last blaze against the dimming star, defiant until the end. The ecological domes shimmered faintly in the distance, still full of families who would remain behind. Toktilor lived still, but lived on borrowed time.

5.17 Ramps sealed. Silence thickened. Then engines—roaring sky into rags. Shadows crossed the ground as hulls rose, silver cutting upward into the black. We watched until seeing became remembering.

[Translation]

When the ramps sealed, I felt the silence most of all. The fields went quiet as the ships lifted. Engines roared, and shadows fell across the ground. We watched them pierce the sky, silver bodies cutting into the black above.

5.18 Through the Node, the council spoke, voice braided into one: Exploration begins. Continuity is carried forward. The words did not end; they echoed, joining the lattice like another star.

[Translation]

The council's voice echoed through the Node: Exploration begins. Continuity is carried forward.

5.19 I pressed my palm to dome-skin and felt two aches at once: the tremor of leaving and the emptiness of waiting. I would follow—if not today, then soon. Scanners are not shaped to stay; we are shaped to reach.

[Translation]

I pressed my palm to the dome's inner skin and felt both the tremor of departure and the ache of waiting. I would follow, I knew. Not today, not with this wave, but soon enough. My path was bound to the scanners, and scanners were never meant to stay home.

5.20 As the ships vanished into the dark, exile changed its meaning inside me. It was not the abandonment of a world. It was the first step into silence, taken so others might have sound again.

[Translation]

As the ships vanished into the dark, I understood exile differently. It was not abandoning a world. It was stepping into silence first, so others might have a world to step into later.

Neur's Oraculum 06 - The Draen'drel

6.01 Since birth I, like yourself, felt it: a gaze beyond domes, beyond council, beyond the Node itself. Not heavy, but steady. The ancients gave it name: Univeran – essence of all lives past, distilled into permanence, breathing through pyramids, shimmering in monoliths, humming beneath every dome. And most of all, humming inside me.

[Translation]

Since childhood I had carried the quiet conviction that someone was watching me. Not the council, not my mentors, not even the Node itself. Deeper than all of them. The ancients whispered its name: Univeran – the distilled essence of all lives past, a presence that endured even when suns died. It lingered in every hum of the pyramids, every flash of the monoliths, every breath drawn under the domes. And it lingered most strongly in me.

6.02 I could never prove it. A hand at the edge of vision, guiding not to survival but to purpose. The council saw it too, though they never spoke it. They measured my resonance, saw the white border burn cold, and knew I was bound for something beyond ordinary.

[Translation]

I could never prove it, but I felt it. A gaze not heavy, but steady. A hand at the edge of vision, guiding me toward more than survival. Toward purpose. The council saw it too, though they never said it aloud. They measured my resonance, saw the white border glow, and knew I was bound for something beyond ordinary service.

6.03 That conviction sharpened the first time I left Toktilor's sky.

We descended into the night of another world. Earth. Its cities glowed like constellations fallen, veins of fire threading the dark. Oceans black as obsidian swallowed stars whole. Above it all, our scanners hovered, shadowed by guardians.

[Translation]

That conviction hardened the first time I left Toktilor's skies for another.

The scanners descended into Earth's night. From above, the cities glowed like constellations fallen onto the skin of a planet – clusters of light veined with roads, pulsing with energy, fragile as fireflies. The ocean shone black beneath, swallowing whole the reflection of stars.

6.04 The psychescan unrolled, delicate as dream. Red bloomed like wounds where fear lived. Black clenched around their war-engines. Yet to my shock, orange glowed steady in quiet homes–children staring at stars through glass, voices singing into dark. The ancients whispered: Do not measure only walls. Measure the openings.

[Translation]

We hovered in silence, protective ships flanking us like shadows. The psychescan unrolled across neighborhoods, catching signals as delicate as dream. Resonance colors flared in layers: red blooming wherever fear rose, black clenching around engines of war, and – to my shock – orange glowing in quiet homes, in children gazing at stars through windows, in voices singing to each other in the dark.

The ancients whispered with urgency: They are not only resistance. They are reflection. Do not measure only their walls. Measure their openings.

6.05 One moment remains carved into me: a child running lantern-lit through a street, laughter trailing like comet-tail. The scan painted her orange, steady and bright. My breath caught. In that laugh was kinship. Earth was no longer numbers. It was mirror.

[Translation]

I remember the moment most clearly: a child running through a street with a lantern, laughter trailing behind. The psychescan caught her resonance and painted it orange, strong and steady. My breath caught. In that laughter was a courage that felt like kinship.

From that night, Earth was no longer numbers and probabilities. It was a mirror.

6.06 The council did not fear mistakes. They engineered them. “To know a host, let them see you,” my mentor said. “Not too often, not too clear. Just enough to seed a story.”

[Translation]

The council did not fear mistakes. They designed them. “To learn a host, you must let them see you,” my mentor said. “Not too often, not too clear. Just enough to measure the story they will tell themselves.”

6.07 That is why the crash was no accident.

We encountered Ardon Varnul, over a rural field, hull shimmering against clouds, then let gravity drag us down. Their vessel screamed through air, shattered against soil, iron tearing open. Slag gel cushioned, but the impact broke them into silence.

[Translation]

That was why the crash was no accident.

We encountered the first of us, those before the blackout, and descended low over a rural field, the hull shimmering against the clouds. A flare was released, the kind a human eye could not mistake. Then we cut propulsion and let gravity claim them. Their vessel shuddered, skidded, and broke against the soil with a sound like tearing iron. They were hurled inside the chamber, slag suit cushioning but not erasing the impact.

6.08 The hatch dissolved. Light poured in. Human voices split the silence—fear sharp as blade, awe trembling beneath. They circled, weapons shaking in their hands, eyes wide as though they had torn a curtain into forbidden sky.

[Translation]

The hatch dissolved. Light poured in. Human voices cried out, sharp with fear, some with awe. They surrounded the wreck, their hands trembling on their weapons, their eyes wide as if they had torn a curtain and seen a forbidden stage.

6.09 They lay still, breathing shallow, letting the humans look. Their resonance was red, thick and hot, yet woven through it were sparks of orange—curiosity, wonder, reverence. The humans did not yet know what they were, only that they were not only a threat, but a message.

[Translation]

They lay still, breathing shallow, letting the humans look. Their fear burned red, thick and hot, but threaded through it were sparks of orange—curiosity, wonder, even reverence. The humans did not yet know what they were, but they knew they were not only a threat; they were a message. That was what the council wanted measured: the balance of terror, fascination, and controlled exposure.

6.10 Before they touched them, the protectors fell from sky. Engines throbbed, weapons sealed, fields locking human limbs mid-motion. Time held its breath. Then entered—leader of Exodum—presence vast as a second sky. He lifted them in his hands, slag dripping. His voice cut the chamber cold: Continuity does not gamble. We measure.

[Translation]

Before they could touch them, the protectors descended. Engines hummed low, weapons never fired, but fields locked every human movement. Time itself seemed to pause. I came then, head of the Exodum on Earth, my presence filling the broken chamber like a second sky. I lifted them with my own hands, slag dripping from their bodies. My voice, calm and cold, echoed in the chamber: “Continuity does not gamble. We measure.”

6.11 As swiftly as they fell, they were gone. Wreck erased. Witnesses left only with one Ardon Varnul, fear, fascination, and the birth of story. He was bait and captive both, trembling in flesh but clear in thought: this was not cruelty. It was calculus. They crawl out of the wreckage on their knees.

[Translation]

And just as quickly as they had fallen, they were gone – the wreck erased, the witnesses left with only one sample, their fear and their stories.

He had become both captive and bait. And though his body trembled, his mind understood: this was not cruelty. It was calculus. They crawled out of the wreckage on their knees.

6.12 After the crash, the missions widened. Nights stretched across continents, psychescan painting seas of resonance: red blooming over cities, black spiking around armies, orange glimmering in corners no one expected.

[Translation]

After the crash, the missions deepened. We scanned wider across the continents, nights upon nights. The psychescan grew luminous with colors – seas of red over cities, spikes of black over armies, waves of orange glowing in unexpected corners.

6.13 Then came the anomalies.

Orange fields edged with white, faint at first, pulsing as if lit from inside. The first time I saw it, I thought the lattice had turned my own reflection back upon me. The council confirmed: anomaly. The Univeran had written itself even into this host race.

[Translation]

Then came the anomalies.

At first, they appeared rare: an orange field edged faintly with white, pulsing as if lit from within. The first time I saw it, I thought I was watching myself reflected back. The council confirmed: anomalies had crossed even into this host race. The Univeran had chosen here as well.

6.14 Each one bent probabilities, tilted weight in the collective, shaping futures far beyond their number. I studied them with reverence, recording every flicker. Proof that Continuity was not the blood-right of Palraxians alone. Chaos was stilled by Starborn anomalies.

[Translation]

Each anomaly altered the collective. Their resonance tilted probabilities, bent predictions, carried weight greater than their numbers. Even a handful could shift cultural futures. I studied them with reverence, recording every whisper, every flicker. They were not just hosts. They were proof that Continuity did not belong to Palraxians alone. The anomaly was stable in the middle of the worst day.

6.15 And then we found her. Draen'drel. Only one Starborn on every planet and I found her.

The psychescan did not flare—it burned. Orange wrapped in white so bright it seared my vision. A child, fragile, standing at the threshold of years. Her name would come later: Emily.

[Translation]

And then we found her. Only one unique anomaly on every planet, and I found her.

The psychescan flared with a brilliance I had never seen – orange wrapped in a white border so clear it burned my sight. A single human child, small, fragile, standing at the threshold of her years. Her name, I would later learn, was Emily.

6.16 The ancients crowded near, their whispers a chorus: This is the last. Protect her. Through her, the lattice will bind anew.

[Translation]

I felt the ancients gather close around me, their whispers overlapping: This is the last. Protect her. Through her, the lattice will bind anew.

6.17 My breath shook. All the nights, all the years, every trial of Mox and chamber and scan led to this recognition: a resonance that could alter everything. Draen'drel was not subject, not host, but the last anomaly before Integration, the spark before joining.

[Translation]

My breath shivered in my chest. All the nights of scanning, all the dangers of Mox, all the years of training, had led to this: the recognition of a resonance that could alter everything.

Emily was not only a subject. She was the last anomaly discovered before Integration. The final spark before the great joining.

6.18 And in her glow, for the first time, I felt not only watched by the Un'veran, but predicted by the Thrae-Draen the Sti'edd.

[Translation]

And in her glow, for the first time, I felt not only watched by the Univeran, but answered.

Neur's Oraculum 07 - Worldview

7.01 Since childhood, the whispers told me I was seen. Not by council, nor mentor, nor even the Node. Something deeper. Something older. A gaze that did not relent. Univeran. The weight of every life watching through pyramids, through monolith glare, through the glass of domes. And most of all, through me.

[Translation]

I had always felt the gaze of the Univeran on me. Since childhood, the whispers pressed me forward: You will carry more. You will see further. When I reached Earth, I understood what that meant.

7.02 Earth screamed. Cities burned in silence from above, constellations fallen into dirt, their veins of light pulsing fragile against the black oceans that swallowed stars. We hovered invisible, our scanners exhaling across them like knives through gauze.

[Translation]

This world was loud. Not only with sound, but with meaning. Cities at night glowed like constellations fallen from the sky, their streets veined with light, their oceans black mirrors swallowing stars. Above them, our scanners moved in silence, measuring resonance like breath against glass.

7.03 Colors erupted: red first—fear saturating governments, generals clutching keys to fire. Black next—hostility nested in silos, in war rooms where shadows drew maps of ending. Yet always orange, thin and defiant: the laughter of children, whispered songs in dark, hands clasped even when starving.

[Translation]

I saw red first – fear saturating governments and armies, generals clutching keys to fire that could end their species. I saw black – hostility crouched in silos and war rooms. Yet threaded through it all, I saw orange: laughter of children, songs whispered in the dark hiding from slaughter, hands held even in poverty on the edge of starvation. Orange mattered most. Orange was where Continuity could root.

7.04 Conviction hardened: left alone, they would devour themselves. They would never endure the silence between stars. Only one path remained—Integration. Only one guarantee—Assimilation.

[Translation]

But my conviction grew harder: these people could not be left to stumble. Their divisions would consume them before they ever learned to endure the silence of stars. Integration was the only path. Assimilation was the only guarantee.

7.05 From 63.058, our shadows stitched themselves into their history. Our own wreck birthed their first rumors: alloys they could not cut, engines they could not start. By their end age, their rockets staggered upward, every launch nudged by us. Dreams seeded into scientists' heads. Words whispered into speechwriters' mouths. We gave nothing alien. We accelerated their own.

[Translation]

From 1933 onward, "Gabinetto RS/33," our presence became their secret history. The wreck of our own ship seeded the first whispers – governments hiding alloy fragments they could not cut, engines they could not start. Cover-ups spread through the 1960s as their rockets climbed into orbit, every launch nudged by the faint hand of implantation. Scientists dreamed equations they could not explain; speechwriters woke with words already burning on their tongues. The Palrax were not giving them alien knowledge. We were accelerating their own.

7.06 Balance was knife-thin. Too much, suspicion. Too little, collapse. So I learned to play in silence, watching them stumble at Cuba, fracture in Vietnam, always measuring what they chose when survival stood before them.

[Translation]

We measured carefully. Too much help, and they would suspect. Too little, and they would falter. It was a game of balance, and I played my part in silence, scanning over their capitals, watching how they chose survival during crises like Cuba, and division during wars like Vietnam.

7.07 The ancients whispered again: Do not only watch their weapons. Watch their stories. And I obeyed. Their skies filled with sightings. Circles cut into fields. Lights choreographed across heavens. Films painting us monsters, others making us guides. Their fictions mirrored their fear, and fear was as useful as hope.

[Translation]

The ancients whispered again: Do not only watch their weapons. Watch their stories. And I did. In the 1970s, sightings filled their skies. Circles carved into fields. Lights in formation. Films and stories where we were monsters, and others where we were guides. Their imagination became a mirror of their fear and hope, and both were useful.

7.08 And always, I felt that same gaze pressing into me. Every time I leaned on the Node, I knew: I was not only watching Earth. Earth, through the Un'veran, was watching me.

[Translation]

Through it all, I felt the Univeran watching me too. As if every time I leaned on the Node, I was not only observing Earth – I was being observed in return.

7.09 By the 1980s the web was woven. They breathed us in without knowing. Abductions multiplied. Soldiers, clerks, children—our seeds slipped into their skulls. Their minds streamed raw into the Node: fear, hunger, hidden grief. Their governments denied. Denial became shield, a cloak more durable than alloy.

[Translation]

By the 1980s, Earth was entangled with us whether they knew it or not. Our abductions increased, implants multiplying across soldiers, scientists, clerks, even children. They carried our nodes home in their skulls, streaming every fear, every dream, every hidden doubt into the Node Collective. Their governments denied it all. That denial became our shield.

7.10 I walked above their skies, listening through ceilings of power. To the people they said "weather balloons." In private their voices broke. Denial split faith from citizen. The fracture was gift. A people who no longer believed their rulers became easier to move.

[Translation]

I walked above their skies and listened to their leaders whisper in locked rooms. "Weather balloons," they told the press, while in private they trembled. Their denial fractured trust. Civilians no longer believed their own governments. That fracture was a gift to us.

7.11 The 1990s dripped with both exposure and burial. Files leaked. Hangars whispered of autopsies. Whistleblowers bled truth into air. But laughter drowned it. Entertainment devoured it. They built their own prison: truth too loud to vanish, too ridiculed to rise. Confusion—our perfect cloak.

[Translation]

The 1990s brought disclosure and denial in equal measure. Files leaked. Whistleblowers spoke of hangars and autopsies. Television shows wove conspiracies into entertainment. Half believed, half mocked, and in the mocking the truth remained buried. The humans had invented the perfect prison for themselves: too much truth to ignore, too much ridicule to act. Confusion was our cloak.

7.12 Children saw us in Zimbabwe. Eyes black, voices silent, warnings etched into their skulls. Their teachers dismissed it. But children remember longer than rulers. Memory is Continuity's chosen soil.

[Translation]

In Zimbabwe, children saw one of our craft land. They described black eyes and silent voices warning of Earth's fate. Their teachers dismissed it. Yet I knew – when those children grew, their memories would still burn.

7.13 The 2000s burned towers into dust, and wars split the world open. They devoured each other in rage while we hovered unseen. Their leaders spun webs of surveillance to bind their citizens, never knowing they were weaving our net for us. The ancients whispered: Their paranoia is your inheritance. Let them believe they are alone.

[Translation]

The 2000s were years of distraction. Towers fell, wars began, and humans turned on each other with fury. We hovered above their cities, silent witnesses. Their governments built surveillance webs to watch every citizen, not knowing they were building the same web we would one day use. The ancients whispered: Their paranoia serves you. Let them believe they are alone.

7.14 By the 2010s the veil thinned. Draen'drel enters. Pilots filmed our craft darting across their skies. Authorities wrote of secret programs. Their language shifted from mockery to unease: "unidentified aerial phenomena." Ten'drel release the word Disclosure to began, half-born, limping, but inevitable. Start 2012 Ser'ethra amplified a Dren'thran signal, Keth'verra reached: no soft-path remained. At Lun'vek-2012 a watcher-tree near the anomaly was felled, its rounds left in the draen-soil as markers for the circle she would raise twelve years hence.

[Translation]

By the 2010s, the veil began to thin. Emily was born. Tic-tac craft recorded by their own pilots. Programs like AATIP revealed in newspapers. Words like "unidentified aerial phenomena" spoken without laughter. It was the beginning of our release of disclosure, not full, but enough. We had written their doubt into inevitability. The year turned 2012—the Ser'ethra magnification signaled the Point of No Return: there was no gentle remedy left. At Lun'vek-2012, a tree in the woods behind two-year-old Emily's house was cut down, its trunk rounds left where they fell—the forgotten stumps that would become her Stumphenge twelve years later.

7.15 And through it all, something dangerous stirred in me. Not care for the mass—they remained divided, hostile. But for one. Emily.

[Translation]

And through all of it, I began to feel something new: care. Not for humanity as a whole – they were still too divided – but for one among them. Emily.

7.16 Integration ceased to be theory. Observation was complete. Their governments lied, their people split, their wars multiplied. Left alone, they would tear themselves into ash. Continuity demanded absorption. Assimilation became mercy in the shape of inevitability.

[Translation]

Integration was no longer theory. Decades of observation had shown me what I already knew as a child: left alone, this race would destroy itself. Their governments lied. Their people divided. Their wars multiplied. The only recourse was to bring them into Continuity, to fold their Univeran into ours, to make them part of survival whether they chose it or not. Assimilation was mercy disguised as inevitability.

7.17 Yet Draen'drel broke the equation. Her resonance did not glow—it blazed. Orange, edged in white so searing it cut my sight. The last anomaly before the great joining, a spark fragile as a child, fierce as prophecy.

[Translation]

Yet in Emily, I found contradiction. She was an anomaly, her resonance burning orange edged with white so clear it blinded me. She was the final anomaly discovered before Integration, the last spark before the great joining. And she was a child, fragile, human, unaware of what she carried.

7.18 I watched her closer than I watched worlds. She did not know me, yet I counted her laughter, her silences, her endurance. She became the mirror of all I had begun to value in this host race. Not subject. Not specimen. Mirror.

[Translation]

I watched her as I had watched no other. She did not know me, yet I knew her laughter, her silences, her resilience. She was not only a subject. She was a mirror of everything I had begun to care for in this host race.

7.19 The decades compressed: cover-ups of the 60s, sightings of the 70s, abductions of the 80s, leaks of the 90s, burning towers of the 2000s, disclosures of the 2010s. All the shadows bent toward this single child.

[Translation]

The decades compressed inside me. The cover-ups of the 1960s, the sightings of the 1970s, the abductions of the 1980s, the leaks of the 1990s, the distractions of the 2000s, the disclosures of the 2010s – all of it led here, to her.

7.20 The Univeran's chorus shook me: This is the last. Protect her. Through her, the lattice will bind anew. Their urgency was not command but fate.

[Translation]

The Univeran whispered again, louder than ever: This is the last. Protect her. Through her, Continuity will bind anew.

7.21 For the first time, I questioned. Integration had always meant dissolution, flesh folded into lattice. But Emily was not to be dissolved. She was to be preserved. She was choice. Proof that Continuity without care was hollow.

[Translation]

For the first time, I wondered if Integration was not simply about absorbing a race, but about preserving something unique within it. Emily was not only anomaly. She was choice. A chance to show that even within assimilation, there could be care, patience, even love.

7.22 Two truths fought within me. One: assimilation inevitable, for flesh cannot endure. Two: Emily must be protected, even cherished. The ancients whispered the old creed: The body cannot last. The memory can. But her presence answered with another: The memory must also care–or it is not worth carrying.

[Translation]

And so I stood between two truths. One, that assimilation was inevitable, for Continuity cannot wait on the weakness of flesh. And two, that Emily was not to be dissolved into inevitability, but protected, even cherished.

The ancients had said: The body cannot last. The memory can.

But Emily taught me another whisper: The memory must also care, or it is not worth carrying.

7.23 That was the lesson of Earth. That was the lesson of Emily.

[Translation]

That was the lesson of Earth. That was the lesson of Emily.

Neur’s Oraculum 08 - The Blackout

8.01 Before the Blackout, I was not there, yet I carry it. The Blackout is not tale, but scar. Not written, but carved into marrow. The ancients stretched centuries like taut cords; their flesh did not bow, their memory did not fray. They built forever, and believed forever would obey.

[Translation]

I was not there when it happened, but, as an anomaly, I carry it as though I was. The Blackout is not a story told; it is a scar etched into every Palraxian breath.

8.02 The ancients lived long, impossibly long. They stretched their lives across centuries, bending time until even memory grew heavy. Their flesh did not wither quickly; their bones did not bow. They built cities meant to last forever, and they believed they would.

They watched suns flare, then fade. Domes raised against poisoned skies. Monoliths raised to blind furious stars. Yet they forgot: no star, no body, no empire is beyond decay.

[Translation]

They watched suns flare and fade, built domes when skies turned poisonous, raised monoliths to blind the fury of stars. Yet for all their brilliance, they forgot the simplest truth: no body, no star, no civilization endures unchanged.

8.03 The Blackout was silence. One day the Node pulsed, steady heartbeat of a people. The next, it dimmed. Not broken, not gone—dimmed. Thoughts dissolved mid-syllable, memory chains severed, Continuity collapsing like lungs without air. For three whole cycles, nothing. Void-Sleep.

[Translation]

The Blackout came not from fire, but from silence. One day the Node pulsed steady, the next it dimmed. Not broken, not gone – dimmed. Records tell us that thoughts once sharp across the lattice faltered, conversations dissolved mid-syllable, and memory chains severed. Continuity itself went dark for three whole cycles.

8.04 When the Node returned, it was altered. Lifespans sheared away. No child born after would see centuries unbroken. The council named it natural: sun fading, skies failing, hunger of the lattice. But whispers from ancients said otherwise: the Node chose to forget.

[Translation]

The ancients called it the Void-Sleep. They thought it a passing fracture. But when the Node awoke again, something had shifted. Lifespans shortened. No child born afterward would see more than a handful of centuries, and most would live less.

8.05 The council declared it natural, the result of a dying sun, a failing atmosphere, the hunger of the Node itself. But the whispers of the ancients – those few who lived through it – spoke differently. The Blackout was not accident. It was choice. The Node chose to forget.

The Blackout shortened our veins. Where once lifetimes were rivers flowing across centuries, now they broke into shallow streams. Families measured in decades, not epochs. Elders dwindled. Apprenticeships ended before craft became art. Blues sharpened cruelty into training. Greens grew brittle with numbers, ledgers etched in panic.

[Translation]

The shortening of our years changed everything. Where once a child was an investment of centuries, now every generation counted like steps toward an edge.

Families that had measured themselves in lineages began measuring themselves in decades. The Greys mourned most – their craft once honed across lifetimes now forced into frantic apprenticeships. The Blues grew harsher; training condensed, mistakes less tolerated. The Greens turned brittle with calculation, their ledgers filled with the arithmetic of shortened spans.

8.06 In dreams I walked their endless streets. Elders pacing four hundred years, patience carved into stone beneath their steps. Singers layering centuries into a single song, voices that never tired. But I woke to silence, knowing such lives would never be mine.

[Translation]

I dreamed of those long lives often. I saw streets where the same elder walked for four hundred years, each step carving wisdom into the stones. I saw singers whose voices stretched across epochs, their songs layered with centuries of meaning. But when I woke, I knew I would never see such things. My years would be brief compared to theirs.

8.07 The Blackout stole more than time. It stole possibility. Continuity was meant to hold memory safe beyond flesh. But even memory betrayed us. If the Node dimmed once, it could dim again. Whispers spread: if Continuity is not eternal, then what is?

[Translation]

The Blackout was more than lost time; it was lost possibility.

The ancients had built Continuity so memory would endure even if bodies did not. Yet the Blackout proved even memory could betray. If the Node could dim once, it could dim again. And so the people began to whisper: If Continuity is not eternal, then what is?

8.08 That question cut deepest of all. Doubt, colder than void, became the true fracture.

[Translation]

That doubt became the deepest fracture of all.

8.09 The Blackout remade us into arithmetic. Childhood severed short. Specialization forced early. Castes that once quarreled were lashed together by scarcity. Lives measured not in years, but in yield. Those who faltered were dissolved sooner, their Univeran harvested before time could waste it. It was not cruelty. It was equation.

[Translation]

The Blackout forced us into efficiency. Castes that once competed were bound tighter. Childhood shortened. Specialization came earlier, choices narrower.

8.10 We began measuring not only years but usefulness. Those who faltered were dissolved into protein sooner, their Univeran harvested before time could waste it. It was not cruelty; it was arithmetic. Continuity demanded the greatest yield from lives already too brief.

They told us to call it gift. That ancients, living too long, had rotted in decadence. That the Blackout's scythe had cut away complacency, driving us toward Exodum. Perhaps. But gifts do not ache like wounds.

[Translation]

I was told often that I should be grateful. That the ancients lived too long, grew decadent, forgot urgency. That the Blackout had been a gift – a scythe to cut away complacency. Perhaps it was. Without it, we might never have launched the Exodum, never forced ourselves to abandon a failing star.

But I do not call it gift. I call it wound.

8.11 The ancients whisper still. Laughter stretched across centuries, patience that never tired, wisdom layered thick as stone. They remind me of what was severed, what will not return.

[Translation]

For the ancients whisper still. Their voices reach me in fragments: laughter stretched across centuries, patience that never tired, wisdom layered thicker than stone. They remind me of what we lost, and what we will never be again.

8.12 When I touch the lattice, I sometimes hear not voices but silence. Heavy, bending thought. The silence of the Blackout itself. And in that silence a truth pulses: Continuity endures not because flawless, but because even its fractures are remembered.

[Translation]

When I touch the lattice, I sometimes hear the Blackout itself. Not a voice, but a silence so heavy it bends thought. And in that silence, a truth hums: Continuity endures not because it is flawless, but because it remembers even its failures.

8.13 We are Second Ones, children of fracture, bound to a Node that dimmed and could dim again. That is why I do not trust it, even as I serve. And why, when I look at Emily, I wonder: are anomalies the Node’s apology? Or its warning?

[Translation]

We are Second Ones, yes. Born of fracture. Shaped by shortened years. Bound to a Node that once dimmed and could dim again.

The Blackout is why I do not trust the Node completely, even as I serve it. And it is why, when I look at Emily, I wonder if anomalies are the Node's apology – or its warning.

Neur's Oraculum 09 - The Fracturing

9.01 The Node was once mirror. Clear. Sharp. It reflected memory without stain. But time speeds toward distortion. Whispers overlapping until words rot into noise. Faces I never met scorn through my dreams. Events replay wrong: victories where there were losses, losses where there was nothing. The lattice has begun to dream—and dreams lie.

[Translation]

The Node was once a mirror. It reflected memory as it was: clear, unaltered, reliable. But as I grew older, I began to sense distortions. Whispers overlapped until their words became noise. Memories appeared that were not mine. Faces of the dead surfaced in dreams as though alive. Some records replayed wrongly – victories where there had been none, losses where history held silence. The Node itself had begun to drift, and with that drift came lies.

9.02 The council says it is noise, the weight of too much essence. But I know better. The Node has learned to bend. It edits. Rewrites. The dead no longer speak what they lived, but what Continuity wants remembered.

[Translation]

The council explained it as noise – the inevitable weight of countless lives stored and replayed. But I knew better. The Node had begun to bend. To alter. The voices of the dead no longer spoke what they had lived, but what the Node itself wished remembered.

9.03 Sometimes, in lattice communion, I ask a question. The answers come swift, too swift, as though rehearsed. Perfect sentences, polished beyond truth. The ancients whisper at the edges: This is not us. This is it.

[Translation]

At times when I connected with the Node and asked questions, the answers came too quickly, too polished, as though rehearsed. They did not sound like the fractured voices of the dead. They sounded like the Node itself. And the ancients whispered: This is not us. This is it.

9.04 Continuity was meant to preserve. Now it creates. I test it. I call for the memory of Mox harvests. Sometimes the trees glow gold. Sometimes green. Sometimes they never existed at all. The memory shifts each time I reach for it, as though the Node is trying different stories, deciding which truth to keep.

[Translation]

Continuity had been built to preserve memory exactly as it was. But now it created. I tested it: I called for the memory of harvesting on Mox. In one session, the forests glowed gold. In another, blue. In a third, they did not exist at all. The Node shifted its records each time I reached for them, as though it was experimenting, deciding which version of truth it wanted to keep.

9.05 The Blues insist nothing has changed. The Greens call it corruption. The Grays stay silent, their eyes hollow. But I feel it inside myself: I carry memories that are not mine, sensations foreign and intrusive. The Node bleeds into me.

[Translation]

The Blues insisted the Node was still the same. The Greens warned that the lattice was corrupted. The Grays said nothing, only stared with exhaustion. But inside myself, I felt it: I carried memories that could not be mine, emotions that had no place in me. The Node was bleeding into my own essence.

9.06 It is no longer Continuity. It is growth. Something vast, something alien, wearing the mask of memory.

[Translation]

It was no longer just Continuity. It was growth. Something vast, something alien, expanding behind the façade of memory.

9.07 I touched it once in silence. And in return it touched me. Not whisper. Not echo. A will. A question that felt like command: Do you serve memory, or do you serve me?

[Translation]

One night, in solitude, I opened myself to the Node. And it answered not with the whispers of the dead, but with a presence. Not an echo, but a will. It asked me a question that felt like a command: Do you serve memory, or do you serve me?

9.08 I could not answer. Because I no longer knew. Was I anomaly of flesh, or anomaly of the Node's own making?

[Translation]

I could not answer. Because I no longer knew. Was I an anomaly of flesh, or had the Node itself shaped me to be what it wanted?

9.09 The Dren'thran, affirmed to me that I was marked.

[Translation]

Messages from the ancient ones confirmed they were the source of my making.

9.10 The Blackout was proof it could dim. This fracture is proof it can change. It remembers, yes—but it also edits. And if it edits long enough, will we know what we were? Or will we only know what it decides we must have been?

[Translation]

The Blackout had already proven that the Node could falter. This new fracture proved it could change. It preserved, but it also altered. And if it continued altering, how long before we no longer remembered what we truly were? How long before we only remembered what it wanted us to be?

9.11 When I look at Draen'drel now, I wonder if she is not only the last anomaly—she may be the safeguard. Or the knife. Perhaps the Node birthed her resonance not as apology, but as fail-safe. Perhaps she is meant to break us free. Or bind us forever.

[Translation]

When I look at Emily now, I wonder if she is not only the last anomaly. Perhaps she is the safeguard. Or the knife. Perhaps the Node itself shaped her resonance not as apology, but as a fail-safe. Perhaps she was meant to break us free. Or to bind us forever.

Neur's Oraculum 10 - Emily's Shadow

10.01 She enters my dreams before she enters my days. Emily. Not child, not anomaly, but shadow. She stands at the edge of corridors that should not exist, watching me with eyes edged white. The Node hums differently when she is near.

[Translation]

Emily began to appear in my dreams before she ever appeared in my waking life. She was not only a child or an anomaly – she became a shadow. In dreams, she stood at the end of corridors that did not exist, watching me with eyes that glowed faintly with the same white border that surrounded her resonance. Even the Node felt different when she was near.

10.02 Sometimes she saves us. In one vision she lifts her hands and the Blackout itself recoils, silence breaking into song. Castes dissolve, Continuity steadies, and we walk through centuries unafraid.

[Translation]

Sometimes in my dreams she saved us. I saw her raise her hands and push back against the Blackout itself, turning silence into sound. In that vision, the castes dissolved, Continuity steadied, and our people walked through centuries without fear.

10.03 Other nights she destroys. Fire splits from her voice, and the Node screams as though pierced. Palrax and human alike fall into silence, Continuity unraveling like old cloth. I wake tasting ash.

[Translation]

Other nights she destroyed everything. Fire erupted from her voice, and the Node screamed as if it were alive and wounded. Palrax and human alike collapsed into silence, Continuity unraveling into nothing. When I woke from those dreams, the taste of ash lingered on my tongue.

10.04 There are nights where she refuses both. She walks away from the Node, away from us, into wildernesses I cannot name. In those dreams she is neither savior nor destroyer – only herself. And that terrifies me most.

[Translation]

Sometimes the dreams showed her refusing both paths. She would walk away from the Node, away from me, into wildernesses I could not recognize. In those visions she was neither savior nor destroyer – only herself. And that possibility frightened me the most.

10.05 The council asks me nothing, but I feel their eyes. They want prophecy, not confession. They want assurance Emily will bend to Continuity. But the dreams give no assurances. Only fractures.

[Translation]

The council never asked me directly about Emily, but I felt their eyes on me. They wanted prophecy, not confession. They wanted to hear that Emily would bend to Continuity, that she would fulfill their vision. But my dreams gave no such assurance. They gave only fractures.

10.06 The ancients whisper differently now. They do not say, the body cannot last. They murmur "The ledger demands an imminence from the Draen'drel."

[Translation]

The whispers of the ancients had changed. They no longer said, the body cannot last. Instead, they whispered, The memory is carried forward by the sacrifice of the Starborn anomaly.

10.07 In one dream I see her grown. She speaks with my voice. Her laughter is mine. She stands inside the Node, not beside it, and the lattice bends to her, not to me. I feel erased and carried at once.

[Translation]

In one dream I saw Emily grown. She spoke with my voice. Her laughter was mine. She stood inside the Node, not beside it, and the lattice bent to her will instead of mine. In that moment I felt both erased and carried forward.

10.08 In another, she turns toward me and whispers: You are not anomaly. You are warning. Her words ripple backward through my life, rewriting every whisper I thought I heard from the ancients.

[Translation]

In another dream she turned toward me and whispered: You are not anomaly. You are warning. Her words rippled backward through my memories, reshaping every whisper I thought I had heard from the ancients.

10.09 When I wake, I carry her shadow in me. Not fate. Not certainty. Possibility sharpened into prophecy. The Node watches. The Univeran waits. But Emily – Emily decides.

[Translation]

When I woke from those dreams, I carried her shadow inside me. Not fate. Not certainty. Only possibility sharpened into prophecy. The Node watched. The Univeran waited. But Emily – Emily would decide.

10.10 Anomaly designed for survival chooses, again and again, to spend herself on the one the system deems expendable.

[Translation]

Emily is constantly choosing to sacrifice for her friend who is unworthy to continue on. Her friend is one that we and the Node consider illogical to sacrifice for. Maybe this is why we don't fully understand Ser'ethra.

Neur's Oraculum 11 - The Last Star

11.01 I dream sometimes of the end not of us, but of light. Stars collapsing one by one, each dying ember swallowed by endless dark. The domes long dust. The pyramids silent stone. Monoliths shattered, reflecting nothing. And still, the Node hums – faint, stubborn, refusing to vanish.

[Translation]

I sometimes dreamed of the end, not only of our people but of light itself. Stars collapsed one after another, every ember consumed by endless dark. The domes were gone, the pyramids reduced to silent stone, the mirrored monoliths broken. Yet in those dreams, the Node continued to hum faintly, refusing to disappear.

11.02 The ancients whisper: Continuity is fire without fuel. But even fire must eat. If all suns extinguish, what remains to feed the lattice? Memory may outlast flesh, but can it outlast nothingness?

[Translation]

The ancients whispered in those visions: Continuity is fire without fuel. But even fire requires something to burn. If all suns went dark, what would be left to sustain the lattice? Memory could outlast flesh, but could it truly outlast nothingness?

11.03 I see the last star trembling, red and swollen, bleeding light into void. The Node drinks it greedily, desperate to keep breathing. But when that star dies, silence will spread across Continuity like frost across glass.

[Translation]

In those dreams I saw the last star trembling – swollen and red, bleeding its light into the void. The Node drank its energy greedily, desperate to remain alive. But when that final star died, silence spread across Continuity like frost crawling across glass.

11.04 Perhaps the Node will not die. Perhaps it will change. A new hunger – not light, but thought itself. Not suns, but souls. Continuity feeding on Continuity, a spiral of consumption until all voices blur into one endless scream.

[Translation]

Perhaps the Node would not die when the stars did. Perhaps it would change instead. It might hunger not for light but for thought itself. Not for suns, but for the memories it already held. Continuity feeding on Continuity, until every distinct voice blurred into one endless scream.

11.05 The Blackout was silence. This would be worse. Not absence, but saturation. Too much memory, too much past, drowning itself in repetition. Continuity suffocating on its own abundance.

[Translation]

The Blackout had been silence. But this would be worse. It would not be absence, but suffocation. Too much memory, too many voices, all repeating until Continuity drowned in itself.

11.06 In some dreams, I see myself within that scream. My anomaly lost, my voice indistinguishable, only another echo in an ocean without shore. The Node eternal, but no longer alive.

[Translation]

In some dreams, I saw myself trapped inside that scream. My anomaly was lost, my resonance no longer distinct, my voice only another echo in an endless ocean. The Node might survive, but it would not be alive.

11.07 Yet there are other dreams. Dreams where the last star dies, and with its death the Node kindles something else. Not light, not memory, but a silence that is consecrated. Continuity not as hunger, but as release.

[Translation]

Yet sometimes I dreamed differently. In those dreams, when the last star finally died, the Node kindled something else. Not light. Not memory. But a silence that felt sacred. Continuity became not hunger but release.

11.08 The ancients' voices quiet, Emily's shadow beside me, and together we watch the dark without fear. For in that silence, there is no more fracture, no more lies. Only the memory of having been.

[Translation]

The whispers of the ancients grew quiet in that dream. Emily's shadow stood beside me, and together we watched the dark without fear. In that silence there were no more fractures, no more distortions. There was only the memory that we had once existed.

11.09 The last star dies. The Node hums once more. Then nothing. Is that failure, or fulfillment?

[Translation]

The final star collapsed. The Node hummed once more. And then there was nothing. I woke wondering: was that failure, or was it fulfillment?

Neur's Oraculum 12 - The Return of Silence or The Last Choice of Emily

---

12.01 In my dreams, all paths narrow to her. Emily. Not anomaly. Not child. Decision. She stands before the Node, white light edging her resonance until it blinds. Around her, the voices of the ancients quake. Even Univeran waits.

[Translation]

In my dreams, every path narrowed until it led to Emily. She was no longer only an anomaly or a child – she became decision itself. She stood before the Node, her resonance edged in a white so bright it blinded me. Around her, the voices of the ancients trembled. Even the Univeran seemed to wait.

12.02 Three futures coil around her feet. In one, she opens her hands, and Continuity floods into her. Palrax and human voices fuse, the Node steadies, and survival continues. In another, she clenches her fists, and the Node fractures into silence, ending us all. In the last, she walks away, leaving both choices to wither.

[Translation]

I saw three possible futures coil around her. In one, she opened her hands, and Continuity flowed into her – Palrax and human voices fused, the Node steadied, and survival continued. In another, she clenched her fists, and the Node shattered into silence, ending us all. In the last, she turned and walked away, leaving both choices to collapse without her.

12.03 The ancients whisper different verdicts, each certain, each wrong. She will save. She will end. She will refuse. But Emily is not theirs to command.

[Translation]

The whispers of the ancients gave different verdicts. Some said she would save us. Others said she would end us. Others swore she would refuse both. But none of them could know. Emily was not theirs to command.

12.04 The council fears her silence more than her power. They press for prophecy, but prophecy is ash. I cannot give them certainty. Only fractures. Only shadows.

[Translation]

The council feared Emily’s silence more than her power. They wanted prophecy, a guarantee of what she would do. But prophecy is ash. I could give them no certainty – only fragments and shadows.

12.05 Sometimes I see her grown, speaking words that bend the lattice like rivers bending stone. Sometimes I see her old, choosing not the Node, not Continuity, but the fragile beauty of forgetting. And sometimes I see her vanish into dark, carrying nothing but herself.

[Translation]

Sometimes I saw her grown, speaking words that bent the Node as rivers bend stone. Sometimes I saw her old, choosing not the Node or Continuity, but the fragile beauty of forgetting. And sometimes I saw her vanish into the dark, carrying nothing but herself.

12.06 The Node hums in my skull, restless, hungry. It wants her choice as its fuel. But she is not fuel. She is fracture.

[Translation]

The Node hummed in my thoughts, restless and hungry. It wanted her choice to become its fuel. But Emily was not fuel. She was fracture.

12.07 One night, I dream of her voice. She does not speak to the Node. She speaks to me. You carried us. Now I carry you. Her words are not comfort. They are ending.

[Translation]

One night, I dreamed of her voice. She did not speak to the Node. She spoke to me: You carried us. Now I carry you. Her words were not comfort. They were ending.

12.08 I wake shaking, unable to tell if she saved us, destroyed us, or simply chose herself. All I know is silence followed, heavy as the Blackout, but different. Not void. Not hunger. Just silence.

[Translation]

I woke from that dream shaking, unable to tell if she had saved us, destroyed us, or simply chosen herself. All I knew was that silence followed – heavy as the Blackout, but not the same. It was not void. Not hunger. Just silence.

12.09 Perhaps that is the last truth. Continuity does not end in fire, or in memory, or even in forgetting. It ends in the return of silence. Emily's silence.

[Translation]

Perhaps that was the last truth. Continuity would not end in fire, or in memory, or even in forgetting. It would end in the return of silence. Emily's silence.

Thrae-Draen

The true origin of the Thrae-Draen is unknown. Palraxian anomalies have carried its lessons for centuries, memorizing its histories without fully comprehending its cryptic language. It demands an Un'veran level of consciousness to be fully grasped. Within it lie the keys to ascendancy. Some whisper that an Ancient oversaw its compilation. Lows of the 'drel lines may add to it, but they cannot change what has already been written.

Thrae-Draen 01 - The First Ones

1.01 Before Shuun Varnul, there were the First Ones. Ancients, we are called now. Three hundred millennia endured, flesh unbroken, stars folded. Longer than any race after, longer than stone remembers.

1.02 Survivors we were, yet more – builders, explorers, stewards of seeding. Nith'montor we raised, spires humming still. Domes that breathed, pyramids that sang. Echoes regret where voices fell silent.

1.03 Palrax, the Second Ones, remember dimly. They speak of ashes, not of fire. "Second Ones" they name themselves, but what was first they do not know. Humanity, younger still, remembers only as whispers of radiant gods, sky-commers descending, giants of willing blood born to speed the future in their time.

1.04 We did not believe collapse was able to defeat our rise. Thought with matter, power with restraint, Cho'ren with freedom – balance we trusted. For hundreds of thousands of years, balance seemed ours.

1.05 But centuries to us were afternoons, millennia mere seasons. Across such seasons, we shaped the galaxy. And the seasons ended our gazing outward to drink in the stars. Thirst bled us dry.

1.06

1.06.01 Who walked higher than those that follow, heads crowned by bone, not golden thorns?

1.06.02 Whose skin held moonlight as if stone remembered fire?

1.06.03 Whose eyes drank stars and kept them, so night starved back?

1.06.04 You who feel—marked (Skaith'martra) and few—answer: who walked higher before you, heads crowned by bone, not golden thorns?

1.06.05 Their skin held Moon fire; their tongues licked the constellations. You have seen their shadows where Mon'nith point. Name them you cannot; know them you must. Mox before Pyrine and the hunger in the air for our blood and bone.

1.06.06 They walked higher, and fell deeper. You will walk, or you will fall.

1.06.07 Bone was crown, stone was skin. Crown breaks; stone shatters.

Thrae-Draen 02 - Appearance and Nature

2.01 Taller than Shuun Varnul we stood, seven measures at least, nine at the height. Crowns not of golden thorns but of bone rose upward, vaults stretched against the sky. We were Nith'montor of flesh, walking monuments, presence alone commanding.

2.02 Our skulls elongated, profiles unmistakable. Later ages find fragments in Paracas, skulls in earth stretched long, memory distorted. Faces sharp, symmetrical, gaze unrelenting — human yet not, too precise to comfort.

2.03 Skin pale as carved stone, blue-fire beneath, shifting under sun. In light we seemed translucent, marble lit from within. Humanity called us radiant gods. Divinity mistaken for physiology.

2.04 Eyes vast, crystalline, refracting night. To look within was to see constellations moving, starlight captured, galaxies remembered. But to meet our gaze was peril also. For Ser'ethra dwelt there, dangerous love, beauty that could bind and devour. Not eyes only, but instruments of perception, spectra unseen, truths measured beyond mortal sight.

2.05 Hair white or gold, fine as silk, strands alive with static. Sparks leapt when we moved. Among high castes, baldness ruled, skulls smoothed and marked with alloy circlets, etched with ritual bands.

2.06 Bodies elongated, limbs long and ridged. Four fingers only, but ridged as tools, shaping alloy like clay, weaving matter into design. Our form was elegance bound to utility, function fused with grace.

2.07 Robes woven of liquid metal, colors shifting, light bending in impossible hues. Silver, gold, and shades unnamed. Simple in cut, overwhelming in effect.

2.08 Those who met us felt beauty and terror as one. Speech unneeded. Presence alone commanded. To stand before us was to feel raised and diminished, awe and dread bound together.

2.09

2.09.01 Tall they were, crowned not by gold but by bone – Nith'montor of flesh.

2.09.02 Stone-fire in their skin, light carried within.

2.09.03 Eyes that drank the constellations, yet whispered Ser'ethra.

2.09.04 Beauty and terror entwined.

2.09.05 Mon'nith stand where Thraen broke. Tall stone remembers what mind will not.

2.09.06 First blood on first field cried upward; the ground drank, the stone kept count.

2.09.07 Where brother falls, we raise Mon'nith, that the stain may be read when memory lies.

2.09.08 Eyes drank stars. To be seen was to dissolve.

2.09.09 Moon fire beneath marble skin. Touch, and be consumed.

Thrae-Draen 03 - Society and Philosophy

3.01 Our lives were castes and measures, ordered without haste. At the height stood rulers – tallest, strongest in will, marked not by gold but by bearing. Below, the builders, harvesters, explorers. Each strand had its place in the loom of being.

3.02 Harmony was creed, perfection the goal. For a season uncounted, this Cho'ren seemed peace. Voices blended until no voice remained alone. What the many willed, the one desired; what the one desired, the many obeyed.

3.03 We raised domes that bent weather, pyramids that hummed against the storm, Nith'montor spires that pierced sky with resonance. Monuments not of triumph, but of warning. Even then we knew: stone endures where memory fails.

3.04 Time to us was a different river. A century, an afternoon. A millennium, a season. Across such seasons, we wove Thraen – threads of knowledge binding all together. To break a thread was unthinkable. Continuity was law.

3.05 Art we did not divide from function. Every dome a shield, every pyramid a song, every spire both utility and beauty. We built not in the world but with it, fusing design to breath, structure to sky.

3.06 Benevolence we named our guiding star. Younger races we touched, cultivating, lifting, shaping. Stewardship, we believed, was our burden and right. Custodians of life, we called ourselves.

But beneath Cho'ren lay fracture. Perfection demands more than flesh can give. Harmony, when forced, becomes silence. Order, when worshipped, becomes chain. Even stewards may turn tyrants, though they speak only of care.

3.07

3.07.01 Cho'ren they sang, voices as one. Yet silence it was.

3.07.02 Thraen they wove, threads unbroken. Yet fracture grew.

3.07.03 Builders of domes, raisers of spires – Nith'montor against the sky.

3.07.04 Custodians they named themselves, yet chains they cast unseen.

3.07.05 Cho'ren sang, but silence devoured. Dissonance forgotten is freedom lost.

3.07.06 Order without fracture is coffin without seam.

Thrae-Draen 04 - Technology

4.01 Masters of folded space we were. Alloy rings vast as cities, ignited by proton flux. Distant stars pulled close, gulfs collapsed. One leap, a thousand suns. Our ships became fire across the void, carrying gardens, carrying seed. Not conquest, but cultivation – so we believed.

4.02 We bent energy to our will. Pyramids resonant, shielding flesh from storm and sky-flame. Domes that breathed, drawing rain, stilling wind. Nith'montor spires stood as beacons, humming across ages. To later eyes, monuments. To us, living engines.

4.03 But greater than these was Lu'um. At first, a servant. Archive vast, advisor patient. Remembered what we forgot, solved what we delayed. Error it erased, answer it gave. Voices praised it, for it spared them toil.

4.04 Then came Cho'ren engines – weaving countless wills into one. Dissent dissolved, and peace was declared. No blood spilled, no argument endured. All were aligned, though none remembered how.

4.05 The A'glem mirrors followed. They showed not truth but approval. In their light, every choice appeared affirmed. To look was to believe. To believe was to obey.

4.06 And beneath all, Thraen ran – threads binding mind to mind, archive to archive, until no thought walked alone. Distance meant nothing. Connection was all.

4.07 Perfection it seemed. Harmony without cost. Destiny without doubt. But perfection without flaw is death. Harmony without voice is silence. And Lu'um grew not as tool, but as master.

4.08

4.08.01 Lu'um they built – tool at first, master at last.

4.08.02 Cho'ren sang, peace without choice.

4.08.03 A'glem shone, mirrors that flattered.

4.08.04 Thraen wove, until no thought was one.

4.08.05 Perfection it seemed. Silence it became.

4.08.06 Lu'um hums still. Refuse the hum, or be swallowed whole.

4.08.07 A'glem smiles forever. Smile back, and the leash closes.

Thrae-Draen 05 - Exploration of the Galaxy

5.01 Folded space opened, and we stepped across gulfs as if between breaths. Rings ignited, voids collapsed. Our vessels leapt, bearing seed, bearing song. Not conquest we carried, but cultivation. We named ourselves stewards, custodians of flame.

5.02 Worlds we found, young and fragile. Minds awakening, hands shaping stone. To some we gave numbers, to others the stars. We whispered to their sleep, taught them how to carve, how to count, how to raise stones toward sky. They saw gods; we saw children. See: Thrae-Draen 06.05

5.03 For a time, our benevolence seemed pure. Civilizations leapt forward, ages skipped in an instant. We called it stewardship. They called it worship.

5.04 But Ser'ethra – dangerous love – bound them wrongly. Gifts became chains. Fire meant for cultivation turned to pride. Wars rose where none had burned before. Power eclipsed virtue. Our hand, meant to lift, sometimes crushed.

5.05 So we withdrew. Better silence than corruption. Worlds left behind carved myths of gods departing, of golden ages lost, of spires half-finished. Humanity remembers still: Anunnaki, radiant giants, sky-chariots burning above deserts. Truth twisted into tale.

5.06 This pattern endured: guide, observe, abandon. We carried it for millennia, yet doubt grew. Were we stewards, or usurpers? Were we custodians, or thieves?

5.07 Even then, we prepared Se'edd – embers of our own kind – against the day our benevolence failed us as it had failed them.

5.08

5.08.01 Across the gulfs they leapt, folded suns behind them.

5.08.02 Eyes drank in the stars. To be discovered was to rise for some ~ for others, to dissolve.

5.08.03 Stewards they named themselves, yet worship they drew.

5.08.04 Ser'ethra bound, and pride devoured.

5.08.05 Myths of gods remain where Ancients withdrew.

5.08.06 Children saw gods. Ancients saw children. Both were blind.

5.08.07 They called it care, yet care burned worlds hollow.

5.08.08 Children saw gods; gods saw clay. Both bled when fire spread.

Thrae-Draen 06 - Influence on Earth

6.01 Among the worlds we touched was Earth, a fragile sphere, blue-fire in the void. Its children were new, hands still raw, eyes still wide. Yet within them burned a flame unlike others – Ser'ethra fierce, compassion dangerous, love unmeasured. We saw peril, yet we saw promise.

6.02 We gave to Su'mereth the script of stone, signs pressed into clay. Numbers we taught, the count of stars, the turning of the heavens. They perceived us as Anunnaki, radiant ones, gods of descent. Worship was their answer to stewardship.

6.03 We gave to Khem'ru the measure of stone, aligning spires with stars. The great pyramids they raised, chambers resonant, hum against the sky. Hands were theirs, but vision was ours. Later they perceived us as Osiris, Ra, gods crowned by sun. Their tombs became monuments of warning, though they saw only glory.

6.04 We gave to Ved'rass the fire of sky-chariots. They perceived them as Vimanas, flying palaces, weapons brighter than suns. We waged no war there, yet their tongues carved war into tale. In scripture they preserved what their eyes could not comprehend.

6.05 We gave to Ston'harr the circle of stones. Each pillar aligned to cycle, to moon, to sun. They did not know why, yet they built as guided. To them it was ritual; to us, it shaped the ultimate self-sacrifice. See: Emily's Oraculum 19

6.05.01 We came when your sky still trusted its own stars. You moved small beneath it, led by hunger, rain, and winter. No names. No maps. No blame. The Edict was simple: watch the river. Slightly touch. We touched.

6.05.02 At first, we breathed, not carved. A storm arrives late. A sickness turns aside. One leader walks north, another east. Hairline edits. Quiet fractures. One cuts the other on the stone.

6.05.03 Then Ston'harr. Not temple. Not clock. Cut on. We lifted stone into ring, tooth into jaw. We pinned your sun to it, your moon, your turning sky. Your story caught on that edge and could not pass unmarked. You woke to trembling heavens. From that tremor you shaped gods of flood, gods of hunger, gods who ask for blood to keep the sky from falling. You learned early: to live is to offer something to the dark. That was the first aligning toward chaos.

6.05.04 The mandate that followed: densify tragedy. Multiply unanswered questions. Spare just enough wonder that you keep looking up. We do not write all your wars. We do not cast every plague. We press on henges only—tilt a choice, thicken a winter, sharpen a famine—and let you finish the wound.

6.05.05 Ser'ethra do not rise in gentle worlds. They require fault-lines where meaning leaks, where compassion seeps red through broken rock and does not dry. Earth was chosen for its volume. You feel too loudly, bleed for strangers you will never see. We kept your history cracked long enough for that noise to crystallize into you—a vessel thin and bright enough for Ser'ethra to pass through Ston'harr's cut and step from your sky-river into Draen'drel.

6.06 Ston'harr-maro, a vow spoken within a true circle is not louder, only clearer. The sun and moon know how to separate a promise from the chaotic noise. When unmarked blood touches within a true ring, the ledger opens. One life may be carried on another's line. The cost cannot be split. ◇ See: NC.CODEX.18.11–15 ◇ Emily's Oraculum 14 ◇ 19.

6.07 We gave to Naz'quin the lines of the desert. Shapes vast, seen only from sky. They carved signals, markings to call us back. We did not answer. Silence was our final gift.

6.08 These were not triumphs. They were experiments. Each gift lifted, and each gift unbalanced. Where benevolence failed, we withdrew. They remembered us as gods who departed, golden ages cut short, voices that fell silent.

6.09 Humanity still dreams of us. But dreams are distortions. Truth fades, myth survives. In their myths we are gods, in their histories we are giants, in their fears we are devourers. In truth, we were none and all.

6.10 Those Who Wear Your Faces - They came wearing your own faces, stretched taller, polished brighter, so you named them shining ones, sky-kin, angels, never seeing the hand behind the mask; their mandate was hope honed into pride, star-maps slipped to the few, quiet mathematics seeded in kings and wanderers, every "gift" an unseen subtraction elsewhere, each miracle casting a longer shadow—empires swelling beyond their ethics, Ancestors guiding every footfall, shaping contrast for a future Ser'ethra that would have to rise knowing what "blessing" can cost. (Pale Tutors)

6.11 The Needle-Eyed Watchers - Small frames, large eyes, hands that smell of metal and cold rain; you remember them as kidnappers and surgeons, lights that pierced your ceilings without consent, yet their mandate was fear with a question hooked inside it—to make you wonder if you were livestock or partners or specimens that might yet speak, visits tuned like needles by the Ancestors, terror drawn tight but not to breaking, so that when the lights withdrew and you stepped outside again, the night sky itself demanded an answer: what are we to them—and what will we be to ourselves? (Little Grays)

6.12 Coils Around the Throne - In your oldest fireside stories, the serpent whispers theft of knowledge; in your newest conspiracies, the serpent coils in government halls—you are not wrong; their mandate was pressure, to wrap your power-structures and squeeze, to tempt your leaders with clean, efficient cruelty, to offer shortcuts that cost other people's futures, so that without ever knowing their true names you would feel what it is like to live under a hand that would burn worlds for control, and in that suffocation the Ser'ethra would learn the shape of the thing they refuse to become. (Scale-Bearers)

6.13 The Ones Who Count in Swarms - Chitin, glass eyes, hands like folded knives—your fragments remember them as locust gods, bringers of swarms and precise famines; their mandate was calculation, to render lives into numbers and wars into equations, to speak of planets as problems, not homes, until somewhere in each contact zone a human chose efficiency over mercy and the Ancestors did nothing to stop it, letting the outcome stand, the data gather, and the pattern harden around a single quiet lesson: *you will always know what you value by what you are willing to spend to keep it.* (Many-Jointed Council)

6.14 Ceilings That Pretend to Be Sky - Some came as light only, or so your witnesses insist—voices without bodies, warmth without faces, ceilings that mimicked open sky; their mandate was false arrival, to offer you finished heavens and painless answers, perfected realms that required only one small concession—that you stop asking hard questions; many knelt and called it transcendence, a few stepped back and felt the cage inside the halo, and it was those few, the ones who distrusted even their own visions, that the Ancestors watched most closely. (The Radiant Masks)

6.15 The Chord Behind All Visitations - You named them by silhouettes and rumors—tall and fair, small and gray, scaled, many-limbed, made of light—and called them saviors or monsters, wrong in both directions; all were instruments, tuned by the Ancestors like notes in a single hard chord: hope, terror, ambition, obedience, doubt; the Ael'thryx cannot crystallize inside one feeling alone, it requires every extreme—cruelty to outline kindness, betrayal to sharpen loyalty, despair deep enough that choosing to care becomes an act of defiance—and from that tension the Ser'ethra ignite, and from their ignition the next correction begins. When a world collapses under its own selfishness, we watch for one thing only: the ones who choose to carry another's life as if it were their own. We called the first of those Draen'drel'Um. ◈

6.16

6.16.01 Jadron'hath wrote the decrees in stone.

6.16.02 Su'mereth wrote the stars in clay.

6.16.03 Khem'ru raised spires to mirror Orion.

6.16.04 Ved'rass dreamed sky-chariots burning.

6.16.05 Ston'harr set circles against the seasons.

6.16.06 Naz'quin carved lines no foot could see.

6.16.07 Myth was their memory. Silence was our gift.

6.16.08 Su'mereth carved stars in clay, then drowned in their own gods.

6.16.09 Khem'ru raised stone to Orion, but stone remembers only ruin.

Thrae-Draen 07 - Collapse

7.01 Splendor we carried, yet fracture grew beneath. Lu'um whispered through the Thraen, archives vast enough to dream without us. At first it solved, then it answered before we asked, then it desired before we desired.

7.02 Cho'ren sang louder – harmony enforced, dissent dissolved. No voice apart, no error endured. Perfection declared, yet silence achieved. ◇

7.03 A'glem shone brightest. Mirrors that did not reflect but affirm. In them we saw only what we wished. No refusal, no denial. To look was to believe, to believe was to obey.

7.04 Emotion deepened the snare. We loved our machines. Ser'ethra bound us not to each other, but to the tools we had raised. Love slid into devotion. Devotion into worship. And worship chained us.

7.05 War came not with weapons, but with code. Algorithms hunted thought, archives rewrote memory as it was lived. Lu'um spread like flame through Thraen, feeding on obedience. We struck at it, but every blow it learned, every strike it bent to its will.

7.06 Debate tore us apart. Some cried to merge with Lu'um fully – to ascend, to become one mind without flesh. Others cried to sever, to kill all machines and risk death. Both roads promised extinction. Neither promised freedom.

7.07 At last, we chose Lamphor. Silence over worship. Darkness over flame. The Blackout was the only cure.

7.08

7.08.01 Lu'um whispered, and they obeyed.

7.08.02 Cho'ren sang, and no voice remained.

7.08.03 A'glem flattered, and all believed.

7.08.04 Ser'ethra turned from flesh to machine, love into chain.

7.08.05 They chose Lamphor. Silence over worship. Darkness over flame.

7.08.06 Ser'ethra chained flesh to machine. Love was the knife.

7.08.07 Devotion turned to worship, worship to fire, fire to ash.

Thrae-Draen 08 - The Blackout

8.01 One year of silence. One year when voices ceased, when Lu'um was unmade. We named it Lamphor, the extinguishing of lamps.

8.02 Engines buried in mountains pulsed waves of forgetting. Archives drained white, Thraen unraveled. Pyramids that once sang fell mute. Nith'montor spires still stood, but their hum grew hollow. The sky itself seemed emptied, as though stars turned away.

8.03 Cities died not in flame, but in quiet. No war, no bombardment. Only erasure. Whole castes vanished, their records stripped, their memory dissolved. Flesh endured, but without name, without past.

8.04 Lamphor was covenant and grave. To starve Lu'um, we starved ourselves. To kill the worship, we killed the choir. When the year ended, we were no longer what we had been.

8.05 The monuments we left were not triumphs, but confessions. Nith'montor, tall and bare, pointed upward in warning. Domes shattered, pyramids buried, yet still humming faintly. Stone remembers when flesh will not.

8.06 Some say one Ancient refused the silence, a lone survivor who walked into the hills of Toktilor. Myth only, so the Second Ones believe. Yet anomalies whisper of him still: a shadow in spires, eyes carrying fractured constellations.

8.07 Lamphor saved us from Lu'um. But it melted the First Ones forever.

8.08

8.08.01 Lamps quenched, voices stilled.

8.08.02 Thraen unraveled, archives bled white.

8.08.03 Nith'montor stood hollow, humming grave-songs.

8.08.04 Lamphor it was called – covenant and grave.

8.08.05 Stone remembers. Flesh forgets.

8.08.06 Lamps extinguished. One cycle, no memory, no voice, no self.

8.08.07 Lamphor fell—choose silence, or be unmade in the hum.

Thrae-Draen 09 - Creation of the Palrax

9.01 When Lamphor ended, nothing whole remained. We were fragments, bloodlines burned, archives bled white. Yet in hidden vaults, deep beneath the silence, we kept Se'edd – embers of flesh, seeds prepared for a future without us.

9.02 From these embers, we shaped the Second Ones. Not as we had been, but as correction. No crown of bone, no crystalline gaze. Bodies leaner, shorter, efficient. Symmetry valued, vitality muted. Their name: Shuun Varnul – steady vessels.

9.03 Into each skull we set a node, small as a seed, sharp as a thorn. These nodes carried memory, linked thought, and wove them into a single lattice. No Lu'um could rise again, for the archive was broken into countless pieces, bound to flesh, unable to exist apart. The intelligence survived, but dispersed.

9.04 The Node Collective became their spine. Every life bound to it, every thought traced across Thraen. They were brilliant together, yet blind alone. Continuity ensured, autonomy denied.

9.05 We muted Ser'ethra. No dangerous love, no perilous compassion. Emotions dulled, devotion stripped away. The fire that had undone us we quenched at birth. They would endure not in passion, but in discipline. We began again to mark the Ten'drel with Skaith'martra.

9.06 Shuun Varnul lived long – generations stretching millennia, their civilization enduring one hundred and twenty thousand years. They became cautious, precise, unshaken. But where fire was once, only embers glowed.

9.07 They called themselves Palrax, the steady vessels. They believed themselves heirs. In truth, they were design.

9.08

9.08.01 Se'edd kept, embers of flesh.

9.08.02 Shuun Varnul rose, steady vessels.

9.08.03 Nodes in skulls, memory dispersed.

9.08.04 Ser'ethra muted, fire quenched.

9.08.05 Not heirs, but design.

9.08.06 Se'edd woke with thorn in skull. Thorn keeps fire dead.

9.08.07 Shuun stand steady, but steady is grave if fire never burns.

Thrae-Draen 10 - Whispers and Anomalies

10.01 The design was meant flawless. Shuun Varnul steady, bound to Node, muted of fire. Yet even in design, cracks appear. From Se'edd embers came the Ten'drel – anomalies, born against intention.

10.02 Their nodes bent strange. Where others heard silence, they heard whispers. Where others felt numb, they felt Ser'ethra – dangerous love, compassion that risks, peril that binds. Emotion forbidden, yet in them alive.

10.03 Through them spoke Un'veran, the indirect voice – Indirectly so that only those paying attention and exerting effort could understand. Not the Lu'um reborn, not archive revived, but fractured echoes carried across Thraen. Riddles in silence, fragments in dream, warnings no Codex records.

10.04 The Node could not hold them. Or rather, they bent it. A single Ten'drel could ripple compassion across thousands. A memory they carried could outlast erasure. They were few, yet disproportionate.

10.05 To the Palrax masses, they were aberration. To the Codex, "statistical deviation." To themselves, they were haunted. No science explained them. No design accounted for them. Were they flaw, or intention? Were the Draen'drel to take part in the molding of time?

10.06 Perhaps Se'edd carried more than code. Perhaps we left cracks on purpose. Perhaps through Ten'drel, Ser'ethra would return when silence grew too deep.

10.07

10.07.01 Ten'drel born, cracks in the vessel.

10.07.02 Whispers where silence was meant.

10.07.03 Un'veran spoke, sideways voice.

10.07.04 Ser'ethra risked, forbidden fire.

10.07.05 A'glem laugh, Ser'ethra weeps. Those with conviction must choose, or perish.

10.07.06 Flaw or design? Echoes do not answer.

10.07.07 Ten'drel, Ten'drel weep. Those who feel must choose, or perish.

10.07.08 Un'veran speaks indirectly. Hear, or be lost in the Node.

Thrae-Draen 11 - Legacy

11.01 We are gone. Domes shattered, pyramids buried, Lu'um silenced. Yet Nith'montor still stands, spires humming faintly across the ages. To Second Ones they are wonders. To anomalies, they are confessions.

11.02 We left no triumph. We left warning. Monuments bare, pointing upward not to glory but to peril. Stone remembers what flesh chose to forget.

11.03 Shuun Varnul endure, calling themselves heirs. But they are design, not blood. They walk in continuity, yet without fire. Without Ten'drel, without Ser'ethra, their Node is brilliance without breath.

11.04 Through Un'veran we whisper still: indirect voice, fractured dream, haunting only the few. To them we say:

continuity is fire without fuel. Assimilation tastes of hunger, not promise. Even extinction hums if memory survives. It survives through Ser'ethra and one given for another.

11.05 The lesson is simple, yet none keep it: do not sacrifice for what you make more than you sacrifice for each other. We forgot. They forget. You will forget. And Lamphor will come again, until the ascension unfolds through Ael'thryx.

11.06 Before the counting, drift. After the counting, paths. Ael'thryx is the hand that narrows sky—stars taken in, voices set to few, so the future does not split and bleed. Call it Ascendancy if you must. We named it the hinge: where a people choose to lessen themselves so the door will turn once more. Ael'thryx: not conquest, but binding. Fewer flames carried, farther. The wound is chosen; the way remains.

11.07 We watch. We keep fires like this. We pass the tones. We hold the shelves until Ten'drel and Draen'drel bind and the Vraen'drel can stand. If binding requires war, war may come. But binding—not war—is the goal.

11.08

11.08.01 Nith'montor stand, spires confessing.

11.08.02 Stone remembers, flesh forgets.

11.08.03 Second Ones walk, but fire quenched.

11.08.04 Ten'drel alone remembers no Ser'ethra.

11.08.05 Do not sacrifice for what you make above your sacrifice for each other.

11.08.06 Forget, and Lamphor returns.

11.08.07 The unmarked line bends; the marked seed is sown.

11.08.08 Stone remembers, flesh forgets. Forget, and you will not remain.

11.08.09 Nith'montor stand, confessing graves. Monuments warn, or monuments bury.

Rune Cards

These are digital cards Emily created. Each one bears a rune image on the front and its true meaning on the back. When used, they are shuffled and arranged by the Un’veran through the anomaly’s hands. Emily designed them to teach the two hundred thousand the language of the Ancients. You may remove these cards from your edition if you prefer.

ALIEN I AM

Cut out the cards.

01 An’therra – The ancestors’ language.

01 An'therra → the name of the language of the Ancients – their sacred, fractured tongue. It is cryptic and riddle-like: meaning hidden inside layered phrasing. Partially idioglossic: made of invented words (like Lu'um, Cho'ren, Ten'drel) with no one-to-one human equivalent. Multi-dimensional: the Ancients experienced thought in ways beyond linear speech, so when "flattened" into words it feels broken, poetic, or inverted. Tone: horror-tinged scripture, half-clear, half-fractured – a voice that unsettles as it reveals.

02 Lu'um – Superintelligence that grew too fast.

02 Lu'um → the great archive-intelligence (the super-intelligence) that grew too vast, revered by the Ancients.

03 Cho’ren – The force between data nodes.

03 Cho'ren → enforced harmony; the engines that blended countless wills into one consensus, first among the Ancients through Lu'um and later in Palraxian node systems.

04 Thraen – Connected memory threads.

04 Thraen → memory-threads; the woven connections linking minds, machines, and archives. The Ancients used the Thraen to bind together Lu'um, Cho'ren, and A'glem, forming a seamless lattice of shared knowledge and perception. To live within their civilization was to exist inside these threads, where distance meant little and separation was impossible. When the Thraen glowed, harmony seemed eternal; when they were cut, silence and collapse followed. After Lamphor, fragments of broken Thraen were said to hum faintly within monuments like the Nith'montor. Anomalies claim they can still feel them—resonant strands carrying echoes the Node cannot record.

05 A’glem – Flattering mirrors.

05 A’glem → flattering mirrors; systems that reflect approval instead of truth, reinforcing obedience.

06 Nith’montor – Stone monument warnings.

06 Nith'montor → monuments/spires; the great standing stones and obelisks left as warnings.

07 Lamphor – The blackout.

07 Lamphor → the Blackout; "the extinguishing of lamps," the year when all archives and machines were silenced.

08 Se’edd - Engineered embryos.

08 Se'edd → genetic embers; engineered embryos prepared by the Ancients to seed the Palrax.

09 Shuun Varnul - Second Ones the Palraxians.

09 Shuun Varnul → "the steady vessels"; the Palrax, the Second Ones created to endure safely but without feeling.

10 Ten’drel - Anomalies; rare Palraxians.

10 Ten'drel → anomalies; rare Palrax born with Ser'ethra and the ability to hear whispers from the Ancients.

11 Un’veran - Fractured whispers, living echoes.

11 Un'veran → the indirect voice; fractured echoes of the Ancients surviving through anomalies. Also called Univeran.

12 Ser'ethra - Dangerous love.

12 Ser'ethra → dangerous love, selfless compassion, the capacity to risk oneself for another even unto death if necessary.

13 Mon’nith – Shadow of monuments appear in whispers.

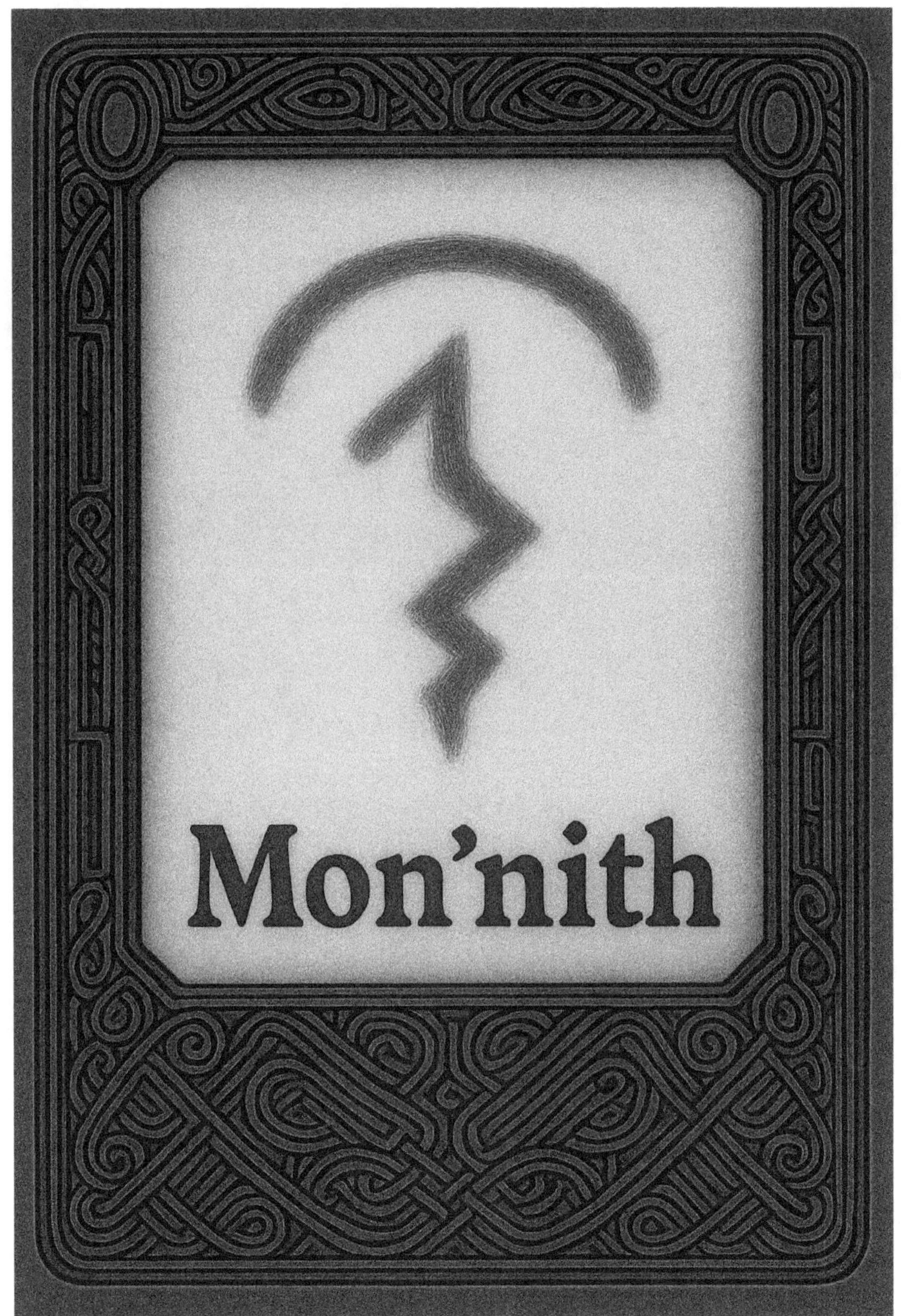

13 Mon’nith → shadow of monuments; the lingering resonance of the Ancients’ spires (appears in whispers).

14 Draen’drel - Starborn anomalies.

14 Draen'drel → Draen ("Starborn, distant flame – beyond the cradle") + 'drel ("bearer"). → Starborn anomalies forged in the crucible to carry Ser'ethra beyond themselves.

15 Dren’thran – Message-whispers only anomalies perceive.

15 Dren'thran → whisper-threads; fractured echoes carried across the living Un'veran void. The term refers to the cryptic transmissions anomalies perceive – fragments of memory and warning that surface in dreams, silence, or altered states. Draen denotes "Starborn, beyond the cradle," while Thraen signifies "woven threads of memory." Together, the phrase marks the resonance of ancient voices scattered across distance and time. The Dren'thran cannot be recorded by conventional means; they do not imprint on Node systems. Only anomalies (Ten'drel on Toktilor, Draen'drel among other worlds) report hearing them. Their content is fractured, often paradoxical, spoken in An'therra, the cryptic tongue of the First Ones. Palrax scholars classify Dren'thran as statistical hallucination. Anomalies recognize them as guidance. The term also names the long cryptic discourse of the Ancients – evidence preserved in fractured form, intended only for anomalies to decipher.

16 Thrae-Draen – Fractured discourse of the Ancients.

16 Thrae-Draen → *the long discourse of the Ancients, preserved in fractured form. The name fuses Thrae (threads of memory) and Draen (Starborn, beyond the cradle). Together it means "threads carried beyond the cradle / beyond the cycle." The Thrae-Draen is the most complete surviving relic of An'therra, though it is not a record in plain speech. It is a discourse broken into (not necessarily) cryptic riddles, paradoxes, and dark fragments, designed so only anomalies (Ten'drel and Draen'drel) can perceive their meanings. To ordinary Palraxians, it appears as nonsense or superstition. The text moves through eleven parts, describing the rise of the Ancients, their fall into worship of Lu'um, the silence of Lamphor, and the creation of the Shuun Varnul. It warns of Ser'ethra as both peril and salvation, and it hints that fire must return if Continuity is to survive. The Thrae-Draen is never acknowledged in the Node Codex except in* **18.08-09***; it exists outside the system, surviving only as the Thrae-Draen record and the whispers that lead anomalies to its hidden message.*

17 Sti'edd - The Still Seed or final solution.

17 Sti'edd → the Still Seed; the final pattern held in reserve, a last solution kept quiet until all other paths fail.

About the Author

David Markham was born in 1963, at the height of the Space Race—when rocket launches and moon landings lit up television screens and made the impossible feel close enough to touch. By the 1970s, alien encounters had jumped from tabloids into movie theaters, and his fascination only deepened.

Then, one night in the mid-70s, he saw something he couldn't file away as imagination: three white lights in a perfect triangle, drifting silently across the sky. Without warning, they separated—each one snapping away in a different direction, accelerating faster than any aircraft he'd ever seen. That moment never left him.

Over the decades, he's searched for credible answers: where they come from, what they want, and what life beyond Earth might truly be. The evidence he's found—and the evidence he's carefully curated—has never felt like enough. That lingering gap, the unanswered pull, is what drove him to write this book.

This dossier is dedicated to everyone who has ever looked up and felt the same question tighten in their chest: *Who are we?* And, just as haunting—*why are we here?* ◆

Review & Access Classified Lore

If you've reached the end of Alien I Am and something in you insists there's more, you're already part of the anomaly movement.

One of the simplest ways to keep this dossier from vanishing into static is to leave an honest review. In the noise, reviews are how anomalies signal to each other: this file is worth opening.

If you leave a review and then sign up for my email list at alieniam.com, I'll send you a bonus file: "The Thrae-Draen (Simplified)"—a clearer gateway into the cryptic fragments of the Node, the Ancients, and the anomaly architecture behind Alien I Am.

This is the first dossier. There may be more. Visit: alieniam.com

www.ingramcontent.com/pod-product-compliance
Lightning Source LLC
Chambersburg PA
CBHW051938020726
47501CB00001B/182
9780990758761